Also by Delia Pitts

Ross Agency Mysteries

Murder Take Two

Murder My Past

Pauper and Prince in Harlem

Black and Blue in Harlem

Practice the Jealous Arts

Lost and Found in Harlem

Short Stories

"Midnight Confidential"
—*Midnight Hour: A Chilling Anthology of
Crime Fiction from 20 Authors of Color*

"The Killer"
—*The Best American Mystery and Suspense 2021*

"Talladega 1925"
—*Chicago Quarterly Review Vol. 33:
An Anthology of Black American Literature*

TROUBLE IN
QUEENSTOWN

TROUBLE IN
QUEENSTOWN

Delia Pitts

MINOTAUR BOOKS
NEW YORK

To my parents,
Helen Lowery Pitts and M. Henry Pitts,
who taught me to love reading, writing,
and books

First published in the United States by Minotaur Books, an imprint of St. Martin's Publishing Group

TROUBLE IN QUEENSTOWN. Copyright © 2024 by Delia C. Pitts. All rights reserved. Printed in the United States of America. For information, address St. Martin's Publishing Group, 120 Broadway, New York, NY 10271.

www.minotaurbooks.com

Design by Meryl Sussman Levavi

The Library of Congress Cataloging-in-Publication Data is available upon request.

ISBN 978-1-250-90421-8 (hardcover)
ISBN 978-1-250-90422-5 (ebook)

Our books may be purchased in bulk for promotional, educational, or business use. Please contact your local bookseller or the Macmillan Corporate and Premium Sales Department at 1-800-221-7945, extension 5442, or by email at MacmillanSpecialMarkets@macmillan.com.

First Edition: 2024

1 3 5 7 9 10 8 6 4 2

LEO'S CASE

CHAPTER **ONE**

I was horny. After a week-long dry spell, the itch was nagging again. A pesky throb teasing my gut. I knew just where to go for a scratch.

Queenstown men were plentiful and lonely at the Kings Cross Tavern, so I quit my office at ten P.M. to navigate Center Street in search of a fresh one.

Private investigator was a new line for me. No sergeant with daily assignments anymore; no academic dean setting my agenda. Now I made my own hours, worked my own cases. Small-bore stuff: divorces, employment backgrounders, process serving. Skimpy dough for measly jobs. A monthly retainer from my partner eased finances, but I was my own boss.

Evander Myrick, Investigations. The tag looked slick on business cards, snappy on the front door. Bearing my father's name gave an advantage to me. Until they met me, most clients assumed I was a man. I lost a few bigots who couldn't swallow the shock, but most people stuck.

Gusts skidded from the frozen surface of Lake Trask, whipping my calves as I trotted against the red light. Snow glare lit the street, mocking the flicker of leftover Christmas decorations dangling from lampposts.

I'd worked late every night this week. I deserved my prize. The tavern promised easy rewards.

At the bar's entrance, I planted my boots on the mat and scraped until little Matterhorns of snow gathered in the treads of the rubber carpet. Icicles lined the roof overhang, their drips seeping inside the collar of my wool coat.

Before I could jerk the handle, a patron barreled out. I recoiled, arms spread to regain my balance. The man pushed a plaid cap off his nose and peered at me.

He slurped, "Baby." More gargles. A leer exposed his tongue. "Oh, baby."

White guy, my height, five-nine, maybe thirty pounds heavier. I stepped right; he followed, arms stiff. The lunge carried his hand to my breast.

He squeezed. "Oooo, yeah, baby." The growl slathered my face with fumes of rye whiskey and salted peanuts.

I chopped the edge of my hand to his throat. His eyes bulged. A fat tear dripped. Jaw wobbling, he swiped his lids.

He swung a fist and grazed my coat button.

I shot a left jab to the point of his chin. No body weight, just a burst of energy from shoulder to wrist. His teeth clicked like castanets as his neck twisted. His head flew sideways, body following. The face-plant was highlight-reel-worthy. In the gray snow, blood dotted a halo around his cap.

I tramped his shoulder with my boot. No groans or twitches. I didn't want him to smother. *Of course I did.* But January was for new beginnings, so I grabbed his jacket collar and pulled him to a sitting position.

Orange stripes of hair slanted across his brow. His lids shivered like mice were running under them. Saliva bubbled at the crack of his lips. Propped against the cement foundation of the tavern, my sparring partner looked like a puppet with his strings cut.

The fight was a nice warm-up round. I rolled my shoulders and shook my hands to release the tension. Now for the main event. I jerked open the green door and stepped across the threshold. I'd shed the icicle water inside, where the bartender, Mavis Jenkins, could rebuke me.

It was our standard game: I'd commit an outrage; Mavis would tut-tut. The moral balance kept us both sharp.

I flapped my arms against my flanks. I took a census of the dimly lit room. Mid-January dragged down the numbers. Five white men sat at tables arrayed along the perimeter; three white men hunkered at the horseshoe-shaped bar. Four Black men and three Latinos clustered at tables near the swinging kitchen doors at the rear.

I polled the racial math of every room I entered. In case I needed allies. Or witnesses. Or alibis.

The bartender and I were the only Black women on the premises. She owned the tavern. I was a private detective. Grit, if not math, was in our favor tonight.

I smiled at my friend and flicked water from my ears. Mavis Jenkins was short, round-hipped, and light-skinned. Lanky and slim, I was her dark foil. I shrugged off the coat, pinched my knit beret, and hung both on pegs to the left of the door.

"I knew your mamá from way back, Vandy Myrick." The bartender's voice rumbled toward me. "And Alma Myrick didn't raise her child in no barn. Stop messing my floor."

"Got it," I said. Not an apology, but close.

I crossed the wide-planked floor at a measured pace. I flexed my left hand, checking for pain. The knuckles stung; tomorrow I'd feel the ache in my rotator cuff. But I rolled easy, arms still, head high. I heard breaths drawn, held, then spewed as I passed. I looked fine for forty-seven, so I gave my audience a good eyeful.

I reached the barstool opposite Mavis and tossed her a wink. I tugged my sweater, smoothing its hem over my hips.

Leaning close, I delivered the news: "You've got a spill on your front stoop." I balled my left fist on the bar top, rolling the knuckles.

Mavis glanced at the scratched skin. "Need to call the cleanup crew?"

"Nah, you're good. He'll find his way home."

"Tidy Sutton was drunk on his ass when I refused him another round. He called me every name, but a child of God. So when Tidy stumbled out, I figured he'd meet some kind of trouble."

"*That* boozehound was Tidy Sutton?" Surprise tweaked my voice. "He anchored the defensive front line for the Panthers' varsity team."

"Always cleaned up, hunh?" Mavis got the old nickname's simpleminded joke. "Well, those high school glory days are long gone." She swiped her cloth over a nonexistent smudge. "For all y'all."

I settled into the green leather cushion, grinning. "When you're right, you're right." My head tilt subbed for regret in our little play. "As usual."

"'Bout time you learned that. You been back seven months and still thick as a side of beef."

Queenstown was my childhood home. Land of skinned knees, Jheri curls, and coke-bottle eyeglasses; science contests and track meets; fried perms and prom snubs. After Q-High, I'd escaped to Temple University in Philadelphia. Seven months ago, I'd returned in pain. When I left at seventeen, I couldn't sneak into the tavern. I'd had to find boys and booze elsewhere. Since returning, I'd made up for thirty years of lost opportunities.

I watched Mavis rummage below the counter: she retrieved an aluminum bowl filled with lemons and limes, a paring knife, and a bamboo slab. Under her pale fingers the fruit fell into neat quarters. "And 'bout time you showed up this evening."

This was Thursday. I'd already hit the bar Monday and Tuesday this week, so the gap was negligible. But I played along. "You missed me? I'm flattered."

"Don't be." Narrowed eyes didn't screen her amused glint. "I got a new job for you. Big bucks this time."

"What's up?" I always wanted fresh clients.

I didn't need to place my order. Mavis knew the drill: simple syrup spiced with finely ground black pepper; a shot of lemon juice, three ice cubes, club soda. A swipe of lime around the rim and a sliver of celery plopped into the drink completed the work. No gin, no vodka, nothing but fizz. A mocktail minus the ironic name. She set the glass on a coaster between my forearms.

I sipped and sighed. "This virgin Tom Collins is the best you've made so far."

"You say that every time," she growled. "And every time I ask you to skip calling it *virgin*."

Dry for a year, I'd quit cold turkey. There were times when my tongue curled with longing and doubts clanged through my head. But I'd made a promise to my daughter. Sticking to that pledge held my life together, like a staple clamped in the corner of a frayed letter. Shredded or ripped, I was going to keep my promise to Monica.

"Lower your voice, girl." Whispering, Mavis swiveled her head. "You call it Clean Collins if you gotta name it, hear?"

I glanced around the bar, antenna up for disturbance. Two of the Black men guffawed when the third slapped their table. The Latinos passed a cell phone between them, pointing at a photo. At the far end of the counter, a white man in a trucker cap raised his glass for a refill. No one paid attention to my conversation with Mavis. As she skated to replenish her customer's order, I tipped my glass until ice struck teeth.

When Mavis took her spot in front of me, I asked, "What's this new job you got for me?"

"Big-time connections," she said. "Large cash. Right up your private eye alley. I got you a date with Leo Hannah, prince of Queenstown."

Lights in the tavern shimmered as I swiveled on my stool. I knew the name. Hannah was a big deal. What could he want with me?

CHAPTER **TWO**

While Mavis fixed her shrewd bartender eyes on me, warmth rose up my neck. If I played this right, Leo Hannah could be my breakout client, my jump to the major leagues. I touched my left earlobe, hoping to quell the pulsing heat there.

"You *do* need the job, don'tcha?" Mavis said the jab loud.

I glanced at the other bar patrons. I didn't want these men to learn I was a private investigator. Personal security dictated that caution. Queenstown, New Jersey, was small, nine thousand souls crammed into twelve square miles fenced by cornfields, warehouses, pharma labs, and tract housing. Privacy was hard to come by in Q-Town, and worth guarding.

"What's Leo Hannah want with me?" Low, to hide the tremor in my voice. Cool, like it didn't matter.

Mavis dropped her jaw to reply. Before she could answer, a fist of January cold pushed a newcomer into the bar. He was tall and underdressed in a fake leather biker jacket that grazed his belt. He clapped hands before his lips like he meant to pray the chill away. Construction-worker grime framed the nail beds. Nice cheekbones, dirty blond hair hanging in ropes across his brow. Eye color indeterminate, not that I cared. The blue-and-gray-plaid flannel shirt and crosshatched jeans were a country song cliché poised to burst.

My future boyfriend took the stool nearest the entrance, eyes wide and neck stiff, as if he intended to bolt. When he raised a hand, then a dimpled chin, Mavis scurried to take his order. She pulled a spigot, scraped the foamy head, and delivered his draft beer in double time.

As soon as she returned, I bit on our previous line. "Don't let sweetness over there turn your head, Mavis. What's this job you found for me?"

"Leo Hannah came in around seven asking if I knew a detective."

"You know him personally?"

"Never seen him before. But when he gave his name, of course I knew him. He's Leo Hannah."

"As in Mayor Hannah?"

"The one and only. She's his auntie."

I bobbed my head. Josephine Hannah had won reelection the previous November to a fourteenth two-year term as mayor of Queenstown. She was the longest-serving municipal leader in Mason County and a key broker in statewide Democratic party politics. Governors came and went; congressmen were bought a dime a dozen; county freeholders fizzled into obscurity. But Mayor Hannah was North Star permanent. Two attributes made her famous: dedicated service to her community and a take-no-prisoners leadership style. When Jo Hannah decided something would benefit Queenstown, she battered the gates of heaven and hell until she delivered the goods. In this state, crossing the mayor was a trick never tried twice. Disturb her, you paid in precious skin. According to legend, trout in Lake Trask grew fat nibbling on people who'd defied Jo Hannah. When anyone in Trenton, Princeton, Perth Amboy, or Newark needed a favor or a rock-solid guarantee, they kissed the ring of the mayor of Q-Town.

"Hannah connections could be a giant win for me," I mumbled over the bar.

Mavis's panting brushed my forehead. She whispered, "When you hit big coins inside those Hannah pockets, just remember ya good old girl did you a solid."

I swallowed the dregs. "Did Leo Hannah want me in particular?"

"He didn't put it that way." She scratched a circle in the curls over her ear. "He asked if I knew the name Evander Myrick. I said yes."

"Maybe he wanted my dad."

"Nah, he said he needed a detective, not a cop."

Mavis knew my father was a retired police officer, now confined to a nursing home. She'd figured Leo was looking for an active investigator, not an out-of-commission cop. I asked, "Did he say why he wanted a detective?"

Mavis poked her tongue inside her cheek. Dryness forced a hack. "He said he wanted to save his wife."

Her lips hitched into a grimace. She dropped her glance to the towel twisted in her fist.

Leo Hannah sounded like a truckload of drama. Toting a butt load of cash. I sucked my teeth. "So you told him I was the woman for the job."

"I didn't tell him nothing. He was muttering and slotting his eyes sideways like one of those old-time crybaby dolls. I could smell the man's crotch sweat across the bar." She rubbed knuckles at her nose to erase the memory. "I fished your card from under my cash register tray and handed it to him before he shit a brick."

"Did Leo say when he'd look for me?"

"He 'bout broke my thumb grabbing that card. He studied it so long, I thought he was going to kiss it. Then he tucked your card in his breast pocket like it was his last valentine. He said he'd stop up to your office tomorrow morning first thing."

"Then I better get this night wrapped fast and tight," I said. To ease the tension, I forced a chuckle. "That Brad Pitt looker at the end of the bar. What's he drinking?"

She squinted at the man in the plaid shirt. "You right, baby Brad, before Thelma and Louise took a header off that cliff." A shrug, a sigh. "Yuengling on tap."

He flashed strong teeth at me. No wink; a sign of class. Maybe.

"Then build a Clean Collins for me," I said. "And tap another Yuengling, so I can tap my new friend."

When she frowned, I paused to let the gripe bloom in her head. As her lids blinked, I figured Mavis was counting the men I'd picked up at the tavern in the past six months.

I stood, turning a slow circle, to remind her I was free. "Bad moves, no strings," I said. "My brand. My way."

Sure, I wanted sincere ties, that web of real connections. I wanted to rebuild a family. Rejoin the human race. But not here. Not tonight.

Mavis puffed her cheeks. She wasn't the Salvation Army. She didn't play the rescue game. When she laughed, I knew we were clear.

Carrying the drinks to my country crooner, I dodged a collision with the white man in the trucker cap. He rolled to the entrance, flung the door wide, and disappeared into the snow cloud draping the street.

Without spilling a drop, I kicked the door shut and slid onto a leather stool next to the chosen one. Itch, meet scratch.

CHAPTER **THREE**

When I opened my eyes, dawn's gooey light frosted the ceiling of my bedroom.

I tugged my camisole from the twist around my throat. Tender goodness surged through my body. Throb erased for now. The essential ache, done right.

I blinked and tried again. Same glare, same silky ruffles at my neck. I pulled until the pink slip glided into place near my hips. The distance from my bed to the bathroom was only ten feet, but I wanted to cross it with dignity.

At the foot of the bed, I stubbed my toe on a cowboy boot. Mud-dappled green alligator skin, two-inch underslung heel. I kicked the boot, then studied its owner, sprawled under the sheets. Dishwater-blond hair curtained the cheekbone whose chiseled contours had enthralled me last night at Kings Cross Tavern. I couldn't see the green, maybe blue, eyes. No telling if they were still fascinating. His face was pressed into the crook of his arm. Despite the sunlight piercing my lace curtains, Derek, or maybe Darren, was still asleep.

"Rise and shine, Captain America," I said.

I needed to get ready for my meeting with Leo Hannah. Time was a-wasting.

I hoisted both boots by their loops, then dropped one beside the bed. The clomp was satisfying. But Dan or Dirk snuffled, then snored. I'd learned last night that behind his baby face was a dim but eager-to-please personality. Slow but steady. Malleable and mellow. Not

saying he was stupid, exactly. But he played follow-the-leader to perfection. I liked that in my one-off boys. I dropped the other boot.
Dion or Dylan refused to budge.

"I'm taking a shower. Be gone when I come out."

I left the *or else* unspoken. If Darryl—that was the name, Darryl—
remembered anything about last night, he'd know better than to mess
with me. Men in Q-Town were fast learners. The ones who'd tried to
cross me knew better. Be smart. Don't challenge the Black lady dick
when she gives a direct order. I wasn't the only bitch in town. But I
was the toughest.

Darryl was smart enough. When I returned to my bedroom fifteen
minutes later, he was gone.

I pulled a tube of ointment from my nightstand and dabbed anti-
septic over the scratches on my knuckles from last night's skirmish.
Nice wounds to show the guys at Mel Diamond's Boxing World. My
sparring partners called me Holyfield, as if the boxing legend who
shared my name had materialized in their modest gym. "How's the
ear, champ?" they'd shout while tugging on mangled lobes. If my interview with Leo Hannah went as I hoped, maybe this evening I'd
drop into Diamond's for a few rounds with a speed bag.

Black jeans were the non-negotiable comfort food of my wardrobe.
I held a navy sweatshirt against my chest—too casual. I studied a
sunflower-tinted blouse, the one my partner, Elissa Adesanya, insisted
I wear when I accompanied her to court. She'd taken some third-year
elective class on jury psychology. According to her, the demure bow
tie helped relax white jurors who were uneasy facing a Black attorney and a Black detective. Maybe Elissa was right: in the past six
months I'd seen her win eleven verdicts when I wore the lucky yellow getup. I pressed the blouse to my waist. I shook my head at the
mirror; insincere, too fussy. Not the look I wanted for my meeting
with Leo Hannah.

I dragged a long-sleeved white tee from the stack in my closet.
That did the job. I needed this sober look for Hannah. He was worried
about his wife. I wanted to fulfill his fantasy of the tough but empa-
thetic private eye. A spade Sam Spade. I needed him to believe I was
the best person to guarantee his wife's safety. I chose a gray tweed

blazer to complement the silver pearls of wisdom sprouting in my black hair. I smoothed a bud of pomade over my unruly kitchen, then waved a brush past my cropped Afro.

My home was a Victorian house on Queenstown's Main Street. I'd purchased the abandoned heap six weeks after I returned. I'd come home with a heavy purse and a burdened heart. If crying could bring back Monica, that miracle would have happened long ago.

But the gut remodel of my new house provided solace of a kind. So did the three-week affair with my architect. His stilted drawings were serviceable, not fabulous. But I did appreciate his other talents, so we enjoyed the hell out of our brief association. The general contractor was smarter than the architect. He built magic out of my sketches. And managed to stay in my bed two weeks after his contract was done.

I turned a 360 in the mirror, then fastened a thin gold chain around my throat. I adjusted the dangling letter *M* so it nestled against the notch of my collarbone. Gold stud earrings. Black ankle boots claimed from Monica's closet, a fuchsia smart watch. Her boots and watch always prompted memories. For a second, I traced circles on the underside of my wrist, remembering.

I was ready to comfort Leo Hannah, reassure his imperiled wife, and slay the dragons threatening her.

As water for oatmeal heated on the stove, I thumbed through messages from Elissa. She was gone for the week, attending a trial lawyers conference in Miami. Her wife, Belle Ames, had extended her own holiday break into January to coincide with the boss's absence. Texted photos proved they were enjoying the beach. In one, sleek Elissa lounged in a teeny-weeny tangerine bikini that made her dark skin glow; in another, Belle rocked a jade one-piece to display her thick curves. Her blond pixie wig was in place as usual, which meant she had no plans to touch ocean. In all the family shots, sun dashed the midwinter paste from Belle's brown cheeks and made Elissa's eyes narrow into sexy glances.

Should I text Adesanya and Ames about my plans to meet Leo Hannah? I wanted to crow I'd netted a big new client. But I ditched the idea as I stirred a second teaspoon of brown sugar into my oatmeal.

Let the A-team enjoy all the fun they'd earned. They'd catch up soon enough.

The drive to the office was ten minutes. I promised when spring hit, I'd stow my Jeep Cherokee. The twenty-five-minute walk was an investment in my health. I needed the exercise. But January was not the time to start a new regimen. Why risk shocking your system after the rough slog through the holidays? March was soon enough. Or April.

Our offices were on Center Street above the Queenstown Pharmacy, an old-time druggist holding the fort against the onslaught of national chain stores. From our break room, we could see the Kings Cross Tavern across the street.

I parked in the cramped lot behind the building, pulling into my usual place next to the slot designated for Elissa. No name on the brick wall for me yet. Our administrative overlord, Belle, would get to it in her own sweet time. Belle was our bookkeeper, data puncher, publicist, hand-holder, brow-mopper. Pushing Belle was never smart. I could wait.

I unlocked the door to our suite, flipped on the lights, and recoiled when stale air lapped at my face.

My colleagues wore expensive fragrances: ferns and velvety moss for Elissa, pushy lilac for Belle. I'd dropped the perfume habit since returning to Q-Town. No point in aimless luxury, was there? But stepping into our offices now, I missed the mingling of their fragrances. Without it, the reception area smelled vacant and unhappy, like a dressing room in a discount clothing store.

I had work to do before Leo Hannah arrived.

After hanging my overcoat and blazer in my office, I dragged the vacuum cleaner from the storeroom and retrieved baking soda from the refrigerator in the break room. Sprinkling the all-purpose deodorant across the blond carpet, I plowed for ten minutes. Furrows careened around the glass coffee table, the six upholstered guest chairs, and the eight-foot-high oak bookcase.

Stooping to thrust the vacuum under Belle's desk, I missed the whoosh of the door.

Wet sniffs jerked me upright. A harsh cough spun me around.

"I'm looking for the offices of Evander Myrick." Not a question, a command for the cleaning lady.

I stepped forward. Leo Hannah was an inch shorter than me, with narrow shoulders and chest flaring to broad hips that strained his camel-hair coat. Waiting for my reply, he stuffed brown leather gloves in his pockets, adding to the bulk at his thighs.

He looked around, brows lowered, searching for someone with authority and rank. He wanted that somebody to appear, pronto. Preferably someone white and male. Anybody but me.

I pressed my lips to squelch the smirk. Privilege stymied was fun to watch.

Hannah wasn't good-looking, but the tilt of his jaw said he'd been told the opposite all his life. Olive skin, clean-shaven around a snub nose and soft mouth. His cologne hinted at spicy forests. Brown eyes framed by fans of black lashes. I knew three college girlfriends who'd contracted eye infections trying to achieve the luxuriant lashes Leo Hannah claimed from birth.

I said, "You've come to the right place." I made him wait two beats. "May I have your name." I wasn't dealing in questions, either.

CHAPTER **FOUR**

The man raked his eyes across the reception area, frowning at the offense of the cleaning lady's demand.

I squared shoulders and chin, fist gripping the vacuum's stick handle.

He snapped, "Leo Hannah." A pause for the magical effect of his name to ooze over me. "I have an appointment with Evander Myrick."

I tilted my head, no smile. I knew the appointment claim was a lie, but let it slide. Mavis had done me a solid by skipping the gender reveal when she handed my business card to Hannah last night. I liked the leg up, however fleeting.

Pointing toward the corridor beyond the reception area, I drawled, "You can wait in the office at the end of the hall. Just past the conference room."

Nodding to dismiss me, Hannah pulled off his cloth driving cap and turned toward my office. His black hair was scraped across a kidney-shaped bald spot. As he stomped by the glass wall of the conference room, I saw him straighten his tie in the reflection.

I let him stew in my office for three minutes.

"Good morning, Mr. Hannah," I chirped as I snatched my blazer from the coat rack. "I'm Evander Myrick. What can I do for you today?"

I settled behind my desk, withholding the smile to let him adjust his racism. The flinch at the left eye was tiny, but I caught it. His gaze clawed the walnut surface in search of sanctuary or explanation:

laptop; owl-handle bottle opener; two unblemished legal pads, a bouquet of black ballpoint pens in a maroon Temple mug.

I speared a stray paper clip and dragged it to the center drawer. The art on the walls clarified nothing, but Hannah studied the black figures in a poster of a Faith Ringgold quilt as if it held the secret to life's mysteries. The broad brown faces of the Diego Rivera print were equally unrevealing.

"I'm glad to meet you, Ms. Myrick." He sounded sincere. Underneath the coat draped on his lap, his hands twisted, so I figured he wasn't. "I hope you can help me. Help my family, really."

"Why don't you tell me what you need. Then I'll tell you if I can help."

Hannah's eyes bulged over a weak smile that dented only the left half of his face. When I nodded, he inhaled for a long spew.

"I want to hire you to protect my wife, Ms. Myrick. I think she's in danger. I mean, she says she's in danger, too. This isn't just my idea. It's hers, too. I can't be with her every hour of every day. I've got an important job. I'm deputy head of research at ArcDev Pharmaceuticals. We create new molecules for use in medicines, cosmetics, food products. Our research is vital to the growing economy of the state and—"

"Is your research vital to your wife's safety, Mr. Hannah?"

A bubble of objection glinted on his lower lip. Deputy head of research Leo Hannah wasn't used to being interrupted. Especially not by a Black woman he still suspected of being the cleaning lady. Or her next of kin. He licked at the saliva and started again.

"No, I suppose it isn't. What I meant to say is that I need your professional services to take on a challenge I can't possibly assume myself."

"Tell me how this menace to your wife manifests itself."

Hannah gulped at the big words. "You mean . . . ?"

"I mean, start by telling me your wife's name. Then tell me as much as you can about who's threatening her."

"Her name is Ivy Mae Hannah." He sighed as if defeated. "She's thirty-seven years old. We've been married fourteen years. We have a three-year-old son, Tomás. We adopted Tommy from an orphanage in El Salvador two years ago. Here—"

He pulled his wallet from a hip pocket and extracted a snapshot. I reached across the desk to take it. Tiny gold script from a photography studio angled across the lower right corner. The family in the shot looked unremarkable. Leo Hannah sat next to his wife; a chubby infant squirmed on her lap. Ivy Hannah's hair streamed in gold waterfalls over both shoulders. A streak of carmine exaggerated the thinness of her lips below an arched nose. Her skin was salt white. If her eyes had been round and blue, Ivy would have looked like a fairy-tale princess. Rapunzel in the tower. Or a mod Cinderella. But the cliché was dashed by the angle at which the brown eyes slanted toward her temples. High flat cheekbones and a strong chin perched on an overlong neck completed the portrait. Ivy Hannah was striking. Not beautiful, but arresting.

"Lots of people say Tommy looks like he could be our natural child." Hannah crossed his arms over his chest as if defending against an expected challenge.

I peered at the photo. The boy's olive skin and black hair matched Leo's, though the baby's hair was stick-straight and Leo's was wavy. Tommy's wide cheekbones and arched nose resembled his mother's. Those "lots of people" weren't far off base. I wondered if Mayor Hannah agreed.

"Yeah, I can see that," I said.

I squared the photo in front of me. "May I keep this?"

Hannah pounced on this slip. "Does that mean you'll take the case?"

He was right. I'd already decided to accept the job, based on nothing more than this photo. But I couldn't concede on such a quick wash of sentiment, so I shook my head. "Give me more details. Then I'll let you know if I can help."

"Okay." Leo's voice rose in uncertainty.

"Be as specific as you can about the nature of the threat to your wife, Mr. Hannah."

"Ivy says someone is stalking her. She's seen a dark-haired, swarthy man dawdling near the church where she volunteers. She's seen him follow her around the grocery store. And she even saw him lurking outside of the day-care center when she went to pick up Tommy. She's scared to death."

Dark, swarthy? Why didn't Hannah say Black if he meant that? Or Latino? This vague sketch sounded like the description of a pirate. Or the standard-issue homie perp from any episode of *Law & Order*.

Instead of challenging him, I played along. "Does Ivy know this man? Have any connection to him, past or present?"

"I don't think so. She said she didn't recognize him. But maybe she met him once somewhere and he started on this stalking campaign." Leo glanced at the photo on my desk, a smile tickling his mouth for the first time. "Ivy is quite stunning, as you can see."

"Mr. Hannah, if your wife is in danger, this is a matter for the police. Have you reported these concerns to QPD?"

"No, I can't. I won't." His voice darkened as the words snapped. When my eyebrows jogged upward, he explained. "You know who my family is. What we represent in Queenstown. If I go to the police without strong evidence, this story gets spread all over town by enemies of the Hannah family. Paranoid, obsessed, racist, ignorant, you name it—that's what they'll call us." He gathered his breath over a whine. "Without solid substantiation, this story'll be used against us, against my aunt."

When Mavis described him last night, she'd said Leo Hannah seemed scared, even near tears. What happened to that guy? The Leo in my office now bristled with anger, entitlement, and resentment. Why the shift? Was he playacting now or last night?

I pushed to close the deal. "That's where I come in?"

"Yes. I want you to track Ivy for a week, ten days. See if someone is following her like she says. If you can identify him, maybe snap some pictures, then we'll go to the police."

"My report will be the foundation of your case? Is that how you see it?"

"Exactly. I want a credible third-party eyewitness to support Ivy's claim. Can you help us, Ms. Myrick?"

"I need to interview Ivy before I begin."

He snapped, "No, I won't permit that." Under his gray gabardine suit jacket, his shoulders twitched with tension.

"What do you mean, *permit?*" My turn to bristle; I jacked up the heat a notch. "This is standard procedure. I need as much information as I can gather from your wife to start this investigation."

Hannah shrank into the chair. Under a slick of sweat, his forehead turned ashen. "I—I don't want you to do that," he whispered.

"Do what? You're the one who came to me. Now you're telling me you don't want me to help your wife?" I figured he was lying about something. I planted both hands on the desk and stood.

"If you're playing games, get out now." For dramatic flourish, I pointed at the door. Corny but effective. "I'm in a generous mood, so I won't charge you for wasting my time this morning."

"No, please. Please don't quit." His spine contracted until his chest disappeared under the jacket. "I really do need your help."

I could see his hands writhe below the coat on his lap. Skim-milk gray crept up his jowls.

I sat down. "Okay, then let's start again."

Hannah sighed, wiping a palm under his nose, to catch sweat, snot, or both. I pulled a carton of tissues from the bottom drawer and thrust the box toward him. He grabbed a fistful of Kleenex and wiped the middle of his face from brow to chin. Warm color returned to his cheeks.

"From the top," I growled. "With the straight story this time."

Clearing his throat, he pushed his chest against the edge of my desk. "It's me in danger," Leo Hannah said. "Not Ivy."

CHAPTER **FIVE**

As he thought of an expanded answer to my question, Leo Hannah dug a fingernail into a groove along the lip of my desk. His nails were long; the wood slivers peeled like skin from an orange. He plucked at his throat. Raising thoughts of his personal peril froze his vocal cords.

I said, "In danger of what?" Repetition was my superpower in this contest.

"I think I'm losing her." Mouth twisted to the side, tongue probing the cheek for the bitter drops of truth. "To another man."

Now I had him. "So you want me to follow your wife to see if she's involved with someone else? Is that why you're hiring me?"

Through gritted teeth, "Yes." Water danced in his eyes when he raised them. "I want proof of her infidelity before I file for divorce. And for sole custody of our son."

This sounded closer to the heart of the matter. Divorce cases were the bread and butter of my PI work. Nasty, lucrative, fun in an unwholesome way. Leo Hannah's would be the tenth divorce case I'd worked since returning to Queenstown.

I speared a legal pad and raised a ballpoint pen. "What evidence do you have so far? Have you intercepted phone calls, texts, emails? Have you spoken to her friends about your suspicions?"

Hannah shook his head with each question. He gripped the bridge of his nose with two thick fingers and pressed until red indentations sprang next to leaking tear ducts.

I kept at him. "Have you seen your wife talking with this other man? Is it a work colleague or a neighbor or a member of the gym, maybe the church choir or country club?"

"No, it's nothing like that. Nothing so concrete or tawdry. You make Ivy sound like a temptress in a B movie. She's not like that."

"Then what *is* she like?" I dropped the pen and folded my fingers.

He gathered a string of boilerplate adjectives. "She's kind and generous. Devoted to Tommy and to our church. She volunteers for several town committees. Ivy's a model wife . . ."

"Except?"

"Except she doesn't love me anymore. That's all. Don't ask me how I know. I just do." Liquid eyes poured into mine. "Are you married, Ms. Myrick?"

"Not since the Ice Age." I quirked my lips to snuff the bitterness.

After a quickie wedding, Philip Bolden deserted me when I was five months pregnant. Greener pasture, tighter ass, fatter bank account. Happiness found and lost in a heartbeat. My father pronounced the verdict: *Bad move, Vandy. Marrying that dog was never going to turn out right. Even Stevie Wonder could see he was big trouble.* My mother attended prenatal classes with me. But she announced these four sessions were all she could handle. Actual labor was a bridge too far, Alma said. So my father's were the knuckles I crushed during eight hours of labor before the doctors decided to perform a cesarean section. I figured I'd earned the right to give Monica my last name, not that of her no-show dad.

"I remember the drill," I told Hannah.

He concluded we were comrades in a forlorn army. "Then you get where I'm coming from. You know how your heart aches when love seeps out of your marriage." Anguish converted him into a poet. "Like sap dripping from cuts in tree bark, it trickles and spills. Until your heart is drained, and you know it's over."

He dabbed the ball of tissue against closed eyes. Which gave me a moment to sniff. Jerk or not, Leo had a way with words. I remembered the moment when I realized my marriage was over. Phil Bolden's exit left me snow-blind in a blizzard. Hurtling downhill on a sled filled with lies. No control or direction. Gutted, with zero confidence and basement-level pride. My shaky purpose refocused on an unborn child. I'd crashed where Leo Hannah was heading now. If I could soften Leo's smashup, I'd try. I blinked, my decision reached.

When his lids sprang open, the pupils were swimming in red. "Will you take the case? Will you help me?"

"Give me a week," I said. "Six days of surveillance will produce enough information to point you in the right direction. I might not have a name. I probably won't have incriminating photos. But I'll have enough data to confirm your suspicions. Or deconstruct them."

"If she's innocent, you mean?"

"Yes, if Ivy is innocent, you'll learn it from my report." A bold claim, but I wanted to deliver clarity and composure for my client. I wished someone had done the same for me when I needed the help.

His sigh rippled across the desk. "Thank you, Ms. Myrick. You're a lifesaver."

"Call me Vandy." I swiveled to fire up the laptop.

"And I'm Leo."

I filled in the blanks on a standard client agreement, daily rates plus expenses, total due upon receipt of my final report, nonrefundable retainer payable in advance. Hannah borrowed my ballpoint to sign the agreement. He used the same pen to dash off a check, which I placed in the center drawer of my desk.

"Will you start tomorrow?" he asked as we walked through the reception area. "I don't know if there's a lot to see on the weekend. Ivy has grocery shopping, playdates for Tommy, church services, committee meetings, Bible study."

"You let me figure it out. I'll follow Ivy as much as needed."

His eyelids stiffened. "But if I see you . . ."

"If you spot me, you ignore me." I smirked.

My confidence was catching. He laughed, too. "You're good at this, I can tell."

"I am."

"Ivy's father is staying with us this week. Visiting from Florida. He leaves Wednesday. I don't want him to know anything about this. Ivy either, of course." He coughed, a flutter in the throat. "I'll come here Friday morning to pick up your written report, if that's all right?"

"Perfect," I said.

I flung open the door of the suite and pressed a hand on the squishy flesh of his back. I didn't shove, exactly. A touch delivering a firm suggestion. Like a hostess urging her guests to call it a night after the bewitching hour faded.

Two pats on the camel coat as the smile hardened on my lips. "Everything will be fine, Leo."

He extended his right hand, then jerked it back. I saw dark stains in the whorls of his fingertips. Blue blotches fanned over the pads; rivulets of blue branched on his palm.

Leo squawked. "God, what a mess." He snatched Kleenex from a box on Belle's desk. As he dabbed at the ink, he said, "One of your defective ballpoints leaked on me when I signed that contract."

"No worries," I said, crumpling another tissue into his hand. His fingers felt like metal tubes against my palm. Where we touched, ink slimed our skin. A chill shimmied between my shoulder blades, then dissolved under a shrug.

I watched him march toward the exit at the end of the corridor, then returned to my office to grab the check and my overcoat.

On the rug below the guest chair, I saw a glint, maybe metal or glass. I stooped to pick up the twisted chunk. It was the carcass of a ballpoint pen. Plastic shaft shattered; metal coil and clasp bent, ink tube split, plunger broken in two. With silent spasms, Leo Hannah had wrenched the pen into a knot as we talked. These brutal contractions of his fingers had been covered by his coat.

He'd lied about the ink stains on his hand. What was contained in this hidden surge of energy?

I balanced the ruined pen on my palm. Powerful emotions drove my new client, no doubt. In our interview, I'd clocked fear and jealousy behind Leo's alternating poses. This fierce destruction of the ballpoint suggested more. I set the pen on my desk. I knew Leo Hannah was determined not to lose. That's why he'd hired me. I wondered what he feared losing most. His wife? His control and status? Power, career, income? Was rage mixed into the soup of emotions? I dropped the tangle of metal and plastic in my desk drawer. A blue cloud stained the creases in my palm.

I folded Leo Hannah's check and slipped it into my pocket. I wanted to run this deposit to the bank before close of business. Maybe hit the boxing ring tonight.

But first I needed to visit my father.

As I buckled into the Jeep, I heard Elissa's courtroom voice in my mind. If she had been beside me, she'd argue that three trips to the nursing home each week were excessive. Glendale Memory Care Center was a fortress of sorrow. Why pick at a scab crusted over old wounds? Elissa asked. Did my father even register my visits? How could I be certain he appreciated my calls? The man never spoke my name.

I gunned the engine for the twenty-minute ride to the edge of town. Of course Elissa was right. That's what besties did: deliver truth when it was least wanted.

Fiddling with my gloves at a stoplight, I rolled my neck to scatter Elissa's voice. Sure, my dad was gone. But I had to try. My debt to Evander Myrick would never be paid this side of the grave. He'd refused to give me the honorific of Junior—that was for the son he never got. Still, I owed him everything.

A parking lot surrounded the Glendale Memory Care Center like an asphalt moat. I circled for seven minutes before I found an empty space. Plodding between the cars, I slipped on a patch of black ice. Oil stains bloomed on the right pocket of my coat. I could hear my father's old reproach: *Bad move, Vandy. Mucked up your jacket again.* As I pushed through the revolving doors into the lobby, I scrubbed at the mess with a tissue.

CHAPTER **SIX**

I always brought snacks when I visited my father at Glendale Memory Care Center. Raisins, popcorn or almonds, beef jerky sticks or cubes of cheddar. Sleeves of pecan sandie cookies or peanut butter cracker sandwiches. Anything chewy and soothing.

Not that I thought Glendale residents were underfed. For the mid-four figures I paid from his pension every month, the meals better be gourmet. But Evander Lionel Myrick always looked skinny to me. Like he barely tasted the three-course lunches and four-course dinners. Like he'd skip breakfast altogether if an attendant didn't arrive at eight each morning to bathe and dress him for the trek to the dining room for waffles, eggs, and ham.

This visit I brought red grapes. I hoped their jewel-like glimmer would tempt my father to pluck a few.

"These are juicy," I said. I held the plastic sack toward his chest and rustled it. "Especially for January, don't you think?"

When he didn't take the offer, I stuffed four grapes into my cheeks, then smacked with obnoxious gusto. I swiped the corner of my mouth as juice squirted into my chin. Rude gestures the old Evander Myrick would never tolerate from his only child. *Not in this house, not while I'm still on this earth.*

My father shifted on the sofa and stared at the broad window. He slanted his black baseball cap to shadow his eyes against the glare and said nothing.

I patted Evander's bony wrist, then threaded my fingers through his. Graying skin hung from my father's cheeks like drapery from a lampshade, pleated and thin, with tiny tags that jiggled on the cords of his neck.

He'd always been lean and well-built, with a light brown complexion and flashing eyes. My mother said when she met him, he was the best-looking Negro boy in their high school. Classmates dubbed him the Bronze Elvis. Alma won him early, but she said she worked every day to hold on to her handsome prize. Women clung to him like flies on spilt syrup, she said. And Evander never bothered to brush them away. "Your daddy loves women," Alma said. "And they love him back." When she told me this, I was twelve, my first period only four days old. Her description of Evander felt less like a warning, more like a reassurance: maybe one day I'd grow into the kind of woman my father could cherish.

As a child, I'd loved feeling his muscles bunch below the short sleeves of his police uniform, biceps, forearms, hand muscles slipping like fish under that pale skin. Along with my name, I'd inherited his strong shoulders, elegant fingers, and slim hips. Rich brown skin and a plush mouth were my mother's contribution to the Vandy Myrick look.

Now I propped the bag of grapes on the coffee table, dripping water onto the weekly *Queenstown Herald*. Front-page photos documented Mayor Hannah's agenda that week: judge a middle school art show; chair a committee debate on sanctuary city status; inspect the eroding iron legs of the municipal water tank; cut the ribbon to launch a new fitness center. She was omnipresent, the fountain of every benefit, the source of all achievements. If we ever forgot Jo Hannah's central role in the community, the *Herald* provided reminders each Friday.

The dripping water smeared her photo. I dabbed a tissue on the newsprint, swirling the ink. Maybe I could tell my father about my new client, the mayor's nephew. I looked into Evander's vacant eyes. He wouldn't understand or care. I skipped the story.

Glancing around the suite, I recalled it was labeled "deluxe" on the Glendale website. When I'd toured the facility, I'd rejected the studio apartments as too small for such a big man as Evander Myrick. He deserved all the space and pride we could afford. From the fifth floor, my father could see the woods that ran like brown streams around the neighborhoods of bungalows. Central Queenstown was a maze of crooked streets, bisected by an avenue leading to the onion-shaped water tank that towered a hundred and sixty feet above the block. I liked the idea that Evander could still survey the town he once patrolled.

The day he moved in, I'd installed Evander's favorite armchair, a corduroy recliner, next to that window. In the three years since, I'd never seen him sit in it. Opposite the recliner was a Windsor chair with a green-checked pad on the seat, Alma's prized antique. I'd placed a box of my father's precious chessmen on the walnut table between the two chairs. Next to it was a silver-framed family portrait: my mother Alma, my daughter Monica, and me, captured for eternity. Two dead women and a live child, looking like dolls cut from the same bolt of lush brown velvet.

Every time I visited, I said the same thing. No reason to break the pattern now.

"Here we are, Daddy. Your three favorite ladies." I turned the picture to dodge the sunny glare. "Me with Monica and Mama. Remember when we took this?"

He always delivered the same grunt. A deep rumble, more barnyard animal than human. Recognition or indifference, I couldn't tell.

I continued: "Morning of Monica's eighth-grade graduation. We went to Heinz Studio for that portrait. We look pretty sharp, don't you think?"

Another grunt, then silence. A glance into the blinding sun.

I jerked on a grape. Its branch snapped and the skin split. Red juice ran between my fingers, down the veins of my hand. "Fuck this," I muttered into my collar.

I glanced at the attendant, sitting opposite us on a gray metal folding chair. "Sorry, Keyshawn. Don't mind me."

He laughed. "Language like that earned me and Bobby quick trips to the bathroom for a Dial soap sandwich."

"Same here," I said. I tilted my head toward Evander. "He was a stickler for manners. No tolerance for foul mouths, dirty books, or lewd clothing." I licked juice from my knuckles.

"I guess being a cop's kid, you had to toe the line," Keyshawn said.

Moving to the kitchenette to rinse my hands, I chuckled. "All day, every day. You know it."

And Keyshawn Sayre knew me. He nodded, eyes twinkling.

Keyshawn had been five years behind me, a rising freshman when his brother Robert and I graduated from high school. I hardly remembered the younger brother from those days, dazzled like everyone else at Q-High by the glamour of the older Sayre boy. Both were built like oak trees, with beautiful black eyes and the sunset-dipped skin my grandmother called redbone. Against all odds, I snagged Bobby's attention. I was sixteen years old. I held on to him for a summer and a semester.

Bobby Sayre played power forward on the basketball team and center field on the baseball team. Keyshawn peddled pot to middle schoolers and majored in shoplifting. Bobby became Robert, now an eighteen-year veteran on the Queenstown police force. Keyshawn did a stint in juvenile detention. For ten years he knocked around Atlanta as chauffeur to his maiden aunt and head gardener at her mansion. When she died, Key returned to Q-Town. Bobby powered through three wives in seven years. The current one had lasted eight. Keyshawn never married.

Now I was grateful to have Keyshawn as an ally in the struggle to care for my father.

Keyshawn stretched to grab a roll of paper towels from the top of the fridge. Seeing my puzzled frown, he explained, "I put them up here because yesterday Evander unraveled three rolls and draped them all over the bathroom and bedroom." He tossed the towels to me with a grin.

I ripped a square of paper, dried my hands, then squashed the roll to my nose. I started to laugh, timid cheeps, then a flurry of squawks, until hollers vaulted across the room.

Evander twisted on the sofa, squinting to locate the commotion. Doubt, then delight creased his face as he watched me. He didn't know who I was, but he sure knew I was having a blast.

"Daddy, look at this," I squealed. I pulled another sheet from the roll, then another and another, laughing until I leaned against the counter, out of breath.

"Yep, he did it just like that," Keyshawn said. "Must be a Myrick family trait. Decorating the halls like it's Christmas, Easter, and the Fourth of July combined."

Evander's order broke through our giggles: "Alma, bring me my soda." His eyes sharpened like trowels, digging into my face. He'd called me my mother's name, but at least he'd seen me.

Keyshawn retrieved two cans of ginger ale from the fridge and handed them to me. I peeked inside: rows of ginger ale integrated by 7 Up and club soda. Only the clear stuff to avoid stains. And caffeine jitters.

Sitting beside him again, I popped the can for my father. He snatched it and guzzled like a desert nomad. "Thirsty, hunh, Daddy?"

When I opened the second can, he grabbed it and took a long gulp. Cans in both fists balanced on his thighs, he stared out the picture window again.

I saw his gaze drop to the photograph. "Thanks, Alma," he said. In four years, he hadn't uttered my name once. But he kept Alma at top of mind. Maybe he saw her face in mine.

I wanted to hold this connection, even if it was false. I needed to share something of me, something beyond the death and sorrow. I wanted to make him see me where I'd landed after all these years. So I reversed course. I told him about my new case, scraping off the shine as I spoke.

"It's not glamorous," I said. "Surveillance for a divorce proceeding is totally without dignity. Crummy borderline-snitch work, to be honest. But at least I'll get out of the office, stretch my muscles, work my sneakers instead of my backside for a change. Maybe I'll even break out that old pair of binoculars you gave me."

Evander snorted and slurped more ginger ale. Back in his chair, Keyshawn's gaze swept my face as if I were a juggler spinning platters in a carnival side show. At least half my audience appreciated me.

To gain Evander's attention, I leaned into his side. "My client is from the Hannah family. Remember them, Daddy?" I felt muscles along his ribs twitch as he raised the can to his mouth again.

With the bill of his cap pulled low, I couldn't see his eyes. I thought I heard him breathe, "Hannah," against my cheek. Did he know them? Recall some buried connection? "Hannah." No inflection in the repeated whisper. Uncertain, I dipped my head for a better look at his face.

Disinterest clouded his eyes like waxed paper. I'd lost him.

I sighed and reached for another grape.

Keyshawn set up the board and chess pieces for a quick match. He'd learned to play in juvie and sharpened his skills on me every time I visited. Evander taught me the game before I was ten. After the basic rules were shared, taunts became his preferred daggers. *Bad move, Vandy. You exposed your queen.* Sarcasm was his trusty sword. *You figure that pawn attack is strong? Bad move, Vandy.* The verbal roughhousing sped my education. By the time I turned fifteen, I beat him regularly. Each time I won, muscles at his jaws would tighten against the sour taste of defeat. I hoped playing chess beside Evander now might awaken ancient memories. But the ploy never worked.

After twenty-five minutes, I called it quits. I counted three blinks of my father's eyes; then I glanced out the window. Snow glare caused water to jump on my lids. I brushed away the tears in case he was watching. He wasn't.

As I stowed the pieces, Keyshawn promised to continue our online chess match. Several weeks ago, he'd proposed we text moves twice a day. The code sharing linked us. We each kept real chessboards at home, duplicating in private the daily progress of our game. The connection was minimal but fun. At the end of a grinding day, I looked forward to Keyshawn's texts. Our chess match was a peaceful prelude to sleep.

Keyshawn trailed me into the elevator and walked me to the entrance of the building. With the automated doors gliding in a slow beat, he said, "You caught him on a good day."

"*That* was good?" I shook my head.

"Sure, better than most. You know how he comes and goes. His mind's like a stray cat. One day, he's at your screen door scratching to get in. Then you don't see him for a week. Then, back he slides again, scratching and purring. This was one of the good times, for sure."

"Thank you for that. Even if you're faking it, the show is sweet."

"No fake, Vandy." Lines beside his mouth softened as he continued. "I remember your dad from before. He was tough on my ass back in the day. Bobby called him a mean sonovabitch. To his face."

We chuckled, shuffling out of the icy breeze as a newcomer barreled through the door.

Key went on. "I know Evander tried. Real hard. How many times did he pull me over, watch me stumble on the yellow line, then dump me on my own front porch instead of dragging me to a cell to dry out like he could have." His eyes glittered. "So I'm always going to look out for him now. Like he tried to do for me back then."

I'd heard stories like this from most of the Black kids of my generation. Growing up in Q-Town was tough: on the daily we pinballed between boredom and exhilaration, with the twin batons of racism and indifference swatting us along our journey. Officer Evander Myrick eased that ride to adulthood. Not all of us made it. The ones who did owed him plenty.

"Okay," I said. When I squeezed his bicep, Keyshawn smiled down at me. He was a good man. I was glad my father had helped him make it.

I thought Keyshawn murmured, "Take care of yourself," as I slipped between the sliding doors.

My visit with Evander rated a C+ grade. Average to okay. But the earlier meeting with Leo Hannah had worked well. Now the speed bag at Diamond's Boxing World sang my name. I pointed the Jeep toward the gym and floored the gas pedal.

CHAPTER **SEVEN**

Ivy Hannah's weekend unrolled much as her husband had predicted.

I figured a mother with a toddler couldn't lounge in bed, so before eight-thirty Saturday morning, I stationed the Jeep a block from the Hannah house. It was a two-story colonial with blue vinyl siding and a pair of Chevrolet Equinox SUVs parked in the driveway. I guessed the blue one was for daddy and the silver one was mommy's, just as nature intended.

Despite a blanket of snow, the wide lawn in front and the curved brick sidewalk enhanced the faux plantation look of the white columns that dominated the façade. The place resembled a miniature Tara, minus the happy slaves in kerchiefs and muslin breeches.

Cotton-ball skies tamped the canopy of gray branches over Allen Street. With temperatures below freezing, I kept the engine running as I waited. I hoped the plume of exhaust would blend with the white glare overhead and not arouse suspicion.

Houses on either side of the Hannah residence repeated its nod to an imagined past. Queenstown had been settled in 1742, so blending elements of American Revolution severity with antebellum frippery wasn't completely off base. But those founding folks would have been baffled by the manicured neighborhoods pitched around the historic town center in the 1970s.

While waiting for Ivy to show, I scanned websites for background on her husband. Leonard Joseph Hannah was born in Portland, Maine, in 1978. Mother, Claire Hannah, father unnamed. Some

kind of scandal there? After public education in Portland, he attended
the Rome School, an elite boarding academy in Queenstown. Pricey
digs with posh connections—our boy was on the make. Debate club
and student council president; wrestling, track, and lacrosse captain.
In team pictures, the green-and-brown Rome colors dulled Leo's olive
skin to yellow. On to the University of Virginia, where he majored in
chemistry. After a few years lighting Bunsen burners for Big Pharma
in northern New Jersey, he returned to Q-Town for the job at ArcDev
Pharmaceuticals. Heartwarming tale. I crafted headlines as I waited:
SMALL TOWN NO LIMIT TO BIG-TIME DREAMS. PRINCE OF Q-TOWN MAKES GOOD,
BAGS SNOW WHITE. Maybe not that last one, too crude.

I'd finished my bagel and tall black coffee by the time Ivy Hannah
and her son popped through their front door. He was encased in a
puffy red snowsuit with no visible means of escape. Complementing
Tommy, she wore red mittens and a red stocking cap pulled to her
eyebrows. But her quilted storm coat and knee-high boots were black.
This was the same outfit Ivy wore every day of the next week, which
made tracking her easy.

The Hannahs clambered into the silver SUV and hit the library for
forty-five minutes, emerging with a *New Yorker* satchel full of books.
Stops at the grocery store and Target dragged into the afternoon. Even
if Tommy wasn't ready for a nap, I sure was.

Did Leo Hannah sleep late on Saturdays, taking advantage of
his wife's absence to putter around the house with a hammer and
paintbrush? He didn't seem like the handyman type who'd honor a
honey-do list of chores. Maybe I was wrong. Could Leo be the DIY
champ of Q-Town?

At last Ivy pulled her Equinox into a parking space at McDonald's.
I needed the bio break, and I figured Tommy did, too. A visit to the
newly reopened play pit kept the boy bouncing in multicolored balls
while his mother nibbled the chicken nuggets her son had abandoned.
I'd saved a coupon for McRibs. I indulged my twice-a-year fetish and
topped it off with a cherry pie sandwich. Fake food, pure delight.

I squeezed into an orange plastic booth. Pulling my knit beanie
to my ears, I watched Ivy and Tommy through the interior window
overlooking the play area.

I was scouting for two kinds of people who might express interest in Ivy Hannah: lovers or stalkers. Of course, nothing prevented these two occupations blending into one overbearing personality. Maybe Ivy's bland good looks inspired a frustrated lover who stalked for kicks. From a distance, Ivy didn't seem like the woman to fire that kind of intense passion. But I never claimed to be an expert on who stirred whose loins.

During the hour she spent at the restaurant, I saw Ivy speak with a young mother whose earrings dribbled onto her neck tattoo, a brunette teenager in a purple-and-white Q-High jacket, and a man shepherding twin girls with runny noses. None of them seemed threatening. Nor likely love interests. When he hired me, Leo first asserted Ivy had a stalker. Unlikely. Then he claimed she had a secret lover. Possible. What did a stalker/lover look like anyway?

I faux-texted with stiff thumbs, taking pictures of Ivy, Tommy, and the people they interacted with at McDonald's. Then I tapped notes for my end-of-week report. Colorful adjectives popped gracefully. No scrimping allowed. Leo Hannah would get his money's worth from me.

Home in their driveway, I watched Leo greet his wife with kisses to the cheeks and nose. Sloppy, wet. Like she'd been gone for months on an Arctic expedition. Perhaps he was performing for my benefit; I saw his eyes shift once toward my hiding spot. But her face glowed like a pink lantern, so I figured Ivy was convinced.

Tommy tramped circles in the snow around his parents as they embraced. Then they ferried groceries into the house. On the final round, the couple was joined in the doorway by a tall man in a sea-green pullover. His hatchet nose and tight-lipped face echoed Ivy's softer features. This must be her father, visiting from Florida. The man might have been blond like Ivy once, but now silver hair sprang above his sunburnt forehead. Professor-chic, he wore round-framed tortoise-shell glasses. Grandpa looked burnished and robust, the way Apollo might if immortality allowed a god to age.

Before they shut the door, I saw the tall man sweep up his grandson for a bear hug. Tommy threw back his head laughing, then buried his face in the man's broad chest.

I felt that squeeze around my own heart. I tried to remember those stormbound Saturdays when my mother had zipped me into navy blue snowsuits so Evander could teach me to pitch snowballs. I was a natural righty, but he made me throw left-handed, like him. Like the boy he always wanted.

I saw Tommy Hannah's grandfather swing him in a circle. Kisses to both cheeks; another squeeze. Had my father ever hugged me with such fierce abandon? Had I ever buried my face in his chest to make sure our moment's joy never escaped?

Maybe so. I couldn't remember.

Sunday's slog put church at the center of Hannah family activity. Top of my mind, too.

At nine-thirty, the family piled into Leo's blue SUV for the fifteen-minute drive to the First United Methodist Church. I watched Ivy, Tommy, Grandpa, and Leo march inside the gray stone heap.

I figured the Hannahs would spend at least an hour in the formal service. Maybe forty-five minutes socializing in the fellowship room afterwards. If they joined committee meetings, the stay at First United would be longer.

Plenty of time to cool my heels. I headed for my own date with the divine. I drove to Bethel AME Church, my mother's chosen path to salvation.

Bethel was located on Quincy Street in the Flats, the Black section of Queenstown. When I was a child, Bethel seemed monumental. Now I recognized its architecture was uninspiring: a redbrick façade with a clumsy stained-glass window. The building extended in a low-slung L, one arm holding the sanctuary, the other an all-purpose meeting hall with a small kitchen. Below the utility wing was a claustrophobic basement. If nuclear war ever struck the Flats, I'd run to this cellar.

Across the street from Bethel was the church's saving grace. A beautiful cemetery sheltered by a mantle of oak and pine trees. Well-tended paths and stone benches with carved lion's paws attested to the loving care of the congregation. I remembered spending third Saturdays each month of high school in a cleanup brigade recruited by the youth pastor. Those neat lawns and walkways marked my gift to the home turf.

The cemetery meant something more to me now. Beyond the black wrought-iron pickets guarding the field of tombstones, my mother and my daughter were buried under a single marker. This graveyard contained my life; everything I'd been, all I cherished was smothered into that cramped plot. I despised the place.

I pulled into a spot near the cemetery gate and doused the engine. I had no intention of visiting either the church or the graveyard. As I studied the building, tendrils of music fluttered across the street. *Wade in the water, children.* I felt the spiritual's notes graze my cheek. *God's gonna trouble the water.* My face grew hot and I pressed my forehead against the windowpane to cool off.

I'd endured eighteen years of fiery services at Bethel, enough to cleanse my soul of all transgressions for eternity.

Fleeing memories, I left the Jeep and walked two blocks to a triangular outcropping of flagstone and grass that divided the street in two.

I sat on a knee-high stone wall. The barrier framed an 1876 monument to the sons of Queenstown who had died in the Civil War. Their names were inscribed on the pedestal supporting a life-size statue of a young man. The marble soldier had keen eyes shaded by a flat Union cap. He gripped a rifle in his left hand and a parchment scroll in the right. Though eroded by time, the words *Union* and *Freedom* were still visible on the scroll.

As a child, I believed this square-jawed soldier, not much older than me, was the guardian of the Flats.

Below the pedestal was an iron replica of a cannon. The artillery aimed beyond the tip of the triangle, pointing down Drew Street toward the heart of Q-Town. Originally, twelve iron balls were stacked in a pyramid below the cannon's muzzle. Every Sunday in spring and summer, my mother let me play on the grassy apron around the monument. I'd pluck dandelions and balance on the low wall after services. I figured she thought this soldier was our protector, just like I did.

When I was a sophomore in high school, marauders defaced the monument, stealing three of the cannonballs. Police never caught the vandals.

But everyone at Queenstown High knew the facts.

This prank was part of spring initiation ceremonies for the Knights of the New Round Table. The Knights were a band of Ku Klux Klan hopefuls, boys eager to start shaving so they could join the senior gang.

Six hundred kids attended my high school. Evenly divided Black, white, and Latino, with a sprinkle of Asians. We all knew the Knights by name. Sutton and Hughes were defensive linemen on the varsity football team. Atkins sat across the lab bench from me in Bio 2. Don Bennett was my study partner in business administration. Kids said Don was the ringleader of the raid on the Civil War memorial.

We were neck-deep in the Klan swamp. Life raft sunk; safety vest punctured. Best to keep dog-paddling with your lip zipped.

No one turned in the culprits. We knew there was no percentage in squealing. The grown-up KKK would protect the recruits from prosecution. Why risk the bruises and earn the label of snitch?

At fifteen, I answered a vital question: which side of the law would I be on? Both at once, if I could pull it off.

And I learned a vital lesson: whose side would the law be on? Not mine, I knew for certain.

I became a cop to fulfill my father's expectations. I became a private eye to satisfy my own.

After the cannonball stunt, my mother told me the KKK history of our town. The Talk—survival techniques like learning protective behavior for when you were confronted by cops—was crucial to growing up Black in Q-Town.

"Trust is like sponge cake," Alma said, "sweet but squishy. You craving that sugar, but the foundation goes soft when you step." We were in the kitchen snapping green beans for Sunday supper. "You can't rely on your gut, Vandy. You best learn early on not to trust nobody."

Were we talking about race relations or something else? Alma's pursed lips didn't give away the game. Then she snatched the pot of beans from the table and banged it on the stove. She cursed the KKK again, so I figured the hood-and-torch mob remained the topic of our lesson.

Alma explained Q-Town was the capital of Klan activity in Mason

County from the 1920s onward. Cross burnings, beatings; broken church windows. Black-owned truck farms and stores destroyed. After supper, we strolled toward the center of town. Alma showed me the vacant lot where Kate's Kountry Kitchen stood on Academy Street. A Klan clubhouse. She noted how the Kozy Klean Kafé bragged of serving fish every day but Friday. I was surprised to learn Catholics and Jews joined Blacks in the KKK hit parade. Alma looked at me with pity, then pressed her hand to my brow as if I was sick. How could a daughter of hers be so naive?

Shaking her head, Alma continued the lesson. By the seventies, brazen acts of bigotry were replaced by subtlety. Pointy hoods, brass knuckles, and rubber cudgels were stowed in attics. Restaurants ditched their Kozy names. The Klan went underground, Alma said. Jersey was hep to the new vibe. Cool, man. Who wanted to be the Garden State Bull Connor?

"But they're still out there, Vandy. Believe it." My mother's eyes turned black as flint. "Your daddy may show you chess and teach you to count your bridge hand. But *I'm* telling you to always count the room." She paused to let the lesson sink in. "You better count how many folks from each camp in that room when you walk in. Otherwise, you can count on a bruising. Or worse."

I never learned if the cannonball raid earned those boys entry into the club. Had Ted Sutton, Jake Hughes, and the others joined the KKK even if they couldn't rock white robes?

When I returned to town last year, I didn't look them up for a reunion. But I did note the cannonballs were still missing.

Despite my parka, the stone ledge below the soldier's monument chilled my ass. As did the trip down memory lane.

I hustled to the Jeep. At the cemetery fence, I tipped a salute toward the graves I should have visited. *Alma and Monica, forgive me.* I cross-my-heart promised to double my stay next time.

I followed the Hannahs home to Allen Street.

Sunday afternoon turned into snowman construction time. Despite his Florida roots, Tommy's grandpa did most of the snow rolling and lifting. Three tiers traditional, no mod touches allowed. The kid fixed twigs for arms and charcoal briquettes for eyes, smile, and buttons. Ivy brought the mandatory carrot nose and Leo donated a blue plaid scarf.

Cheesy, but the normality of the scene lifted my heart. I aimed my phone for a Hallmark photo.

Spoiling the shot, a taxi pulled between me and the Hannahs' front lawn. I watched Jo Hannah, mayor of Q-Town, lumber past the snow-man, a giant pizza box in her arms. Balanced on the carton was a black top hat. The door flew open. I snapped the back of the mayor's camel-hair coat as she pushed past her nephew into the dark foyer. Two minutes later, Tommy burst through the door, top hat clutched to his chest. The mayor joined her great-nephew, placing the hat on the snowman's head with solemn ceremony. Clapping, they rushed inside.

I knocked off for the night. These people were so sweet my molars hurt thinking about them. How could a model family like the Han-nahs be in trouble?

CHAPTER **EIGHT**

I followed Ivy Hannah for the next three days. The weekend had showcased Ivy's devotion to her family. In contrast, Monday, Tuesday, and Wednesday were all about me time. I tracked Ivy through a parade of big-box spending, volunteer work, and self-indulgent splurges. To remain inconspicuous as I trailed her, I made a few purchases myself.

By Thursday afternoon, my shoe leather and my credit card were worn thin. When Ivy headed for home, I retreated to my office for coffee and a consultation with my partner, Elissa Adesanya. As a sounding board for testing my ideas, Elissa always provided reliable insights. Her interrogation tactics involved sarcasm, often directed at my clients. This session, I was the target of her caustic observations. Elissa teased me about the mound of data in my file on Ivy Hannah.

"You mean to say the woman dragged your ass from Monday 'til now and all you've got to show are receipts from TJ Maxx and Barnes and Noble?"

Elissa stretched long legs on the sofa in her office, four-inch patent pumps wriggling above one armrest. Peacock-blue trousers draped from her ankles, the matching jacket thrown across the swivel chair behind her desk.

"Girl, you're tripping," she said. "Or you're slipping."

I couldn't stick to the stiff guest chair while she grilled me. I paced in front of the couch.

"Not all." I waved my hands in defense. "She went to Rite-Aid and ShopRite, too."

"And every other store that uses misspelling as a sales gimmick?" Elissa enjoyed the hell out of this. "You better give me the blow-by-blow on this chick's week. Before you write up the notes for her man."

Elissa was my boss, friend, and conscience. If she nagged, she did it with the best of intentions. She'd saved my ass more than once. Her judgment, in and out of court, was impeccable.

I huffed in mock annoyance. Actually, I was glad to review the data out loud. I wanted to find a pattern, shape the incidents into meaningful clues. Elissa's talk technique could help me outline my report to Leo.

"Right. Monday was Ivy's self-care time," I began. "After she dropped the kid at day care, she drove straight to Bath and Things. I could see her through the window buying a basketful of candles, body lotion, and shower gels."

"Matching sets?" Elissa's giggling exploded into a snort. "Or did she mix it up? You know, one scent for hubby, another for the side boy?"

"I do . . . not . . . know. Okay?"

"Where'd Miss Ivy go next on this self-indulgence tour?"

"She spent two hours at Antoine's Salon."

"Only two? That's white-girl time. I mean, a sister'd take four hours minimum for the full treatment. Head to toe." Elissa snickered. "That's why Antoine won't let us near his place."

"True. And he won't do our hair anyway. As you well know."

I winked to show I remembered Elissa's threat to bring legal action against the salon when they refused to blow-dry her hair before a court appearance. She'd switched to elaborate box-braid styles after that confrontation.

"You know that's right," she said, poking a dagger-length nail under a bun of extensions on top of her head.

I continued: "When Ivy came out, her hair was shaped and styled. Maybe five inches chopped off, with a sleek wedge cut at the nape. She looked fresh. As Belle would say, 'righteous.'"

Elissa bowed to her better half's better taste. "See any sign of a stalker at the beauty parlor?"

"No, but when Ivy left Antoine's, she had a girlfriend in tow. Thick brunette with thick curls. Must have been a celeb client because

Antoine himself followed them through the door and watched them drive off in the other girl's car. They went to that new Thai restaurant in Charlesburg. You know it?"

"Yeah, Belle and I tried it last week. The food was off the chain. Best pad Thai I've tasted in years. And service was on point. You should check it out." She paused to deliver the zinger: "Take one of your little boy toys there for a treat."

I snapped my mouth to bottle a smart-alecky retort. I knew Elissa disapproved of my social life.

Five times since August, she and Belle had lectured me on safe sex. It got ugly fast. They clicked tongues and wagged fingers like the model parents in a 1950s fright documentary on dating dangers. When that didn't work, Mommy and Mama stuck STD pamphlets in the desk drawer in my office. Then they dropped boxes of Trojans in my blazer pockets. What next, a chastity belt?

In December, I shut down Elissa's sixth rant on my lifestyle options. "Bad. Moves. No. Strings," I said, a handclap for each word.

"What's that? The motto on your family crest?" Her sneer was epic, flowing across my office like a glacier.

I countered: "My brand. My way."

To settle the debate, she threw a fountain pen at my head. The punctuation to her closing argument: "Stupid girl."

On Christmas Eve, in front of her overdecorated tree, we made up. If Elissa didn't buy my "bad moves" line, at least she'd swallowed her opinions. Until now.

Despite the truce, this dig about boy toys showed she still objected to my bed partners. Quality, quantity, identity? Whatever her beef, not her business.

I scowled, waiting to cool off before I continued my report on Ivy Hannah.

"Ivy and her friend met two other women at the restaurant," I said at last. "They took a table near the front window."

"So you snapped lots of pictures of the four pretties, right?"

"I did."

I thumbed my cell phone for the gallery of Ivy shots. I showed Elissa photos of the four women laughing, clapping, hugging, and toasting. Auburn mermaid, curly-headed brunette, pixie-cut blonde, and Ivy. Casting straight from the limited imagination of a Hollywood studio executive.

Elissa thought so, too. Sitting up, she straightened her body-con blue turtleneck. "Looks like outtakes from an episode of *Sex and the City,* third season. You remember, the one where things went sideways after the redhead broke up with her geeky boyfriend." She returned the phone to me. "Any idea what they talked about over the Chablis?"

"No, I wish I'd thought to record instead of taking still snaps. Then I could have tried lipreading." I sighed over lost opportunities. "Anyway, after lunch, Ivy split from her friends. She took a taxi from the restaurant back to where her car was parked. Then she picked up the kid and landed at home by three-thirty."

"For quiet time with her papa before Leo returned from a hard day at the lab."

"Probably. In any event she didn't go out again on Monday."

"And did you catch anyone paying undue attention to Ivy?" Bobbing eyebrows. "Aside from you?"

"No. I didn't see anyone of note." I thought over the possibilities: cashiers, taxi drivers, bank tellers, shampoo boys, and waiters. Not a deep ocean to trawl.

Elissa rose, strode to the window, and cranked open a horizontal pane. Frigid gusts pommeled our faces. She said, "You ever think, maybe our Miss Ivy is digging in another garden. Could be her secret boy is a girl."

I bounced upright. "Maybe. But I got no evidence. You could check, right?"

Elissa snorted. "You mean, tap that vast network of lesbian spies I've flung across Queenstown?"

"Yeah, sure."

"Aye, aye, Captain." Elissa chuckled and clicked her heels. "I'll get right on it." She was teasing, but I figured it didn't hurt to ask.

She unwrapped cellophane from a pack of Salems and lit up. Fearing the wrath of Belle, we fanned the smoke toward the cracked window.

After two deep inhalations, Elissa revived the examination of Ivy's week. "Tuesday more of the same?"

"No. Quite different."

"How so?"

"This was volunteer day at First United Methodist."

"Nice . . . I guess. See anything unusual?"

"Not really. Ivy parked in the lot at the rear of the church. I didn't go inside, so I don't know where she works in the building. But I did observe her open the back door four times during her shift."

"Deliveries?"

"Yep. First, I saw a white florist van. Ivy held the door open as the guy carted an armful of cut flowers inside. Twenty minutes later a cab showed up. Ivy helped a dark-haired teenage girl haul two sacks of clothing from the taxi's trunk. At eleven-thirty, a catering van arrived. Ivy propped the door while two service staff carried trays of sandwiches and bowls of salad into the church. The van stayed in the parking lot for three hours."

Elissa puffed a smoke ring. "Lunch for committee members, deacons and such, is my guess."

"Maybe Bible study classes or book club."

"Busy girl, this Ivy." My friend's eye roll was monumental.

"At two-thirty, she opened the back door for a plumber."

"Uh-oh. I'm gonna guess, emergency call."

"Right?" I squeezed out a *yikes* expression and Elissa mirrored me.

She blew a gray spurt toward the window. "Volunteer work is tough going. Any more visitors for Church Lady Ivy?"

"No, that was it. At four-fifteen, she went home."

"You took pictures of all these vans and handymen?"

"For sure."

Elissa nodded. "And how was yesterday?"

"Back to Target in the morning."

"Twice in one week? Girlfriend is capital-S strange. What was Ivy after this time?"

"I couldn't get too close, of course. But I watched her pick out three outfits for her son. In the women's section, she chose a cobalt-blue V-neck, an oatmeal-color cable-knit sweater, and two pairs of leggings, black and gray. Then she hit the greeting card aisle."

"Don't tell me." Elissa's cheeks stretched into a feline smirk. "Early Valentine's Day shopping."

"Nope, birthday. She lingered in the 'From Wife to Husband' section for fifteen minutes before she found the right one. Double-size, crusted with glitter and a pop-up cardboard cake inside." I spread my fingers to show how big the card was.

"Nice. And they say marriage kills romance." Elissa rotated, waving her cigarette toward me. "You think girlfriend was exaggerating with that display of lovey-dovey for hubby?"

"Maybe. Or she's into Leo for real," I said. "Can't read her."

"Did he buy the act? That's the million-dollar question."

Buzzing from the desk phone ended our debriefing. Elissa fielded the call, frowning at the console, though her voice was warm as oven-fresh cornbread. When she hung up, teeth sucking punctuated lip smacking as she slipped into her black reefer coat.

"Thugs and thugettes on the road again," she said, pulling open the door. "I've got to meet the Palko family at police headquarters to pry their daughter from jail. This is darling Megan's second DUI arrest in four months. Talk about a menace to society."

As she swept through the outer office, Elissa dropped a kiss on Belle's forehead. "Sorry, babe, I'll be late for dinner."

The two women faced each other in front of the reception desk, a mini-standoff brewing.

Belle harrumphed, adjusted her ice-blond Marilyn wig, and braced fists on hips. She turned to me. "Veal cutlets, pasta with homemade pesto sauce. Fresh breadsticks from Gino's. You interested?" Her wink was buried in the creases around her eyes. "Perry Masonnette here can eat leftovers."

I shared meals twice a month with the couple. Their whitewashed stucco house had been my first landing place when I retreated to Queenstown seven months ago. I had dawdled in their guest bedroom for the duration of the summer renovations on my place. Elissa had joked that keeping me in the mother-in-law suite prevented their real mothers-in-law from visiting. In those first months, the two women watched me like chefs tending a soufflé, afraid I'd collapse after my career cratered. I grumbled a lot, pretended to balk at the nonstop surveillance. But I slow-walked my move when construction was done. These glimpses of domestic bliss did me good. Made me fantasize that maybe the beautiful things didn't always have to vanish. The way they had for me. And Belle threw down like a pro chef. The warmth of her kitchen would always be a magnet.

"Interested, yes," I said. When Elissa paused, hand on the suite door, I added, "But can I get a rain check? I've got to wrap my report for Leo Hannah tonight. He's due here at nine tomorrow morning."

"Your loss, Leo's gain," Belle chirped.

Satisfied she wouldn't lose any veal cutlets to me, Elissa skated through the door. Belle puttered at her station for another thirty minutes, then quit for the evening.

I knocked off two hours later, the report polished like a river stone.

The next morning, I beat Elissa and Belle into the office. After my first coffee and some tinkering, I printed a copy of my report. Twelve pages, double-spaced; executive summary and timeline annex included. Photos attached to the electronic version. Maybe Leo Hannah preferred paper. If so, I was on it.

I didn't get ready; I stayed ready. No option for me. My need for referrals and clients was everlasting, especially those with high-end connections and deep pockets. My customers were always right.

Leo Hannah might be right, but this Friday he was late. Our nine A.M. appointment came and went. Elissa headed to a client meeting; Belle left for the bank. I fidgeted, ticking the minutes, ruffling the paper report.

My direct line rang at nine thirty-five.

Leo's voice was slow, the diction muddy. "I can't make our appointment. Flu hit me bad last night." He sounded like his head was jammed in a wooden bucket.

"Sorry to hear that, Leo," I said.

"I need you to come by my house. Drop off the report." Was his hand over the receiver? Or was his throat clogged?

His illness sounded contagious.

"Look, you're sick. Let's meet tomorrow. Or next week. When you're feeling better."

"No," he snapped. "Bring it here. Now."

"Sure thing."

Before I could add, "See you soon," the line went dead.

I arrived at the Hannah house twenty minutes later. A black-and-white Queenstown PD squad car was ditched in front, nose on the lawn, rear on the driveway, exhaust fumes pumping from the tailpipe.

As I skidded into the curb behind a parked taxi, two uniformed white officers raced toward the front door, guns drawn.

CHAPTER **NINE**

Blinded by ice flares, I toppled the snowman on the lawn as I sprinted toward the Hannahs' front steps. Leo had phoned me. He must be inside. Ivy's silver car was parked near the garage. She must be home, too. Where was Tommy?

The cops disappeared inside, leaving the front door cracked. Their squad car rumbled in the driveway where it blocked the twin SUVs.

I pressed the door wide. When it banged against the wall, I flinched. I held my breath, balanced on the threshold. I didn't know what the police had found inside. Or how they might react to a Black stranger bursting in unannounced. I didn't want to make a hasty entrance and end up as another BLM statistic.

A shriek punctured the foyer. Male, shrill, and thin like wire. I stepped onto the tile, pausing in front of the gilt-framed mirror. I heard muffled words, then the same male voice dwindled to groans.

I shouted, "Anyone need help?" Two more steps, my hands held palms out at shoulder height. "Leo, are you all right?"

Sobs, sputters. I heard my name in the jumble of words. An officer appeared in the dining room entrance. His face was white as an iceberg, points of red pulsing on each cheek. His eyes pinwheeled in their sockets as he looked at me. He motioned for me to approach.

Before speaking, he caught his breath in two gulps. "You Myrick?" He'd holstered his service weapon, but fingers worried the leather safety snap. Sweat beaded his hairline.

I nodded. "Yes, Officer." I stepped closer, lowering my hands. "I'm a private investigator. Evander Myrick. My ID's in my wallet. Back pocket. I'm reaching for it now."

I matched movements to words, extracting the license and placing it in the man's hand. His fingers shook as he returned the card.

"Okay, Mr. Hannah says he knows you. You better come inside." He caved his chest to let me pass around him into the dining room.

Carnage racked the space. I saw two bodies, sprawled on the carpet, a tide of blood swilled between them. Red covered the right side of Ivy Hannah's head. Her eyes were half-open, the lids batting. Frantic jerks drove her fingers into the hollows of her cheeks. Her mouth gaped, then closed as I staggered forward.

Behind me, I heard the crackle of police walkie-talkies. The first cop was calling for backup. "We need two buses over here."

A second cop yelled into the air in the direction of the walkie-talkie. "We got two down. Female breathing. Male dead."

Garble from the dispatcher, then the first cop replied, "Yes, I said one before. Now I'm telling you send two."

Three yards from Ivy's feet a dark-haired man lay chest down on the carpet. His face was turned toward me. Blood streamed over his forehead and cheek, pooling below his jaw. I saw a gray shadow spread from his lips toward his ears and throat, a leaden stain under his skin. I knew he was dead, even before I looked into his frozen eye. The source of the blood on his face was covered by a thicket of straight hair. A bullet wound punctured the tawny skin of his neck above his jacket collar. The wooden handle of a hammer lay next to the man's gloved fingers. Blood and blond hair caked the hammer's ballpeen head.

Leo Hannah knelt on the floor beside Ivy. His right hand gripped her shoulder, his left was clamped on his mouth. I saw Leo's gray sweatpants and shirt were drenched in blood. He swung his head toward me, eyes drowning under waves of tears.

"You—you came," he sobbed. "You came . . ." Babble dissolved the string of words.

When I crouched beside Leo, the second officer stamped toward me. The metal zipper of his overcoat brushed my ear.

"Don't touch anything," he barked. "This is a crime scene." Unlike the junior officer who'd vetted me, this cop wasn't shaking.

"Got it, Officer," I said. "Just trying to speak with my client here."

As the cop took a step back, melting snow dribbled from his boot laces, diluting the blood on the carpet to pink. I heard sirens wail beyond the picture windows. Red and blue streams from the revolving lights of three patrol cars dazzled the white streaks on the trees.

I touched Leo's shoulder. "Where's the baby? Where's Tommy?"

Leo inhaled. Before he answered, the cop snapped, "What baby? There's a kid in this house? Now?"

"They have a son," I said. "Three years old."

The cop yelled at his subordinate: "Phillips, search the place. Find that kid. Move."

Phillips scraped his hand across his face. Chalk erased the red in his cheeks. Then he scrambled toward the hallway, equipment clanking on his utility belt.

Leo shook his head. "No, Tommy's at school. The day-care center. Ivy took him this morning." He looked at his stricken wife and caressed her eyebrow. "Like she always does. Then she came back. And, and . . ." He lowered his chin to his chest. I squeezed the fleshy pad of his shoulder.

Boots pounded in the hall. Emergency crews pushed cold air through the house as they bustled in with medical kits and equipment. Police officers lined the dining room like blue wainscoting, while the medical staff attended the injured and cleared the dead. As first on the scene, the senior officer directed traffic; his nameplate identified him as W. Torriano.

As colleagues swarmed over the scene, Phillips helped Leo to a chair at the end of the dining table. In the middle of the table were a half-full glass of water and two empty coffee mugs, one with pink lipstick stains. I dragged a chair to sit with my knee pressed into Leo's.

I wanted to learn as much as I could from Leo before the police and ambulances swept him away. Heartless, maybe; gruesome, sure. Under the sweatpants, his skin was still soaked with his wife's warm blood. But I wanted the truth and I needed it fast, before misery distorted Leo's memory and repetition hardened his story.

"What happened after you phoned me, Leo?"

I looked up at Phillips, hovering over Leo's right shoulder. The young cop's frown registered bewilderment.

I wanted him on our side, so I explained: "I was working a case for Mr. Hannah this week. We had an appointment to review my report in my office at nine. He called me shortly after that to say he was sick and I should come by the house instead."

The cop nodded, squaring his stance, his hands clasped behind his back. Beyond us, monitors bleeped as a huddle of EMTs probed Ivy Hannah's throat and arms.

I touched Leo's wrist. Flakes of blood transferred to my fingernails. I wanted his full attention, so I didn't flinch from the gore.

"Leo, tell me what happened after you phoned me."

He swung his gaze to me. "I went downstairs. I have an office in the basement. I thought I could catch up on emails as I waited for you to arrive."

He paused to make sure I was following. "After maybe ten or fifteen minutes I heard a thump upstairs. Then a second one, louder than the first. Ivy had already returned from dropping off Tommy at school. She was back home even before I called you. She'd yelled down to the basement when she walked in the door, so I knew she was in the house. But something about the thumping sounds didn't seem right."

Leo paused, clutching his right fist in his left palm. "You know how petite Ivy was. Thin as a blade of grass. She hardly made any noise at all when she moved around the house. I used to tease her, saying she loved to creep up on me, she was that quiet." Flickering smile of remembrance. Then dread returned. "The sounds this morning startled me. The thumps were loud, heavy. Strange."

He narrowed his eyes as if hearing again the noises that ended peace in his life. "Like boulders falling."

"Okay, then what did you do, Leo?" I repeated his name to keep his attention focused on me, on telling his story. Away from the blood-soaked spectacle in the room beyond us.

"I went upstairs, of course, to investigate the noise." Leo coughed, then pressed a palm to his lips.

Behind him, Phillips the rookie gasped. I was glad for the audience; corroboration of Leo's account was good. But I wanted Phillips quiet. So I burned the cop with my eyes. He clamped his lips shut.

"Go on, Leo. What happened next?"

"I saw him, the stalker. The one I told you about. He was leaning over Ivy. He had a hammer in his hand, and he was hitting her on the head. She was screaming and pushing at him. But he kept on hitting her. Even when I yelled, he hit her again." A sob behind stiff hands. "It was awful."

I leaned to drop an arm around Leo's neck. I pressed my forehead against his. Phillips stepped close, gripping the shoulder of the weeping man. We stayed frozen like that for thirty seconds, maybe more.

I rustled my coat to break the misery. "Tell me the rest, Leo. If you can. I want to hear it all."

He nodded and wiped a thumb under his nose. Phillips pulled a crumpled tissue from his coat pocket and pressed it into Leo's hand.

"I ran to the study. We keep a gun there. In a safe, of course." Leo blinked, his eyes shifting left to glimpse the listening cop. "I grabbed the gun and returned to the dining room. When I entered, the man was crouched over Ivy. He was hitting her with the hammer. The hammer I'd left in the kitchen this morning. Ivy wants me to hang a picture in the hallway, so I left the hammer out as a reminder."

Leo touched his bald spot as if it were a talisman for luck. Maybe it worked, maybe the caress gave him new strength. He shuddered and went on.

"I saw him hitting her. I fired twice. Oh, God. I don't know how I hit him. Or where. But he went down. Then I called 911. I said a man had attacked my wife and I'd shot him. I said I needed help. Then you came. That's all I know." He blew a long sigh, the weight lifted.

At that moment, two burly medical technicians hoisted Ivy onto a stretcher. They covered her body to the neck with a blue blanket. I took off my coat, dropped it over Leo's shoulders, and steered him after the retreating gurney.

From between the white columns, Phillips and I watched him stumble across the lawn to the ambulance. After the EMTs collapsed the stretcher's legs and shoved it into the vehicle, Leo climbed inside, crouching next to his wife.

The ambulance bowled between rows of squad cars as shivering clumps of neighbors watched and muttered. At the end of the block, the ambulance revved its doleful siren.

"Poor guy," Phillips said. "She sure looked like a goner, didn't she?"

I agreed but refused to speak the grim truth out loud. "Could be she pulls through. You never know."

"Yeah, you never know."

When Phillips went inside, I jerked the cell phone from my pocket. My gloves were stuffed in the coat I'd given to Leo Hannah. Cold fingers made me fumble the device into a snowdrift. I retrieved the phone, swiped it on my jeans, and blew a prayer over its black surface. I tapped the glass and the phone sprang to life. Prayers answered. I focused the camera on the red taxi abandoned next to my Jeep across the street. I snapped two shots.

Shivering, I turned toward the warmth of the house, slipping into the clutch of crime scene technicians crowded in the dining room.

My job was not over. Leo Hannah's case had taken a left turn. But he was still my client. I had more evidence to collect and a report to finish.

CHAPTER **TEN**

I snapped eight shots of the death room, then darted through the Hannah house, leaving the first floor to the team of crime scene technicians.

I wasn't squeamish; I'd seen death on the job as a New Brunswick city cop and as campus police at Rutgers. But familiarity didn't breed comfort. After catching the initial examination of the dead man, I wanted breathing space.

From the dining room entrance, I watched two techs roll the man on his back. His sleeve hiked from a brown wrist, flopped across his chest. The leather jacket was flimsy protection—too little, too late. When he was flat, a cop patted the jacket, then the pants pockets. He found a fistful of keys, some coins, a cell phone, and a pack of chewing gum. Each item was stowed in a separate plastic evidence bag. He pulled out a thin billfold and extracted an ID card and a driver's license.

"Says here he's Hector Ramírez."

"Run it through the databases. I want everything we got on this asshole. Now. Township, county, state. Where he gets his hair cut, where his granny buys her tortillas, where he busts his balls. Everything. Got it?"

"Yeah, Sarge."

"Address on the driver's license is local. FitzRoy Street."

"Don't mean shit."

"Sure. Card says he worked for one of them local spic taxi companies."

"Which one?"

"Compadre. You know, fleet of red Priuses with black lettering."

The taxi parked outside was from that company. I figured the cops had noticed it. No need for me to comment. I'd let them make the connection on their own.

"Like fucking cock-a-roaches all over town," the sergeant said.

"Yeah, that one."

"Run their records, too. I want whatever they got on this Hector González."

"Ramírez."

"Yeah, okay, Ramírez. Whatever. Get on it."

I blew a stiff sigh. Loud enough Torriano eyed me. I counted the house: twelve white officers, four white technicians. And me. My dining room photos were enough for now. I wanted out of there. Before the racism—casual like flip-flops down the shore—swamped me. Blowing up at the cops was a punk move. I'd end up on the wrong end of a fight with no way out. I didn't need the sour stomach and sore heart. Or the diversion. My goal was to collect evidence to bolster Leo Hannah's story. He'd claimed self-defense in the face of domestic violation. I wanted to prove his case.

I sneaked down to the basement. Leo's home office was small, ten feet by twelve, carved from a corner of the original rec room. He'd preserved the 1970s dark paneling and mustard carpeting in the windowless office. When I entered, the overhead light—a two-bar fluorescent fixture—was flickering amid pocked tiles. I could see where the faux maple wall had buckled, revealing tufts of pink wadding.

A black swivel chair featured a tall executive-style back rest. Squeezed into one corner was a bookshelf with a printer, reams of paper, and boxes of jet ink cartridges. Yellowing issues of the *Queenstown Herald* were stacked next to an unopened package of legal pads. On the desk, a Dell laptop stood at attention, the 21-inch screen upright and dark. If he'd jumped from the desk, startled by noises from the first floor, this was how the computer should look: open and abandoned.

I photographed the computer and the ring light clamped to its lid. An old-style gooseneck desk lamp craned over the laptop, which sat on a black blotter. The mouse pad featured his company's logo, Arc-Dev Pharmaceuticals. The office was murky, as if draped in a shawl. Even with the overhead light on, I couldn't read the titles of file folders scattered on the desk beside the laptop. I wondered if Leo had conducted his early morning work session in this gloom. The circle lamp was extinguished. Had Leo taken time to douse his desk lamp before running upstairs? Or maybe he didn't need extra light to read emails. An orange and blue mug labeled UVA idled next to the laptop. No coffee dregs or drying tea bag. Maybe, despite his head cold, Leo had skipped morning caffeine.

Upstairs, I dodged around the duo dusting the kitchen for prints. I figured they'd find plenty of DNA samples from all the Hannahs. Plastic bowls with dinosaurs were stacked in the dish rack next to a sparkling set of small plates. I detected no crumbs on the toaster or smears on the blender. The Mr. Coffee machine was cold and empty. If the Hannahs had eaten breakfast that morning, someone had cleaned up with a vengeance.

I took a quick look in the hall powder room. I wanted to find clues to Leo's sudden onset of flu symptoms. The bathroom looked like a model unit in a show house. The bar of mint-green hand soap was spotless, the towel crisp, and the medicine cabinet empty.

Four upstairs bedrooms were just as tidy, all freshly painted in bland cream, except for Tommy's room, which was splashed with circus wallpaper. Red molding around the ceiling matched the painted slats of his crib. Three years old and still behind bars. I didn't take any pictures. The violence of the dining room seemed a galaxy away from these stuffed giraffes and tigers. I wondered if Tommy would ever play in this room again. Or would his father whisk him away with a fairy-tale explanation about Ivy's disappearance? I didn't know what I'd do in these awful circumstances. But inventing a story about Mommy's never-ending vacation trip might be my fallback position.

In the first-floor library, I joined a police officer to stare at the open maw of a small safe on the second row of a bookshelf. The steel walls were two inches thick; the dial lock rotated smoothly when the officer grazed it. Inside were a carton of .38 cartridges snuggled next to a Tiffany ring box and a thin black hinged case for a necklace.

The cop said, "Must be nice." He jabbed the blue box with his thumb. "My wife would kill for one of these."

When he swung the safe door on its silent hinge, I asked, "How long you figure it'd take to open this?"

"From a standing start? Four, five revolutions might need twenty seconds. Fumble, try again, and you push it toward a minute. Why?"

"Just wondering." I peered at the mahogany shelf on either side of the safe. "Was the safe open when you got here?"

The cop tugged at his hat. "Yeah, the lock wasn't engaged. But the door was pushed snug against the body of the safe." He twisted his lips to one side. "Not slammed shut. Just eased closed, gentle like."

I blew at the parade of encyclopedias and volumes on European art that flanked the vault. "You see the same dust I'm seeing?"

"Yeah. I don't figure they do a lot of reading in here."

I guessed they rarely touched the safe, either. Why would they? Pistols and designer jewelry were not everyday accessories. Without practice, unfamiliarity with the lock might make quick use problematic. Was Leo nimble-fingered or a klutz? Did he freeze under duress? Or was his mind clear and his grip automatic when he reached for the gun in this vault? I snapped photos of the safe open and closed.

The cop glanced around the room, taking in a dainty desk with scrolled legs, two heavy armchairs, and a sofa upholstered in red-striped fabric. He pointed at a wall covered by a large oil painting of two ladies in wide hats boating on a sun-dappled lake.

"Wanna bet there's a flat-screen TV hiding behind there?" he asked.

I shook off the bet. He was right. Sony smart screen mounted on a retractable arm. Like the cop said, nice.

When I returned to the dining room, Hector Ramírez had been removed. I found a familiar figure examining the bloodstained carpet where he died.

Robert Sayre was Q-Town's chief of police. Barrel fists on waist, legs wide, he stared down his glasses at me as I reentered the death room. In his black puffer jacket, he claimed all the space his title allowed.

"What're you doing here, Myrick?"

In high school he called me Vandy, using a sweet voice and flashing dimples to plead his cause. I called him Bobby then and we dated for a sweaty minute or two. Kids' play, but memorable.

Now the bark was strictly official. "Make it good."

"A case brought me here." Firm, quick, no smile. We were thirty years past batting lashes, so I returned the stare. "I'm doing follow-up."

Sayre grunted, then swung on Torriano.

Glaring daggers at me, the officer in charge rumbled, "She's legit, chief."

I'd known Robert Sayre since eighth grade, when he was still chubby Bobby and his brother Keyshawn peddled bootleg copies of *X-Men* movies. Both boys had grown tall and hard since we left high school. To disguise his scanty hair, Robert shaved his head now, highlighting the jut of his brow and the width of his nose. With the salt-and-pepper beard, he looked good: meaner, but still alluring.

He leaned close. "What case you working?"

Torriano slunk from the room as I inhaled to answer. A newcomer's arrival cut me off.

Josephine Hannah rushed into the space between me and Sayre. She was compact and agile, with heavy hips. Her helmet of black hair framed her face like a small-town Cleopatra. Frigid air wafting from the lapels of her camel-hair coat made me shiver. I caught hints of lavender and lemon on the icy draft.

The mayor swung her head from side to side, like a predator sizing up the herd. "She's working for my nephew." Energy bristled around her, forcing us to retreat. "What she says to you, Bobby, she says to me."

"Sure thing, Mayor, whatever you want," Sayre purred. I remembered those undulating tones from years ago. He tried a half-smile.

Hannah squared on him, her voice a lash. "Driving here, I took a call. Ivy died on the operating table ten minutes ago. This is a murder investigation now."

CHAPTER **ELEVEN**

Standing in the living room, I gave the mayor and the police chief a condensed version of the report I'd prepared for Leo Hannah. I'd left the printed pages in my car. I didn't have a document on me they could confiscate. I figured that report belonged to Leo until he instructed me to hand it over. So I neglected to mention it.

Sayre stood like a statue as I talked. Jo Hannah shifted her pear-shaped figure from side to side, her gaze focused on the frozen landscape beyond the windows. Wrapped in their silence, I rattled off the details of Ivy Hannah's last week: errands around Queenstown were mundane; contacts with friends, service staff, and church volunteers were routine. I'd seen nothing to suggest she was in danger. I deleted the snarky quips I used during my review of this material yesterday with Elissa Adesanya. Now the grim finale daubed every detail in somber strokes.

"What was her mood?" Mayor Hannah's question was abrupt.

I saw Chief Sayre startle at the touchy-feely inquiry. His frown said the investigation would hinge on forensic facts and eyewitness testimony, not woo-woo instinct or suspicions. How was I supposed to read the mind of a woman I'd never spoken to?

Wrinkles softened around the mayor's eyes. This question meant a lot to Jo Hannah. "How did Ivy seem this week?" She twisted her thick fingers as she waited for my answer. "Happy, troubled, distracted, content?"

I said the first word that leapt to mind: "Purposeful. That's how

I'd describe her. Resolute. Of course, I don't know Ivy. Never spoke to her. But she seemed focused and firm. Like she was headed somewhere."

I closed my eyes, trying to picture the woman I'd followed. Instead, the ruby wounds on her body subverted my thoughts. I lowered my voice. "The Ivy I watched this week was loving to her father, tender toward Leo, and devoted to their son."

I thought that account of domestic peace sounded as upbeat as one could hope for in such dire circumstances. I'd wanted to comfort Mayor Hannah in this moment of unimaginable family grief. I expected to see a measure of relief run across her face.

Instead, her mouth sagged, a dark gap splitting the lips. Her tongue darted to one corner and her large eyes shone like moons. "Thank you, Ms. Myrick. That is helpful." Her head dipped left, but the waves over her ears and the black bangs didn't flutter, as if her hair had been carved in onyx.

Jerking her head up, Hannah squared on us. "Here's what I want." She shot her eyes at Sayre. "Bobby, I want to guard my family. Leo is devastated. He's suffered enough. And the baby . . . My God, the baby." She gulped. "I want this case closed before the media drag our name through a shitstorm. I want you to work with Dave. Can you bring in a verdict before Monday?"

David Lindquist was the county prosecutor. I remembered meeting Lindquist years ago at a QPD Christmas party when I was home from college. He was one of the few white people there who talked with my father. After the party, Evander told me Dave Lindquist was a straight arrow. But like most public figures in Mason County, my father said, the prosecutor owed his fortunes—political and personal—to Mayor Hannah.

Now her bleak words ricocheted against the plate-glass window. "Leo, Tommy . . . They're all I've got. I need your help to protect my family. Understand?"

"Yes, Mayor." After snapping the reply, Sayre slanted his gaze to me.

Before he could speak, Hannah said, "Myrick, I want you to help them wrap this case." Her hands shook; tremors rolled from wrist to nails. She thrust the wayward hands in her coat pockets. Lines on her forehead smoothed. "I've been friends with your father for a long time, Vandy. I know you'll do the right thing." A smile twitched, then flattened. "Share all the information you've collected. Understand?"

Of course formed on my lips. I wanted to ask why the appeal to my father's friendship. Was her connection to Evander supposed to make me do my job better?

But the mayor angled her shoulder away, cutting me from her line of vision. She swept toward the hall without another word.

Sayre hummed, whether in appreciation of my performance or in surprise at his boss's swift exit, I couldn't tell.

We watched Mayor Hannah stride across the trampled snow of the front lawn. A bullet-shaped man in a gray coat leaned against the marine-blue Lexus. As the mayor neared, he ran to the street side of the car and got in. She took the rear seat and leaned forward to speak with the driver.

As they sped away, I said, "That guy looks familiar."

"He should. Ted Sutton was the beast of the D-line when we were in high school."

I hiked my brows. I remembered my brief fistfight with Tidy Sutton at the door of the Kings Cross Tavern one week ago.

"He has the same job now," I said. "Only working for the mayor this time?"

"Right. Him and his old pal, Jake Hughes. Still squad mates—now they're private muscle on the mayor's team." Sayre's eye twitched as if he'd sucked a lemon.

I wondered why Q-Town police officers weren't detailed to protect the mayor. But I stored that question in my "check ya later" file.

A sharp gust of wind rattled the windows. We moved toward the center of the living room. I shivered. He tugged his coat collar.

Sayre cleared his throat. "You did good work briefing the mayor." A slight trill at the end of the sentence, like he was surprised by my competence.

I thrived on being underestimated, so I nodded and stuck my hands in my pockets.

He dropped the hammer: "Now you get to do it all over again at headquarters."

When I groaned, he added, "And you turn over your written report. I know you finished your homework on time, like always. Plus, the photos. Everything you got, we review."

"Let me talk with my client first." A weak ploy but worth a shot.

"Nothing doing. Leo's been through an awful shock. The worst thing a man could face. You don't disturb him when he's traumatized and in mourning."

He was right. I owed Leo that privacy. Like the mayor said, her nephew had suffered enough. The idea of meeting him at this moment made my stomach clutch. I didn't want to see Leo, not yet. I didn't have embraces enough or sufficient words to deliver the comfort he required now. Could I pull some nuggets from the avalanche of condolences I'd received after Monica died? We were grief-kin, Leo and I. Now more than contracts and cash united us. We shared suffering, too. Maybe if I dug into my own memories, I'd come up with the right phrases to soothe the pain Leo faced now.

But I didn't want to spend the rest of the day in Queenstown police headquarters. "Then let me come to the station tomorrow morning."

"What you got to do this afternoon that's more important than assisting a police investigation?"

"I want to visit my father. That's what." Before the mayor mentioned Evander, my plan had been vague. Now it hardened.

Sayre's lips pressed together until the pink at their center disappeared. "Yeah, Keyshawn told me how you make regular visits to see Chief Myrick. It's good, you keeping close to him like that, Vandy."

I thought I detected water glimmering at the corners of Bobby Sayre's eyes as he thought about his old mentor and champion. Chief was an honorific title he'd bestowed on my father.

Then the sentimental haze lifted. He snapped, "You call Keyshawn now. Tell him to let your father know you won't be stopping by today. You can catch him tomorrow or Sunday." He thrust his chest toward mine, jabbing my collarbone with a stiff index finger. "I intend to make my preliminary report on this case to the county prosecutor tomorrow. We need your formal statement plus supporting documents tonight."

He glared, I stared.

Sayre broke the standoff. "This is simple. I want to keep my job. I want you to do your job. No fault, no problem. Got it." He bobbed his head. His non-question echoed the mayor's request.

I gave in and made the call to Glendale Memory Care Center.

Keyshawn asked if I thought he should tell my father about the Hannah family tragedy. After all, the old man knew the Hannahs from before the dark curtain descended; maybe he'd appreciate learning the news as soon as possible. Perhaps this death would brush aside the decade of webs draping his memory.

I told Keyshawn to use his judgment, tell the grim story in his own way, at the best time. I doubted Evander Myrick would have any reaction at all. He didn't know Alma or Monica or me. Why should he remember Jo Hannah and her family? But I kept that cynicism to myself.

I had work to do: a case to unpack for the cops and reassemble for my client, Leo Hannah.

When Chief Sayre turned to his team, I fled the murder house. I drove home for coffee and another coat to brace me for my interview with the Q-Town police.

CHAPTER **TWELVE**

The cops kept at me until eleven-fifteen that night.

Police headquarters occupied the first floor and the basement of Queenstown's municipal building. Upper floors held city council chambers, departmental offices, and the local court. Four stories high, this circular fort of pebbled concrete had narrow windows and wide buttresses tapering toward the surrounding parking lot. When we were kids, we invented stories about the alien invasion that dropped the odd structure in our town. To us, the building looked like a spaceship straight out of a *Star Trek* movie. We claimed the city hall, like the spindle-legged water tower, was a relic of the Romulan–Federation wars.

News of the murder of Ivy Hannah rocketed around the municipal building. From the mayor's fourth-floor suite to the sunless basement, city employees bent every effort to wrapping the case. I was the focus of their work, a convenient receptacle for their energies and ambitions. I handed over my written report. Relinquished my phone so the relevant photos could be printed. I dictated hours of testimony and signed four copies of my statement.

I wasn't a suspect, but I received the perp treatment anyway: an interrogation room furnished with an ass-bruising chair; ominous thumps echoing behind one-way mirrors; temperatures dialed to near freezing. Five teams of officers rotated on forty-minute shifts, practicing their good cop/bad cop routines to extract every drop of information. QPD had forty-three sworn officers, all white. I must have seen each one. Only the handcuffs and blazing overhead lamps were missing from the third-degree routine.

Twice I asked to speak with Chief Sayre. I even played the school friend card. No dice. I was told he'd be around to see me. He never showed. I decided Bobby hadn't snubbed me; his subordinates kept him in the dark. I felt better believing that. When I asked to call my lawyer, Elissa Adesanya, I was reminded I was a cooperating witness and not a suspect. I had no need for an attorney. When I demanded my cell phone, I won a chuckle. At the end of my ordeal, a Black assistant returned the phone, dangling it like it was infected before she dropped it on my palm.

Between grilling sessions, I was allowed four toilet breaks and two ten-minute mealtimes. Jamming wrinkled dollar bills in the vending machines, I heard the city hall chatter about my client: Leo Hannah left the hospital at two or maybe three; picked up his son from day care, and retreated to his aunt's brick bungalow, the gossips said. Could he be under sedation? Probably working on a second bottle of rye or vodka, someone snarked. I heard nurses had been dispatched to tend to father and child. Or Ivy's girlfriends were watching Tommy. Or admin assistants from the mayor's office had been assigned to babysitting duties. I wondered if anyone had contacted Ivy Hannah's father. According to rumor, a relay of city employees spontaneously formed to deliver hot casseroles to the mayor's house. Or maybe fast-food joints Chipotle and Popeyes entered the fray. The gossip mill was energetic but uncertain. I watched a fifteen-gallon coffeemaker hoisted from the municipal break room, on its way to the Hannah kitchen to accommodate the hordes expected to descend from across the county and state over the weekend.

When I trudged to my bedroom at eleven-thirty that night, the coil in my stomach refused to unwind. My knees ached, my hips shouted as if I'd been pounding the dance floor for hours; even my knuckles crackled with complaints. If I'd been clubbed with a nightstick by Q-Town's finest, I would have felt better. I tried the needle setting on the showerhead, angling my neck and spine for maximum pounding. No joy. Water slipped between my lips and under my eyelids.

I wanted bourbon, one smoky dose to wash the taste of the day from my tongue.

Using my stiffest towel, I scraped water from my back and thighs. I found the sweatshirt I'd saved from Monica's collection. Eggplant with gold swatches dashed across the front. How had my tiny, beautiful daughter looked so fly in this monstrosity? The sleeves hung below my fingers, the hem cupped my ass. The mirror whined I looked old, depleted.

As I slipped downstairs to the kitchen, my promise to Monica receded. I flung open the door to the upper cabinet. Full bottles of Jack, Old Turkey, and Beam glistened in the shadows. One gulp to soothe the rasp in my throat, one taste to sponge the swill of blood floating on an oatmeal carpet. One more to put me under. I unscrewed the cap of the Jack Daniel's bottle and lifted its mouth to mine. Fumes of caramel and burnt oak carried new images to my mind.

I thought about Tommy Hannah scampering around the snowman his grandfather had built. I saw Leo Hannah drape his scarf below the snowman's carrot nose. I remembered the grin on the face of Ivy's father when he welcomed his family into the warm house. In my little way, I'd helped this family. Monica was right: I hadn't earned this cup of sorrow. Not tonight. I sealed the cap and stowed the bottle beside its brothers in the cabinet.

The next afternoon, thirty-six hours after Ivy Hannah died, the prosecutor for Mason County declared she had been murdered by Hector Ramírez. No charges would be pressed against her husband, Leo Hannah, who had committed justifiable homicide in defense of his wife and home. The mayor's wish to protect her family and name was achieved.

Three Saturdays later, I attended Ivy Hannah's memorial service. Cremation removed the opportunity for a full-blown funeral. From what I remembered of her battered skull, this choice was for the best.

I sat in the rear of the sanctuary of First United Methodist. I took an empty pew where I could prop my elbow in the carved armrest and watch the assembly without having to interact with anyone. Scores of neighbors, friends, coworkers, and classmates filled the church. I recognized Governor Sullivan, the congresswoman from Trenton, and two Democratic party pols, one from South Jersey, one from Newark. I figured other heavy hitters were in the lineup, but I couldn't name them without a scorecard.

Leo Hannah and his aunt arrived on a flurry of murmurs and rustling programs. He wore a long black coat and gloves. She wore the camel-hair coat I'd seen earlier, this time topped with a stiff black hat. He was bareheaded. The balding crown made him seem exposed. I wished he'd also worn a hat to cover his vulnerability. As he marched down the center aisle, I thought Leo's eyes popped when he saw me. Maybe the sudden impression was a trick of the light beaming through high windows behind the altar. His puffy face was mottled with yellow, like a piece of wax fruit. His aunt's cheeks were distended around a pursed red mouth. As they took their seats in the front pew, the Hannahs laced fingers.

In the space below the pulpit, waves of peonies embraced a color portrait of Ivy Hannah. The pink and white flowers harmonized with the bloom on her cheeks. In this picture, her blond hair was long, straggling over her shoulders school-girl style. This look was nostalgic, not the sophisticated bob I'd seen her wear as she emerged from the salon four days before her death.

Between hymns from the church's adult choir and the children's chorus, three friends read passages from Old and New Testament verses they said Ivy loved. I recognized their faces. Or rather their hair: auburn, curly brunette, pixie-cut blonde. I'd seen these women join Ivy for lunch four days before she died. As they spoke, I scanned the program, matching names to faces. I shrugged off my coat to release the humidity gathering under my turtleneck sweater. From my perch, the tributes landed as distant droning. The minister's words were warm, but vague. I wondered if he knew much about Ivy's volunteer work in his church office. Or anything about her at all.

I scanned the crowd for Ivy's father. According to Elissa's city hall contacts, Samuel Decker had been at an academic conference in Europe when a municipal secretary located him to deliver the dreadful news. *Five long days after Ivy's death.* He'd basked in ignorant joy for five days before that call. I didn't wonder how Samuel Decker had taken the blow. I knew for a stone-cold certainty. I'd been on the receiving end of a similar summons to an untimely ceremony. The memories clenched my stomach. I bent to suppress the pain; sour nausea invaded my mouth.

As the organist thundered a recessional, I veered from the crowd. I didn't want to join the reception in the fellowship room. I angled my shoulders to slice through the throng. My connection to these people was tangential, my presence an unhappy reminder of Ivy's death, not a celebration of her life. I pushed across the stone foyer, which echoed with relieved chatter. I heard a muffled laugh as I shoved past the carved double doors to the outside. I wanted to wait to see what happened. On the limestone steps, I drifted into a triangle of sunlight near the wrought-iron railing. I stamped my boots to drive out numbness.

I watched two bodyguards in charcoal overcoats flank the mayor's sedan. Exhaust plumed around the blue Lexus. Sunbeams bounced from their fair heads. From my distance I couldn't see their features, only jets of cold air spewing from their mouths. I figured these were footballers Tidy Sutton and Jake Hughes. In unison, they shifted their aviator sunglasses to follow the departure of a black-haired girl on a bicycle. Her purple-and-white Q-High jacket rippled in the glare. Then they snapped to attention as Mayor Hannah and Governor Sullivan lumbered down the church steps, elbows entwined. After he spoke for a minute, she ducked into the Lexus and it peeled from the curb.

I was alone. Mourners slipped away in quiet clusters. I pulled the folded memorial service program from my coat pocket. Smoothing the paper, I studied two pictures of Ivy Hannah. Both were in somber shades of sepia. On the program cover, Ivy wore a sweater with a ribbed mock turtleneck collar, a thin smile curving her lips. I remembered this outfit. She'd worn the same pullover in the full-color photo Leo had given me during our interview in my office. Was this picture taken at the same session? Maybe Leo was holding their son, just off-camera. The second photo showed a younger Ivy in her wedding dress. Under elaborate lace, princess seams corseted her waist. Her golden hair was twisted into an ornate knot at the nape, her bare shoulders and throat dulled by the russet tones of the photo. She gazed at a distant horizon, her face smooth and unsmiling.

I wondered if these were pictures Samuel Decker would have chosen to represent his child. Out of reach for almost a week, he'd arrived in Queenstown too late for the private service preceding his daughter's cremation. Had he been consulted on that decision? Had he declined an invitation to speak at this memorial service? Maybe he'd returned home to Florida, evading a public confrontation with this unnatural calamity. That's what I'd done when it happened to me. Disappeared from sight. Locked myself away to mourn in private. Maybe Samuel Decker had tried the same escape. Had grief clawed at him behind those sealed doors? Or had his misery—like mine—seeped through the keyhole as poisonous fog? I touched my thumb to the pulse of my right wrist and rubbed a circle, searching for comfort in the gesture. I folded the program and returned it to my pocket.

Warm breath pressed against my neck. I turned, cigarette smoke and mint brushing my face. I collided with a dark coat, buttoned to the chin against the frost.

"She was so beautiful, wasn't she?" Samuel Decker said.

I nodded. "Yes, she was."

He gulped, then fished a black knit cap from his pocket. He snuffed the glow of his silver hair, pulling the wool to cover the tops of his ears. "Will you have coffee with me, Ms. Myrick?"

How could he know my name? What did he want with me? I was exhausted. I had nothing to give this stranger, no bandwidth for comforting another grieving parent.

I shook my head, raising my hand as a barricade between us. I meant to decline the invitation, push away the pain.

Before I spoke, Decker answered the second question, but not the first.

"I know you're a private investigator, Ms. Myrick." Gray shadows wreathed his eyes; I couldn't catch their color. "I want to hire you. I want you to prove Leo Hannah murdered my daughter."

SAM'S CASE

CHAPTER **THIRTEEN**

I drove Samuel Decker to a coffee shop in a hamlet six miles from the center of Queenstown. Privacy was my goal. Six miles wasn't far, but after the Starbucks opened in Q-Town a year ago, few neighbors trekked to Grover's Mill for their coffee fix. I figured Decker and I could talk there in peace.

Before we entered the Red Planet Beanery, Decker hunched against the wind to smoke a quick cigarette. A polite addict, I guessed. The shop was rustic: brass-embossed cash register, antique coffee bean grinders displayed on wooden shelves. Pastel chalk on blackboards above the butcher-block counter described thirty-five variations on caffeine. I chose a mocha latte called the Orson. Double shot of espresso. Decker ordered Americano straight up. Grande, he said, so he didn't have to return for a refill. As he paid for our coffees, I selected a table beyond the glass-fronted cabinet of pastries.

We'd done the small talk in the car. It was sunny and 73 degrees in Tallahassee. Maybe the groundhog would deliver six more weeks of winter, but only for us poor suckers up north. One week before the Florida State University spring semester began. But he wasn't teaching this semester. The chair of the English department had granted his request for compassionate leave. The plane ticket to Newark was cheaper than flying into Philly. The flight was a blur. The airport was a shambolic embarrassment.

I broke the silence covering our table as he stirred a second sugar packet into his mug. "How did you find me, Dr. Decker?"

He winced. "It's Sam, please."

"Okay, Sam. Where did you come up with my name?"

A sigh, then long fingers loosened the black tie's knot. "I read your report. The one you made for Leo."

"Then you know he's my client."

"Yes."

"He gave you my report?" The squeak sounded shrill to my ears, but Sam didn't blink.

"After I pushed. A lot." Maybe a twitch at the corner of his mouth, more triumph than amusement. "First, Leo claimed the report was his property. Then he said he felt squeamish about divulging Ivy's movements during the last week of her life. Then he argued giving up the report was a violation of Ivy's privacy."

"You dismissed his arguments."

"You make it sound like genteel discussion at some faculty sherry party, Ms. Myrick." Now he was smiling. "I called his bullshit. Table pounding and book throwing, peppered with liberal use of *fuck* work wonders on most people. But especially on a self-righteous bully like Leo Hannah."

"Call me Vandy." I liked his style, but I was wary of this new assignment. I still was on the job for Leo.

When he nodded, I continued: "Did your distaste for Leo come before the wedding? Or later?" I didn't want to mention the death of his daughter. Not yet.

"Or after Ivy's murder. Isn't that what you want to say, Vandy?" Calling out bullshit was Sam Decker's specialty.

"You're right. The possible turning points are multiple. So which was it?"

He settled in his chair. "I met Leo Hannah when I visited Ivy during her junior year at Charlottesville. She'd been dating him for several months at that point. I didn't think the relationship was serious. How could it be? She was beautiful, funny, with a 4.0 average in engineering. He was a middling student in chemistry. Wavy hair and not much under it."

"Leo wasn't good enough for your daughter." A smile quirked my lips.

"Of course I sound like every doting father since the dawn of time. No man good enough for my darling child and all that. But Ivy dated other boys, so I didn't see anything notable in this one. In fact, I underestimated him."

"How so?"

"The next time I saw Leo Hannah was when Ivy brought him home to Tallahassee during Christmas break of their senior year."

"She'd fallen in love and wanted her boyfriend to meet the 'rents. Perfectly normal."

"Except they were already engaged by the time they landed in Florida." Red flared along Sam's cheekbones. He rubbed the bridge of his nose. "And her mother had been dead for sixteen months by that point. Just so you know."

"I'm sorry." I blew to scatter the foam from the middle of my cup.

"Nothing to be sorry about. Cancer steals the best of us." He pinned me with clear eyes. Brown like the coffee. "I'm just grateful Sophia isn't here to suffer through this now."

I waited while he wrecked a napkin. When he dropped the scraps next to his spoon, I said, "Did you approve of the marriage?"

"They didn't need my approval and didn't ask for it. Proclamation, not discussion. Edict, not finesse. That's the Hannah style, I discovered."

"Maybe he gets it from his aunt."

Sam Decker frowned. "You nailed it. I learned their playbook years ago. The Hannahs are about control and command. No room for discussion. Rage before compromise." He shook his head to scatter ugly thoughts. I wondered if he'd clashed often with his in-laws in the past. Images of twisted metal flashed through my mind. I remembered how Leo had twisted that ballpoint pen in my office. And the way he lied to cover up his violent gesture. Was Leo hiding even deeper rage than he'd shown in our first conference?

Sam glanced at the display of pastries across the aisle, the grimace lifting from his brow. "I haven't eaten all day. That lemon custard pie is calling to me. Do you want anything?"

"Nothing, thanks."

When he returned with a double-wide slice and two forks, I jumped to an earlier point in our exchange.

"You read my report."

"Yes."

"And decided you wanted to speak with me?"

"I knew I wanted to hire you." Off my raised eyebrows, he added, "I'm not impulsive. Quite the contrary. I'm pretty bottled up. At least my students say so. But there were certain points in your account that struck me. Questions your report raised I believe deserve further examination."

"Points you feel indicate Leo murdered your daughter?"

He flinched at the stark construction. But I was echoing the tough phrase he'd used to introduce himself. Now was my turn to pin him with a stare.

"Yes, one in particular," he said. "You wrote that when he hired you, Leo claimed he wanted to discover if someone was stalking Ivy. You concluded there was no evidence to support that fear. Yet you never interviewed her. Why didn't you ask my daughter if she felt she was in danger?"

I sniffed and looked at the dregs of my latte. "Leo told me I wasn't to speak with her." The excuse limped over my tongue. I'd flunked the exam, leaped to conclusions based on sentiment. Leo and I were fellow travelers on the marriage failure trek. So I'd given weight to his account. But now I wondered if there were other questions I should ask about Leo. Maybe I needed to take another look at Leo's account. Sam Decker knew the Hannah family through years of interaction. I'd met them a few weeks ago. Maybe Sam had identified trends I'd missed, spotted clues I'd skipped. My ignorance was a thin justification. Knowing I'd relied on such dumb-assery made heat prickle the tops of my ears. To avoid touching them, I gripped my fingers below the table.

"That's what I guessed," Sam snapped. "Leo never concedes control. His wife, his life, his way."

"I'm not going to take your case." I stuck with my position, although I could feel fresh doubts shimmy through my mind.

"Why not?"

"Because it conflicts with my responsibility to Leo Hannah. He's still my client." That sounded super-professional. I felt like a fool. *Because you read me, Sam Decker, and it stings like a goddamn hypodermic needle.*

The lines beside his mouth deepened. His eyes seemed to retreat until only pinpoints of light remained. Their glow hit the mugs, the crumbs of pie crust, then my face.

I looked away. The interview was over. "Where are you staying while you're in town?" Polite, smooth—only my croak gave away the phoniness.

His voice softened to a whisper. "Queenstown Motor Inn."

"Near the turnpike?" I knew where the motel was, of course. But making conversation was tough.

"Yes." He spoke into his tie as he tightened it.

"I can give you a lift." This was a business meeting, and though he bought the coffee, I was the host. Formality worked like armor.

"Thank you. I can call a cab."

"Nope. Not the way we do things in Q-Town." I tried a smile. "I brought you, I carry you home."

"Like a date?" No reciprocal grin, but I caught a warm hitch over the last word.

"Sure." I ground my molars at the shift, but rolled with it. "Which is why I'll finish the rest of the lemon custard pie. I'm starving."

He pushed the plate and spun the second fork until its handle pointed at me.

While I scarfed the pie, Sam bought a second slice to go. Outside the Beanery, he consumed another cigarette, dropping the stub into a flowerpot in the parking lot. He balanced the clamshell carton on his knees during the twenty-minute ride to the motel. Silence worked for both of us. I chewed over my new doubts about Leo Hannah; Sam fiddled with an unlit cigarette.

Under the carport sheltering the entrance to the inn, I turned off the engine. I wanted him to hear me plain. "I'll take tomorrow to think things over. Come to my office Monday at ten. I'll give you my final answer then."

"Thank you," he said. He was smart enough not to question my swerve in direction.

He removed his glove to take my business card, held it close to his eyes, then squinted as if looking for spelling errors. "I'll see you Monday, Ms. Myrick."

One last cigarette, this time inhaled next to the revolving doors guarding the motel lobby. When he flicked the stub into the box-woods, he glanced at me without smiling.

I puzzled over the change of designation all the way home. Had he called me Ms. because I'd opened the possibility of taking his case?

CHAPTER **FOURTEEN**

Elissa Adesanya boiled with lawyerly opinions when she confronted me in the office Monday morning. She was dressed to convict: emerald pantsuit, ivory silk shirt, doorknocker hoops, gold rings on thumb and pointing finger. I was in the witness stand.

"You can't take the Sam Decker case." Elissa's second cup of coffee fueled her tirade. "You already said it: conflict of interest. Aren't you still on the payroll for Leo Hannah?"

She was behind her desk; I was sunk into the sofa, eyes down to avoid further provoking my friend.

"I deposited his last check ten days ago. Paid up and done. Case closed. So no, I am not double-dipping."

She wagged her finger at me. "Conflict of interest still pertains. You gathered information in private communication with Leo when he was your client. Now you'll be tempted to use that information in this new case. An investigation that may run counter to the interests of your former client. You are still bound by confidentiality rules, you know." A pronouncement from the high bench.

"I'm not the lawyer here, but I don't believe private eyes are held to the same rules as attorneys."

Elissa waved a hand as if batting cobwebs. "Okay, then think of yourself as a priest: the Reverend Father Evander Myrick. Mild-mannered rector of Center Street parish." She curved fingers around her eyes as clerical spectacles to complete the picture. "You interacted with Leo in an implied ecclesiastical relationship. Seal of the confessional." She pressed her palms together in a mock prayer, dagger nails clicking. "He spoke with you assuming the rights and protections of the priest-penitent connection would prevail over anything he told you."

"Bull. Shit."

She chuckled. "Yeah, but I made you think, didn't I? You can't do it, girl."

"I don't know, Liss. This is going to bug me."

"Because you missed something? Or because this zaddy Decker has soulful eyes and broad shoulders?"

"You're ridiculous." I shooed imaginary smoke from my head.

"But he *is* cute, amirite? Girls creaming their jeans for him by mid-semester, hmm? And the boys, too. Tell me I'm wrong."

"Not cute. Plus, he's twenty years older than me." Doubtful, but I refused to concede an inch.

"And he's white. But what's that got to do with the price of manioc in Lagos?" She stuck out her tongue.

"Sam Decker is grieving and lost. Angry and frustrated. And not looking for a hookup. That's why."

Describing Sam out loud strengthened the affirmative case. He needed my expertise. I'd deliver. I made my decision then in the face of Elissa's grilling.

I said, "Follow me on this." I rubbed the ache throbbing behind my right ear. "Maybe I screwed up. Missed the deeper dive. Decker understands the family dynamics in a way I don't. Could be I overlooked key facts or relationships."

Elissa sighed and closed her eyes. I'd seen her do this when taking depositions from clients. She'd lower her pen to the legal pad, press an index finger against her lip, and close her eyes. In this mode, she listened to the undercurrents of conviction in my argument. She heard my heart.

"Maybe I sloughed off." I worried flakes of skin from the corner of my mouth. "Ignored hints, leaped where I should have looked. Now I owe my best effort."

Her eyes sprang open. "You're taking the case, aren't you?"

"I'm taking the case."

Samuel Decker arrived three minutes early. Under the black topcoat, he wore a tweed blazer and a gray sweater over a blue button-down shirt and dark jeans. Casual Friday at the English department meeting. Cue the sherry and madeleines. I hurried him through introductions to Elissa and Belle, hoping he'd ignore the cold wafting from both women.

When I steered him toward my office, I lagged behind to catch their first impressions. As I walked by, Belle frowned, scrubbing the back of her neck; Elissa mouthed *no*, punctuated by narrow eyes. I respected my partners' views, but I planned to disregard them.

Since he arrived in my office before me, I figured those ten seconds were enough for Sam to survey the space and make assumptions. He could see I liked minimal decor, bright colors, no plants, and lots of ballpoint pens. He didn't need to know more.

Before he settled into a visitor chair, I darted two questions at him. "Why do you believe your son-in-law killed your daughter? And why do you think I missed the clues?"

I squared my body behind the desk and leaned forward.

"No chitchat?" He dropped his coat on one chair and sat in the other. "That mean you're taking the case?"

"Yes. But if we're going to work together, you have to follow my lead."

He thrust his hand across the desk. We shook, deal done. "That's hard to guarantee," he said. "I *am* a tenured full professor."

"God's gift to humankind. I know. I worked at a university in my previous life. But here, tenure means squat. You pull rank, we're through."

He dipped his chin. I saw his eyes muddy as he blinked. "I believe Leo murdered Ivy because accepting the house invasion story as he told it is impossible."

"The police bought it." Beat for the obvious. "I bought it."

"Then you're all fools."

"Explain."

"How did this man, Hector Ramírez, enter the house? Were there any signs of forced entry—a broken window or a jimmied door latch?"

"No." I fiddled the plunger on a ballpoint. *Click. Click.* Until the sound filled the room.

"So someone let him in."

Sam grabbed a pack of Marlboros from the breast pocket under his pullover. When he fished a lighter from his jeans, I shook my head. No smoking rules operated in my office, even if Elissa violated them in her own space. He balanced the unlit cigarette on his palm, reading it like a textbook.

"If Ivy was truly afraid of a stalker, does it make sense she would let a stranger in the door? My daughter was kind, trusting. You'd say *naive*. But she wasn't stupid. She never opened that door to her killer. The domestic disturbance story doesn't hold."

I nodded. Sam's points were ones I'd churned through in the weeks since the double deaths. His views on his daughter's character were based on affection, of course. But their logic fit my own inclinations. Still, I countered his argument to test our new direction.

"Maybe she knew Ramírez," I said.

"You followed her for a week. Did you run across Hector Ramírez?"

"No." Confession time had arrived. Sam was shooting square; he deserved the same from me. "But maybe I missed him. Took my eye off the ball in my focus on everyday events."

He expelled a whoosh of air. "Thank you." I saw a tear dazzle through his lowered eyelashes. He ran a hand along one sideburn, then down his jaw. A gulp before he spoke: "It means a lot to hear you admit that."

"You may be tenured, Dr. Decker, but you're not crazy," I said.

With a short laugh, he accepted my bid to break the mood. He flipped the cigarette to his mouth and bobbed it. "So what's next?"

"I fill in some blank spaces. You sign some dotted lines. We file the contract with Belle. And we're official."

"Then?"

"I want to get into Ivy's house," I said. "Can you make it happen?"

"Leo and Tommy moved two weeks ago. To an apartment some-where out of town." His mouth turned down, as if the cigarette suddenly tasted sour. "But I have the key Ivy gave me when I visited last month. We can get in. What're you looking for?"

"When I tailed her, your daughter bought new clothes in several stores. Women shop with a purpose. Sometimes the goal is entertainment, but sometimes it's serious as a heart attack. I want to examine those purchases. And anything else she might have kept in her closet."

"You think you'll learn about her state of mind?"

"Perhaps. Or maybe I'll find evidence of her plans for the future."

"If she spree-shopped to cover misery." He plucked the cigarette from his lips and snapped it in two.

"Yes, retail therapy. Or was Ivy buying to spread happiness?" I squared my jaw over the sting of the next words. "I messed up by not talking to Ivy when she was alive. I hope I can backtrack to determine her thoughts now."

Sam had driven to Center Street in a rented Kia. I didn't ask if the lease was by the day or week. With a semester at his disposal, I figured he planned to stay in Queenstown until we solved his daughter's murder.

As we drove to the Hannah house in my Jeep, I let him smoke that abused Marlboro.

Ivy's key, dangling from a pink plastic daisy, slotted easily into the lock. Sam stood aside until I entered. His footsteps didn't follow, so I turned in time to see him stride across the brown frozen lawn. He bent to retrieve the snowman's scarf from a sink of mud. Inside the foyer, he coiled the scarf and set it on the table below the mirror. Figuring he wanted the sliver of privacy during this ritual, I didn't meet his eyes.

As if by morbid instinct, Sam walked toward the closed doors separating the dining room from the hallway. I hurried to intercept him.

"You don't want to see it," I said.

CHAPTER **FIFTEEN**

For a moment, Sam and I swayed in unison, our breaths rolling through the entrance hall. "You really don't want to go in there." I gripped Sam's elbow as he reached to open the door to the murder room.

Images of the blood-splattered dining room darted through my mind. Shards of his daughter's skull dotting the carpet, strands of blond hair scattered among the inflamed smears.

"There's nothing for you there," I said. "Please. Trust me."

He bowed his head until I could see red on the knobs at the back of his neck. Hitching his shoulder to shed my grip, he said, "Where to?"

"Ivy's closet in the master bedroom."

The room was tailored and strict. It felt like Leo Hannah's idea of a parade ground, controlled and dour. Denim-blue sheets were covered by a gray-and-navy-striped duvet. A blue armchair tufted with buttons bullied one corner of the room. At the foot of the king-size bed a bench stood sentry duty.

Ivy's closet was a rebuke to the military stance of the bedroom. Cashmere, silk, bouclé, and tweed mixed with pastel blues or pinks; faded jeans, flowery blouses, straw hats hanging on the walls. The walk-in gave us plenty of space to work side by side. I shuffled hangers on the pole lining one long wall. Sam crouched over a shoe rack, then rifled through a laundry hamper. We ferried piles to the bed: pants, dresses, shirts, jackets. Everything looked like Ivy.

Sifting these bits of a lost life reminded me of the chore I'd undertaken nine months ago. Sorting through the shelves and boxes in

Monica's closet was the toughest task I'd ever performed. I rubbed circles on the underside of my wrist as I remembered that day. Every cardigan I lifted, each sandal I unbuckled, every frayed hem and tee spouting a cheery slogan reminded me I'd never see my daughter wear them again. I could dream about Monica, cry for her, rage at her. But she'd never come back to me.

I picked up a patent leather slingback from a Nordstrom box. Monica had worn a kitten heel like this. I held the shoe in the air and turned toward Sam. I wanted to tell him about Monica. Tell him how I lost her, how she died. Let him know we were at different milestones on the same path. But his expression—brows bent, eyes foggy with his own memories—stopped me.

He saw me staring at him. "What are you searching for?" He ran a finger along the waistband of a lemon-and-white polka-dot dress.

I dropped the shoe in its box and replaced the lid. "I want to find the things I saw Ivy buy the week she died. Sweaters, leggings, tights."

He pointed at a chest of drawers wedged at the far end of the closet. "You fold knits, don't you?"

Chagrin twisted my face. I should have known that. "Tonight. I turn in my fashionista card tonight."

My eye roll won the first grin of the day from Sam. He sat on the bench at the foot of the bed to watch me tackle the dresser.

I hit pay dirt in the second drawer. I pulled out a stack of sweaters, price tags still attached. In the drawer below were five pairs of leggings, also unworn. I checked the labels and found what I was looking for, but I dumped the lot in his lap for confirmation of my discovery.

Sam held a mint-green pullover against his chest. "Does this look big to you?"

I nodded. "Size large. The six other new sweaters are all either large or extra-large."

Creases lowered his brow. "I don't think Ivy wore a large, do you?"

"Of course not." I snatched a dress from the pile on the bed. "Look at this, a six. Here's another, four. Nothing in this closet is more than a size small. There're even a few blouses that are extra-small."

"Then why would she buy new clothing several sizes too big for her?"

"That's the puzzle, isn't it?" I had my guesses, but I wanted to see where he went with this anomaly.

"Could they be gifts? Maybe a girlfriend has a birthday coming up. Or a lady at church? Maybe she was shopping for someone who worked with Leo?"

"Yeah," I drawled. "That might explain why she hadn't removed the labels and price tags yet."

"But you don't think that's it, do you?"

I shook my head. "These new purchases are in the same pastels and prints Ivy loved." I stretched a pair of black leggings festooned with pink and sherbet-orange tulips.

"You think these were for her."

"I do."

"Because?"

"Because she was pregnant," I said.

Sam shot from the bench, scattering clothing on the floor. He strode to the window overlooking the front yard. I could hear the panes rattle when he pushed his palms against the window. He touched his forehead to the mullion dividing the glass panels.

I crossed the room the way I approached the deer who grazed in my backyard at dusk. Arms around my waist, knees flexed, breath held. Sam was injured, and I didn't want to startle him into running.

When I touched his forearm, he glanced at my fingers. I expected to see tears when he looked at me. But his eyes were clear and hard.

"She couldn't be pregnant," he said. Simple, direct. End of story.

Beginning of the story for me. "Why not?"

Gray bristles along his jaw jumped as he bit on the words. "They were married for fourteen years. They never quit trying to get pregnant. Even when they began the adoption process for Tommy."

I gulped to swallow the apology and backed off a pace.

He shook his head. "I know they couldn't get pregnant. That's a fact . . . But . . ."

"But what? What do you know?"

He shook his head. "It can't be relevant to her murder."

"You don't know that for certain," I said. "And neither do I."

As he leaned against the window, his panting brushed warmth

across my face. "Sophia told me something. Once . . . a long time ago . . ."

"About Ivy?" I guessed at the mother-daughter secret a father never wants to learn.

The truth rushed out. "She said Ivy'd had an abortion. During her freshman year at UVA. No complications, no lasting injury. A simple procedure in a Charlottesville women's health clinic. Sophia went up for the week. She told me the visit was girl time with Ivy. An antiquing trip. I was department chair that year, swamped with candidate interviews, budget quarrels, tenure reviews."

"I get that."

"So I didn't ask to join them. Late that summer, Sophia told me about the abortion." Lips pressed tight. A swallow. "She made me promise never to let Ivy know I knew."

"And you never did."

Eyes on the bare branches of the oak outside. "No, I didn't. Ever."

"And the boy wasn't Leo Hannah?"

"No. Some asshole she met at a frat party. They dated for two months. Or maybe two weeks. As far as I know, the kid never learned he'd gotten Ivy pregnant."

A fraternity party. The thought sent shivers racing across my shoulders. I didn't want this to be part of Ivy's story, too. I rested my hand on the windowsill. When I coughed, the tremors passed.

Sam picked up a dress from the bed, hooking its hanger over his wrist. Then more until the garments festooned his arm to the elbow. He returned the clothing to Ivy's closet, replacing each item with care. When everything was in its proper place, Sam stood in front of me at the window.

He spoke the conclusion we had reached together. "If they couldn't get pregnant all those years, the problem was with Leo, not Ivy."

"She could have been pregnant," I whispered.

"But if so, Leo wasn't the father."

I nodded. "We need to find out who Ivy was seeing."

Metallic scraping from the hallway broke our exchange. I eased toward the bedroom door. Sam mimicked me, closing the space between us. His shoulder grazed mine. I pressed my finger against my lips.

CHAPTER **SIXTEEN**

I heard the front door lock slide, a hinge squeak. Slow steps clomped to the foot of the stairs.

"Myrick, you in here?" Leo Hannah's shrill voice charged up the stairwell. "I saw your car." Louder: "You have no right breaking into my house. Get out."

I squared my shoulders and stepped to the top of the stairs. Guilty as charged, I watched the shiny bald patch on Leo Hannah's scalp rise through the gloom as he climbed.

"I should call the police," he said when he reached the landing.

Sam Decker moved from the bedroom doorway to loom over his son-in-law. "Go ahead, Leo. Do it."

Leo gasped, tears coating his eyes as he blinked at Sam. Both men reddened. Specks of chalk and pink dotted Leo's face. Sam's cheeks flushed under gray stubble. Four fists trembled at their waists. Leo stepped forward.

I darted between them. "Leo, don't try it." My back to Sam, I pushed a palm into Leo's soft chest. His shirt smelled like wood on a rotting pier. I shoved; the sweat stink rose.

Leo retreated toward the entrance to his son's room, mouth buried in his collar. His panting filled the hall. When he raised his head, he complained at me. "You have no business here. None. I didn't ask you to come here."

"I did," Sam said. "Myrick is here at my invitation."

"You . . . you?" Leo's voice lifted to a squeak. "How did you get in my house."

"Ivy's house, too. Remember." Sam's growl erased the question mark. "She gave me a key. I kept it."

The two men squared on each other.

Leo snapping, rough: "What were you looking for? Nothing here belongs to you."

"I wanted to gather a few of Ivy's things," Sam said. "Something to take home. Something to remember her by." He wiped a hand over his mouth, then stubbed a shoe against loose threads in the carpet.

The words sounded sad. The quavering delivery was real. But I knew he had larger aims, goals masked by this partial truth. The grief was authentic. But the contrition was an act to disguise the real purpose of our search. I wondered if Sam's ploy worked to soften the other man's heart.

It didn't. Leo fired back: "You want in my house, you ask, understand? *I* control who comes and goes here. *Me*." Anger raised a sheen on his forehead. "I find you in my house again, you will regret it."

He poked a finger at my nose. "That goes double for you. Understand?"

I said, "You threatening me, Leo?"

"Call it what you want. Break in again and I'll get your license revoked."

Not waiting for my response, he swiveled to Sam: "Give me that key." He extended his hand; the arm shook with rage.

Sam switched tones. "I want to see Tommy." Eyes wet; voice heavy. "I came to Queenstown to see him; see how he's doing. Let him know I love him."

Leo shouted, "After a stunt like this, you think I'd let you near Tommy? You're out of your fucking mind." He gathered air for a cyclone of invective. "You hate me. You always did. I won't let you see Tommy under any circumstances. You'd try to poison him against me. I know you would." He blinked; fists clenched at his thighs. For an instant, Leo's face contorted with the anger I'd glimpsed in my office during our first meeting. I felt as though a veil had been snatched aside to reveal the surging, unruly emotions he usually held close. Was this fear of changes he couldn't control? Or brute rage?

A vein throbbed above Leo's right eye. Would he strike Sam? Lash out at me, too? I stepped forward.

Maybe my move worked. I saw the curtain drop: Leo's face smoothed, veiling his roughest emotions again. His breaths steadied. "I transferred him to a new school, near where we live now. Tommy's happy there. Making friends, playing, laughing, even reading a little."

The whirlwind abated, words raining softer now. "I've got him seeing a therapist. She says he's doing fine, adjusting. Moving on." He sliced his gaze toward Sam. The look was surgical, the words cold as steel. "Seeing you would bring it all back. Tommy's lost his mother. If it was up to you, he'd lose me, too. No way in hell will I let you send him into a downward spiral now."

Though the fury wasn't directed at me, I gulped in shock. Sam ducked his head, but I saw red lines pop around his pupils.

"Give me that key." Leo held his hand out flat.

Sam reached into his pocket, fishing out a steel ring garlanded with keys of many shapes and metals. Using his thumbnail, he pried open the hoop. He slid a brass house key off the ring and dropped it in Leo's palm. This wasn't the key Ivy had given him. The one hanging from her daisy ornament was still in his pocket.

Leo stowed the key and padded downstairs. We followed, silently buttoning our coats. In the foyer, he flung aside the door and stood at attention until we crossed the threshold.

As we buckled our seat belts in the Jeep, I saw Leo slosh through mud to reach his neighbor's house. He spoke with a white woman in turquoise yoga pants who answered the door. I figured this was the snoop who'd alerted Leo to our unauthorized invasion of his house.

When we reached the end of the block, I asked Sam, "What was that back there? For a minute Leo seemed unhinged." I wondered if his son-in-law's grief had been transformed into the fury we witnessed. Perhaps Leo's anger was his way of coping with unbearable sorrow. Or maybe there was something more sinister beneath the façade. Something I was missing; something I needed to uncover.

Sam pounded the dashboard. His take on Leo was harsher than mine.

"That asshole stole my beautiful girl. Now he's stealing my grandson." Grit clogged Sam's throat. "I want Tommy. Amend your contract, Myrick. You've got two jobs now: prove Leo murdered my daughter. And help me get custody of my grandson."

"Job accepted," I said, flicking my gaze from the windshield.

His lips tilted in a half-smile. "The bastard got one thing right."

"What's that?"

"I'm going to do everything in my power to turn Tommy against him."

In silence we drove the fifteen minutes to the parking lot behind the Queenstown Pharmacy, me scheming, Sam fuming.

His knuckles were still waxen and stiff when I slanted into my spot facing the brick wall. I rotated the key. "That was cool."

"What was?"

"The way you juked Leo out of that key," I said. "Smooth."

"You think I fell off the turnip truck yesterday?" He smirked. "In some high-tone neighborhood bursting with McMansions and gold-lined swimming pools?"

"Sure, I figured you grew up in a compound in Palm Beach with Kennedy cousins on one side and Versace spawn on the other."

That got the laugh I was looking for. He twisted in the seat to face me.

"Figure again. I grew up on Chicago's Far South Side. You heard of Evergreen Park? Cicero? In my neighborhood our Irish gang battled Ukrainian jerks who fought Italian punks who attacked Polish thugs. The only thing we all agreed on was beating up any Black kid who dared bicycle across Kedzie Avenue into our territory."

I hummed. "Impressive. And scary." I rubbed my chin, as if deep in thought. "That's why you weren't intimidated when you walked into our office and faced three strong Black women."

He raised his eyebrows but had the brains not to answer.

I continued: "So when you suited up for the tenure track, you possessed all the necessary skills."

"You better believe it. I scaled the ivory tower armed and ready."

I hitched a shoulder toward the window. "We need to apply those street skills toward plotting our next moves. Let's eat and talk."

"Scheming requires fuel," he said. "Empty stomach, empty head. Why do you think every faculty meeting is stocked with groaning trays of sandwiches and cookies?"

"I've got just the place for you, Professor."

"Lead on, Myrick."

We knotted our scarves against the stiff breeze swirling fresh snow on Center Street. I steered Sam to Kings Cross Tavern and the tender attentions of my friend Mavis Jenkins.

I was good at plotting; Sam was better.

CHAPTER **SEVENTEEN**

The next afternoon, Sam Decker and I trudged uphill three blocks from my office parking lot. When we arrived at the courtyard of the First United Methodist Church, we were blowing like steam engines, perspiration beading on the hems of our knit caps.

"This is the highest elevation in Queenstown," I announced in a tour guide voice. "Unless you count the catwalk on the water tower. One hundred and sixty feet high. One million gallons." Like a game show hostess, I flung an arm toward the reservoir, five blocks away. Its blue tank loomed over the roofs of sprawling Victorian houses and humble frame cottages.

"Okay. Good to know," Sam said. He squinted at the landmark, then quirked his lips. "They paint the name up there so everyone knows they live in Queenstown?"

"Hey, it works," I said. "No one's forgotten yet."

We turned to look down Abbott Street, beyond the tavern, toward the ice floes drifting on Lake Trask. Sam pounded his gloved hands together—not applause, circulation-restoring blows against frostbite.

Tourism over, we pushed through a gate in the wrought-iron fence separating the church property from the sidewalk. We crossed the service driveway and rang a button beside the back door. Unlike the imposing limestone slabs bolstering the façade of First United, the rear elevation was sheathed in frayed brown shingles.

Five weeks ago, I'd watched Ivy Hannah greet a parade of delivery drivers at this door. When I called to make the appointment, I hoped to interview people who shared volunteer duties with her. At the very least, I wanted to give Sam insights into his daughter's charitable work and community involvement. Perhaps we'd learn something of the life she'd led beyond the control of Leo Hannah.

After introductions and expressions of condolence, a hunched woman in purple corduroy pants and flowered smock led us to the office Ivy shared with other volunteers.

"Ivy could have put on airs," Georgette Cornell said, smoothing the ends of her waist-length braid.

We looked over three desks crammed next to four metal file cabinets and a bookcase. Sam picked a volume from the sagging shelf and stroked its spine.

Mrs. Cornell continued. "She was director of volunteers. Lots of executive responsibilities. Organizing, scheduling, planning. Even budgeting. She could have demanded her own space. She deserved it. But Ivy wasn't that way. She never put herself above the rest of us. Even if she was Queenstown royalty."

"Where did Ivy sit?" I asked.

Mrs. Cornell pointed. "She always used the desk farthest from the door." A wistful smile shaded her face. "Said she liked having the bookcase behind her and the cork bulletin board on the wall at her shoulder. Said she could think better in her little corner of peace." She sniffed. "That's what she called it. Her corner of peace."

When Sam nodded, the old woman dabbed a tissue to her nose, muffling a sigh. "We miss her. More than I can say. It's just awful, awful business . . . the way . . ."

Sam coughed to interrupt the flood of anguish. "Thank you, Mrs. Cornell. I know Ivy loved her work at the church. She told me how much she enjoyed her time with all of you."

Mrs. Cornell beamed. Sam narrowed his eyes until they twinkled, either from tears or charm. "Can you show me around the rest of the church? Ivy used to speak about the kitchen with special fondness. I'd like to see it, if you have the time."

This was our plan. As soon as the two left the office, I sat at Ivy's desk. I wanted to see if she'd kept any useful notes or files. I hoped the staff hadn't cleaned this desk in the weeks since her death. Out of respect or neglect, I didn't care which. Either excuse served my purpose.

I tackled the center drawer of the wooden desk first. Pencil stubs, pocket packages of tissue, folded newspapers, pads of sticky notes, hand sanitizer, scissors, and a box of Bic pens. On top of a stenographer's pad was a framed photo of Tommy, looking grown-up in a red bow tie. Over his head was the banner of the school, the Blue Bird Day Care Center. No shots of Leo or of the family together. I wondered if Ivy always kept Tommy's picture in the drawer or if she set it on top of the desk when she worked. I put the photo aside, a keepsake for his grandfather.

In the deep side drawer, I found a pair of black high-heeled pumps, body lotion, sanitary products, and a bag stocked with lipsticks, mascara, foundation, and a powder compact. I crouched to reach the farthest corner of the drawer. I withdrew a bottle of perfume, YSL Paris. It seemed extravagant. And romantic. I wondered who Ivy primped for? A member of the congregation, a fellow volunteer, the assistant youth pastor, the choirmaster? Herself?

I spritzed my wrist; heady scent coated my skin. Lush roses tumbled through the room. I rushed to lift the double-sash window. Fanning cold air with a manila envelope, I hoped to clear the office of Ivy's secret perfume before my snooping was discovered.

Retaking the chair, I studied the bulletin board above Ivy's desk. Thumbtacks pinned the expected: a calendar, postcards of the Wildwood boardwalk and the Manhattan skyline, and a stapled spreadsheet of volunteer names, phone numbers, and email addresses. I wanted that list. So I took it. I stuffed the rolled pages into my waistband at the small of my back. If anyone missed the volunteer list, they could print out a new one.

When Sam and Mrs. Cornell returned, I was settled at a different desk, my hands clasped on the blotter like a model student. I saw her sniff, frown, then hiss as she scurried to shut the window.

I smiled sweetly, looking around the office for a distraction. "Mrs. Cornell, what is that a photo of?" I pointed at a four-color display on the wall over the bookcase. "It looks important."

She lifted the photo from its hook. "Oh, it is. This is the ceremony where the First United volunteer program was recognized for our outstanding contribution to the community last year." Her eyes lit and her concave chest expanded. "We were so proud that day. Last October it was. Ivy insisted every volunteer should attend the event so we could get the recognition as a team."

She thrust the photo toward me. "See, here's Ivy, in the front row with the rest of us behind her. And of course, you recognize Mayor Hannah. She made the loveliest speech that day, thanking First United for leading the way in community service. Our volunteer program set the standard for the whole of Mason County, she said. After her speech, she handed Reverend Kent a wonderful medal. See it here?"

An arthritic finger traveled across the photo to indicate the mayor and the minister, teeth flashing in the middle of the volunteer ranks. Between them, they clutched a round medallion and a framed certificate. Ivy was at the far end of the first row.

"Later Reverend Kent gave the certificate to Ivy. He said she earned the honors, not him." Mrs. Cornell paused. "Of course, he keeps the medal in a display case in his office." As a delicate huff escaped her lips, she glanced at the photo. "And you'll never guess who took the picture. It was Leo Hannah. He was so proud of Ivy that day."

I craned over the photo, trying to distinguish the faces in the crowd.

"Do you have a copy?" Sam asked. "I'd love to have one to take home with me."

"We don't have a copy of the photo," she said, wrinkles veiling her face with disappointment. Then the creases smoothed. "Of course you're welcome to take a copy of the newspaper. The *Herald* printed this picture front and center that week."

Mrs. Cornell tugged on the top drawer of Ivy's desk. She extracted the pile of newspapers I'd seen earlier. "Here you go, Mr. Decker."

She unfurled the tabloid. Spread above the fold was the shot of the First United Methodist volunteers with Mayor Hannah. The credit line at the lower right edge read: *Photograph courtesy of Leonard Hannah.*

Sam took the newspaper and a second copy, pressing them under his arm. "This is very good of you, Mrs. Cornell. I won't forget your kindness today. You've been most generous with your time and your insights."

I detected a Florida drawl sweeping the South Side edge from his voice. He was good at this.

"It's been my pleasure, Mr. Decker. I am so sorry for your loss. As you can tell, Ivy meant a great deal to us. We loved her."

We escaped before the flood of tears.

At the intersection where Abbott dead-ended into Center Street, I gave Sam new marching orders.

I pointed to the Geoffrey Heinz Photography Studio on the northwest corner. I remembered the gold script engraved on the corner of the Hannah family photo Leo had given me at the start of my investigation. That formal portrait had been taken in the Heinz Studio. I figured the wedding photo of Ivy used on the program at the memorial service had been shot there as well.

"Let me guess, Heinz is the only studio in Q-Town," Sam said.

I corrected: "The best . . . and the only." I wrapped my arms around my waist to ward off the knifing wind. "Your job is to learn as much as you can about those photo shoots. Geoff Heinz is a chatterbox. It shouldn't be hard for you to pump him like an alumni donor."

"And where will you be?" The tip of his nose was pink with cold.

I jerked a thumb over my shoulder. "Up there in my cozy office. I've got paperwork to tackle."

This wasn't true. I had a hunch to follow and I didn't want Sam trailing along. He didn't fight me, pushed to action by the snow swirling around our boots.

"Tonight, I drive," he said. We'd agreed to make a second raid on the Hannah residence under cover of darkness. "That nosy Yoga Lady next door clocked your Jeep. So we'll go in mine. Nine-thirty good?"

I agreed and ran across the street toward my office. As I skidded past the Queenstown Pharmacy, I peeked through the cluttered window display to be sure my quarry was behind the counter. He was.

I stood in front of the reception desk begging for Belle's assistance to find the back issue of the *Herald* I wanted. I knew she could locate it faster than I ever would. I wanted the edition that ran the first story on the double murder at the Hannah house. I zipped and unzipped my puffer coat as Belle rifled through a stack of newspapers on a table behind her. Her side-eye halted my nervous twitch. I ran to the break room to find a box of plastic sandwich bags stored over the fridge. By the time I returned, Belle had found the issue I wanted.

I scanned the *Herald*. Amid towers of black type, I saw the photo of Ivy Hannah in her pristine sweater, a half-smile playing across her face, Rapunzel hair cascading over both shoulders.

Below the fold was the smaller picture I needed. In black-and-white, Hector Ramírez looked haunted. His cheekbones rose like sand dunes above gray depressions framing a tight mouth. His eyes were large, maybe beautiful, with heavy lids, long straight lashes, and swaths of white below the dark irises. With Belle's scissors, I snipped the photo from the newsprint.

I had many questions about Hector Ramírez. Armed with this photo, I hoped the druggist at the Queenstown Pharmacy could answer one of them. I folded the picture in half and sealed it in the Ziploc baggie. The three-minute scamper to the corner store was warmed by my blistering certainty that my hunch would pay off.

CHAPTER **EIGHTEEN**

Three Latina women and five kids were shopping in the Q-Town Pharmacy when I pushed through the door.

Alerted by the jingle of the bell, the kids giggled behind their mittens as they assessed me. I guess my height was funny. Or maybe the snowflakes on my eyelashes looked silly. I rubbed my nose; the laughter bloomed. The mothers hushed their children and smiled apologies at me. I idled for five minutes in the cosmetics aisle, waiting for the other customers to leave. Malibu Coral or Sag Harbor Sage? Nail polish choices were supposed to transport me to cruise mode. But I was shipwrecked on the Isle of Irked.

I wanted to find out if Hector Ramírez had been a customer in this pharmacy. The changing population of the neighborhood made that seem likely. I knew from newspaper accounts that Hector had come to Queenstown with his family from Honduras several years ago. Maybe Hector didn't live here in Abbott's Landing, the immigrant community that stretched along the streets bordering Lake Trask. When they examined his wallet in the death room, police had found an ID with an address in Abbott's Landing. But Hector could have moved elsewhere. Maybe he'd found a whiter neighborhood miles from the center of town. I knew he worked as a driver for a local taxi company. Why would he move so far away? I guessed convenience and familiarity were powerful influences. My gut said Hector had made his home here in the heart of historic Q-Town.

Flipping through *Vogue* and *New Jersey Bride* ate up five more minutes.

I stared out the front window. In the gathering dusk, I surveyed pedestrian traffic: a squat man toting a dog; a black-haired teenager pushing her bicycle; two boys munching burritos; a suit angling for the tavern. The three women took plenty of time finding their purchases. When they left at last, the kids waved goodbye at me. They might be future clients, so I smiled back.

With the field cleared, I moved to play my hunch. I approached the counter empty-handed.

The pharmacist recognized me. "You're here to refill your Metformin prescription already, Ms. Myrick?"

Dr. Rajaram turned to consult a computer, summoning my contact information before I could deny I needed more diabetes medicine.

Frowning at the screen, he continued: "No, you should not have run out so quickly. You had a three-month supply. The insurance company will reject this request for a refill without your prescribing physician's approval. Do you want me to contact Dr. Klein?"

"No, that's not why I'm here today." I smiled and the pharmacist did, too.

Creases around his mouth relaxed as he pressed both hands to his chest. Behind wire-rimmed glasses, Satish Rajaram was movie-star handsome: tall, dark, and chiseled. He co-owned the pharmacy with his wife, Nina, who was equally stunning.

He pushed aside a stack of pamphlets on shingles vaccines. "Are your allergies kicking up again?" he asked, tilting his head. "Most people find the winter weather brings relief. But I suppose you might be the exception to the rule."

Small-town life, where everybody knew your name and had the inside line on all your business. I hoped I could turn this bug into a feature to aid my investigation.

"Dr. Rajaram, I'm not here for allergies. I need information. For a case."

He looked down at me, dark eyes glowing. "You are on an investigation? I knew you were a private detective. But I never encountered anyone who knew of cases you were working on."

A dig, the politest put-down I'd received in years. I let it slide. "That's the way it's supposed to be. Private."

"Ah yes, I see." He nodded and leaned across the counter, craning his neck to check that we were still alone. "How can I help?"

I pulled out the baggie with the photo of Hector Ramírez. "Have you seen this man? Has he ever visited the store?"

"Yes, of course. I know him." Voice tight and scratchy.

I feared Rajaram would say he'd seen news articles on the murder of Ivy Hannah and recognized Ramírez from those reports. But he went in another direction.

"Hector often comes in to pick up medicine for his mother. Over-the-counter, mostly for arthritis and migraines. Sometimes his little sister runs the family errands for common items like toothpaste or hand soap." The pharmacist dropped his bass to a murmur. "I see them at least once a week for one thing or another. Is that what you want to know?"

I tried to stifle the sigh of relief, but it dribbled out. "Did Hector ever come in with anyone other than his sister?"

Rajaram straightened, then bit his lower lip. "Once. Yes." His chattiness evaporated.

I smoothed my voice to penetrate the resistance. First, an appeal to professional collegiality. "I know you have a code of confidentiality, just like I do."

"That's right. Hector Ramírez and his family are patients."

I wondered why Rajaram referred to Hector in the present tense. Was the misuse of tenses a way of avoiding an ugly subject? I wanted to break the fetter on Rajaram's speech with some harsh truths.

"You are aware that Hector Ramírez is dead? Right? And you know he is accused of murder?"

He hissed at my sacrilege. "Yes. Sure, I know." The pharmacist's eyes watered, but he didn't flinch. "I don't believe it."

"Why not?"

"Because I know the family. They've been good customers for years. I don't believe Hector could have done such a thing as murder. And . . ." He raked the hair at the nape of his neck. Through a sigh, he finished, "I can't say more."

"You are a professional. I respect that, Dr. Rajaram. So am I. I wouldn't ask these questions if I didn't think the answers might give important insights."

"But you won't share what I'm saying, will you?"

"I'll keep it between us." That wasn't true in a strict sense. I would use whatever data he gave me any way I could.

His shoulders relaxed; the pledge seemed to soothe him.

I added, "I won't share anything until you give me permission to do so."

He removed his glasses and fiddled with the plastic cushions of the nose rest. He buffed the lenses against the lapel of his lab coat. When he scratched a fingernail over the embroidered name on his left breast, I broke through the rituals.

"What do you know, Dr. Rajaram?"

Direct worked. The dam shattered.

"Hector came here once with that poor young woman. The one who died. They came in together."

More euphemisms. I hoped clarification wouldn't interrupt his flow. "You mean Ivy Hannah? You saw Hector with Ivy?"

"Yes, in late October, just before Halloween. I remember because she bought a bag of candy corn."

"How do you know the woman with Hector was Ivy? Couldn't it be some other woman?"

Rajaram sniffed and lowered his lids as if I'd insulted him. "Ms. Myrick, I know my customers. Almost all of our clients are Latino. In fact, you are one of the few non-Hispanic customers I see on a regular basis. She was a stranger, but she was white. So I remember."

"How did you know they were together?" Another insulting question, perhaps, but I wanted precision.

"They came in together. They left together. Hector spoke to the woman several times. He showed her a magazine and they laughed at a headline. It wasn't difficult to conclude they were together."

"And was Halloween candy the only thing they bought?"

"No."

Rajaram's hesitation caused new gray hairs to sprout on my head. I thought the pauses meant he was coming to something important, so I pushed.

"What else did she buy?"

Big breath, huge answer. "A pregnancy test kit. Two, in fact."

I slid the photo of Hector Ramírez into my coat pocket. The move covered the trembling in my hand. I gripped the counter. The pharmacist stared at my clenched fist.

"Is this information you can use, Ms. Myrick?" Below glittering eyes, a smile flickered across his lips. "Now you see why I do not believe Hector Ramírez could have done away with that woman."

I gulped like an amateur. Heat swept from my throat to my cheeks. Hoping to distract him from my excitement, I burbled clichés. "Yes, this is useful. Thank you for your candor."

When he tucked his head in a short bow, I asked the obvious. "Did you share this information with the police?"

"No, they never inquired." He pressed his mouth into a line. "And I did not volunteer."

Rajaram had a doctorate in pharmacology. And brown skin. He followed the time-honored protective practice of most people of color. When confronted by police, speak little, offer nothing. Guard your family, save your neck. The hurried official probe into Ivy Hannah's murder missed many fruitful lines of investigation.

One last question, the same one Mayor Hannah had asked me about Ivy: "What was her mood? Did you get an impression of how she felt about the pregnancy test?"

"They seemed happy. That's what I thought when I watched them leave the store. Excited, bubbly, buzzing. That's what I saw."

I swallowed a breath I didn't realize I'd been holding. "Thank you, Dr. Rajaram."

He shook his head over stiff shoulders. "This is why I will never believe Hector committed the crime they accuse him of."

When I reached the Jeep, I looked for Sam Decker's car. He'd gone, his interview with the photographer over. I was relieved. With the burden of this new information, I needed time before I saw him again. I sat for a moment in the dusk, letting the chill seep from the leather cushion into my thighs. I gripped eleven and one o'clock on the steering wheel, then touched my forehead to the cold plastic between my fists.

I thought about the array of oversize sweaters and pants I'd seen in Ivy's closet. How long had she known of her pregnancy? Was the

October test a confirmation of her condition? Had she suspected for several weeks prior? Who had pushed to buy the test, Ivy or Hector? Had she shared her news with him? Did Leo Hannah know of his wife's pregnancy? Had he even suspected? I wondered how to break this discovery to Sam Decker.

Before meeting Sam later that night, I wanted to see my father, so I made a lightning trip to Glendale Memory Care Center. The visit with Evander rang up zeros on all counts. My father had no connection with me; sighs, burps, and grunts were his only input. I found no clues about how to share my new information with Sam. Distracted, I bungled my chess match with Keyshawn Sayre.

As usual, Key walked me through the lobby. He caught my arm at the sliding doors. "Something on your mind?"

"Did I seem out of it today?"

"Yeah, kinda like . . ."

"Like Evander, you mean?" When he winced, I joked, "Makes you wonder if my dad inherited dementia from me, hunh?"

We chuckled, the dour mood broken. I added, "Sorry for the 'tude, my job's giving me fits at the moment." He knew I was a private detective, though I never shared details of my cases.

"At least your work keeps you engaged, right?"

"Engaged, crazy. Same-same." More quips. To smooth the frown line between his eyes, I asked, "You like your job here, right?"

He glanced around the lobby. Clusters of guests grabbed the elbows of shuffling residents headed toward the dining hall. You could tell the visitors by the white ringing their pupils and the stiffness of their necks. Anxiety rolled off them in torrents. In contrast, the residents carried the soft smiles and fluttering fingers of perpetual calm.

"I like my job here well enough," Key said. His eyes raked pots of ficus trees towering in a corner of the lobby. "But I want something more . . . more useful."

"Like what?"

"I want a job where I build things with my hands, see something grow, finish something big. Like I did when I worked on my aunt's garden in Atlanta. That's the kind of work could keep me engaged. Like you are."

He dipped his head, sucking his lower lip until it disappeared.

"You'll find something." My assurance sounded light as a fern leaf, but I doubled down. "You'll get what you want, no worries."

He smiled when I pecked his cheek with a dry kiss.

The ride home gave me no clues how to approach my story for Sam. How do you tell a man his murdered daughter was carrying his grandchild? The microwaved bowl of chili was empty of ideas. Two cups of coffee, nothing.

I sat in my darkened living room, gazing past the front porch to the pools of lamplight on the street, waiting for Sam to arrive. We had a break-in to execute and a test to complete. I decided I could delay this conversation until we returned from the Hannah house. I'd fished a mini flashlight from the junk drawer next to the stove. I pressed the torch's head against a sofa pillow, flicking the beam on and off to mark the seconds.

When Sam pulled into my driveway at nine-thirty, adrenaline sparked heat under my ribs. This night raid was forbidden and freighted. Good trouble, as civil rights warriors used to say. I hoped to find evidence to unravel the case against Hector Ramírez. If we succeeded, we'd reshape the investigation into Ivy's murder.

Dragging my knit cap over my ears, I charged down the porch stairs.

CHAPTER **NINETEEN**

The plastic daisy jiggled as Sam worked, using touch rather than sight to insert the door key. In the dark, we slipped into the foyer. Our rubber treads squeaked on the tiles as we crossed toward the rear of the house. The air smelled brackish, as if our movements had disturbed water at the bottom of an unused well.

I saw Sam glance at the closed doors blocking the dining room. I pushed a palm into the small of his back and waved the flashlight beam to steer him toward the kitchen. We didn't have time for sentiment or distraction. Our job here was simple: we wanted to test Leo Hannah's account of the killings of Ivy and Hector Ramírez.

According to Leo, he was working in his basement office when the domestic invasion began. He said he heard strange thumps on the floor above his head. Those thuds had drawn him upstairs, where he found Hector pummeling Ivy with a hammer. We wanted to find out if sounds traveled through the floorboards the way Leo described in his testimony at the inquest. The police had accepted Leo's account of the incident without challenge. But I had explored the basement that day. My memory was I had not heard tramping footsteps during the time I was belowground. Of course, my recollection was clouded by an avalanche of emotions and sensations. An experiment now could give us valuable data.

In the kitchen, Sam and I stood on either side of the island. I doused the flashlight. I hoped the moonglow coating the windows in the breakfast nook was sufficient for our needs. I didn't want to alert Yoga Lady next door to our snooping.

"You make the first run," I said. "Stay downstairs five minutes. I'll knock around the dining room and living room. Then we switch."

"Yep." Sam nodded and unbuttoned his coat, hooking it over a stool at the counter.

I dropped the flashlight in his gloved palm. I figured a torch would be needed belowground. I watched the pool of light waver around his feet as he navigated the basement stairs. When he disappeared, I returned to the front hall.

I tried different treads in each room. High-kneed clomps like a show horse. Marching band plods. Boot heel stomps. I whacked fists on the parlor carpet. I dropped a chair in the dining room.

The furniture was positioned as I remembered from the day of the killings. Credenza, glass-fronted cabinet, chairs crowded against the dining table. The drinks glasses and coffee cups had been removed. But everything else was just so. I knelt near the table, then crawled on all fours. I stroked the rug's carved ridges, searching for indentations where furniture feet might have been shifted. But each piece was placed with precision. I could see patches of ivory shimmer against the wheat-colored carpet. These were the bleached swatches where forensic cleaning crews exercised their gruesome task. When I lowered my face, a whiff of chemical solvent brushed my nose.

The murder scene writhed in my mind. I wondered if Ivy had cried out during the struggle. Had her scream brought Leo from the basement? Should I risk a shout to test the scenario? I decided against the attempt—too gut-wrenching for me, too cruel for Sam.

As I reentered the kitchen, sweat lathered my neck. Leaning against the fridge, I dabbed paper towels to my cheeks and throat.

Sam slipped through the basement door thirty seconds later.

"Anything?" I asked. I was panting, as if I'd raced a four-hundred-meter relay.

He shook his head. "Nothing."

I puffed upward to cool my forehead. "My turn, then."

He passed our baton, the flashlight.

I wanted to warn him against entering the murder room. To tell him he'd never erase those images from his mind if he did. But I clamped my mouth shut. I couldn't make that judgment for him. I figured he'd know if now was the right time.

At the bottom of the basement stairs, I heard Sam's footsteps retreat toward the hall. Then silence. I followed the bobbing spotlight to Leo's office. He had cleared the space of essentials. The laptop and printer were gone. The bookcase was bare and dust-free. The gooseneck lamp still anchored one corner of the black blotter on the desk. I waved my torch over the desk. Why had Leo neglected to take the mouse pad with the ArcDev Pharmaceuticals logo? I tugged at the spongy square. It was gummed to the blotter. I figured a coffee spill had wrecked the mouse pad. No need to save this—it could easily be replaced with a new one from the lab. As I lifted the pad, the blotter peeled from the desk.

Underneath, I saw a ragged edge of paper. I shifted the blotter. Four identical clippings from the *Queenstown Herald*. Newsprint, yellowed with age. Photographs of people assembled in three ranks. I recognized Mayor Hannah in the center, next to Reverend Arthur Kent of First United Methodist Church. Ivy Hannah stood at the far left end of the first row of volunteers. Everyone grinned as the volunteer program received their community service medal from the mayor. I tapped a finger to the credit line: *Photograph courtesy of Leonard Hannah.*

Why had Leo saved four copies of this picture? I figured he'd taken the shot with his cell phone. If he meant to celebrate the achievement of his wife and her volunteer team, wouldn't he paste a copy in a family scrapbook? Or frame a high-quality print for display? Ivy had proudly hung this photo on the wall in her church office. Why had Leo clipped multiple images from the newspaper and then hidden the pictures below the blotter? I figured the photo must be important to him. My guess: the meaning was negative.

I replaced the clippings beneath the blotter. Then I set the desk lamp on the corner as before. If Leo returned to his office, I didn't want any disturbance to reveal we'd been here. Sam had this issue of the *Herald*. We needed to study the picture closely. Maybe we'd find insights into Leo Hannah's intentions. Or uncover something new about Ivy's connections.

My five minutes in the basement were done. I'd heard nothing from Sam's efforts upstairs. When I returned to the kitchen, he raked my face with hard eyes. I shook my head. He turned both palms down, then stretched his arms wide. The signal for bust, flunk, fail.

We now knew Leo lied. He did not hear a disturbance from the first floor of his house on the morning his wife was attacked. Or if he did hear noises, he wasn't in the basement at the time.

A silent exit from the house. The crunch of snow accompanied our walk across the neighbors' lawns. When we reached the pavement at the corner, Sam skidded on a patch of ice. I gripped his elbow, steadying him. In the Kia, we buckled seat belts before he lit the ignition.

"Where to?" He shifted his torso to catch my reply.

"My house. We need to talk."

As we pulled from the curb, I heard another engine grumble behind us. I looked in the side mirror at the blackness surrounding our car. "I think someone's back there."

"I heard it, too." Sam glanced at the rearview mirror without shifting his head. "Let's see if he follows."

CHAPTER **TWENTY**

The ghost vehicle trailed us for fifteen minutes after we pulled from in front of the Hannah house. I didn't expect the surrounding homes to be ablaze with domestic cheer. It was ten-forty, late for a school night. Most residences were dark, their leftover Christmas tinsel and deflated reindeer decorations giving the block a neglected feel.

We eased toward the first corner, then around the second. Behind us, the tail kept pace. The headlights were doused; the vehicle's dark finish shed dull reflections of moonbeams across snow ridges in the intersection.

Sam said, "Late-model Dodge Ram. What do you figure, red or black finish?"

We passed under a streetlamp. I said, "Take a left here. And it's red."

"Not going straight home?"

"Not yet. Testing his resolve."

We took four more corners in a zigzag route. We passed an all-night Wawa and a GM dealership. Another turn past a pocket playground bordered by residential streets. We crawled into the shadow of the giant water tower, its legs casting broken stripes across Windsor Street. Our headlights startled a bundled figure walking a dog who jittered in the cold outside an autobody shop.

"You think he knows where you live?" Sam's voice was pitched high, the squeak of a boy on his first date.

I figured he was excited or scared or both. "Of course he does," I said. "Welcome to Smallville."

"Then your fan club president will drop the chase once we get home."

"Probably," I said. Some questions are better left unasked, such as why he'd referred to my house as *home*.

I directed Sam around Tidwell Park. The central gazebo was swallowed in shadows, its cupola floating like a yacht on a black ocean. When we pulled into my driveway, our escort stopped, then whipped a Y-turn. Front bumper toward my house, he ramped his headlights to high beam. We walked to my porch in a white spotlight, the glare blocking our view of the driver's face. As I switched on the lamp in the entrance hall, the shadow truck sped away.

"Any idea who that was?" Sam asked as we hung our coats on hooks near the front door.

"Nope. Leo drives a Chevy Equinox. That wasn't him."

"If he wanted us out of the house, he'd have confronted us. Like he did last time."

I corrected that thought. "He was angry but scared, too, after that meetup. I figure he'd recruit reinforcements. He didn't want to risk a second run-in. Maybe Leo tagged local muscle to do the job."

I balled up my gloves and stuffed them in the pocket beside the photo of Hector Ramírez. I'd pull this photo when the time felt right.

Sam crossed the hall toward the living room. "This was someone who'd been watching the house. Waiting for us to come back." He stood in the archway, his back to me. "Any ideas?"

"Nope." I hated the repetition. I'd come up empty. Failing at my basic private eye job. "Give me time to work my hunch machine on this one."

He wasn't looking, but I tried a smile anyway. It faltered. Shift topics until I got my bearings was a well-thumbed page in my playbook. "Debriefing time," I said.

When Sam didn't answer I moved to the kitchen, raising my voice. "What's your pleasure? Coffee, tea, or something warmer?"

He said nothing. He intended to inspect my house. Ignoring my question was his strategy.

I watched him glide by the deep sofa near the front windows. Fawn leather sections were grouped into an L meant for lounging. I wondered if he recognized that the patterns embroidered on the pillows mimicked traditional African mud cloth. A giant throw knit from nubbly cream yarn sprawled across the back of the sofa. When I needed soothing, I stroked the exaggerated tassels on each corner of the throw.

I didn't believe in table lamps—too grandma-style—so a brass globe hung over the sofa from a curving metal tube anchored in a marble stand. I remained amazed by the four brass cubes I'd scored for coffee tables. *Aspirational* was the term; they were sleek and sophisticated. Not like me at all. I'd placed a carved bronze figure, a Benin Oba, on one cube. Cool and international. Someday. When I flew over the rainbow.

I watched Sam slide his gaze across the living room. If he wondered where I kept magazines, photos, catalogues, and books, he'd have to ask. Maybe I'd show him the side room. Not grand enough to be labeled a library, it was a retreat painted midnight blue, furnished with plush sofas, bookshelves, a sound system, and a flat-screen.

He sketched a finger along the backs of the upholstered chairs that marked the division between living and dining rooms. The seats were creamy wool with yellow accents, like the Moroccan rugs. This house was my breakout moment, my split with the past, my nothing-to-lose statement. I'd knocked down all the partitions on the first floor. I'd had the walls painted eggplant, which read black at night. I'd chosen Carrara marble slabs to reface the brick fireplace. I'd bought the boldest paintings and the most precious silk drapes I could afford. I'd purchased a warehouse of high-end appliances I'd never cook with. Crates of translucent porcelain I'd never eat on were crammed in my cabinets. This was my *Architectural Digest* fantasy, my dream house without a dream.

Pausing at the glass-topped dining table, Sam peered at my chess set, carved bone and ebony pieces arrayed on a board of tawny squares. Keyshawn hadn't texted his new move yet. In the press of work, had he'd forgotten our match? I hoped not.

I hoisted the empty carafe, repeating the offer: "Coffee, tea?"

"You said 'something warmer.' What do you have?"

I flung open the door to the upper cabinet. "Bourbon, scotch?" I stretched to push aside the front row of bottles. "Or rum?"

He leaned on the marble counter of the island separating the dining area from the kitchen. "Scotch and soda, please. No ice."

I drowned the Glenlivet with a healthy splash of boring, then filled a tumbler with ice and club soda for myself. He hiked an eyebrow at my choice, but he didn't ask and I didn't tell.

He pulled from his jeans waistband the folded copy of the *Queenstown Herald* we'd taken from the church that morning. Adjusting reading glasses on his nose, he spread the tabloid on the counter.

He flattened the creases. "You said Leo had four clippings of this photo in his desk?"

"Hidden under the blotter. A secret stash."

Sam peered at the blurry faces. "Hard to make out anyone except the mayor. She's crystal clear." He poked the paper. "You think that's on purpose? By city ordinance or something? 'Thou shall worship no other officials before me, thy mayor.'" Wrinkles flew at the corners of both eyes as he intoned the sacred commandment.

"Now you're catching on." I rummaged in a drawer on my side of the island. I parked a long-handled magnifying glass on the marble. "This could help."

As he skimmed the photo, I went to the hall to retrieve the plastic baggie from my coat pocket. I placed the picture of Hector Ramírez next to the ranks of church volunteers.

"Here's where my hunch engine goes into overdrive," I said.

Taking the magnifying glass, I passed the lens over the rows of volunteers. Faces bulged and shrank, twisting like images in a funhouse mirror. I scanned each row twice. On the third run, I settled on the face I wanted.

"This is Hector Ramírez." I tapped the newsprint. "See? Second row, fifth from the right. He must have been a team regular to score an invite to this ceremony."

Sam looked through the lens. He stood, bumped his glasses on his nose, and straight-armed from the counter. "Yes, they wouldn't include someone who only lent a hand once in a while."

I stated the case, ticking off each point on a finger. "Ivy was director of the volunteer program. She knew all the volunteers. Arranged their training, managed their schedules, issued assignments, supervised work, evaluated results."

"She ran the whole shebang," he said, eyes downcast, wistful.

I continued: "She knew Hector. We can check the printout of the volunteer list I took from the church. I'm positive we'll find Hector on it. We can get an address for him, too."

Sam gulped the heel of his drink and shoved the glass toward me. I poured a second dose of scotch, more booze, less soda. He swallowed half.

He asked, "You think this is where Ivy met Hector?"

"I do, yes." I swirled ice, killing the last bubbles in my glass. No way could I look Sam in the eye now. I had more to tell him. After he finished the second round of scotch.

"Then she wouldn't have feared he was stalking her, would she?"

"I doubt it." Softening my certainty felt like the kindest move. I coughed, then blew a long sigh.

Sam said, "That puts a new spin on what I picked up from the photographer, Geoff Heinz."

Good. On track, but in a new direction. "What did you learn?"

"Heinz said the studio session with Leo, Ivy, and Tommy was pretty routine for the first twenty minutes. Mom and child sit on stool, dad stands. Dad sits, mom stands with hand on his shoulder. Mom and dad hold child, heads together. Usual stuff."

"But what changed?"

Sam removed his glasses, rubbed the lenses against his sleeve. "Leo wanted some shots with just him and Ivy. They put Tommy in a play-pen off to one side with a mountain of toys. Up 'til then, Ivy had been smiling, easy, tickling the baby and all. But when it was her and Leo alone, she clammed up. Heinz said the change felt like walking into a meat locker. Ivy flinched when Leo touched her arm or shoulder. Her smile looked painful, stiff."

"Okay. Siberia-level tension." I shivered. "Then what? More trouble?"

Sam blinked and drew his hand over his mouth. "Heinz took a series of solo shots of Ivy. He said she relaxed when posing by herself."

I said, "When you visited last month, did you sense this tension?"

"No." He shook his head. "I was focused on Tommy. I hadn't seen him in six months. He'd changed so much, grown so big. It was pure joy connecting with him again." He gulped scotch, wincing as the burn descended. "Ivy and I didn't get a chance to really talk, just us together."

There was no good time to tell him what I'd learned during my visit to Queenstown Pharmacy. Without asking, I poured Sam a third drink. I bulled straight ahead, summarizing Dr. Rajaram's observations in five phrases.

I wrapped with a single sentence: "I think Ivy was having an affair with Hector Ramírez, and that by late last fall she was pregnant."

He dropped the eyeglasses on the counter. Yellow draped his cheeks. "I missed everything going on in her life." He lowered his chin and raked hair back from his forehead.

"You couldn't know," I said.

'Every. Last. Thing." Tears hovered, but didn't fall.

Voice rough, I said, "I missed the clues, too." Breath, over breath, over sigh. "In my daughter's life. Maybe it's what we parents do. Miss the signals, botch the connections. Maybe that's the fucked-up way we deal with their growing into adults."

I licked my lips, tongue catching on the cracked skin. Flecks in the marble beneath my fingers swam and dodged. Blood pounding in my ears muffled his words. He asked something, wanted an answer. I saw his gaze drop to the gold chain at my throat. He wanted a name.

I touched the dangling letter M. "Yes, Monica," I said. A charm for a dazzling life. "She was my everything. Brave, funny, smart, beautiful, kind. She was nineteen when she died."

I saw his lips form the question. I couldn't hear through the roar. I answered by walking to the midnight-blue room beyond the kitchen. Sam followed, carrying both glasses.

I sank into the sofa, taking the left cushion so he could drop onto the right. I pulled a carved box from beneath the couch and set it between us. The smell of sandalwood rose from the lid when I lifted it. Photos drifted like leaves as I tilted the box. I sifted through the treasure, running my fingers over the piles of memories. Pictures of Monica from every year of her life.

As the sweet fragrance twined around our shoulders, I talked.

About her childhood and school years. About her birthdays and Christmases. About her prizes and recitals and contests and awards. I showed him photos of our trip to France: Eiffel Tower, Versailles, the bridge at Avignon, Marseille's grubby port.

Sam hummed, "Perfect."

"It was." I closed my eyes. "Our trip was a gift from my dad for Monica's high school graduation. Three weeks of bliss before Rutgers freshman orientation."

When I paused, Sam was as blunt as I had been. "And then she died. How?"

Direct questions required courage. I honored that bravery with straight answers.

"Her nineteenth birthday was January a year ago. She celebrated first with me, then with student friends. Our dinner was a quiet affair in a fancy Italian restaurant in New Brunswick. Mommy and Me with Sangiovese."

I rubbed one eye, remembering. "Monica tried to avoid being seen on campus with me. As a first-year student, having a parent on the university staff was awkward enough. To hear Monica tell it, having a mother on the campus police force was beyond embarrassing: 'A narc, Mom, jeez!' she'd say."

I imitated her drawl to perfection, the neck snap, the eye roll, the long sigh. Sarcasm was Monica's love language. I sounded just like her. Of course, Sam couldn't appreciate the realism. But the echo of her voice made me laugh.

He smiled and hummed to draw me on.

"Monica preferred to downplay our relationship. She insisted on living in a dorm even though our house was only a few miles from campus. So going to Due Mari for her birthday was a compromise: I pampered her with a fancy meal; she dodged the gossip patrol. Win-win."

I picked a photo from the pile and passed it to Sam. "Friday night. Lobster ravioli, braised asparagus," I said.

He studied the picture of us. Monica and I grinned above the white draped table as the waiter snapped. She'd wanted to eat early, so I'd met her straight after work. I wore my uniform: stiff navy shirt, hideous buttons on the breast pockets, metal insignia on the collar points; bulky radio and gun holstered below the table top. My hair was pulled into a tight bun at my nape. Did Sam notice the drastic change from long hair to chopped? I figured he was focused on Monica's style, not mine. In the photo, she flaunted polished shoulders in a sequined dress supported by black spaghetti straps. The gold M danced from the delicate chain at her throat. A birthday gift from my father. Her hair was caught in a dramatic pouf high on her head. She'd worked the winged eyeliner and sculpted boy-brows to perfection. Her lids and cheeks gleamed. A chocolate cupcake with six tall sparklers sat between us. Leaning toward each other, we raised wineglasses to salute the camera. We wore identical rosy lip gloss; I looked tired, she looked radiant.

Sam said the right thing. "You could be twins."

A sarcastic snap died on my tongue. "Yeah, we got that a lot." I executed another Monica eye roll to cover a sniffle.

He replaced the photo in the box and sipped his scotch as I continued.

"When we parted, Monica said she planned to meet her girlfriends for dessert. I dropped her in front of the Scarlet Castle. I remember stopping at the red light and turning to see her enter the place with two women I didn't recognize. Later, I learned the girls quit the bar after one round and landed at their real destination: a fraternity house party two blocks off campus."

I took a swig of club soda, hoping the flat drink would soothe the sting of memory.

"I was in bed at home when the call came in that night. Disturbance at a townhouse on Griswold Street. Dispatch gave few details, just the address, members of campus community involved, backup officers called to the scene. I was on the duty roster that weekend, so I skipped the uniform, scrambled into slacks and sweater. Arrived at Griswold Street fifteen minutes after the call. Three squad cars and an ambulance were on the scene. At the door, a cop sketched the sit rep: two white females plus one white male unconscious, alcohol poisoning suspected. Possible unknown drugs ingested. One Black female, identified as a university student, dead at the scene."

I stopped. Sam filled in the gap. "That was Monica?"

"Yes. She was lying on the couch in the front parlor. When I arrived, they hadn't covered her face. I recognized her right away. I knelt beside the sofa, touched her cheek, her throat, feeling for a pulse."

I traced circles on the underside of my wrist, remembering. "Her eyes were closed, her mouth open. I saw bile dripping from her chin onto the flowers of the sofa. She'd aspirated her own vomit. Drowned, suffocated, ignored on that couch."

I gripped the cushion beneath me. I was shaking.

Sam hummed, then pressed a hand over my knuckles.

I continued. "I know I didn't cry. Not then. I know I screamed. I shouted, 'Cover her!' At the cops. The EMTs. The kids huddled in corners of the room. The detective in charge. I screamed, 'Cover her.' Again and again. 'Cover her.' They brought a canvas from the ambulance. Draped it over the couch. When Monica's face was protected, I shut up."

Sam said, "You don't have to tell me this."

"And you don't have to listen."

"But here we are." He sighed.

I shifted my shoulders—left, then right. Tension flowed out. "I want you to know."

He ducked his head. "Go on, then."

The words rolled out of me. "I saw the techs hoist her onto the gurney. That hurt my stomach. I screamed at the kids perched on the staircase. Sitting two by two up the steps. Heads bobbing. Big eyes staring. Watching the show. Seeing her beautiful body jolted. Over the doorjamb. Down the cement steps. Kids looking. Twitching video-gamer thumbs. Fiddling cell phones. Watching me follow her to the curb. I hated them. For living."

Sam knelt in front of me. His face was tight like a fist. He stroked fingers under both my eyes, wiping tears I hadn't felt fall.

"Don't say it's okay." The last word hitched in my throat. "It's not all right."

"I would never say that," he whispered. "You know I couldn't."

He'd traveled where I'd gone, lost what I'd lost. I said, "I know."

I rolled my head on the sofa back. The wail rose through my arched throat. "I want my girl. My baby. I want her."

"I know," he said.

He covered the box of photos, smothering its rich fragrance. A shove returned the memories to their place under the sofa. Then he doused the overhead light. The cushion sagged when he sat beside me.

We rested in the dark, wrists and elbows touching. From the tremble of his shoulders, I knew he was weeping.

After a while, he passed a hand over his face and spoke. "There's a Robert Frost poem I've returned to in these troubled weeks. Maybe it will mean something to you, too."

"What's it called?"

"'Nothing Gold Can Stay.'"

"How does it go?" I turned to catch his profile in the pale glow from the main room.

"It's short, only eight lines."

I curved my spine against the cushion, as if bracing for some new hurt. But I said, "Go on then."

His fingers tapped rhythm against the sofa arm as he recited:

"Nature's first green is gold,
Her hardest hue to hold.
Her early leaf's a flower;
But only so an hour.
Then leaf subsides to leaf.
So Eden sank to grief,
So dawn goes down to day.
Nothing gold can stay."

I let the silence wash for a moment, missing the bright cadence of his voice. "What does it mean?"

He sighed. "Each person can read it differently, bringing their own temperament and life experiences to the interpretation. Years ago, I used to teach that Frost was writing about the inevitable changing seasons. Or about losing youth and beauty to the inexorable passage of time." His grunt was harsh. "Do I sound too much like an egghead English prof?"

"No." I leaned against his arm. "Go on."

He cleared his throat. "But now, for me, it's about losing the one thing—that one person—you cherish the most."

"Nothing gold can stay?" I plucked the necklace at my throat.

Tension rippled along his jaw. "Yes."

I sighed, sipping the silence.

Drifting on our misery, we lost minutes, maybe hours. First he fell asleep; then I followed.

Rumbles from a distant vehicle woke me.

Steadied by a hand on the dining table, I watched headlights sweep from the street through my house. The contours of white furniture and marble counters shimmered in the beams. The searchlight plunged from living room to kitchen, probing the dining room and bath to the sunroom at the rear of the house. After two passes, the truck departed.

Cloaked in darkness again, I fetched a blanket and pillow from the cupboard next to the bathroom. Covering Sam's torso and legs, I placed the pillow below his right hand. He clenched his fist once, then relaxed.

I checked my phone on its dock in the kitchen. Two-thirty. Keyshawn had texted another chess move. An audacious castle attack. After moving the pieces on my board, I texted a low-risk retreat to protect the king and powered off.

When I dropped into bed upstairs, my sheets felt warm to the touch. I smoothed circles on the skin of my wrist until I slept.

CHAPTER **TWENTY-ONE**

Nutty odors of simmering butter drew me downstairs the next morning.

I wore gray sweats, almost clean; Sam wore yesterday's jeans and pullover. Bare feet for us both. We had no precedents or ceremony, no guardrails for the situation, so Sam's crisp words matched mine. *Good, fine, scrambled, rye, grapefruit. Yes, sugar; no, cream.*

Checking my phone, I found a bug-eyed emoji from Keyshawn; he wrote last night's chess move was cowardly, unworthy of me. I zipped an exploding head in reply. Separate texts from Elissa, Belle, and Mavis Jenkins shouted a single message: attend town hall meeting this evening, or face wrath and eternal damnation. And no more lasagna from Belle.

When I chuckled at the texts from the power trio, Sam mumbled through the last bacon slice: "Something good?"

"Early morning reminders."

"From who?"

"My partner, my assistant, and my bartender." I sipped grapefruit juice and grimaced.

"The Three Furies. What do they want?"

"I promised to attend a town hall meeting with them this evening."

"Now you want to duck out?"

"Yes."

"But you're too smart to do that, right?"

"Or too scared." I laughed. The first real laugh in two days felt good. I tried it again. Still good.

"How tedious can it be?"

"Not boring. The opposite, in fact. The topic is important: The city council is considering a resolution confirming Queenstown as a sanctuary city."

"What's that?" His piping voice sounded almost sincere.

"If approved, the resolution means the town could shield immigrants from ICE agents."

"And the police won't assist Homeland Security raids?"

"Exactly. Some are for it. Lots are against it. That's what the council meeting is about."

"Hot time in the old town tonight." He bit the corner of a rye triangle, chewed, then washed it down with coffee. "What side are your friends on?"

"Mavis and Belle plan to speak in favor of the resolution. Elissa will keep quiet, but only because being a lawyer makes her careful. She's in favor, too."

He lowered the mug to peer at me. "And you?"

"I'm in favor. But zipped lip is my policy." I dragged thumb and forefinger along the seam of my mouth, twisted the imaginary key at the corner, then tossed it.

Sam pretended to catch the key in two hands. "Her Majesty, the mayor? Where does she stand?"

"She hasn't said." I collected plates, glasses, and utensils, piling them in the double sink. "We'll find out tonight. Lots of citizens are enraged. They claim it's sanctuary today, tomorrow socialism, communism, gay orgies, and free love. Taco tyranny, hip-hop autocracy. Decline of Western civilization. Details at eleven."

"White citizens, no doubt." Sam poured coffee into both mugs.

I dribbled blue soap over the dishes and cranked the spigot. KP duty was on me. I usually delayed for three days, maybe five, if I could. This morning I embraced the chore. Fair exchange for breakfast well delivered.

"Ten-four, good buddy," I said, flipping a mound of suds. I glanced over my shoulder. "You betcha. Preserving our Q-Town way of life, one burning cross at a time."

Sam tugged shaggy strands over his right ear. "This makes me want to get Tommy out as soon as I can." He pulled at his chin and sighed. "I hate the thought of him growing up here. Without Ivy."

I turned from the sink to face him. "I know." When his eyes clouded, I said, "We'll make it happen."

"You can't guarantee that." I heard his teeth click on the last word.

He knew the truth. I was a minor-league PI, a Black woman with few friends and no resources. Wading in troubled waters. Working for outsiders and immigrants against the bullnecked aristocracy of the town. Logic pegged my chances between slim and hell no.

But I was stubborn. Fuck logic. I amended the pledge: "I guarantee your case will be rock-solid, Sam."

"Thank you. That's all I ask."

Twenty minutes of scrubbing and sipping; then Sam left. He begged off for the day, saying he needed time to recharge his batteries, clean his spark-plug points, reset his speedometer. I clasped two hands, pleading for an end to the barrage of automobile metaphors. When I guessed the town council meeting would end by ten, he promised to come by at ten-thirty for a Glenlivet refill and an update on the investigation.

I was glad of the break, too. I wanted a silent morning to myself. I intended to study the photos I'd made of the murder scene at the Hannah house. A grisly job I couldn't perform with a grieving father clamped on my shoulder.

After I showered, I redressed in stiffer clothing: a button-down Oxford shirt and slacks with a leather belt. Formal outfit for a grim task I'd avoided earlier. At the kitchen island, I made a fresh pot of coffee. I needed to examine the photos I'd taken at the murder scene. But when I grabbed my phone, I seized on a delaying tactic. I searched for the Robert Frost poem Sam had shared last night. The lines, short syllables, simple images, dashed through my mind in Sam's warm voice: *Then leaf subsides to leaf. / So Eden sank to grief, / So dawn goes down to day. / Nothing gold can stay.* After repeating the poem aloud twice, I turned to my ugly task. Scrolling through the gallery of photos sent sour waves through my stomach. Grisly images ignited horrific memories. The extra caffeine was a bum idea, but I guzzled anyway.

I slowed when I found the sequence of photos I wanted. Flexing thumb and middle finger, I expanded the shots of the two bodies on the dining room floor. The distance between Ivy and Hector looked like seven to nine feet. Certainly more than arm's length. But Leo said that when he entered the room, he found Hector bent over Ivy, pounding her with a hammer. The two would have been close together when Leo fired at Hector to stop the assault. They should have been only inches apart when they fell. Leo's story disintegrated in the face of the photographic evidence.

I scrolled to a close-up of Hector. He was lying on his right side, torso curved. His left arm covered his face, but I could see the wounds on his head. Sliding the image into maximum close-up, I saw blood caked around two bullet holes to the skull. I scrolled to other pictures. In each photo, I saw the same position of bullet holes. One was on the top right quadrant of the head. The second hole was in the center back, approximately three inches above the hairline at the nape.

This juxtaposition did not fit Leo's story, either. These shots weren't fired from the side at a distance, as he'd claimed. I could see the two bullets entered the skull from above and behind. At close range. Nothing defensive. This was an execution.

If they'd looked, medical examiners should have seen this, too. They would have seen the crust of gunpowder indicating a point-blank shot. Forensic specialists would have noted the trajectory through the brain from the point of entry. If they looked, they would have seen Hector was either lying on the floor or kneeling when he was shot. The man had flung his left arm over his face in a defensive gesture. A desperate move against a gun pointed at his head. But no one examined the dead man with precision. The county prosecutor delivered his verdict less than two days after the deaths. Nobody applied scientific skepticism or humble disbelief. All incentives weighed in the other direction. No one challenged the story of the man who lived to tell the tale.

I pushed the phone to the edge of the counter, waiting for its sleek face to shimmer to black. More questions galloped through my head.

I wondered if Ivy was elsewhere in the house at the moment Hector was shot. Did she hear angry shouts, perhaps a thud as Hector dropped to the floor? Had she run to the dining room to see Leo bent over the prone man? Maybe she'd thrown herself at her husband in a futile effort to stop him. Had Leo struck her with the hammer before he'd killed Hector? Or after?

When the cops arrived on the scene after Leo's call to 911, Ivy was struggling to speak. I remembered seeing her twist on the carpet, hands plucking at the air. I saw her lips quiver around bubbles of saliva. Had she been trying to tell us the true story as she died?

In a reflexive jerk, my hand swept over the counter, striking the phone. I lunged, grabbing it in midair. These photos were evidence. My ideas were conjecture. But the inferences were grounded in the facts of these pictures. I needed to share these shards of evidence with someone who would use them to reconstruct the case; someone who could reopen the investigation of Ivy Hannah's murder.

I punched numbers for the switchboard of Queenstown police headquarters. I wanted to speak with Chief Robert Sayre. When I clawed through the bureaucracy to reach my friend, I heard warmth surge through his voice as he greeted me.

I cut short the welcome. "Bobby, give me thirty minutes this afternoon. I need to talk with you."

"You got five minutes at four-thirty." Gruff, the numbers gargled in the throat. "My office. Be on time."

When I stepped off the elevator on the second floor of the municipal building at four twenty-five, Bobby's broad chest blocked my view of the hall. His navy dress shirt and black tie seemed to absorb light from the fly-specked lamps overhead, casting a shadow that swallowed me.

I said, "You didn't have to throw a welcome party, Bobby. I'd have reached your office without an escort."

Uniformed officers clomped around us, their eyes glued to the walls or ceiling to avoid attracting the chief's attention.

Bobby rolled his weight from one foot to the other. "You're not going to my office, Myrick." He lowered his head to meet my gaze. Last-name stiffness was a bad sign.

"Why not?" I whispered, as a civilian in a sweater dress and knee-high boots bumped my arm. I knew demanding reasons for the change in plans was obnoxious. So I softened the presumption with a smile.

Bobby frowned. But he did explain. "I got five department heads at my conference table and a tech guy setting up PowerPoint. They're briefing me in advance of the town hall meeting tonight."

I scanned the busy corridor. "What I want to say requires a door, Bobby."

He grunted, then swung his head to the left. Using his bulk, he crowded me into the service stairwell next to the elevator. "This'll work," he said. When he'd pushed the door shut with his hip, Bobby turned on me. "You got four minutes left."

I pulled my cell from my pocket and fiddled the screen with trembling fingers. When the gallery of shots showing Hector Ramírez's mangled head appeared, I stepped next to Bobby. Shoulder to shoulder, we scrolled through the photos. I noted the angles of the bullet wounds, the distance between the dead man and the woman he was supposed to have attacked. Bobby huffed, his lips pursed to reject my claims. But when he took the phone from my palm, I counted that a plus. He'd rolled his shirt cuffs, exposing both forearms. As he worked the magnification on the photos, I watched long muscles glide and ripple, veins bulging near his knuckles.

"I can text these photos to you," I said.

"They're in the file, aren't they? Didn't you hand them over?"

"No. The photos I attached to my report were ones I took during my surveillance of Ivy Hannah. I figured the QPD forensics team took better shots than I did at the murder scene." I kept my tone mild to muffle the criticism. I guessed Bobby heard it anyway.

He dragged his hand from brow to beard, then squeezed the bridge of his nose. "I'll look at the file photos. You got anything else?" His eyes slotted from side to side, as if he sensed a clock ticking in his head. Dismissal neared.

I didn't want to share with Bobby my speculation about a romance between Ivy and Hector. Or the pregnancy theory. Conjecture like that could fly through the steel doors of the staircase, penetrate the municipal building walls, and sprint around town before the sun rose tomorrow. I knew Bobby was discreet and professional. But gossip that juicy would run amok all the same. Hector and Ivy were dead, but their families were not. I wanted to hold my theories close until I needed to unleash them.

I'd give Bobby something smaller. A crucial scrap of information I hoped would steer the official investigation in a new direction. I pulled from the inside pocket of my coat a copy of the photo I'd clipped from the *Queenstown Herald*. The celebratory shot of the church volunteers receiving commendations from Mayor Hannah.

"You can add this to the file." I slid a finger along the rows of blurry faces. "Here's Ivy." I tapped her pale image. "And this one, in the back, is Hector. I figure they knew each other through their church work."

"So what?"

"They were colleagues, friends. Why would he bludgeon her to death?"

"Don't play simple, Myrick. You never heard of acquaintances, co-workers, even close friends, killing each other?"

I stiffened. Bobby's insult to my professional instincts stung. "I'm simple? Okay, if it makes you feel big, you go with that. But I don't think that's how it went down." I grabbed his hand and slapped the newsprint into his palm. "Keep the photo. Give your team of crime gurus a new crack at the case." Interview over. I jammed both fists in my pockets and lurched toward the door.

I saw Bobby's eyes widen. He gulped, then twisted his mouth right. When his jaw dropped, I raised a palm to block the apology speech. "Save it, Chief." I jerked the door open. Dipping into a bow, I swept my hand toward the hall. The sneer was my weapon: "Don't you have department heads waiting in your office?"

As he barreled past me, I said, "Catch you this evening at the town hall meeting." When Bobby disappeared, I plunged down the stairs two at a time.

CHAPTER **TWENTY-TWO**

The town hall meeting that evening was as raucous as I'd expected.

Discussion of sanctuary city status pushed the desperation button on everyone's dashboard. Bluster and fear swilled like ammonia through the air in the third-floor auditorium of the municipal building. When I opened the swinging door at the back of the hall, the stink bit my nose.

I surveyed the room: maybe three hundred sweaty people packed like hogs in a slaughterhouse. Mayor Hannah sat behind a long table in the front, dressed in dark gray like a judge or a nun. Her fingers flexed around the handle of a Paul Bunyan–size gavel. Six council representatives flanked her. The men were all white and all furious, their faces frozen in jack-o'-lantern grimaces.

I stood next to the side door in the back of the hall. As I leaned against faux-wood panels, I noticed the mayor's personal bodyguards, Jake Hughes and Tidy Sutton, bracketing the entrance on the right. We raised chins at one another but kept yards between us.

When the agenda flashed on a screen above the mayor's head, the crowd groaned. The first item on the program was the decrepit condition of the municipal water tank. Nobody cared about the city engineer's report on the fragile struts and rusty pilings of the old structure. Chicken Little's account drew jeers from the throng. No one wanted to discuss infrastructure troubles. Sarcastic slow claps drove the man from the mic. Everyone was primed to rage about the top bout on the fight card: the sanctuary-city proposal.

Microphones were fixed on stanchions at the head of two aisles dividing the rows of theater chairs. My friends Belle Ames and Mavis Jenkins stood stiff as bowling pins waiting their turns to speak. Their forward progress toward the mic was painful. Scores of residents had opinions; no one had patience. In the creeping line, I spotted Darryl of the green alligator-skin boots. My former chum had leveled up: blond hair dipped over one eye; blue shirt tight against chiseled pecs. His jeans reminded me of candy—good and plenty. My insides twinged in celebration as he stepped toward the mic. But when Darryl opened his mouth, my ardor fizzled. He spouted the anti-sanctuary rant of the majority. Who knew bigotry was such an effective buzzkill?

Arguments in favor of the resolution to declare Queenstown a sanctuary city rested on two claims: first, the founding fathers wanted us to uphold the principal of equality for all men; and second, we were a nation of immigrants, benefiting from the diverse contributions of people who had arrived on our shores from all across the globe. Lots of eye rolling greeted that claim. A brave few dared to cite the biblical injunction to treat your neighbors as you would wish to be treated. Finger-wagging recitations of the Golden Rule generated grumbling, the shuffling of feet, and a tide of catcalls. Reminders of Sunday-school lessons were out of favor this night.

The anti-sanctuary crowd found biblical precedent too, even if they botched the interpretations. An eye for an eye. Splitting Solomon's baby. Give unto Caesar—in this case meaning we should let the feds capture and deport immigrants, stay out of the mess. Mayor Hannah's only intervention of the night came in support of this point. With damp eyes and pointing finger, she warned that the federal government might cut off grants to Queenstown if we defied the immigration laws.

Her conclusion was stirring. "All of you know me, know my record of service to our community," she said, her voice rising. "I've devoted my life to creating safe neighborhoods where we can raise our children, strong schools where we can watch them flourish, vibrant establishments where we can shop and entertain. Building a better Queenstown is my life's work."

Hannah stopped as applause thundered across the auditorium. Head bop, then palm pressed to chest. Finger flick to catch a tear. I saw her lower lip tremble. This passion wasn't show. Her emotions were real. I felt my own heart soar as she resumed speaking.

"Thank you, my friends. I value the confidence you have placed in me over the years I've been your mayor. I assure you now, that confidence will not go unrewarded. Queenstown is as precious to me as my own family. Indeed, you *are* my family. I will defend Queenstown with every fiber in my soul." Fist clenched on the table, jaw jutting with resolution. "I won't allow Queenstown's unique character, grounded in our patriot past, to be tarnished. Nor will I permit Queenstown's exciting future to be corroded by rash appeals or unfounded claims."

Applause, louder than before, greeted this pledge. I saw color rush across Hannah's cheeks, warming her sallow skin. She blinked rapidly, the collar of her dress rippling against her throat. At last she bit her lower lip, bottling the raw emotions. The mayor raised her hand to quiet the throng. "Thank you for your patience and attention, my friends. Now let us continue our discussion of this important issue."

After her speech, I figured we knew where the mayor stood. Her conviction was compelling. My heart pattered like a snare drum. If an election were called that hour, I'd vote for Josephine Hannah. If she pointed at a hill, I'd lead the charge up it. She had me. Heat pumping in my cheeks, I pushed through the auditorium door. I trotted left toward a water fountain. Three long gulps, then a splash to chill my face. As I reentered the assembly hall, swampy air washed over me.

The sanctuary city debate wore on. Some people spoke about being replaced. They wouldn't say by whom. Left the blank empty for neighbors to fill in with their favorite bugbear: foreigners, dark people, elites. Hannah made no further remarks, simply bobbing and smiling like a sphinx.

The heated hours rolled and the stench in the room mounted. The mayor said nothing in response to the avalanche of appeals to the traditions and culture of that wonderful era when Queenstown had been safe, clean, and affordable. Q-Town the untroubled haven, the unblemished citadel. Everyone who made this argument was white. The rest of us remembered things differently, but we took the mayor's tactic: we said nothing. According to this pale view, Q-Town was great when everybody spoke English as a first language. Applause and foot-stomping rocked the room whenever a speaker struck that old-time chord.

At one point, I thought the mayor might gavel the room to order as the white-paradise reminiscing swelled. She stroked the hammer but didn't raise it. She only nodded and tapped her shoe under the table. I wondered if Jo Hannah was not just on board the supremacy ship. Maybe she was first mate, bo'sun, and captain. Did having a brown-skinned great-nephew make a difference to her? Maybe she figured her family was the exception to the rule.

The crowd was boisterous as the final thumps of the gavel ended the meeting at ten-fifteen. Lots of laughter from shiny red faces, plenty of backslapping and high fives. I figured most of the attendees smelled victory, or at least vindication. I lost track of Mayor Hannah as she disappeared into a knot of cheering supporters.

Since Belle had been a prominent speaker, I played bodyguard, walking her and Elissa to their car. They shrugged off my concern. But Mavis, returning to the tavern, welcomed my offer to escort her to her SUV. As a bartender, she knew plenty about the unpredictable nature of triumphant crowds. Happy and vulgar one minute, overturning cars and smashing windows the next. Mavis wanted my attention.

By the time I turned toward my Jeep, the parking lot was almost deserted. I counted three sedans, four pickups, and a station wagon. No people in sight.

Bobby Sayre intercepted me before I grabbed the door handle. Dressed in black, he'd moved like a cat, catching me woolgathering as I dug for my key.

"That was something, wasn't it, Vandy?" He pressed his height over me. Full police-chief mode.

"Yeah, something else."

I didn't know what I was agreeing to, but the urgency in his voice made me shiver despite the heat rolling from his body to mine.

When we'd talked at police headquarters five hours earlier, Sayre had seemed calm, even reticent. His eyes had remained mild as I discussed my revised theory of the Ivy Hannah case. Even when I showed him the photos of Hector Ramírez's damaged head, he kept his focus on a point beyond my shoulder. As if my views were reruns of played-out scenarios. I remembered how his voice marched around the stairwell to a stately cadence. Slow and deep, as if I'd exhausted his daily measure of energy. *Simple,* he'd labeled me. Like I was a busybody harassing the police tip line with a crank call. As if nothing I said mattered.

Now I wanted to needle him about his silence in the town meeting. He'd had a chance to be a big shot, strut his official stuff. But when the mayor asked him for a comment at the end of the meeting, he shook his head.

"I thought you'd give us a drop of your wisdom, Sayre." I snapped his surname, distancing, the way he'd used mine in our earlier talk. "Why'd you beg off?"

He removed the left glove and twisted it in both hands. "Yeah, I could have said my piece tonight. Maybe I should have. Had the numbers ready and everything." I figured his department heads had armed him with data-filled reports that afternoon. I wondered why he'd decided not to speak in the town hall session.

He hitched a sigh. "Every time those federal boys raid a house in Abbott's Landing, I get calls at midnight from some poor woman frantic because la migra is hauling away her man."

"What do you say?"

He shot a jet of frosty air. "What can I say? I don't have jurisdiction over ICE. So I listen, I mumble, I take a phone number, I promise to send someone from social services to help the family."

"And do you?"

"Sure. But what's the point? Her family is broken, her life torn apart. She's not going to be right. Ever. Nothing I can do about it." Each word dropped lower in his chest. I crowded close to hear him spit the next sentence. "Every time I get a call like that, I cringe."

"These raids take a toll." *On you,* I wanted to finish.

"On the people, on the cops, on everybody." He jerked the black knit cap from his scalp to wipe sweat from his brow. "Sanctuary status would take QPD out of the raid business. We could build trust in the community. Make solid connections. Work together with neighborhood leaders to solve problems. We can't do that now because we're despised as narcs for the feds."

"Why didn't you say that tonight? You might have made a difference."

He snorted in disgust. "My nuts are already in the vise. You think
I'm going to give *her* a lever to twist the screw tighter?"

He swiped the wool cap from eyes to chin, a momentary mask.
Then he dragged it onto his head.

I inhaled. Bobby didn't have to say the name. I got the picture.
He was a town employee; the mayor signed his checks. He was free
to quit, to try for a career elsewhere. But as long as he was Q-Town
police chief, he answered to Jo Hannah.

He glowered at the sky over my head. "You want a life in this town,
you need to learn the facts."

"I learned that lesson decades ago." My mother's kitchen-table
warnings flashed through my mind. *Trust is like sponge cake,* Alma said,
*sweet but squishy. You craving that sugar, but the foundation goes soft when you
step. You can't rely on your gut, Vandy. You best learn early on not to trust nobody.*

"Then this is your refresher course. Around here, you got a choice:
you can do your job, or you can keep your job."

"Where's the conflict?"

He ignored my question. "Fourteen years back, working a break-in
at a local contractor's office, I ran across notes showing how much he
paid in kickbacks for each construction job."

"Pay-to-play?"

He nodded. "Simple shit. Low amounts, but regular. The skim all
went into one particular pocket."

No need to strain my imagination. I muttered, "The mayor's?"

Shrugging, the chief continued. "Two days after I collected that
contractor's shoebox of notes, I got a call from her office. We had a
nice chat: plain, clear, sincere."

"She warned you off the case?"

"Not in so many words. She said she was looking out for my long-
term professional interests. I had a bright future in Q-Town. I could do
my job, take my shoebox of evidence to the county prosecutor, push
for an investigation."

I supplied the kicker. "And get busted to patrol duty and fired
within six months. I got it. Or . . . ?"

"Or I could bury the shoebox." He polished sweat from his nose with a gloved finger. "And keep my job."

"Where'd you dump it? Lake Trask? Delaware River?"

Sayre's mouth tilted. "How stupid you think I am, Vandy? I wrapped that shoebox in a canvas tarp and tucked it under my bed." His lower teeth flashed like whitecaps on a night ocean. "And I kept my job."

He leaned into me, his puffer jacket bumping my shoulder. "I still want to keep my job. I want to protect my town." He gazed across the lot, toward the lake and the silhouettes of low buildings crowded on its shore. "And I want you to take care of yourself out here."

"What do you mean, Bobby?"

"I said what I said," he growled. "Be careful. Watch your back."

"Am I in trouble?" I could see the white corners of his eyes slide as he looked at me.

A puff of warm breath against my cheek was his answer. Not good enough.

"What am I supposed to watch out for?"

"You're messing in deep shit. You're churning more muck than you know how to handle."

"Ivy's murder? You think someone's coming for me?"

"If I had anything specific, I'd tell you." Three slow blinks shuttered his eyes. "I'm on your side."

I thrust my jaw. "You say you're on my side." I stabbed a finger into his chest. "But you won't have my back. Is that it?"

"Get in your car, Vandy." He jerked open the door. "Go home."

The bite of Sayre's dismissal ate at me each block I drove. Simple, he said. I could feel the sting poisoning my system, one angry thought building on another. My rant filled the Jeep: he discounted my ideas and ignored my research and experience. He wanted to scare me into dropping the case. Maybe he'd noted something worth considering in my ideas. But his default position was a refusal to acknowledge my contribution. Because I was a woman? Because once upon a time, I'd been his girl?

Heat surged to my throat as I chugged into the driveway and killed the engine. Unzipping my coat, I freed warmth from my chest. I felt Sayre's insult swell to injury; my fury grew into purpose. I wanted to rush to my laptop. With a solid hour of writing, I could outline my hypothesis and elaborate my notes on the case. Simple, he called me. I'd make him pay for dismissing me.

I tramped the icy brick path. As I passed, wind shuddered through the rhododendron bushes flanking the porch steps. Snow dusted from bare branches to my pants cuffs.

I felt a hand on my bicep. The grip was small, the squeeze firm. I kicked straight; my shoe struck metal, then rubber. I heard gears whir. Off-balance, I twisted to break the fall with my hip. The small hand pulled on my elbow, then wrist.

"You hurt?" Squeaking skipped from alto to soprano. "I didn't mean to surprise you."

On my knees, I steadied one hand on the bottom step, the other swatted snow from the hem of my coat. I squinted up at a heart-shaped brown face framed by a waterfall of bushy hair. Toppled on the path, her bicycle's rear wheel spun like a dervish.

"Let go of me." I tried to thunder, but only gasps emerged. "Who the hell are you?"

"I'm Ingrid Ramírez." She bit her lower lip, eyes scanning my face to see if the name registered. It didn't.

I scrambled to my feet, arms extended toward the scrawny bushes. I wheezed, "Who the hell is Ingrid Ramírez?"

The girl squared her shoulders inside a purple-and-white varsity jacket with the Q-High School panther leaping on the left breast.

Her voice punched the night air. "I am the sister of Hector Ramírez. I want to hire you. I want you to prove he never murdered anybody."

INGRID'S CASE

CHAPTER **TWENTY-THREE**

Ingrid Ramírez requested tea. Coffee or chamomile were the only beverages on the Myrick menu. She announced chamomile tasted like hay. She required four fingers of milk and two spoonfuls of sugar to improve the coffee. I found a carton of doughnuts in the pantry, and while we talked, she devoured the three with chocolate icing.

Sitting at the kitchen counter in a green sweater and purple tie-dyed leggings, Ingrid looked undersized for a sixteen-year-old. I thought high school sophomores ran bigger. She was five-three, with two-inch platforms on her black combat boots. Maybe 105 pounds, lots of leg, and enough chest to make her classmates drool.

As I studied her, I caught the resemblance to her brother. I'd only seen Hector dead; my opinions were based on close inspection of the photos I'd taken at the murder scene. But Ingrid looked like the man in the driver's license photo the *Herald* published after his death. She had the same sharp cheekbones framing a tight mouth. Her brown eyes tilted toward her temples; the heavy lids and long lashes could have stunned an army of Instagram followers if she played in that world.

I asked Ingrid how she'd found me. My name hadn't appeared in the media coverage of Ivy Hannah's murder case.

"I clocked you following her before she died," Ingrid said. When she wagged her head, black hair billowed over her shoulders. "You were tracking her. Like a stalker or something."

I didn't try to swallow my surprise. "When did you see me with Ivy?"

"I first saw you in McDonald's. It was a Saturday afternoon. You watched Ivy and her little boy in the play zone."

"You were there?" I sounded stupid. Heat rushed in my cheeks. "I didn't see you." That wasn't true. I remembered a teenage girl in a Q-High jacket, the same coat now dumped on my living room couch. "Were you with your brother?"

"Sure. That was Hector with me. We were babysitting a friend's kids."

A dark-haired man trying to corral twin girls leaped to my mind. I had seen Hector speak with Ivy that day. What else had I missed early in this investigation, before I knew there was a case?

Ingrid dabbed chocolate from the Cupid's bow of her lip. "I saw you a few days later at the Methodist church. You were hanging in your ginormous Jeep, snooping at the back door like Harriet the Spy."

I remembered the brunette girl delivering sacks of clothing to Ivy at the church. "You think Ivy saw me?"

"Doubt it." Ingrid scrunched up her nose. "She never caught much, ever. She was always go-go, rush-rush. Charity work was her jam. That lady *loved* clothing giveaways. Each month she'd buy cheap stuff to donate. Leggings, blouses, sweatshirts. Always mega-baggy, like she figured all us poor people are fat." The girl chuckled at the curious ways of the donor class.

I blinked at this simple explanation for Ivy's mysterious purchases of the oversize clothing Sam and I'd found in her closet. Another swing and a miss.

Ingrid poked at my scratched ego again. "That day you were spying at the church, Hector and I delivered bags of old clothing. We weren't supposed to use the taxi for that, but nobody ratted on us, so we did it when we could."

I understood the pattern now. Ingrid was the black-haired sprite who bicycled into my peripheral vision in the weeks after Ivy and Hector died. She'd hovered near Ivy's memorial service. She'd pushed her bicycle along the sidewalk outside the Queenstown Pharmacy when I interviewed Dr. Rajaram, the pharmacist. Time and again, I'd seen but failed to observe. Sherlock Holmes would strip me of my PI credentials. Waves of humiliation heated my neck.

"Did you attend the town hall meeting tonight?" I figured she followed me home from the municipal building.

"Nah, I knew it'd be a total drag. Nobody does white-people bigotry like Q-Town old-timers." She sucked her teeth. "I biked here and waited on your porch. I figured you'd show eventually. Took your time, though." She pulled the turtleneck to her chin and shivered.

"How did you know where I lived?"

Ingrid looked at me like I had a giant L stamped on my forehead. *Loser, lame, ludicrous,* take your pick. The comical intensity of her sarcasm reminded me of Monica. This was how she used to tease me, challenge me. My heart clutched on a downbeat. I squeezed my lids to mask the surge of pain. Then I smoothed circles in the skin of my wrist. This girl had my daughter's sass, the identical fire of youth and superiority burned in these eyes.

I watched as Ingrid rotated her index finger in the air between us, raising her eyebrows to urge me to solve the puzzle for myself.

When I fumbled the exercise, she sighed. "I followed you from the office a few times, obvi. And anyway, we live on FitzRoy Street, not far from here." Teacher leading a dear but dumb student.

Rattling at the front door interrupted my reply. I heard someone tromp into the hallway. When I stood from the island, Sam Decker shouted a greeting. Smooth and cheery. Like he was Ricky Ricardo, and I was Lucy. More heat—humiliation or something else—flowed to my throat. He hung his coat on the hall hook, as if it belonged there. I'd forgotten his morning promise to come by for a catch-up meeting. I cringed and glanced at Ingrid. She made a *yikes* grimace, but said nothing.

"Oh, I'm sorry," Sam said when he strolled into the living room. "I didn't realize you had company." Polite, but he gaped at Ingrid like he required an explanation.

She stiffened on the barstool and returned the stare, dragging her gaze over Sam from head to toe. Tough girl.

I coughed, ready to make the awkward introductions. *Victim's father, meet victim's sister.* Private eye etiquette escaped me in the macabre moment.

But Ingrid beat me to the punch. "No, I'm the sorry one. I didn't realize you had a hot date tonight." Her wink traipsed across the kitchen counter at me.

I said, "No date."

"No date," Sam echoed. He wore a chambray shirt—three buttons popped—and dark jeans; the hot prof look supported Ingrid's guess.

He walked to the corner of the island and loomed over the girl. Tall men believe their height scares the shit out of us. We let them have their fantasies.

Ingrid's lip bent around a drawl: "Okaaay. No date. It *is* after eleven. I was trying to be polite."

Her jaw shifted as she searched for alternative terms. I imagined the teen dictionary unfurling in her head: booty call; slam the hen; lay pipe, hook up.

Time to seize the conversation. I glided my hand in the air between them. "Ingrid, this is Sam Decker. He's Ivy Hannah's father. I'm working with Sam to find out who killed her."

She gasped; green stained her cheeks. Her eyes clouded and she drove her tongue in search of moisture. "Oh, God," she whispered, lowering her forehead to the counter.

Sam's brow crumpled as he absorbed the girl's distressed reaction. Wide-eyed, he looked at me.

I said, "Sam, this is Ingrid Ramírez. She's the sister of Hector Ramírez. She wants me to work for her. To prove her brother's innocence."

A groan surged from deep in his gut. He turned toward the refrigerator, extending an arm to steady his body against its bulk.

We held our positions for thirty seconds, maybe a minute. Frozen by the horror of what we'd experienced, the anguish of what we knew, the injustice of what we suspected.

Sam broke the silence. He stepped to my side. "Will you take the job? Can you help Ingrid?"

I looked at Ingrid. "First, I need to hear from you." I reached across the marble to her, palms up. "I need to know why you picked me. And what you think I can find if I take this case."

She began with a whimper. "I chose you because I saw how carefully you followed them. I think you can know my brother. Not as a relative or friend. You're not one of us." She swung her tearstained face toward Sam. "And you're not one of them, either." Blackness made me neutral like Switzerland in her calculus. "That's your advantage. You have no ties. That's what I want from you. Fairness."

I swallowed the dregs of coffee, looking into the mug to avoid Ingrid's shining eyes. Her artless faith warmed the kitchen. She knew nothing of my Queenstown family and history. That ignorance stoked her belief in me. I wanted to be the impartial guardian she imagined. The paladin she needed. Clutching the counter, I stiffened my knees to stop their wobble. Did I have the skills? Could I help this troubled girl and ease her suffering?

She continued, her voice rising: "Mr. Decker, I know my brother didn't kill your daughter. He never would. I know it. Here. Where I carry him." She touched her heart, plucking the sweater with two fingers.

When Sam nodded, she pinned me. "My mother and I need your help. We want you to prove Hector didn't do this horrible thing. We want you to clear his name."

Eyes bright, lips firm, Ingrid leaned toward me, her plea converted to a challenge.

I accepted the job.

We sorted the details of tomorrow's work. Sam insisted he'd join me to interview Ingrid's mother at their apartment on FitzRoy Street. I saw a flicker of doubt dance across Ingrid's brow as she slipped into her coat. I wondered if she believed this was the best approach to her mother. But Sam's eagerness and sincerity committed us to this plan. When Ingrid stepped onto the porch, he pulled me aside. He whispered he'd pay for the billable hours I racked up on Ingrid's case. I protested, but without vigor. He was right: I needed the money; Ingrid had none, Sam had plenty. Our course was set.

I closed the door and leaned against it, listening to the clank and laughter as Ingrid shoved her bicycle into Sam's car. I heard the Kia's engine putter toward the corner as I returned to the kitchen in search of the last doughnut.

I dabbed fingers into the empty box, retrieving chocolate crumbs. Sweet, with a bitter aftertaste. I squeezed arms around my waist. Did our strange alliance have a chance? Could a man and a woman who'd lost their only daughters unite to help a girl who'd lost her only brother?

CHAPTER **TWENTY-FOUR**

Sam and I arrived separately at the Ramírez apartment the following afternoon.

FitzRoy Street was in the heart of Abbott's Landing, the neighborhood where most of the town's Latino residents lived. Dumpy houses on crooked streets; low-slung apartment buildings with balconies guarded by railings painted puke yellow. The trees in Abbott's Landing were two and three hundred years old; beautiful cathedrals of oak and birch softened the ramshackle vistas near the lake.

Sam was already seated on a lumpy couch in the front room when Ingrid opened the door to me. His coat was unfastened but still bunched at his neck, as if he might flee at any moment. Relief flushed his cheeks when I entered.

I glanced around as I unbuttoned my jacket. The apartment was crowded with flowers: a riot of blooms covered the sofa, the curtains, the rug, and a plastic cloth on the kitchenette table. A dahlia festooned the ballpoint pen poking from a notepad clipped to the fridge with a magnet. Matching the decor, the apartment was as hot as a solarium. I pulled at the collar of my blouse to cool my throat as I sat.

In contrast to the flowers, Carmen Ramírez wore a navy pullover and slacks. Her black plaits were pinned into a bun at her nape. She sat in an upholstered chair that swallowed her slim body. The reading lamp over her right shoulder was lit, even though bright sun streamed through the room. Maybe Mrs. Ramírez wanted the extra light for warmth. Her forehead was dry; flakes of skin lifted from the black stripes of her eyebrows. Her hands were clasped in her lap, a thumb rubbing circles across green veins. Both her children had inherited her beautiful heavy-lidded eyes.

Ingrid motioned me to a place next to Sam, and she sat in a wooden chair beside her mother.

The girl made no move to introduce us. She didn't offer soft drinks or water. In case we were in doubt, this wasn't a tea party. Sam hunched with his hands glued to his thighs, misery squeezing his face.

After a minute of silence, I sighed, then launched into a rehearsed speech. I thanked Mrs. Ramírez for receiving us in her home. I regretted the circumstances that brought us together and offered condolences for the loss of her son. I gave a thumbnail professional résumé and explained who Sam was; I assumed Ingrid had shared these details with her mother before we arrived, but I wanted to frame the interview in favorable terms.

During my speech, Carmen Ramírez studied a point on my left shoulder. Never my hands, my eyes, or my mouth. She wouldn't look at Sam at all. The interview was a bust. I hitched my knee, ready to rise from the sofa and depart.

Ingrid leaned on the arm of the chair, pressing her lips to her mother's ear. Then Carmen Ramírez spoke in Spanish.

Her daughter translated: "I'm grateful you have come to our home. We arrived here from Honduras twenty-five years ago. My son was nine when we came. My daughter was born here. My husband died here. We have lived and worked in Queenstown in the schools and restaurants and warehouses." As Ingrid spoke, her mother studied a calendar on the wall. The formal speech closed with expressive contempt. "You are the first gringos to visit our home in all this time. Except for the police."

Ingrid's eyes darted to me. "Sorry. She knows you're not white."

"I get it," I mumbled. Shifting from one hip to the other, I sank deeper into the cushion. I couldn't dodge Sam, though I wanted the distance.

The girl cleared her throat. "My mother is prepared to answer your questions."

The exchange was stilted. I asked about Hector's employment history. Mrs. Ramírez gave a phone directory of curt replies: Olde Towne

Diner, Target, Campanella's Nursery, the Wayfair warehouse, Gordon's Landscaping, Stubby's Tacos, Patel's Grocery, and Compadre Taxi Company.

Mrs. Ramírez paused between each post, giving Sam time to write in his notebook. Scratching from his pen filled the silences. She watched his fingers move, waiting until he stopped before adding to the list.

At one point I interrupted. There were two Campanella locations, I said, one in Q-Town, one in Hamilton. When I asked where Hector worked, his mother replied before the translation. I figured she understood and spoke solid English. Twenty-five years in Jersey delivered plenty of tough lessons in language and life. But she kept a purposeful distance by reminding us we were visitors in her Spanish-speaking home.

I wanted more. I needed to learn about Hector as a man and a son. But I knew we were pinned in a difficult corner. I stood and squeezed Ingrid's shoulder. When I tipped my head toward the front door, she followed me outside to the balcony.

I went direct: "Your mother won't talk with us, will she? I mean, really talk."

"No. She won't speak in front of Mr. Decker." Ingrid's eyes welled with tears.

"Because he's white? Or because he's Ivy's father?" I stepped closer, hoping we could share body warmth and break this impasse.

"Both," Ingrid moaned. "Last night when I told her I'd invited you here, she was super angry. She yelled at me. She said I had no right involving outsiders—gringos—in our troubles. I said you were already involved. You were trying to uncover the truth. She was still mad when I went to school this morning."

Ingrid pressed her hand against her temple, pulsing her fingers against the headache caused by her mother's fury.

I asked, "Do you think she'd feel better if Sam left?"

"Yeah, that would help."

"I'll speak with him. He'll understand."

"I'm sorry." She sobbed, pulling the sweatshirt hood over her hair.

"Nothing to be sorry about, Ingrid. Five hundred years of culture don't get wiped off the books in an afternoon." I hugged the girl and rubbed her back. "Neither do twenty-five years of experience. Or five weeks of grief."

My teeth were chattering when I leaned through the doorway to gesture at Sam. He bolted from the couch as if stamped by a branding iron. Ingrid left us on the balcony.

"Sam, this isn't working," I said.

"You're telling me." His shoulders slumped inside the coat. "She hates me."

No contradiction from me. I wasn't going to give a mini lesson on colonialism and oppression. We had work to do and limited time to do it. He could nurse his wounded privilege later.

I said, "I need to question her about Hector's private life. I want to generate new leads, learn more about his relationship with Ivy. And I can't do it with you here."

He bobbed his head but stood still.

I grabbed his forearm. "We split up; we get more done." My breath burst like foam in the air between us. "I want you to pursue the taxi company angle. Go talk with the people at Compadre. Find out what they know about Hector. His friends, coworkers, bosses. Did they like him? Hate him? Trust him? Fear him?"

"Yeah, I can do that." His eyes narrowed, calculating. "I'll see how many people I can reach now. I'll phone you this evening."

"Perfect," I said.

"You think I should tell them I'm Ivy's father? Will that help or hurt?"

"Play it by ear. Ease into the conversation. See who wants to talk about Hector, who won't. Then if you feel sympathy will make them open to you, drop the news."

Sam stared at me. "Your lips are turning blue." He pointed at my face. "I've read about that. But I've never seen it in real life." He wrapped his arms around me and squeezed. "You get inside and warm up. I hear frozen detectives are no good."

Carmen Ramírez watched her daughter bring me a mug of hot tea when I returned to the sofa. The dangling yellow tea bag tag matched the tulips on the mug. I let the fragrant steam thaw my nose as I prepared to restart the interview. She spoke to me in English.

Hector's transition to life in Queenstown was difficult. A nine-year-old can't make friends easily, his mother remembered. Especially if he's brown-skinned, nearsighted, chubby, and non-English-speaking. Hector stayed out of trouble by playing soccer and baseball with the Police Athletic League. He learned English at school; after-hours tutoring helped, as did working jobs for neighbors. He liked washing cars, raking lawns, shoveling snow from driveways and sidewalks in winter.

When he graduated from high school, Hector began the series of short-term jobs she had listed earlier. Difficulties with the police? Nothing serious, she said. Parking tickets, running red lights, failure to signal a turn. Once he was stopped for the cardboard air freshener dangling from his rearview mirror. Once he was pulled over because a rear taillight was broken.

I understood these were minor infractions, nothing to prevent Hector from getting a new job when the old one ended. I wondered if Ingrid knew of any serious blemishes on her brother's record. Had he been picked up for pot? Disorderly conduct? Vandalism or shoplifting? Something had kept Hector from settling into a steady position with a permanent employer. To learn more, I needed to talk with Ingrid on her own.

Mrs. Ramírez said Hector worked at Compadre Taxi Company for eighteen months. He was proud of the service they provided to the community. So many Latinos in Queenstown couldn't afford to own private cars. People needed taxis to get to work and shopping, to attend church, to go to the health clinic, or to visit relatives. Hector liked wearing the red Compadre jacket in public. It was a uniform of distinction and pride, he always said.

And his volunteer work? Did Mrs. Ramírez know Hector worked with Ivy Hannah? Another question to ask Ingrid in private.

When the girl retreated to the kitchen for more tea, Mrs. Ramírez sat on the edge in her chair.

"In your work, I think you have met many bad people, Ms. Myrick." Arms extended, palms open. Her lower lashes were damp. "Does this seem to you the description of a killer?"

I gulped and shook my head. She was right, I had seen murderers.

I knew killers ranged along an arc of dispositions, a spectrum of motives. Some were indifferent to their victims; some were consumed by self-justifying fury. A few were overcome by remorse; three laughed in my face.

"Mrs. Ramírez, thank you for sharing your son with me." I took the hot mug from Ingrid. I wanted to say I could see Hector as clearly as I saw my own dead child. That wasn't true, but it was a comfort I wanted to share. "You have let me know him. See him, even understand him."

The woman's throat bobbled. Her hand flew to the indentation below her jaw as if feeling the pulse there. Ingrid leaned over her mother and whispered into her hair. The woman nodded.

I said, "I do not think your son killed Ivy Hannah. I want the tools to prove that case." As if I were translating from a new language, my words stiffened as we closed our interview. "You have pointed me in the direction I will go to find that evidence."

Mrs. Ramírez bent forward, pressing her face into her open hands. Ingrid rubbed her mother's back. Circles of comfort like the ones I traced on my wrist when Monica rose in my mind. Then Ingrid straightened and beckoned me toward the rear of the apartment. She whispered, "I want to show you Hector's room. You'll understand more."

CHAPTER **TWENTY-FIVE**

I wanted to speak with Ingrid in private, so when we reached her brother's room. I tipped the door closed.

"Has your mother rearranged things here . . . since . . . ?"

She filled in the blanks. "Not much." She glanced around the narrow space, leading me on a tour with her eyes. "We gave away his sneakers and his overcoat. But Mamá wouldn't let me touch the jeans and shirts. Everything else is the same."

A blue-and-green plaid quilt was draped over the twin bed. A chair with metal legs held a flashlight and a phone charger cord. The mirror on the closet door tilted on a nail. A three-drawer chest formed the foot of the bed. On one wall I saw a calendar with bird photos, frozen on January's red-tailed hawk. Posters of the Philadelphia Eagles and 76ers papered another wall.

I stepped to a corner next to the closet. On this wall, Hector had pinned a front page of the *Queenstown Herald* from last October. I studied the familiar picture of the medal ceremony honoring the volunteer team from First United Methodist Church. Mayor Hannah and Reverend Kent grinning in front. Ivy relegated to the end of the first row. Hector squeezed at the rear.

Ingrid said, "He was so proud that day."

"Did you attend?"

"Of course. Mamá, too." She sniffed. "She was so happy. He had such a screwed-up time of things. There weren't lots of days like this."

I put my finger on Hector's smiling face. "Do you think this is where Hector met Ivy?"

"At the ceremony?"

"No, at the church, as a volunteer?"

"One hundred percent. He enjoyed working at First United. Our home church is Saint Anthony of Padua, but Mamá didn't mind Hector spending his free hours at a gringo church." Ingrid chuckled. "Protestants are Christians, too, she said. In their own way."

"What did Hector do?"

"Lots of stuff. He collected clothing and appliances, books, and furniture. Once a month, he joined in food drives, collecting canned donations at drop-off depots around town."

"You helped him?"

"When I could."

"Do you think your mother knew about his relationship with Ivy Hannah?"

"His relationship?" Ingrid's eyes darted right, to a stack of sweaters on the dresser. "No, I'm sure she didn't. How could she? There's lots my mother doesn't know about."

Lips tight, Ingrid stepped to the sweaters. Question time on pause. She pushed her fingers between a red pullover and a teal blue. She held the red one by its shoulder seams, tilting it from side to side, her body swaying with the dance.

I saw a store tag dangling from the collar. Size extra-large. Hector had never worn these sweaters. Were these gifts from Ivy? Maybe some of the sweaters I found in Ivy's closet were meant for Hector— not for donation, not for herself. Was I mistaken in thinking she'd been pregnant? But then why did they buy pregnancy test kits?

Ingrid opened the closet door wide, so I could look at her brother's meager collection. One black wool suit, four pairs of jeans neatly folded over hangers beside three pairs of gray slacks. He'd kept his shirt assortment to white, pale blue, and gray.

"Compadre took back his red jacket. The one he wore driving the taxi." She hitched over the last word. "He loved that jacket. I wanted him to be buried in it. But it belonged to the company."

She pointed to the closet floor. "What do you think we should do with these?"

I saw a set of free weights mounted on a floor rack. Black iron stacked in a pyramid of red plastic. "Your brother liked to keep in shape."

Not brilliant, but the remark won a smile from Ingrid.

"Yes, he was fanatic about his workouts." She bent to touch an iron dumbbell. "Never missed a morning. Upper body one day, lower body the next. Six-thirty, after coffee, before his shower. He'd run through this routine he'd developed with Carlos. First the five-pounders, flies and bicep curls to warm up. Then down the stack to end at eight reps on each arm with twenty-pound weights."

"Impressive," I said.

"Carlos had it all figured out. This daily plan. They'd phone each other each morning at the end of the session. Encouragement, you know. Like a team."

"Carlos was a good friend?"

"The best." Happy crinkles flicked at the corners of her eyes. "You ought to meet Carlos. You could learn more about Hector from him."

"I'd like that. Can you fix it?"

"I'll text him. See if he's around." Ingrid seized the knob but stopped before opening the bedroom door. "I need to make these arrangements outside."

"Outside?" Playing dumb worked sometimes, a major tool in my private eye arsenal.

She whispered, "In your car."

"So your mother can't see or hear?"

"Uh-huh." Relief smoothed wrinkles from her brow. I wasn't as adult dense as Ingrid feared.

In the Jeep, I lit the ignition. "So make the call. Can you set up the meet for tomorrow?" When Ingrid pushed up the bill of her ball cap to peer at me, I explained, "I've got an appointment now. I'm already late."

"Then hit the road," Ingrid said, sounding like a drover on a Texas cattle drive. "I text, you steer."

"You can't go with me."

"Why not?"

"I'm going to see my father." The weak explanation dribbled from my lips.

As soon as I said the words, I realized that having a new girl join our father-daughter party might be just the ticket we needed to ease our conversation. I knew this was Keyshawn's day off. The prospect of navigating even a brief visit with Evander was daunting. *Coward.* I wanted a go-between. There was only so much I could say about the old photos of me, my mother, and Monica. Headlines from the Q-Town *Herald* had limited appeal. Maybe there was a basketball game on ESPN. If not, I hoped Ingrid's fresh gab would save the visit.

Even without knowing her role, she was ready for the challenge. "Great, I'd love to meet him." The grin split her face. "Ándale, chica."

She settled the cap on her hair, pulled up the hood of her sweater, and cradled the phone to her waist. Flying thumbs said the issue was settled.

In a few words, I explained to Ingrid that Evander Myrick's advanced dementia prevented him from recognizing me or any element of his former life. The girl nodded and sucked her teeth in sympathy. There wasn't much else to say. In between my sentences, she tapped a furious exchange with her brother's friend. Carlos Baca worked as a phlebotomist in a local medical practice. He had the day off tomorrow, but multiple errands to run. After negotiations, we agreed to a five-thirty meeting at his apartment.

I snapped a right turn signal. "I could have met Carlos alone, you know."

"Yes, you could have." Slow and clear as if I were mentally limited like my father. "But Carlos would have given you the cold shoulder. He only agreed to see you because I'll be there, too."

I sighed and steered into a parking spot in the crescent driveway fronting Glendale Memory Care Center. Yellow lights from the upper floors shone like birthday candles in the dusk. I could see residents gathered in twos and fours in the dining room to the right of the lobby. It was only five in the evening, but supper came early for people without history or recollection. For my father and his mates, meals marked the passage of the hours, manifesting progress from one day to the next on their journey through oblivion.

Ingrid pushed on the handle and shoved the door open. The whip of cold air returned me to our exchange. As did the crispness of her next words. "We are in this investigation together."

In case I thought we were a mother-daughter tag team for the ages, she clarified: "And I'm the client. Which means I'm the boss. Right?"

I grunted. Teen arrogance was easier to handle than adolescent angst, so I said nothing. We'd straighten out our relationship soon enough.

As we rotated in the revolving doors, I remembered I'd forgotten to bring the usual snack for my father. I hoped he would accept Ingrid as an adequate distraction.

The lobby was crowded with residents edging toward the dining room. The French doors had been flung wide in welcome. I could smell pot roast, fried chicken, baked potatoes, green beans, even apple and cherry pies. My stomach grumbled in appreciation. I walked to the reception desk and signed the visitor book with both our names, as required.

I turned to find Ingrid. She was standing next to a breadbox-shaped woman dressed in a yoga outfit. The silver spandex was splashed with pink and black slashes on leggings and a tight shirt. Her ginger hair partially obscured the *Glendale MCC* embroidered across the shoulder yoke. The woman and the girl bent toward a large man in a wheelchair. With powerful strokes, he rolled the chair toward Ingrid.

As he spun, I saw Evander Myrick's profile sharpen below a purple baseball cap. He flung his head back, chin jutting, nose shiny with perspiration, eyes on fire. He studied Ingrid, then flipped the footrests on the wheelchair and rose from the seat.

With a sweeping gesture, my father lifted the cap from his crown, looked straight at Ingrid, and proclaimed, "Ivy!"

CHAPTER **TWENTY-SIX**

My father patted the ball cap on his head, then raised it again. "Ivy," he said, triumph warming his voice.

"Dad, this is Ingrid," I said, crouching to bring my face to his level. "She's a friend."

He waved the hat like a flag, hiking his eyebrows. "Ivy," he cooed. His gaze caressed Ingrid's face.

The girl looked at me. I shook my head and shrugged. I had no explanation for my father's outburst, for his cheerful expression and squared shoulders. He smiled, years dropping from his face as energy flowed through him. Like Ingrid, I wanted answers. I hoped a mix of hot food and lively talk would draw meaning from Evander's clouded mind. I pointed toward the dining room doors, urging Ingrid to lead the way.

The Glendale supper wasn't as good as my nose and stomach imagined it would be.

The blocky yoga instructor joined us for the meal. "I'm Laurette Brandt. I fill in when Keyshawn has the day off. Usually I stick with chair yoga, pottery, and watercolor painting classes."

I was glad for her assistance, but I missed Keyshawn Sayre. His presence both calmed and stimulated visits with my father. Without Keyshawn, I expected the time to drag.

Laurette wheeled Evander to a table for four, cooing and clucking as they rolled. I bristled as she patted his shoulder and stroked his neck. Like he was a lapdog. But he didn't seem to mind, so I kept shut. Ingrid and I gathered grub from the islands of hot and cold food at one end of the dining room. We distributed our bounty onto three plates, setting the dish with the smallest amounts of food in front of Evander. Laurette drifted toward the buffet, returning three minutes later with a heaping platter.

As he picked at the pot roast and speared his beans one at a time, my father stared at Ingrid.

"Ivy," he said for the fifth time. He lifted the cap and doffed it in Ingrid's direction. Then louder, "Ivy."

"Dad, I told you this is Ingrid." I struggled to come up with a reason I was hanging out with a sixteen-year-old. To compensate for his skimpy appetite, I shoveled up a double load of mashed potatoes. "She's a friend. She works part time in our office after school." That sounded almost plausible. I swallowed the potatoes in hope.

He said, "Ivy." This time followed by a grin as he flourished his hat at the girl. Evander had his flirt on.

When I frowned, Laurette took pity. "He thinks she's Ivy," she whispered. "You know, Ivy Hannah." She bowed her head. "Poor thing." I wondered if she meant my father or the dead woman.

"Why in the world would he think that?" My voice rose, but Evander looked past my ear toward the diners at the next table.

"Ivy used to come here every week. She was a regular volunteer. Usually Thursdays, when Keyshawn was off. Part of her church's outreach program. Your father and Ivy became fast friends."

Now I was intrigued. I lowered my fork beside the turkey pot pie. "When did this start? The visits, I mean."

Ingrid leaned against the table, her head tipped to catch Laurette's words above the din of the hungry horde.

"About a year ago. Their usual trick was to play at exchanging baseball caps." The woman crunched on lettuce soaked in French dressing. She spoke about my father as if he wasn't in the room. Which was true in a way, but still rude.

"He would lift his hat, show it to her. Then Ivy would lift hers. And they'd trade. She'd help him fit her cap to his head, then she'd wear his. Sometimes they'd switch again. Sometimes Ivy would go home with a new ball cap. Depended on his mood that day." Laurette chuckled.

"I get it. Like a potlatch," I said.

"Hunh?" The yoga teacher frowned.

"Symbolic exchange to solidify relationships."

Laurette shrugged and swirled a forkful of meatloaf through a gravy pool. "Yeah, sure."

Ingrid narrowed one eye. "And now, Evander, do you want to switch with me?"

She held her black cap across a corner of the table, within reach. As she smoothed her frothy hair, he grabbed for her offering. Once he'd secured his treasure, Evander returned the favor. Ingrid took the purple hat and clasped it to her heart. Evander smiled and fiddled with the plastic tabs at the back of his new cap.

Laurette said, "Ivy always had to fix the straps to fit his head. He's got a bigger head than she does."

I watched Ingrid perform the adjustment. She stood behind Evander, sitting the cap on his close-cropped scalp twice before finding the right hole in the plastic strap. Tears pricked my eyes. I coughed to cover wiping a finger beside my nose. Her gesture was so little, but so comforting. The whims of a confused old man, accommodated with bighearted kindness.

"Perfect, isn't it?" Ingrid said. She squeezed Evander's forearm, then resumed her seat and dug a fork into her cherry pie.

He sighed and tapped the bill of his new cap. Ingrid was his forever sweetheart.

Laurette gave a thumbs-up. "Ivy was kind. Just like you are. He really misses her."

Ingrid smiled—a strained flicker, not a grin. "Sure, I bet he does."

Laurette chirped, "But it's nice he gets visits from other members of Ivy's family, isn't it?"

My heart jumped. "What other members?" I asked.

"Mayor Hannah stops by on the regular, every other week. She talks with him for a time, all friendly-like. Hard to tell if he enjoys her visits. The way he is, quiet and all. But she comes by regular, all the same. Nice lady."

I wondered why Keyshawn never mentioned these visits to my

father. Had he ever seen Jo Hannah with my father? Maybe the timing of the mayor's social calls wasn't an accident.

I studied the woman's rusty hair and freckles. Her amber eyes reminded me of someone. Curiosity drove me. I asked, "How long have you been here, Laurette?"

"About eighteen months."

"Have I seen you before? You look familiar."

The woman's lips stretched around gray teeth. "You don't remember me, do you?"

"No, I'm sorry, I don't." I stiffened my tone to match the two grooves between her eyes. "Have we met?"

"You went to Q-High with my older brother, Ted Sutton. Back then, most kids called him Tidy."

My stomach swirled, then dropped. This woman putting her hands on my father was sister to Tidy Sutton, who put his hands on me outside Kings Cross Tavern last month. The Tidy Sutton who, with his teammate Jake Hughes, served as personal bodyguard to Mayor Hannah. I wanted to jump from my chair, shove the table, and run from the room.

Instead, I forked the tip of my sweet potato pie wedge. "Ah, yes, I see." I didn't lift the piece to my mouth.

Ingrid swallowed the last crumb of her pie as ice descended on the table. A few polite minutes later, she and I kissed Evander and left Glendale Memory Care Center.

In the parking lot, Ingrid slipped into the Jeep. "Well, that wasn't weird at all." She shivered.

I explained the connection between Laurette, the mayor's security team, and the Hannah family.

Buckling her seat belt, Ingrid asked, "You think Laurette was spying on Ivy?"

"Yes, I do." I craned my neck to ease the car from the parking spot.

Ingrid let me finish the maneuver, then said, "But what could she have told the Hannahs? What could Laurette have seen Ivy do that would be worth reporting?"

"I don't know," I said. "But I will figure it out."

After dropping Ingrid at her apartment, I chugged off home. As I stepped onto the porch, Sam Decker phoned. I asked for five minutes to settle inside. I hoped he had important information from his talks with Hector Ramírez's bosses and colleagues at Compadre Taxi Company. I wanted to clear my mind to get the most from our debriefing. I wanted a drink, bourbon to smooth my ruffled fur and ease my troubled gut. But I settled for a cup of chamomile tea instead. Promises, promises.

When I called him, Sam picked up on the first ring.

I asked what he learned at Compadre. He said QPD returned Hector's vehicle to them the morning after the murders. The first thing the boss checked was the tool kit under the front seat. Company property. According to the boss, the canvas satchel contained its usual complement of tools: wrenches, screwdrivers, a flashlight, a utility knife, and batteries. Even a rasp, a tape measure, and a box of paper clips. Nothing was missing.

This was significant, I said. The cops believed Hector came to the Hannah home to kill Ivy. If that was his plan, why didn't he use one of the weapons he had on hand? Why not take a wrench or knife from the tool kit? Why would Hector rely on the off chance of finding a hammer in the house? This made no sense. Another hole in Leo's argument that Hector was the assailant that day.

I asked if the boss had found Hector's cell phone in the vehicle when it was returned to the shop. No, they hadn't found it. Just his red jacket and his time sheet. He hadn't recorded any passengers for the morning of his death.

Sam told me the drivers, mechanics, and supervisors at Compadre liked Hector. They said he was clean and polite. No, they didn't know if he had a girlfriend; they'd never heard him speak of a woman. But they agreed Hector was a quiet, reliable man. Not a macho show-off or bully.

"Did they think Hector did it?"

"I didn't ask," Sam said. "Not directly. I couldn't. I didn't tell them I was Ivy's father. And I didn't ask them that." His words crept as he recalled this wrenching day of interviews. "But one driver volunteered this: he said *no way* was Hector capable of murder."

"Did they have a theory?"

"Yes." I heard him cough. First loudly, then muffled, as if he'd covered the phone with his hand. "They think the husband did it."

"Sam, I'm sorry. I should have done those interviews. Not you."

"I'm not sorry. Don't you be."

I heard him take a long slurp. I hoped it was booze.

"Tomorrow is another day," I said. He couldn't see the tears dripping from my chin, which was a good thing.

I told him of my plans to meet Hector's friend, Carlos Baca. Thanks to Ingrid, we were piecing together a compelling portrait of Hector, I said. And its boldest strokes outlined the case against Leo Hannah. I didn't invite Sam to the interview, and he didn't ask. Lessons learned.

After we hung up, I read text messages from Keyshawn Sayre. His chess move floored me with its elegance and power. He was beating me like a rented mule. I tried a rejoinder, but apologized in advance if the countermove fell flat. I said tonight my game was more clown than Kasparov. But I promised to do better tomorrow. Heat needled my throat as I signed off. I didn't want Key's opinion of me to matter, but it did.

The following afternoon, I met Ingrid Ramírez in front of the first-floor home of Carlos Baca. I wanted another angle on Hector, and I hoped his closest friend would supply details to strengthen my case.

This apartment block on Fitzgerald Street was identical to the one on FitzRoy Street where Ingrid and her mother lived. A failure of architectural imagination on a large scale. Squat structures faced in red and yellow brick. Flimsy wooden railings on the upper balconies, iron bars at the windows of the lower floors. Prison design without the efficiency of the real article.

When Carlos dragged open the door, he scowled at me. Then he stepped aside to let Ingrid enter. He slipped an arm around her waist for a quick hug and several phrases in Spanish. Without a word to me, Carlos followed her into the room, leaving the door ajar. Cold air streamed around my body and into the apartment. I hesitated. I was visiting the home of a man who drew blood for a living. But I was no vampire; I didn't need a direct invitation to enter. I crossed the threshold and slammed the door behind me.

CHAPTER **TWENTY-SEVEN**

Hector's friend Carlos Baca didn't warm to me until the twenty-minute mark of our interview.

He made matcha tea for me and Ingrid, served in glass mugs. He sipped a concoction of turmeric, whey protein, honey, and bean sprouts with a chaser of apple cider vinegar. The smell shut down my stomach. Carlos was a health fanatic, which I suppose was a good thing in a medical professional. His body—coiled muscles under brown skin— was convincing testimony to his regimen's success. He kept his shiny hair trimmed army short on the sides, fashionably spiked on top. His narrowed eyes and tight mouth radiated discontent, as if I was infecting his home with trouble.

We sat at his kitchen table, fiddling with simple questions and shallow answers that boiled my blood. I let Ingrid lead the interview, figuring she might have a better sense of how to draw him out. In English, she asked Carlos about his job. He liked the doctors, nurse practitioners, and assistants at Queenstown Medical Associates. He was happy to be starting his third year with the group practice. He made drawing blood samples sound more boring than I'd imagined.

Ingrid asked Carlos to outline how he'd met Hector. At the Tiger Fitness Center, a storefront gym on Route 130. And how their friendship had developed. Pumping iron, spotting each other on the weight machines, *Lord of the Rings* movies, Dungeons & Dragons video games. The men liked craft beer, 76ers basketball, repairing car engines, and following national politics.

His apartment was sparsely furnished. A sofa and two matching armchairs in maroon leather. A round wooden coffee table held a fishbowl filled with matchbooks from dozens of restaurants, clubs, and bars. The wall over the sofa was a checkerboard of framed photos. Two pictures showed Carlos with Hector: a shot in T-shirts and cargo shorts; and another taken outside a bar, showing the two men in well-cut slacks and polo shirts. They looked handsome, relaxed, happy.

Most of the framed images featured two little girls in various costumes and stages of development. Mermaids, princesses, pumpkins, gymnasts. Riding on ponies or tricycles or hay wagons.

I figured asking about the girls was a safe entry into the conversation.

"Your daughters are so cute, Carlos." With their father's bulging eyes and gaping mouth, they resembled miniature frogs in tiaras. But my opinion didn't matter. "How old are they now?"

Worked. "Thank you for asking." A big smile threatened to separate his jaw from his face. "Isabel and Jennifer turn five next month."

"Five? They're twins?" Playing stupid drew out the best in parents. As did repetition: "They are *so* cute."

Ingrid chimed in. "Hector and I used to babysit the twins. We took them to the playground, McDonald's, even the science center in Metuchen one time, remember, Carlos?"

That comment was drawn out, to remind me I'd seen Hector corral the girls during their playdate. The same Saturday I'd followed Ivy Hannah and her son to McDonald's. She was rubbing my nose in my mistake, but in the nicest way.

"Yeah, Hector was so good with the girls," Carlos said. "They adored him. They called him Tío Hector." He threw smiles at the photos of his friend on the wall. "They still ask about him every time they stay with me. Last Sunday, Jenny complained Tío Hector had been gone on his vacation for too long." A frown blanketed his face.

I pivoted from the sadness. "Don't your daughters live here with you?" I looked around the living room. One corner exploded with pink plastic: dollhouses, telephones, play stoves and ironing boards, fairy wings, tricycles, scooters, even a rocket ship. Two plastic stethoscopes dangled from the neck of a stuffed hippo. "I thought with all their toys . . ."

Carlos jutted his chest at what he took as a dig. But he gave a direct reply. "I'm divorced. Three years now. The girls live with their mother in Robbinsville. I get them every other weekend."

"And you told them their uncle Hector was away on vacation?"

"Yes," Carlos said. "What could I say? They're so young. They'll forget about Hector after a while." His face stiffened like cardboard. "I won't. But they will."

Ingrid raised her eyebrows with the go-ahead sign. Now was my shot. I needed his insights.

I said, "What do you think happened, Carlos?"

"Does it matter what I think happened to Hector?" His sigh twisted into a low cackle. "Everyone has it figured out. No one cares."

"We do." I drew a circle around Ingrid and me. "I do."

Carlos stared at me. My gut clutched. I thought he wouldn't talk.

After an hour, a year, he whispered, "No way Hector killed that poor woman. He liked Ivy, admired her. Why would he murder her?"

"Tell me about their relationship."

Confusion cut a furrow between his eyes. "Relationship? They worked together on church volunteer projects. More than that, they were friends. Is that what you mean?"

"Yes." It wasn't what I meant, but I was flowing with Carlos now.

"Hector told me he liked talking with her. About books, movies, careers. Things like that. She encouraged him to think about applying for an associate's degree program at Mason County Community College. He was shocked when she said that. I used to say the same thing to Hector. But when he heard it from her—a white woman—that made a big impression on him."

"Did they visit outside of the church office?" I asked.

"Sure. Sometimes she met him for coffee. Even met at McDonald's when she took her kid there sometimes. Is that what you mean?"

"Yes. But did they visit each other's homes?"

"You're joking, right?" Carlos screwed one eye shut, the better to see into my loco head. "No way that was happening. Ever."

I leaned forward. "Then why did Hector go to Ivy's home that day?"

CHAPTER **TWENTY-EIGHT**

My question about his friend jolted Carlos Baca to the edge of his chair. He glared at me for maybe twenty seconds, as if I were a Martian unzipping my space suit.

"I've been wondering the same thing." He slapped the tabletop.

Mugs jumped, tea sloshing as he remembered the last days of his friend Hector Ramírez. Memories drove tears to Carlos's eyes. Strong feelings: friendship or something deeper? I glanced at Ingrid. She studied the pile of toys in the corner of the living room.

Carlos pulled at his lower lip. "I think Hector got a call inviting him to the Hannah house."

"What makes you say that?"

"The day before . . . before he died, Hector came over here for dinner. He said he had an appointment the next morning."

"Did he give any details?"

"No, just that he had a meeting he couldn't miss. He said he was going to clear up a misunderstanding. Something like that. I asked what misunderstanding. He waved his hand like he didn't want to talk about it. So I dropped the subject."

Carlos's mouth twitched, maybe a happy thought tickling his memory. "Hector could get bullheaded when cornered, so I didn't push." He smiled at Ingrid, who tried to return the smile but failed.

"I saw him text somebody for a minute," Carlos continued. "He looked at me, then poked at the screen some more. He angled the phone so I couldn't peek. You know, like a kid does." Carlos glanced at Ingrid, as if she could confirm teen phone manners.

This was the information I wanted, the missing piece of the puzzle: on the day before the murders, someone had invited Hector to the Hannah home. Who had arranged the meeting? Could the invitation have come from Ivy? Or was her husband responsible?

Ingrid sniffled into the cuff of her sweatshirt. She stood from the table and walked into the kitchen. I heard water rush in the sink. Seconds later, she returned with a half-full glass.

After gulping two swallows, she stared into the space between me and Carlos. "If Hector got a call or a text, that message would still be in the phone memory." Then she glared at me. "That's why you asked me if the cops had returned Hector's phone with his other effects. Right?"

"Yes."

She banged the table. "We have to find the fucking phone."

Eyes wide, Carlos glanced at the heap of pink toys, as if worried his daughters might hear the rough language. He looked at his own cell, then at me. "I need to go pick up my girls in thirty minutes."

"This is fucked," Ingrid yelled. Tears dripped from her mouth and chin.

She shoved from the table, her chair toppling backwards. Dragging her coat over her shoulders, she stamped toward the door.

I righted the chair and pushed it under the table as she dashed from the apartment.

I exhaled, a soft whistle for sorrow and regret. I didn't think Carlos needed an apology for Ingrid's outburst. But I wanted to end our interview on a gentler note.

"Your weekend with the twins starts tonight?" I asked. Softball question to ease my departure. I pushed one arm through a coat sleeve.

Carlos looked toward the door, his gaze vague, as if he still heard the slam of Ingrid's exit. Water blurred his eyes, then he shook his head and answered me.

"Yes, I pick them up tonight. I have to drive to Robbinsville. It's a bit of a hike." He herded me toward the door. "Blue Bird is super strict. Last pickup is six sharp. If parents arrive late, we get charged extra."

"Your daughters attend Blue Bird Day Care Center?"

"Yeah, you know it?"

"There's one in Q-Town, isn't there?"

"Yep, the main center is here. The Robbinsville branch opened two years ago. Why?"

"Nothing, really," I mumbled to block the rise in my voice. "The Hannahs' son was at Blue Bird."

"That's right. Tommy was at Blue Bird here. Then last month, he transferred to the one in Robbinsville. Jenny and Isabel were super excited when he showed up. They treat him like a baby brother."

I remembered watching the three children play together the day I tracked Ivy to McDonald's. Why was Tommy Hannah enrolled in the Robbinsville school now? I assumed only his father had the authority to make the switch. But what prompted the change? I knew Leo had moved from Queenstown. Had they landed in Robbinsville?

Questions flying through my head, I shook hands with Carlos and left. I found Ingrid leaning against the Jeep, her arms folded around her torso.

I gathered her against my chest. "That was tough. Real tough."

Wet snuffles rose between our bodies. I cupped the back of her head, pressing her brow against my throat.

I whispered into her knit cap. "Does your mother know about Carlos and Hector?"

Seeing Carlos's anger and sorrow over the brutal death, I knew the men were close. Brother close? Or more? The photos of their restaurant outings and the collection of bar matchboxes were souvenirs of many happy times together. The routine morning phone calls suggested an intense relationship, as did Carlos's choice to include Hector in his daughters' lives. Sam said Hector's colleagues reported he never mentioned dating women. I figured at some point Hector's friendship with Carlos had bloomed into romantic intimacy. I imagined being gay was a truth Hector hid from his mother. I hoped he'd shared his authentic self with his sister.

Ingrid shook her head. "No, Mamá doesn't know."

Her muffled phrases drifted upward. "Hector came out to me eighteen months ago. I scoped it on my own before that. But I was so happy when he talked with me. He looked relieved. Free. But he begged me not to say anything to Mamá. He said he wanted to do it in his own way. In his own time."

She hugged me then raised her tear-stained face, sipping the cool air. "There's lots my mother doesn't know."

Although she lived only ten minutes' walk from Carlos Baca's apartment, I drove Ingrid home. In the dark, she wept silently for two minutes after we parked.

I asked the hard one: "If Hector and Ivy weren't having an affair, why did they buy pregnancy test kits together?"

"How do you know about that?"

"Snooping. It's what I do." First time in this case I felt guilty for my work product.

"Yeah, you're good. Real good." She said it like a curse. After a sigh, Ingrid continued, "It was for me. The kits were for me. All clear. But I wanted to be sure."

"You couldn't buy them yourself?"

"Yeah, right." Eye roll plus twisted lip. "I'm going to skate into the drugstore and blab my business to the whole world. What planet do you live on?"

"I'm a mother, too, you know." Present tense, the way I still fooled myself sometimes.

"And your kid discusses their latest hookups with you?" Eyes narrowed to scope the lie. "Doubt it."

"You're right." I stroked my throat to halt the wobble. "Monica didn't share that part of her life with me."

Ingrid caught the tense. "Didn't?"

"She died last year."

"I'm sorry. I didn't know."

"How could you?"

"Jesus, I'm sorry." A cyclone of sniffles battered the windshield. Ingrid swiped her cheeks with a mitten, puffed three long breaths. "Like I said, there's lots Mamá doesn't know about me."

I flicked the button to unlock the door. Ingrid slid from the car and marched up the stairs. I saw the soft planes of her face shuffle into an innocent mask to greet her mother.

Heading home, I considered the shredded details of my case. I still felt certain Leo Hannah had killed his wife and Hector Ramírez. But my theory of his motive took a direct hit from Carlos Baca's story. If Hector and Ivy weren't lovers, then a key cause for Leo's fury evaporated. I wasn't sure he knew of his wife's innocence. Maybe he'd been as mistaken as I was. My assumptions had tripped me. Now I needed to find other pressures, different reasons for Leo to end these lives.

In my driveway, I slipped on the uneven ice grooves crisscrossing the pavement. Fifteen minutes with a pickaxe would demolish these ridges in the morning. The exercise would help me thrash out a new strategy for the case.

I inched toward the porch. Shuffling beside the bushes, palms outstretched, hoping to avoid a tumble.

Two blows thudded at my left ear. Sparks dashed between my eyes. Blue streaks fired left, right, left. Blazes of white crackled behind my nose. I raised my elbow. The next strike hit bone.

I batted snowy swirls in my head, the whorls clawing darkness. I heard yells. My own shouts? Hands lifted my arms. I felt my ankles jerked through the hot air of exhaust spew. Hip, then knees hit ridges on a flatbed. My spine twisted. Wires of pain burned both thighs. Metal ruts jolted my head.

The truck rumbled me into space.

CHAPTER **TWENTY-NINE**

I slammed against the coffin walls of the truck bed for ten minutes. Maybe less. Roll left, around one corner; slide right, around a second. Vaulting a cement curb jolted new pain through my jaw. Everything above the shoulder hurt. Neck, skull, left temple. Pain wrung my brain, torque after twist, until nothing was left but agony.

The truck stopped; my stomach lurched. I heard two men, maybe three, grunt as they cranked open the gate of the truck bed. Squawks like raven laughter invaded my ears. They were talking, but I couldn't make out the words.

Hands dragged the collar of my coat. I felt leather gloves strip my knit cap. Iced turf bumped my bare head. I worked my tongue to shout. I tasted snow and dirt. I shifted my face until hurt radiating from the nose snapped my lids open. I needed this pain to clear the fog smearing my sight.

We were at the cement base of a metal pole. I recognized the aqua paint, rivets, rusty seams. The old water tank. Between work boots, I saw another of the tower's four supports. A ladder scaled its length. Could I run that far? Climb to escape? Could I move my legs? I scraped my boot on the ground. The shin caught fire. I puffed to douse the pain.

I rolled my right eye, catching the underbelly of the water tank. I saw the scaffolding that girdled the reservoir. The tank blocked the moon. Its deflected light silvered the tin shed and chain-link fence at the end of the yard.

Shoes crunched the snow near my hip. Chin tucked, I glanced

toward the sound. Wet dripped from shoelace tips onto black leather. I tried to see the face above. Only shadows pinned against shade. A kick to the ribs forced me into a protective comma. I gasped.

"You listen and you listen good." The white man's drawl seemed amused, maybe stretched for disguise. "It's too cold out here for a long chat."

A pointed toe probed my knee. "You need to quit your snooping, understand?"

The nudge switched to a kick. Pain shot to my ankle. I groaned into the snow. Briny grit coated my tongue.

"That's right. Pay attention when I talk."

I hacked, then spit. Saliva laced the snow with blood. Yellow spots popped in the gloom.

A deeper voice burst over my head. "She don't get it, Ted." He slammed the lug sole of his boot against my spine. Two white men. Bad racial math.

"Dumb nigger, slow on the uptake." The first man chuckled. "Let me spell it plain, bitch. You're messing where you ought not mess. You fuck around, you find out. If you don't quit, this little date tonight's gonna seem like junior prom next time we meet up."

The second man pushed my shoulder until I sprawled facedown, my coat bunched at my shoulders. I raised my head to inhale.

"Think she needs a little taste tonight?" the second man snarled.

His partner answered, "Something she won't forget?"

I felt hands grab the belt loop of my jeans. Cold soaked the small of my back. I twisted. My knees scraped the frozen ground. More cold air wrapped my waist. Suede leather fingers brushed my skin.

A new voice growled, "Leave her alone, Ted."

I craned my neck. Muddy boots with a tooled green alligator-hide shank. I recognized the two-inch underslung heel on these cowboy boots. My twelve-hour boyfriend Darryl ran with this ruffian crowd?

The gloved fist released my waistband. I flopped to the ground, hitting my chin.

Darryl said, "She got the message. Let's get out of here."

"You fucking kidding me?" The first man's words snapped like brittle branches.

"Think I'm kidding?" Green alligator boots stepped into the snow dented by the first man's dress shoes. "Come on. Try me."

I saw Darryl shove the first man, who stumbled. Both men were panting. Darryl closed the gap.

Another falter. Then the man said, "Fuck you, Darryl."

The work-boot man stepped between them. "Okay, all right, fellas. Knock it off."

The double-barreled beam of a passing car swept across the yard. I heard gravel skitter as the men turned toward the headlights.

Work Boots said, "Bitch got the message. Let's get outta here."

He herded his pals toward the cab of the truck.

Exhaust fumes slathered my face as the engine whirred. I coughed and scrambled to my knees. Hands on my thighs, I watched the red Dodge Ram disappear around a corner. In a panic, I grabbed at my throat. Monica's necklace was still there. I exhaled.

The water tower was a fifteen-minute stroll from my house on a sultry summer evening. This wasn't a stroll.

My head rocked, my ankles and knees ached. Every inch hurt. Each step pounded home my humiliation. I clasped my arms around my waist. I could still feel gloved fingers rubbing my skin. I'd been kicked, beaten, one ugly move short of rape. I staggered onto my front porch half an hour after the boys in the red Ram deserted me.

Inside the entrance hall, I stripped off my wet clothing. Maybe the pile of soaked jeans and sweater would stain the hardwoods. I didn't care. I walked into the living room.

I pulled the knit throw from the sofa and wrapped it around my body. My toga covered the rude marks. I wouldn't look down. No need. I felt bruises blooming on my thighs and belly. Raw purple and cordovan stained the floor and my skin. I hid these signs under the wheat-colored throw. In the shadow of the water tower, my investigation had cratered. I didn't want to see the evidence.

The throw's long tassel dangled over my breast. I stroked the twisted fringe and headed to the kitchen. Bourbon from the upper cabinet was the perfect comfort to end this night. Jim Beam or Jack Daniel's, barkeep's choice. It didn't matter which gentleman did the trick.

I drizzled a shot down my throat, then another. Hot volleys, no ice. Quick doses of the medicine I craved. Was pain evaporating from my ribs? Good old stuff. I executed three rounds standing at the kitchen island. For the fourth, bellying up to the bar wasn't practical. I needed to sit. Tugging at the stool was hard, tougher than I remembered. Evil furniture, who knew? I gripped the round seat like a steering wheel and wrangled it four inches from the edge of the marble counter. I patted the stool and sat on my conquest.

In the distance, over my shoulder, I heard pounding. Then clattering, then scrabbling in the hallway. Someone was barging through my house. Maybe a friend, maybe a neighbor, maybe an enemy. Overhead lights wavered like vapor above a waterfall. I scrubbed my face to clear the mist.

Keyshawn Sayre clapped a hand on my arm. He squeezed hard. I jerked against the pain. He stared into my face. I thought he looked fuzzy and sad. Or maybe that was me reflected in his eyes. With mad skills, he eased a stool from under the counter. *How did he do that?*

Keyshawn said stuff, then gabbled more. His words washed in a slurry through my head. I reached for my glass. Missed. He sharpened his voice.

"Vandy, what happened?" Keyshawn's teeth were bright, his voice low. He gripped my chin and tilted my head to the right. My neck muscles shrieked.

I scrambled fingers along the marble, searching for the shot glass. I grabbed air; stupid glass had dodged. I growled.

In my head, words erupted. *How are you here? Who invited you? This is a private party, Key, with velvet rope and bouncers in lug-soled work boots. Only my good buddies Jim and Jack allowed. Who let you into my show?* Maybe I wailed. Someone did.

Keyshawn stood, legs wide, eyebrows bent like a lion tamer watching his wild partner. With a grunt, he wrapped his arms around my toga. I floated up the stairs.

CHAPTER **THIRTY**

Clocks ticking in my brain chimed for every step we mounted. One second, one minute, one hour. Time burst, then collapsed as I drifted upward, wrapped in Keyshawn's arms. I didn't register sinking into the bed. Somehow I righted myself, then touched my throbbing forehead. Sitting, I swallowed a glass of water Key brought from my bathroom. My stomach churned at the cold surprise. He loomed over the bed, chin rising and falling as I gulped. Miming or talking, hard to know. When I paused, he pointed at the bottom of the glass. Twice, until I finished the whole tumbler. His shoulders blocked moonlight from the window beyond the reading chair.

When he returned with a second portion, I scrambled under the quilt to avoid the drink. I pulled the cloth to my neck and shivered.

"I'm fine." I wriggled one palm from beneath the coverlet and held it out like a shield. "No waterboarding." I tried a smile, but the move hurt my jaw.

He took my hand, spreading the fingers. "How'd you get these cuts, Vandy? What happened to you?"

I studied the red welts on my knuckles. "Nunh-unh. You first. Tell me what you're doing here. Then I tell you how I got banged up." Shaking my head ignited sparks behind my eyes, so I blinked.

He moved toward the edge of the bed.

Raising my hand like a visor, I added a new condition. "Turn off that overhead first. Light's killing me." I dropped my hand when darkness hit.

The mattress sagged under his weight as he sat. "You know I send my new chess move every day. You always answer within a few hours."

"Yeah, well, I was busy." My head wobbled. Muddy tides sloshed in my gut.

"When you didn't play, I texted. No answer. I called. No answer. More texts, more calls. I got worried. So I drove over here."

Simple enough. But idiot me, I asked, "How do you know where I live?"

I was stalling; I didn't know how to tell him about the beating. Maybe the booze would knock me out before I had to answer. I glanced at the door, hoping Jim Beam would waltz in to rescue me. No luck.

Key looked at me like a tunnel had opened in my forehead. "Your contact information is in the Glendale office. In Evander's file. I've known your address for months."

Delay tactics exhausted, I told him about getting jumped in my driveway. I used clinical terms to describe the beating and showed the bruises on my back and torso, like we were doctors scrubbing in for surgery. When I hiked my bra strap to display the marks on my shoulder, I heard him hiss. I was glad darkness masked his expressions. As I finished, the booze cloud lifted, replaced by a tin drum filled with gravel.

Long strides carried Keyshawn from the window to the closet and back. As he moved, I could see fists flexing at his flanks. Two more circles around the room until he dropped into the reading chair below the window.

"What did they look like? Sound like?" Gritted through clenched teeth. "How many? White? Black?"

"White voices."

"You know who they were?"

I lied. "No. I didn't get a good look at anything but their shoes."

Pebbles rattled inside the tin drum. I didn't want to mention the cowboy boots I recognized. Or the name Ted, which I linked to my high school classmate, Tidy Sutton.

"So you're not reporting this to the cops?" The bubble of argument rose in his throat.

"Nothing concrete to report."

"What did they want?"

"They warned me off the Hannah case."

"You know too much? You coming too close?"

"Combination, I figure." Stretching my legs, I sank until my head hit the pillow. *Plink, clank, thunk.* I squeezed my eyes shut.

"Vandy, I got to know . . . did they . . . I mean, did they touch you . . . umm . . . hurt you?" Stuttering engulfed his last words.

"You mean, did they rape me?" Nausea and exhaustion swelled in alternating waves through my body. "No, I'm all right, Key."

He flung his head against the chair back. I heard a hiss, then a low whistle like calling a guard dog. I could see his fingers grip and release on the arms of the chair.

"You own a gun," he said. "I heard you talk about it once with your father. Why don't you carry it?"

I snapped: "You saying I could have prevented this?"

"Not what I'm saying. Not at all. Three of them. One of you. There's no blame on you. You saved your life. That's what matters to me." He leaned forward, elbows on his knees.

I rolled onto my side, propping my head on one hand. "But you still wonder why I don't carry a weapon if I've got the license?"

"Yeah. I do."

I flopped on my back, hands over my face. "Short, sad story."

"I can listen if you can tell. I want to know you, Vandy Myrick."

Perhaps the urgency in his voice convinced me. Or maybe the ache ricocheting in my skull drove out old doubts. Whatever the reason, I was ready to tell my story. Knees curled to my chest, I touched the flayed skin on my cheek and began to tell Key how I'd abandoned my gun.

CHAPTER **THIRTY-ONE**

My words unspooled as darkness drifted like webs around the bedroom. I heard scrabbling outside the window; frozen branches or perhaps a barn owl resting on the gutter. Keyshawn was listening. I was talking. At last.

"I went back to work a week after my daughter died. I should have taken more time. The captain said so, my colleagues urged me to use the weeks to heal myself. I said no. I told them I was all right."

I gulped as those lies pommeled me once more. "What I wanted was the rush of my job. I needed that rush to blunt the dog's teeth eating my insides. Every moment I slowed was a moment that beast tore another chaw."

I glanced toward the window. I couldn't read Keyshawn's face. His neck was a rigid column.

His chest moving at a steady pace, he said, "I hear you."

I drew circles on the veins of my wrist, probing for that old comfort. "I went back to work. First in the station, answering calls, filing reports. Easy stuff, minimal contact. Gradually I started on the people stuff again: attending committee meetings, conducting wellness checks on students, conferring with deans."

When the circles didn't soothe, I pushed my fingers into my mouth, gnawing on ragged cuticles. "People tiptoed around me, speaking in whispers, as if loud words could send me over the edge. They hadn't been to the edge. Turns out, neither had I. But I got there. And plunged over without a parachute."

Hot tears dripped from my temples to the pillow. I knew Keyshawn couldn't see them in the dark. I brushed the wet from my cheeks anyway.

"One Saturday, I was on the duty roster. I volunteered to pull weekend shifts to give other officers time with their families. I didn't have a family anymore, so why not give the lucky ones a break? The call came in. Noisy party in an off-campus frat house. I recognized the address. Griswold Street. The same block where Monica died five months before. I should have asked for backup; I shouldn't have gone there at all."

I shifted, knees poking the quilt. Rustling sounds filled the air above the bed. The hinge of my jaw ached. Was this the bourbon talking? Or fear spewing some ugly calculus with anger in the denominator? I kneaded my cheek and continued.

"But I went. I drew my gun on the kid who opened the door. I waved him into the parlor and made him lie on the sofa in front of the others. I shouted at them to turn off the music. I kneeled on his chest and pointed my gun at his nose. He reeked of booze. I said I'd shoot him if the music continued. It stopped. I hit him in the mouth with the muzzle of my weapon. Two teeth dangled on bloody threads from his jaw. I reared to hit him again, but a cop grabbed my arm. Two officers wrestled me to the floor."

Fury strained my vocal cords. "I wanted to kill him. I would have beat his brains to pulp if they hadn't stopped me."

Keyshawn lifted one shoulder, then the other, like a boxer loosening neck muscles. I heard his fingernails scrabble in the crevices beside the cushion. His head ducked below the outline of the chair back. A long sigh spewed from his chest.

"Hear me, Key. I wanted to *kill* that boy. My baby—my beautiful girl—was dead, and this drunk, entitled monster was alive."

He raised his head. "You don't have to tell. It's okay if you don't."

Silver light streamed around the silhouette of his head and shoulders, turning the rosy pink of my curtains and bedcover into an ocean of steel.

I said, "I want to tell. This shit happened." I gasped and shook my head. "No, that's not right. It didn't just happen. I *did* this shit. Me.

Virtuous, upright Evander Myrick. *Me.* And I want to tell you. I want you to know this about me."

"Then it's all right." He scrubbed his face, pulling at the lower lip. "What happened after?"

I laughed. Pain ripped through my gut. "Bosses dropped the hammer on me quick. But not as fast as my own conscience. The morning after the incident, I turned in my shield and weapon to my chief. We both cried when he took them. He said I needed to deliver my letter of resignation to the university president. That's when I called Elissa Adesanya."

"Your lawyer friend."

"Yeah. We've been besties since college. I teased Elissa about setting up a law practice in Q-Town. I said she picked the ten square miles on the planet I'd been running to escape my entire life." When I snorted, my ribs hurt. I panted to lift the ache.

Keyshawn eased deeper in the chair. White glinted from his mouth as his head tilted toward me. Making him smile felt good. The first good this whole night.

I continued. "Elissa was a beast. She negotiated the terms of my separation package. She arranged the sale of my house."

"And she suggested you come home?"

"My girl Liss does not play. She *dragged* me home."

"I'm glad she did." The whisper floated so briefly I almost didn't catch it.

"Me, too," I said. Wiping wet cheeks, a cough stitched pain in my lungs.

Memories of that ragged exchange with Elissa swept through me. *"I'm scared, Liss." "Of what?" "Of starting again. Of losing again."*

I shifted on the bed, raising my voice. "The day I resigned, I made two promises to my daughter: I'd never carry a gun. And I'd never drink alcohol."

I cringed, expecting Keyshawn to sniff at my broken pledge. Didn't bourbon still stink on my skin and mouth? I could see his jaw shift as he held silent.

He exhaled. "Tonight you sleep, Vandy. Tomorrow you relaunch that promise."

I thought to invite him to lie next to me. For the comfort, the convenience, the friendship. Keyshawn was right: I could restart. The future wasn't promised, nor was the past frozen. My stomach uncoiled for the first time since I'd stumbled home that night.

But fear blew a chilly draft across my neck. I wanted the closeness, but I couldn't risk the loss. Not again. I shivered and pulled the quilt to my ears, letting the invitation evaporate unspoken. I stared at the sky beyond his head until I slipped into sleep.

The next morning, I awoke with a start. Sunlight bolted through lace curtains, stabbing my face with rude cheer. My eyelids burned, my tongue was crispy, joints protested along the length of me. Thrashing plus hangover equaled misery.

I heard bangs and thumps in the kitchen below. Keyshawn on breakfast patrol. He cursed an appliance, then stomped. I figured I had ten minutes until he rose up the stairs, like Santa out of season, bearing gifts and glad tidings. That gave me thirty seconds to piss, five minutes to shower, four minutes to fly into black sweatshirt and leggings, thirty seconds to ruffle my matted coils. I could do this.

Eleven minutes later, I sat cross-legged on my bed, smiling like a fool as Keyshawn angled through the door, a bamboo tray clutched in both fists.

"Good morning," he boomed.

When I winced, he purred, "Sorry, good morning."

He settled the tray near my knee. Pointing, he toured the meal: "Muffins, blueberry or chocolate chip. Squishy banana. Sorta brown. Still good. Prunes, toast, hot grits with butter, yogurt, chamomile tea. No coffee, 'cause I couldn't find the canister. No orange juice, 'cause acid on your stomach is murder."

My gut twinged, but I said, "Looks perfect."

His handsome face shone with pride. Three paces into the bathroom and back, bearing the dreaded water glass and two tabs of Tylenol.

"Don't fight me," he said when I frowned. "After the carbs, you take the painkiller and as much water as you can guzzle."

I nibbled on the blueberry muffin; he chomped toast, banana, prunes, and chocolate muffin. We passed the mixing bowl of grits between us until it was finished. The tea worked its magic, as did the Tylenol.

"You need to see a doctor today," Keyshawn mumbled around a spoonful of yogurt.

"Not happening."

He tipped his head to one side for a new angle on my face. "Your nose could be broken. You ought to get it looked at."

I touched the end of my nose. "It feels all right to me." A bald-ass lie. The lower half of my face hurt like hell.

The smirk said he knew I was lying. "You let it set like that, you'll have a permanent bend. Not bad, just a little tilt to the left. Kinda cute." He paused for the punch line. "And the purple under your eyes will disappear in a week, ten days, tops." He held up two prunes as illustration. Nice.

I prodded the tender swellings beside my nose. Even temporary ugly was a strike to my ego. But I still refused to see a doctor. He'd make the same pronouncements as Keyshawn with half the expertise and none of the charm.

I asked, "You think cold tea bags could help under the eyes?"

"Probably. Give it a shot."

Key sat the tray on the table next to the armchair. He lifted a corner of the curtain and looked at the roof next door. Without turning, he said, "Last night . . . I-I don't know what that was."

"It was nothing." Deep growl to deliver my lie. The next part, softer, was true: "I got beat, I got drunk. I wanted to talk about shit. You listened. That's it."

"You okay?" His whisper patted the windowpane. I wanted him to look at me, but instead he studied two cardinals flirting on the drainpipe.

"Not yet." I hiccuped to hide a sob. "I will be."

He turned around, a sigh drifting below wet eyes. "Okay, Vandy. You lead. I want to follow."

Markers laid, hopes planted, he stiffened his shoulders and walked toward the bathroom.

What was I supposed to do with this upside-down declaration? Return the sentiment? Tell him to scratch the mush as a nonstarter? I scrubbed fingers through my hair. I wanted to erase whatever I hadn't said. An impossible task, like proving a negative. Instead, I pointed toward the hall. "Clean towels in the linen closet. Help yourself to the shower gel. Moisturizing cherry blossoms or guava citrus." Black-belt-level deflection.

As he bent before the oversize mirror, he stroked his chin and yelled through the open door. "Thanks, I'm good. I'm heading straight to Glendale. On Saturdays I start late. I can shower in the staff locker room before my shift." He fingered bristles on his upper lip and jaw. "But I could use a shave. Don't want to show up looking like King Kong after a bender."

Eyes wide, he glanced at me, as if I'd hear an insult in the imagery. "Sorry."

I had been drunk the fuck off my ass, so I chirped, "No apology needed."

"You have a razor I could borrow?"

"Sure, if you don't mind pink and plastic." I limped from the bed to dig into the Aladdin's cave of beauty essentials under the double sinks. I handed him a fresh blade. "Untouched by female leg."

I crossed my arms and rested my hip against the counter to study his shaving process. First, he beat the soap bar until it lathered. Pat the foam. Then up, down, around; tug right, pull left. In my experience, men looked especially alluring when they shaved. Something about the concentration, the adorable grimaces, the precision, the intense delicacy. Keyshawn confirmed my research.

When he'd finished the scraping, but not splashed water on his cheeks, he startled me with a question from left field. "You think I should shave my head?" He peered into the mirror to catch my glance, then dragged a palm over his cropped hair.

"What for?"

He traced an index finger along the coves and inlets of his hairline. "See this? I'm going bald. Losing it fast. You know how Bobby shaves his head?"

"Yeah, he's going for the chic, sleek look, right?" I figured police chief Sayre wanted to project authority. His shaved dome created a fearsome appearance, the bullet shape designed to intimidate perps and junior cops alike.

"Nah, Bobby's hiding baldness. We inherited it from our old man. Lester had a big bald patch on top before he was fifty. After that, his forehead kept growing and growing 'til it linked up to the bald spot." He shivered in horror. Not mock, real.

"Hereditary male pattern baldness," I spouted like WebMD, breezy abandon lifting my words. "Nothing to fear, Key."

"Yeah, easy for you to say." He grinned and splashed streaks of soap from his face.

"Hey, my father has a pretty impressive bald spot on his scalp."

He laughed. "You may have inherited his name. But you have zero worries about inheriting Evander's bald head."

He patted his cheeks with a hand towel, then zipped it at me. I caught the cloth against my chest, chuckling. This felt right, laughing with a good man after a bad day. Scary as fuck, but nice. When Key marched from the bathroom, I glanced at the thinning hair on top. He wasn't bald yet, but he was heading there. Something in that concern niggled at my mind. I rubbed my own crown, grateful for the full thatch of curls.

When we hugged at the front door, Keyshawn's grip made me wince. "You staying home today, right?"

"Sure," I lied. I wanted to make a quick stop in the office, check a few files. Saturday was not playday. With my brain churning on high, I couldn't bear the slack time.

Key rested his clean-shaven chin on my head, holding me to his chest. The heat of his embrace carried me all the way to my office.

Where the welcome from the A-team was more wail than warm.

Adesanya and Ames were seated in the conference room, sipping coffee and scribbling on notepads when I entered the suite. An unhappy surprise. I'd expected to have the place to myself. I lurched along the corridor, hand angled to screen the view through the glass wall. I hoped to reach my own office unobserved. Fat chance.

Elissa jumped from the table, screech cranked to earsplitting: "Good Lord, what happened to you? You look chewed, stewed, and re-fused." She turned on her partner. "Like that dead-mouse trophy the cat brought home last week. Remember?"

Belle nodded. "But more ooze, less cute." She clapped a hand to her mouth.

I thought the gagging was too loud to be genuine. I sighed and kept limping.

They pursued me into my office, empathy and revulsion windmilling on their faces. I settled into my chair, braced for the onslaught.

CHAPTER **THIRTY-TWO**

My partners gave me scant seconds to ease my aching bones into my office. Elissa Adesanya and Belle Ames faced me, arms stiff to support their weight as they leaned over my desk. They wanted an explanation for my damaged mug, ramshackle gait, and skewed posture.

I slumped in my chair, legs extended under the desk, fingers clenched on my lap. I figured with caved chest and hunched shoulder, I looked as bent as macaroni. With a kisser as pounded as tenderized steak, raw and unappetizing.

I was a fledgling private eye, but I'd mastered one key skill of the trade: I lied like a world-class champion.

I looked up from my chair. Because vivid expressions led to nagging pain, I kept my face still. "Rough Friday night, girls."

"Joking won't cut it." Elissa clucked and pointed. "This is beyond bad. The damage is real."

"Who did this?" Belle's pageboy wig dipped off-kilter as her brows flew heavenward. "What did the doctor say?"

The women clutched their fists and leaned closer. Like avenging angels in designer denim, my partners wanted to know who to destroy in their flight of retaliation.

Careful lying was my best refuge. I knew when to deliver the critical point in a report, how to delete the speculation. I calculated how much of my sorry tale to give. I wanted to satisfy their curiosity and incite their sympathy. But I withheld elements, just as I had with

Keyshawn last night. My ideas about the identity of the thugs who assaulted me were still guesses.

If I told Elissa I thought members of the mayor's personal entourage were involved, she'd have filed a lawsuit within the hour. Belle would organize an anti-Hannah picket line by lunch.

I also knew how to distract. If I got them working on a task, I might avoid more grilling. "Belle, you gotta help me out here," I said, pointing to the bruises on my face.

Hideous, she'd called them. Getting her to apply camouflage was only logical. Unlike me, Belle adored cosmetics. Using fake lashes, highlighter, and a Picasso palette of eye shadows, she rocked the full beat every day, even weekends. I heaped praise as thickly as I hoped she'd plaster on the foundation. Tugging pink cashmere cuffs, she bustled from my office to search for her gear, Elissa a step behind. I figured they wanted to confer about me out of my earshot.

When they left, I opened the center desk drawer and pulled out the twisted ballpoint Leo Hannah had mangled weeks ago. I balanced the knot of metal and plastic on my palm. What sort of man contained such reserves of rage? And exercised this ferocious control to hide his anger from me? I tilted my hand and a drop of ink dribbled onto my skin. I knew plenty about both anger and control: fury had consumed me after Monica's death. And on the daily I needed iron will to avoid falling from grief into dereliction. I studied the blue specks on my palm. Had I been as furious as Leo? Yes. As tempted by thoughts of murder? Yes. Were we really so different? Sweat prickled my hairline as I dodged the answer. I dropped the wrecked pen into the drawer and shoved it closed. Dashing a Kleenex across my Heart line, I erased the blue stain.

Three minutes later, the team returned. Belle hauled a black satin kit shaped like a carpenter's toolbox and set up shop on my desk. She and I shared similar coloring—good and brown. Her Tawny Deep No. 2 liquid foundation worked for this emergency.

Elissa had grabbed her coffee mug and quilted biker jacket from the conference room, ready to supervise the beauty labors. She had perfect skin, smooth like a dolphin. Did she wear any makeup more complicated than mascara and ruby lipstick? Her interest in Belle's effort was strictly academic.

I leaned back in my chair, swiveling as Belle directed. She fussed and hummed, tilting my chin for expert assessment. I followed her on Instagram. According to her fans, Belle's lip game was goals, and her eyebrows were on fleek. A thousand followers couldn't be wrong. I was in good hands.

As Belle daubed and painted, Elissa fired questions. "You said these thugs told you to quit. What does that mean?"

I kept it simple. "Stop digging into the Hannah murders."

"Did they mention the case in particular?"

"No."

"Then you don't know for certain what they wanted." Her braids rustled over the chain embellishment on her collar. She sighed. She puffed. She didn't trumpet her doubts, letting me stew for a moment.

After an ugly pause, I gritted, "No, I don't. Just my gut. The gut those white boys stomped." I touched my tender side.

Elissa sat on my desk, hiking a leg over one corner. "They weren't playing. My guess is they know something. Or they work for some-body who knows something. Or they did something." She tapped her sequined sneaker on the arm of my chair. "Or they owe somebody."

"Could be. Or maybe I'm headed down the wrong track." I squinted as Belle smeared concealer under the left eye. "What if I'm digging in dirt unconnected to the murders? Garden-variety gossip. The kind that's nasty but not criminal. Maybe they want me to quit to protect someone's reputation."

"True that. This town's full of juicy nonsense." Elissa ticked the possibilities on fanned fingers. "What if you unearthed some old-style embezzlement? With a side order of drug addiction? Any votes for adultery?" She blatted a raspberry through pursed lips. "How many Q-High kids paid seniors to get test answers? How many parents bribed Coach Kissmyass so little Wallace could add varsity sports to his col-lege application?"

"This town's got corruption out the ying-yang," Belle said.

She warmed foundation in her palms. She spread the mixture over my cheeks and forehead, her careful taps soothing, calming. When I winced as she grazed my chin, she stopped. She cooed, then chirped, eyes soft. The seagull sounds worked. I relaxed and nodded for her to continue.

Ever the sharp lawyer, Elissa plunged, without skipping a beat, into examination of the opposing side of her argument. "But if you're on the right track, then the Hannah killings are at the heart of it all."

"You convinced me I was off base," I mumbled around Belle's fingers.

"But let's say you aren't."

"Okay." I sighed. "Next moves, Counselor?"

"I don't know." Tossed at me with an airy shrug. "Specifics are your department." Elissa lowered her gaze to pin me. "Here's my take. Have you spent too much time with the living?"

I sat upright. "What the fuck does that mean?"

Elissa flattened a palm to curb the storm. "So far you've focused on live clients: Leo Hannah, Sam Decker, Ingrid Ramírez." Her eyebrows lifted. "Who are you ignoring?"

I wanted to scream. She was an idiot. This Socratic bullshit was tearing my last nerve. But I knew Elissa wasn't stupid. She was dragging me for a purpose.

Still, I snapped, "Of course I work for the living. What the hell am I supposed to do? Dig up cemeteries?"

"Hear me out." Elissa's summation voice poured slow and creamy. "Maybe you've got another client in this case. Maybe two. But they're dead, so you ignored them: Ivy Hannah. Hector Ramírez." She nodded, agreeing with herself. "What if you flip the script? Inspect the other point of view? Maybe the dead have a case, too."

Remembering the ruined pen in my desk, I wanted to scrub my hands over my face. I started the move, but Belle seized my wrists. "Sit with it a minute, baby." She pressed her fingers against my pulse points.

Did she mean the makeup? Or Elissa's idea? I groaned and flung my head against the chair back. Bad move. My shoulders and neck griped; pain zipped left to right. Lowering my lids helped. But in the darkness my stomach protested with flutters.

I thought of what I knew and what I still didn't understand. I was confident I knew how Ivy had been killed. But did I know *why* she died? Not yet. I had a clear idea of how Hector had been killed. But I couldn't piece together why he had to die.

My stomach flutters revved to lurches. I pressed my belly, as if *that* could help.

If I didn't find a motive, I'd be stuck in an endless spin, a frustrating cycle with no answers and no satisfactory resolution. I didn't have to start over, not if I proceeded with care. I didn't need to dump every element of the cases I'd developed to this point.

I had something. Leo and his goddamned pen. My lids flew open. Belle cursed. I'd botched her shadow application. I closed my eyes again. She resumed tapping.

Leo's case pointed me to the details of Ivy's last days. But I'd looked at those moments from his vantage point. I'd even interpreted my own observations through that lens. What if I flipped the script, as Elissa suggested?

Drawing me from my thoughts, Belle feathered a brush from my temples to cheeks. "Bronzer to contour, blush to highlight."

She misted goop to fix the makeup. "Setting spray." I smelled like strawberries.

Elissa stood from the desk and crossed her arms over her chest. "You look good." When her wife frowned, she amended, "On point." Top marks from two discerning judges.

Belle flourished two lipstick bullets: "Kalahari Red or Pink Martinique? Your choice."

I waved them off. With a shrug, Belle dropped the tubes into her makeup kit and dragged the zipper.

"Frankenstein audition over?" I asked. I scrubbed fingers through my hair, then smoothed the nape and sideburns. "Almost human?"

The artist handed me a pressed powder compact. According to the little mirror, I'd avoided Joker status by an eyelash.

"Honey, you clean up nice. The glam look suits you." Belle's chest puffed with pride. "You need to take this show on the road."

I harrumphed and checked the mirror. Still Ronald McClown, but presentable.

"Then you won't be shocked when I tell you I'm heading to Antoine's Salon," I said.

Belle gasped at the mention of Q-Town's most prestigious beauty shop. Elissa sucked her teeth.

Grinning at their confusion, I added, "The resolution of Ivy's case starts there."

I needed to retrace Ivy's steps in her last week, the movements and appointments I'd witnessed. I wanted to find new contacts. Through their eyes, maybe I could reinterpret Ivy Hannah's actions and intentions.

IVY'S CASE

CHAPTER **THIRTY-THREE**

Armored with my painted mask, I drove to the strip mall where Antoine's Salon huddled between the Star Indian bakery and a Subway sandwich shop.

Despite its cramped location, Antoine Edgar's spa was the height of elegance for white Queenstown. Women booked appointments months in advance. Local influencers dropped hundreds of dollars to be trimmed, shaped, dyed, and waxed by the Queen of Chic, as Antoine called himself. Black women relied on Wynonna's Beauty Spot for our hair needs. Belle Ames had her ever-expanding flock of wigs styled by Wynonna herself. Elissa Adesanya booked all-day sessions to refresh her braids every two months. I'd chopped my hair the day after Monica's funeral. I didn't want the fuss or memories of that old style. Since my return, I'd hit Wynonna's twice for shape-ups. No one in the Flats trusted Antoine to master the newest techniques for weaves, silk press, or no-lye relaxers. How was he going to style a full-lace premium Indian virgin unit if he couldn't handle our actual hair?

Ivy Hannah had entered Antoine's Salon during the final week of her life. She'd left with a fresh cut and her curly-haired friend in tow. I wanted to learn about that visit.

At the front counter, I informed the receptionist I didn't need an appointment. She objected, but I shoved by her arm tackle and barreled into the narrow salon, my eyes peeled for the proprietor.

Snap survey: twelve white clients, eight white stylists; four Vietnamese nail technicians. Saturday was peak time at the pleasure dome. I swept through a swarm of hisses and gasps.

At the rear of the room, I spotted my quarry. ID'ing Antoine was simple. His glamour shot dominated a quarter-page ad in the *Herald* every week. Face shaped and colored like a fresh scallion. Shoots of green-tinted hair above gaunt cheeks. His throat sprouted from a black turtleneck. Gold chains cascaded under a black cloth smock.

As I approached, his button eyes widened.

"We need to talk, Antoine." I looked around at the parallel rows of black swivel chairs filled with goggling customers. "Here, with your clients as witnesses, or . . ."

I leaned; his pupils glittered.

"Okay, okay." He pointed the stalks of hair toward a black curtain at the rear of the salon. "In the back, the shampoo sinks."

We hustled to the hidden room. As Antoine caught his breath, I explained I was working on behalf of his client, the late Ivy Hannah. I wanted details about her final appointment.

He tried to deny he remembered her visit. Some bogus argument about stylist-client privilege. I mentioned the date and hour of her appointment. When I described the hairstyle he'd given her, Antoine relented.

"Yes, I remember. Poor girl, so tragic." He sighed, the bags under his eyes dulling to tapioca.

"For months I recommended she try that wedge cut. She wouldn't budge. Every month, all she wanted was a trim. Quarter inch off the ends, deep protein conditioner, and ash-blond highlights. I said the shorter style would accentuate her gorgeous bone structure. But every month, she resisted."

"What made her change her mind in January?"

"She didn't say. Not exactly."

"What did she say? Inexactly."

"Ivy was a private girl, closemouthed like you wouldn't believe. Most women come here to talk their heads off." Antoine whispered this observation with a glance toward the closed curtains. "They spill everything. Boyfriends, husbands, girlfriends, lovers, bosses. Potions, prescriptions. Perfumes, positions. Nothing's off the table here."

"But Ivy was different?"

He nodded. "She rarely spoke about her family. I remember this one time because it was so unusual. Ivy said she wanted to try the new Spanish olive oil treatment we were featuring as September's discount deal."

He pointed at a framed poster on the wall above the sink. Sunny olive groves, romantic castles, shiny hair blowing in the wind.

"When I said the treatment would add eighty-five dollars to the total, Ivy said no, she couldn't do it. Her husband would throw a fit at the cost, she said. I asked if her husband paid for the salon visits. 'Yes, of course,' she said. 'Why do you think I keep my hair long?'"

"Because her husband liked it that way." I clenched and released my fist.

"That's what I concluded." Antoine rolled his eyes toward the ceiling. "Tragic."

I said, "But then something changed. In January, Ivy changed her mind about the haircut."

"Yes, she stormed into the salon that day, her eyes flashing. Usually she was white as rice, but that day her cheeks were pink. Even her lips were flushed. I remember, I said to Minh the manicurist, 'Ivy is very angry. Or very drunk. Or very scared.'"

"Scared? What made you believe that."

"Not belief. Fact. She told us."

"She told you she was frightened?"

"Not in so many words. That's not how women talk." He raked his gaze over my frame, as if I might need lessons in femininity.

I unzipped my puffer jacket. Despite the twinge of pain, I straightened my spine so he'd get some clarity. "Tell me what Ivy did."

"It was after the other girl arrived."

"What *other* girl?"

"A friend, I guess. She came into the salon after Ivy'd been here for ninety minutes."

"What did this other woman look like?" I had an idea, but I didn't want to lead the witness. He was giving me intel I could use. No need to botch it now.

"Plump, short, five-three or -four. Dark brunette with caramel highlights." The expert eyed my head. "Curls thicker than yours. Growing out a shag. She was pulling a solid Little Orphan Annie impersonation. I expected her to burst into 'Tomorrow' at any moment. Ack." He made a gagging noise. Antoine was my kind of petty.

This was the woman I'd seen exit the salon with Ivy. They'd driven to a cocktail-fueled lunch with two other friends.

"Did this woman seem chummy with Ivy? You suggested there was tension. Maybe they weren't really friends, just playacting."

The stylist reached to a ledge above the shampoo sinks. He pulled a wooden paddle from the shelf and thrust it toward me. It was a hand mirror with a square of ivory paper taped on the glass.

"We keep this if we need to question clients without letting on. To learn if they're in danger. That day, when I finished the styling, I handed this mirror to Ivy."

I read the handwritten sentence on the paper slip: *If you are in fear of the person with you today, put the mirror on the counter facedown and someone will come over to check on you (pretending to be a senior stylist).*

The message was chilling. The fact this mirror was a commonplace tool here caused goose bumps to needle my neck.

I returned the mirror to Antoine. I'd discounted him. He brought perception and empathy to his service. He protected vulnerable women, reaching them in places social workers and law officers couldn't venture. Heat surged into my throat and cheeks. Antoine was a warrior on the front lines. He served with courage and distinction in this hidden war.

I asked, "What did Ivy do when you handed her this mirror?"

"She looked at the curly-haired woman for a minute, hard, a smile jumping on her lips. Then she placed the mirror facedown on the counter."

"Ivy was in danger? She wanted help?"

"I don't know. Maybe." He leaned against the sink. "But then she changed her mind."

"What happened when you approached her?"

"I bent close and lifted the hair beside her cheek. I smoothed it behind her ear, as if I was showing her how to style the new cut. I whispered, 'Do you want me to call the police?'"

He poked a finger into the stiff roots above his left temple as if scrubbing at a question he still couldn't answer.

"What did Ivy say?" I asked.

"She didn't say anything. She shook her head no." He sighed. "I asked again. And again she said no."

"Did she leave then?"

"Yes, ten minutes later. She paid her bill at the front desk. Both girls booked future appointments and they left together. I remember thinking Ivy was grinning like a lunatic at that other girl. I followed them out the door and watched them drive off in Little Miss Annie's Toyota."

I'd seen the two women smiling, shoulders touching, heads thrown back in laughter as they walked from the salon to the car. I remembered how Antoine studied their departure from the front door. Had I misinterpreted the scene so badly?

"Like friends?" I asked.

"More like faux friends." He bared his teeth in a gargoyle grimace. "Ready to rip each other's throats out. Grinning all the way to the knife fight. Frenemies. Smiles sweet, blades sharp. That's how I saw it."

"After Ivy's death, did you share this with the police?"

"The *police?*" He jerked his neck, pursing his lips as if I'd farted. "Girl, you think the cops came here?" He sniffed. "You don't look like a fool. Maybe I read you wrong."

I nodded, cringing inside. If he'd read me wrong, then for sure I'd misunderstood Ivy and her circle of friends. To correct my fumble, I wanted more information, fast.

"Can you give me the name and address of that woman who was with Ivy? I want to speak with her. Find out if she knows anything to shed light on how Ivy died and why."

A smile crept across Antoine's face. "*Now* you're talking. You track down Little Orphan Annie. She knows something, I bet my gold fillings on it."

At the front desk, Antoine instructed the receptionist to pull the electronic file on Orphan Annie—real name: Pepper Sheridan.

When he wrote Sheridan's address and phone number on a pad, I realized the handwriting was identical to the careful block letters of the rescue note on the mirror.

Antoine handed me the folded page. He leaned close, brushing my face with spearmint puffs. "Go get 'em, sister," he murmured.

As I tucked the paper in my jeans pocket, he laughed. I saw he did have a mouthful of gold fillings.

In the Jeep, I inserted the key, but suspended the seat belt buckle above my lap. I wanted to approach Pepper Sheridan with caution. I believed she knew something of value to Ivy's case. For sure their troubled interactions held clues. I could phone and hope an impersonal conversation would draw the information I needed. Or I could bull my way into her place and hope to overwhelm her. Which approach would yield quick, complete results?

I slotted the buckle and glanced at the paper on the seat beside me. Sheridan lived in Robbinsville. A ten-mile trip south on Route 130. On a Sunday morning, the journey might take twelve minutes. Weekday evening rush hour could blow that time to forty-five minutes or worse. Today I was sliding into the magic Saturday moment when the stream of red taillights hadn't yet congealed.

I reached to the back seat and pulled a padded Amazon envelope from under a stack of advertising flyers. The stretch fired twinges in my rotator cuff and neck. I dry-swallowed another Tylenol tab as I examined the empty envelope. This book-sized package would do the trick. My emerging plan wouldn't quite violate federal postal law, I hoped.

I dialed Pepper Sheridan's landline. No need to travel to Robbinsville if she wasn't at home. When she answered on the third ring, I offered an irresistible time-sensitive deal on solar panels for her roof. She declined my offer. So sorry, she lived in an apartment and had no roof. Her voice was soggy with apologies. Maybe she truly regretted frustrating my efforts to save the planet.

A glance in the rearview mirror. Belle's plaster-and-paint job was still in place. Dirty blue splotches swept under both eyes, but the swelling on the bridge of my nose had receded. I licked my finger and smeared concealer to hide the bruises. I looked borderline trustworthy.

I pulled into 130 traffic, happy with the steady clip. No jams, no snarls. The drive gave me time to plot. And time to wonder: Ivy's son Tommy Hannah had been moved to a day-care center in Robbinsville. Was this simple coincidence or an important connection?

CHAPTER **THIRTY-FOUR**

I tucked the flat Amazon envelope inside my coat as I limped through the lobby of Pepper Sheridan's modern high-rise building.

The soaring atrium was empty. I guessed most of Sheridan's neighbors were out running Saturday errands. Or hitting shopping malls between Trenton and Philadelphia. Four-thirty was early for the homeward rush.

I glanced through the lobby's floor-to-ceiling windows to an interior courtyard paved with weathered gray wooden planks. The enclosure was littered with Adirondack chairs in lollipop colors. Boardwalk style for the striving class. Indoors, sandy tiles, rattan furniture, and sea-glass-green walls helped residents imagine they lived down the shore, instead of in a bland suburb of the state capital. The elevator was upholstered in almond linen framed in brass. I was careful to not brush my soiled puffer coat against the pristine walls as the car rose to the tenth floor.

I found Sheridan's door and propped the envelope on the welcome mat. Adjusting it to an alluring angle, I snapped several shots. Close enough to capture the trademark smile on the package. Far enough to show the doorframe but obscure the address label. I sent Sheridan a text with the best picture. I figured she'd had experience with thieves; she'd move fast to grab this delivery.

After six minutes, she opened the door, her eyes bent on the prize. I surged from my hiding place in the adjacent doorway. As she crouched, I slammed a forearm against the panel and stepped across the doorjamb.

She gasped and straightened into defender pose, envelope before her chest like a shield. But we were already inside her apartment. Advantage: Myrick.

I sidestepped her and took the middle of the room, legs wide. Open-concept space: kitchen to the right, dining zone defined by a Navajo-style rug, a living area with four upholstered armchairs surrounding a glass coffee table.

I squared my hips and expanded my chest. As if our positions had flipped: she was the intruder, violating my space. I lowered my arms. Hands open toward her, I backed two paces. I was weaponless and meant no harm. I kept my gaze level, blinking slowly to avoid an aggressive stare. I relaxed my mouth but didn't try a smile. Grinning would look crazy.

"Who are you? What do you want?" She tossed the empty package to the floor between us, as if it were contaminated.

"Pepper, my name is Vandy Myrick. I'm a private investigator."

"A private . . . what?" She coughed, fingers flying to her throat. "How do you know my name? What do you want?" Her eyes ricocheted from the ceiling to the walls and the balcony beyond the dining table.

"I'm from Queenstown, Pepper. I work for your friend." I hammered at her name to keep her attention focused. I wanted to let the location and relationship land.

The jitterbugging eyes stopped. She looked me in the face for the first time. Her jaw slid left, like she was chewing on the news. "What friend?"

"Your friend, Ivy Hannah."

She gulped. Her eyes closed, their bulges rolling beneath freckled lids. She squeezed her lips to a knot.

I remembered Antoine's catty sneer: Pepper as Little Orphan Annie. Bouffant curls, rosy cheeks, and now the blank spaces in her eye sockets. The taunt fit.

"You're lying," Pepper snapped, lids jumping open. "Ivy's dead. You don't work for her. You-you can't."

"Yes, I can, Pepper. She is my client." When she gurgled to interrupt, I held up a hand. "Let me explain. Then help me. I need to learn about Ivy's last days. Where she went, who she saw."

Pepper's gaze narrowed. She was trying to decipher my aims. "Her last days?"

"I need to know Ivy."

"What can I tell you? You think I can help?" Fingers tangling, she bit her lower lip.

"Yes, I know you can." My voice rose with conviction. I stepped closer. "Help me, Pepper. Help me understand Ivy."

She exhaled. "I don't know . . . anything." Her wail was soft, inward.

"I think you do, Pepper. You can help me." I held up my fingers to tick off the questions: "What did Ivy want? What was she thinking? What did she hope for?" I ended on a whisper: "Please, for Ivy, help me understand."

Pepper nodded, a brisk ruffle of the curls on her crown. She pointed with her chin at the dining table. "Sit there."

I moved as she'd indicated. If I could shift from invader to ally, we'd make progress. I didn't need to be her best pal. Just the best private eye she'd ever imagined.

When I pulled a chair, Pepper said, "We don't have much time. Fifteen minutes, maybe twenty."

I almost asked what appointment was more pressing than her friend's murder. But I curbed my tongue. Pepper was cooperating. That was as much as I could demand.

I studied the woman across the table. She was short, with generous curves above and below a snatched-in waist. Chocolate curls fell to her shoulders, tipped with butterscotch highlights framing an oval face. Rice pudding skin, round eyes, pointy nose, thin lips. Pretty in a down-market catalogue way. Woman Within, not Neiman Marcus. She dressed in casual luxe: the fawn tracksuit was cashmere adjacent. Her scent was matronly lavender, cut with citrus. I figured Pepper was younger than Ivy, around thirty-five. Old enough to feel desperation lurking over the next hill.

For three minutes, I delivered an edited version of my investigation.

I sketched my work for Leo Hannah. Pepper hummed through this part of my story, her neck and shoulders relaxing. I didn't share my theory about Leo's involvement in his wife's death. Pepper didn't need to know about Sam Decker or Ingrid Ramírez. The clock was ticking, but I wanted background, so I guided the conversation into the past.

"How did you become friends with Ivy?"

"I met her at an office party at ArcDev Pharmaceuticals."

"Where Leo works as a research chemist?"

Her eyes flickered, then darted to the trash bin near the sink. "Yes, I'm an assistant in the front office, handling payroll, procurement, grants administration, other financial matters."

She shifted on the chair seat, then tugged at a curl behind her ear. I wanted to know why the mention of Leo Hannah made her twitch.

I leaned on the table. "And that's where you met Leo?"

"Yes. He was—is—deputy head of research. So I worked with him on project management and budget development for grant applications." She flicked a drop of sweat from below her nose.

"You got on well?"

"Yes."

"More than well?"

She sucked her lower lip. "What do you mean?" Big eyes, fluttering lashes.

"We're grown women, Pepper. You understand what I mean." Co-conspirator, I dropped to a murmur. "Leo is smart, good-looking. I don't know him well. But I can see he's warm and funny. Kind, too." Delivering lies in brief spurts wasn't so tough. "Isn't that what you learned when you worked with him?"

Pepper dribbled honey: "Yes, you can see that, too? Most people don't get him, but I do."

"Is that what Leo said? That you understood him?" I hoped my eyeballs wouldn't lock in a violent roll.

The oldest line in the history of sex games, invented by some Neanderthal creeper to placate his side-cave cutie. *Only you get me, baby.* But maybe Pepper really was as innocent as Orphan Annie. Or as needy.

She nodded, fond smiles tripping across her face. This might be love. Lucky Leo.

"He told me I understood him like nobody ever had before."

I said, "When did it begin, this connection between you and Leo?"

Affair seems like a sordid term to the lovers inside a relationship. So I'd employ language she preferred. I'd call it a connection as long as she kept delivering facts I could use.

"Last February. A year ago. We'd get off work at the same time. But we'd walk separately to our cars. Then he'd follow me back here." She looked around her boudoir of stainless steel and granite. "He said he liked the quiet of my place. And the way afternoon sun streamed in over the terrace. And how the traffic noises sounded like surf down the shore."

Pepper stared through the sliding doors to the treetops beyond the wrought-iron grillwork of the balcony.

"Leo brought me those plants." She pointed at nine terra-cotta pots bristling with philodendrons, spider plants, begonias, and ferns. The houseplants occupied a sunny rectangle on the floor next to the balcony door.

"To replace Mischief," she said.

"Who's Mischief?"

"My kitten. Darling orange tabby. Leo hated her fur and dander." She sniffed in imitation of her boyfriend. "He said he wouldn't visit if the cat stayed."

"Kitty or me, hunh?"

"Yeah." Pepper bowed her head. "So he took her away. He brought me the plants instead."

"Sure," I said. Command and control, Hannah style.

"Leo says we can set them outside again as soon as the weather's warm."

I zeroed in on the case. "Did you make friends with Ivy after you began seeing Leo?" I almost said *screwing Leo,* but I was too good a dick to make that slip.

Pepper walked to the refrigerator and opened it. In search of an excuse or justification, perhaps. She brought two cans of Diet Coke to the table and thrust one at me. She popped the top of her can.

Through the fizz, she answered. "Yes. I knew Leo was married. He never hid that from me. My eyes were wide open from the start." Her lids flew up to demonstrate. "Then I met Ivy at the company Fourth of July barbecue. We both brought potato salad and compared recipes."

I snapped my pop top. "Simple as that?"

"Simple as that." Not defiant, but not ashamed, either. "We found lots in common and started seeing each other regularly. For lunches, shopping, dinner, coffee. Once, sometimes twice a week. Ivy was a good friend." Her brown eyes were clear of guilt; Leo was wrecking the marriage, not her. Tough lady. She sipped Coke, waiting for more questions.

I wanted to catch her off guard, hoping the challenge would stun her into blurting the truth. I shot a guess. "When did Leo promise to marry you?"

CHAPTER **THIRTY-FIVE**

My ambush question worked: when did Leo propose marriage? Surprise splashed pink under the freckles on Pepper Sheridan's cheeks. Her lips quirked in admiration. I wasn't as dumb as I looked.

She combed her gaze over the mini jungle of plants near the balcony door of her apartment. As if the ferns were shrieking for relief, she jumped from the table to grab a plastic watering can from below the sink. She filled the can with water, anxious eyes on her chlorophyll pets. I could almost hear them mewling like the kitten she'd surrendered to Leo. Pepper showered her precious charges with a sweeping motion. Stalling in the service of Mother Nature.

I took a swig of cola, leveled my eyes, and repeated, "When did Leo pop the question?"

Pepper sat at the table, dropping the watering can with a thud. "Last fall. September 30. I remember because I was closing the books on the end of the fiscal year that night." She inhaled to demonstrate the tyranny of corporate life: damp, heavy, relentless. "Leo stayed late at the office with me. Even though he didn't have to. The work was on me. But he wanted to be there. Moral support, he said."

Blushing, Pepper dissolved in giggles. "That's when he asked me to marry him."

She was panting, excited. This Leo was some special prize. Who knew?

Time running out on our appointment, I sharpened my tone: "To marry wife number two, he had to free himself from wife number one. What was the plan, according to Leo?"

"I don't know." Eyes darting left, sagging mouth said this was a lie.

"That's not good enough, Pepper. You're not that kind of girl. Neither am I."

I paused. Would she buy our instant sisterhood? Ebony and ivory twins under the skin? I stared into the sun until the trick forced wet to my eyes. With my pinkie, I dabbed tears from my lower lid.

She nodded, fingers pulsing dimples into the soda can.

I continued. "You wouldn't go for an indefinite affair. I know *I* wouldn't. Not with Leo, not with any man. You wanted prospects. You wanted a future. You needed plans."

I thought she'd deny my characterization, but she tightened muscles along her jaw. I was in.

"What did Leo promise you, Pepper?"

"He said he'd ask Ivy for a divorce. It would be quick, no-fault, easy on everybody. Especially on Tommy. He was worried about that. He didn't want a long divorce fight. Or a bitter custody battle."

"He intended to keep Tommy?"

"Of course. He'd never give up his son."

I hadn't figured Leo for a devoted father, but then I hadn't seen him as a passionate lover, either. The world kept dealing surprises.

"And when he asked Ivy for a divorce? What happened?"

"I don't know. But Leo said she came at him with demands. Lots of them."

"Demands for what?"

"She wanted a big settlement. Plenty of alimony. Enough to cripple Leo unless she remarried."

"And Tommy?"

"Yeah, she wanted Tommy, too." Pepper chugged her soda. "She said Leo was unfit to be a father. She'd never let him have Tommy."

Bitter, vindictive wife. Determined, persistent girlfriend. Leo Hannah was caught with his neck and his balls in the vise. Abundant motive for murder. But what applied the turn of the screw?

Pepper set the Diet Coke beside her cell phone and glanced at its face. Time was ticking; this interview was near done.

My probe turned blunt. "Did Ivy suspect you were involved with Leo?"

Pepper winced. Accordion lines framed her eyes. "I didn't think so . . ."

"Until when?"

"Until just before Christmas." Pepper screwed her mouth to one side. "I think she figured it out then."

"What did Ivy do?"

"She invited me to join her for a charity event at United Methodist. Church members had donated hundreds of new toys for those poor Mexican children. You know, the ones in Abbott's Landing. We were supposed to sort and wrap the toys. They were to be distributed by Santa at a party two days before Christmas. I was happy to join the gift-wrapping. Then the night before, Ivy phoned me. She said I shouldn't bother to come."

"Did Ivy tell you why?"

Pepper sniffled. "I asked. She said, 'You know exactly why.'"

"But she continued to see you."

"Yes. We had friends in common. Entangled social calendars. Ivy didn't break with me. She put distance between us. But no break."

"You met her at Antoine's hair salon the week before she was killed."

"You know about that? How?"

"I'm a private eye. It's what I do."

"When Ivy asked me to join her at the salon, I thought it was her way of repairing things between us." Rapid blinking to conquer tears. "But when I got there, I realized she wanted to show off her cool new hairstyle. This smart, sophisticated cut. I think she wanted to announce she was a new woman, starting on a new path."

"A path without Leo?"

"Maybe. But more than that." Pepper shook her head. "In the car ride to lunch Ivy told me something strange."

"What?"

"She said she had new information, big news that would guarantee her fortune for life. She told me not to worry. Leo would get his precious divorce. She said thanks to this new information, the child support payments would be sky-high. And the alimony would be permanent."

My heart raced, forcing heat to my throat. I pressed, "What was this big information?"

"I don't know. In the car, Ivy smiled and winked. Cheerful like a kid before her birthday. But she wouldn't say what she meant. I don't know what she learned. She talked in vague words. She said lots of people would be interested in what she knew. Even Leo's aunt would want the news."

Pepper looked at her phone, tapping a quick message. Then "It's time for you to go. I've already said enough." A puff, like exhaling cigarette smoke. "Maybe too much."

We pushed from the table in sync. I swallowed the last of my Coke.

"I have another question, Pepper." I didn't wait for her consent. "Why is Tommy Hannah enrolled in the Blue Bird Day Care Center across the street from this building?"

"How do you know that?" She gulped, then answered her own question. "I know, it's what you do."

"Right." Fists on the table, I leaned forward.

She said, "He's enrolled there because Leo rented an apartment in this building. They live on the eighth floor."

I suppressed the gag reflex. "Cozy. And convenient."

"I didn't ask Leo to move to Robbinsville." Her voice pitched higher. "He said he wanted to get out of the house where Ivy was murdered. He said he couldn't stand the echoes, the smells, the sights. The memories."

"He wanted to be near you." I didn't stifle the sneer this time. "How romantic."

"I never asked him. He decided on his own." Pepper traced a finger through water drops on the table. "The night before . . . um, before Ivy died. Leo called me. He asked if I would always love him. No matter what happened." Her eyes softened to match her whisper. "I said of course I'd love him. Nothing could happen to tear us apart. He said, 'Soon we'll be together always.'"

"Did you share this with the police? After Ivy died." I knew the answer. The tremor in her voice told the story. But I let the question hang.

"No. The police never interviewed me." Giant eyes, still and direct. "Why would they? I'm not involved in her death."

Nothing I could say to strip those blinders. Pepper was in the middle, the embodiment of motive. If she couldn't see that, I had no way to break through. If she ever assembled the puzzle pieces, she'd need years of therapy to recover.

I'd come to Pepper wanting insight into Ivy Hannah's mindset, mood, and actions during the months leading to her death. Now I had important data on Leo. His motive, basted in desire and frustration; his cause, driven by compulsion. Now I wanted to discover what had twisted his motive into murderous action.

At the door, I thanked Pepper for her time. She extended her hand, as if we were ending a business meeting. Perspiration dampened curls into dark commas along her collarbones. She panted in shallow sips; her fingers trembled as we separated.

Pepper didn't linger on the mat. The door whooshed closed, sending humid air in the corridor eddying around me as I walked to the elevator bank.

When the brass doors slid open, I heard the chirping and clucking first. A child babbling joyful nonsense. Eyes down, I shuffled aside to let the family exit.

Leo Hannah stepped toward me. "Pepper said you'd visited." He breathed against my cheek. "I'm surprised you're still here."

His advance pushed me against the wall. I heard the elevator doors whisper shut. Spicy fronds of Leo's aftershave brushed my nose.

He bent to his son, freeing the child's hand. "Go on, you know where Pepper lives." Leo pointed to the far end of the corridor. "Knock on her door all by yourself. Daddy wants to talk with this lady."

CHAPTER **THIRTY-SIX**

I watched Tommy Hannah skip along the hall, trailing a red balloon. His knock at Pepper Sheridan's apartment door was sharp, like an adult's. Command technique was learned early in the Hannah family.

The door flew open. Pepper stepped onto the mat; her hand found Tommy's head. She ruffled his hair. When he pointed, she looked in the direction of the elevators.

Her mouth dropped into an O when she saw me with Leo Hannah. She grabbed the boy's hand and pulled him inside.

The smile fell from Leo's face. "What're you doing here?"

"My job."

"I sent you your last check weeks ago."

"I didn't say you owed me."

"Then who are you working for?"

"I'm a private detective. With a capital P."

"Is it Sam Decker? That asshole is bad news. Dishonest, crazy prick. Keep him away from me. And from Tommy. He's filling Tommy's head with lies and dangerous ideas."

Sam visited his grandson on the regular. Good. Leo was bringing Tommy to playdates with his mistress. How could he complain about proprieties? I didn't throttle the smile flickering across my lips.

"I'm not answering your questions, Leo." I flattened two hands against his chest, ready to push. "I'm sure you'll get an earful from your girlfriend."

"My *girlfriend?*" His eyebrows scooted so violently the bill of his driving cap tilted back.

"Oh, I get it," I sneered. "Is this you acting the grieving widower? And is Pepper playing the role of friend to your late beloved wife? The dear friend you turned to for comfort in your time of sorrow and pain?"

His eyes ping-ponged to the ceiling and back to my face. He grunted and stepped off.

I moved closer. "Okay, Leo. Sure, you stick with that phony story. I bet everyone will buy what you're selling. Almost."

"Almost?" His echo was faint, from the well of his throat.

"Yeah, why not? Your story almost hangs together, right?" I clenched my fists at my side. I wanted to jam him now. "Like that story you shoveled in my office the day we met."

"What story?"

"You acted like you had no idea who I was."

"I'd never met you."

Careful answer, cute construction. He was covering up something. I wanted to explore.

I said, "Never met me, maybe. But you knew who I was."

"That's not . . . not quite, um . . . right."

"Then why did you come to the tavern looking for me?" I held up a cautioning finger. Lies were off the table.

"I wanted a private investigator. You were recommended to me."

Begging the question. I bit. "Who recommended me?"

He growled, a low hum behind his molars. Eyes roamed over the wall beside my head, then angled to the fake palm tree between the elevator doors.

Stepping closer, I barked the repeat. "Who recommended me to you, Leo?"

"My aunt." Small voice, like a prayer.

"How could she know me? I returned to Q-Town only eight months ago." I assumed the mayor's connections spread deep and wide. I wanted to know how they netted me.

"She said you were a smart detective."

Nice praise, but fishy. "Why would she know that?"

"I don't know," he snapped. "She said you came from a good family. She told me investigation and police work ran in your blood."

"My father."

He frowned. "Yeah, the great Evander Myrick." Sarcasm coiled around the word *great*. "Aunt Jo said you'd learned lots from your dad. Said I ought to get to know you better. Hang with you. Like we'd become pals."

I fluttered fingers at my side to release the shudders rolling over my spine. I didn't want Leo to see I was spooked. Josephine Hannah was the reason I was entangled in this case. Her prompt inspired Leo to hire me. How had she hoped to gain from my involvement? What was important to her about bringing me closer to Leo? Why did she believe Leo needed me in the days preceding his wife's death?

"Auntie Jo wanted you to hire me to be your best buddy?" I snorted. "Not cool, Leo. Buying Black people fell out of fashion in 1864."

Dusky orange blotched the slopes of his cheeks. Beads of sweat clotted the dents beside his nose. He whipped the cap from his head and twisted it.

"Fuck you," he barked.

He jammed an elbow into my sternum. I thumped against the wall. Leo grunted, then walked toward Pepper's apartment. The shove hurt. Pain fired from ribs to neck as I sucked air. Watching him retreat, I jabbed the down button.

Bent to one side, I crept through the lobby to the parking lot. A blister pack of Tylenol waited in the Jeep cup holder. Two tabs down the dry hatch would lift me through Route 130 traffic to Queenstown.

The pain meds stuck on the hump of my tongue. I hacked, cradling the Tylenol in my palm as the cough sent new shocks rattling through my chest. The spot where Leo Hannah hit me hurt like a bear. I settled my skull against the headrest, hoping to ease my aching chest. I thought about what I'd learned from Pepper Sheridan. Thanks to her affectionate babble, I'd discovered Leo had a strong incentive to escape his marriage to Ivy. He wanted to be with Pepper. Of equal importance, Leo wanted to keep custody of his son. Tommy was the family he wanted, even as he ditched Ivy.

I stroked the tender skin on my chest. Pain radiated from the swollen bruise, my gift from Leo Hannah. I'd watched his anger rise and subside during our first office interview. The twisted ballpoint he'd left behind was proof. I saw the fury again when he confronted Sam and me at his house. Maybe if he'd found only one person instead of two that day, Leo would have joined the fight he was itching for. Now he'd walloped me. I realized Leo's ire was buried under a veneer of civility. But not all that deep. I'd seen it flare into violence when he was cornered or threatened. I guessed Ivy challenged Leo's pride, an affront he couldn't bear. She was a rebuke to his authority, thwarting his dream of a new life with the compliant Pepper. Had Leo felt the deepest offense was Ivy's refusal to surrender custody of Tommy? He deceived; she taunted. He betrayed; she teased. A pact of mutual denial sealed by disdain. If I was right, Leo murdered Ivy to clear the path to his goals.

With my thumbnails, I split both Tylenol tablets. I crunched the four halves until the bitter powder dissolved on my tongue. My mind eased even before the meds landed. I'd made progress, but I hadn't cleared Ivy's case yet. Discovering her murderer's identity was only half the job. There were more pieces to this puzzle. Before I could stop, I needed to know the complete story, all the whys behind the crime. The slurry of painkillers slipped down my throat, promising relief. I started the engine, aiming the Jeep for Route 130 and home.

Stretching before me, red taillights sailed away from the fading sunset. I gave myself to the stream of cars. Gliding north, I felt pain subside the way sleep dissipates from the mind. Drop by drop, calm seeped through my limbs until the hurt eased. I exhaled. Maybe I'd won a portion of quiet rest for tonight.

When I reached the turnoff for Walmart, about four miles from the center of Q-Town, Sam Decker called.

"I've been trying to reach you all afternoon." This whine was a new feature, one he'd either suppressed during our earlier visits or developed during his stay at the inn. "You didn't pick up."

He could have added, *I'm paying for your time, missy,* but he kept to the civil side of sulky.

"Sorry. New investigative leads boxed me in today." I glanced at the dashboard. Five forty-five, kiddie supper hour, but worth a try. "You up for early dinner tonight?"

"For some reason, the Queenstown social swirl has passed me by." Whine erased; I could hear South Side snark undercut southern graciousness. "Yes, I'm free this evening."

"See you soon, Professor," I said. I threw a hard right across two lanes of traffic and steered toward the Queenstown Motor Inn.

CHAPTER **THIRTY-SEVEN**

Sam Decker was standing under the motel carport when I pulled up twenty minutes later. I thought the white cloud circling his head might be cigarette smoke. But when he slid into the Jeep, he smelled of Altoids, not nicotine. I hoped grandpa time was cutting into Sam's cigarette habit.

Without asking permission or offering options, I drove toward the Queenstown Diner. "You can't spend time in New Jersey without sampling real diner fare. It's state law," I said, tourist-brochure style. "Saturday night, diner booth, pure Jersey."

Sam grunted but didn't comment further. I'd invited, so maybe he figured I was footing the bill and picking the spot for our meal.

We drove along Center Street past the tavern and the First Federal Bank, curved in front of the First Congregational Church into Mott Street, with its row of consignment clothing stores and repair shops for shoes, computers, and appliances. The diner occupied the long edge of a triangular parking lot opposite the post office. Like its cousins across the state, the Queenstown Diner was a narrow railroad car set on concrete blocks. A semicircular step of bricks and cement led to the door. Stainless-steel panels interrupted by fluted red siding made the façade festive, bursting like the Fourth of July even in midwinter.

Frost hustled us from the car. I stumbled when Sam held the door for me. Who does that anymore? Inside, we blew into our fists to warm up as we waited for a hostess to return to the cramped cash register counter. I hadn't eaten at the diner since Christmas Eve lunch.

The silver tinsel garland draping the countertop was gone. The plastic wreaths, Santa wall decorations, and mini trees topping the cake stands had vanished. But the jolly persisted. Red swivel stools along the chrome-clad counter, red vinyl padded booths, and red checkerboard flooring. Feeling glum was forbidden at the Queenstown Diner. I'd tried, but the gloom got thumped out of me every time I visited.

A mile-wide grin split the hostess's face when she wriggled into view. I smiled, but her delight wasn't for me.

"I know'd you'd be back," she shouted at Sam. "I told you, taste us once, you come running for more. Twice, you can't stay away. Amirite?" Her blue eyes grabbed at his face as she tucked yellow strands into the tipsy bun on top of her head.

Sam beamed down. "Roxanne, you were so right." He winked at me. "I told my friend Vandy we had to get a taste of your peach cobbler tonight. I hope you saved a slice for me."

She threw a dirty look my way, but sprinkled the sugar on Sam. "Don't worry, sweetie. If it's gone, I'll slide into the kitchen, strap on an apron, and bake you a fresh one myself."

Despite his modesty, Sam had in fact conquered one corner of Q-Town society. By the time we slipped into a booth, my vaulting eyebrows had settled into place. Fangirl Roxanne dropped laminated menus on the table between us and recited the specials while she poured coffee in two mugs. She implied that leaving the whole carafe was a special favor for Sam. I figured more than coffee was on offer, if only he'd ask.

After she ambled away, I said, "You've made quite an impression. Been here more than once?"

"Every other day for the past two weeks. The motel restaurant is an abomination." He scrunched his face into a knot of nausea. "I explored the local options. Alternating between Kings Cross Tavern and the Q-Town Diner was my best play."

My laugh skidded into a wince. Before I remembered to cover up, I touched a finger to my aching jaw.

Sam caught the move and grabbed the opening: "What happened to you?"

"Nothing." I closed my eyes to avoid his. I wasn't having this conversation. Not the pity, the worry. Not again.

"Looks like three rounds, welterweight division. Only you entered the ring with your hands tied behind your back." His gaze raked my face from hairline to throat. "What happened?"

"You're not going to drop this, are you?"

"No. I'm a persistent little fucker." He narrowed his mouth and eyes. "At least, that's what the provost says."

I gave him the watercolor version of the beating. Blood and gore grayed to pastel tints. Before he asked, I said I hadn't been raped. As designed, that announcement shut down the cross-examination.

"And no, I'm not seeing a doctor, Doctor." I smiled to draw one from Sam. Didn't work.

"This was about our case," he said.

"Yeah, that's what I figure."

"You need to quit."

"Not happening."

"I'm your client," he growled. "I order you to quit. I'll stop paying you. You're off the case."

"You're not my only client."

"Ingrid?" He huffed to dismiss her. "She'd tell you the same thing. Quit."

I raised my eyebrows, slowed my breathing. "I've got another client now. Not you, not Ingrid. Same case, new client."

"Who?"

"Ivy." When he gasped, I continued: "I'm working for Ivy now. She deserves my best effort. I'm not quitting." I'd wanted to thump him and I had.

Sam's jaw slotted left to right. I saw a droplet of perspiration slip down his neck to disappear below the collar of his shirt. His Adam's apple bobbled as he dragged long fingers over his mouth. When he raised his eyes, they were clear. He nodded once. We were clear, too.

After his fried flounder and my gyro platter arrived, I asked about Sam's visits to the Blue Bird Day Care Center.

"You know about that?"

I could have smart-assed about private eye skills in my wheel-house. But I stuck with simple: "Leo gave me a heads-up."

I didn't unload details. Sam's sneer said he understood how his son-in-law must have described those dates.

"Ivy put me on the approved visitor list when Tommy was at Blue Bird here. So when he transferred to Robbinsville, I didn't have any trouble getting to see him."

Sam picked flakes of fish from its golden crust. "I try to arrive at lunchtime. Tommy and I sit at one end of the main room, eating from our plastic lunch pails."

"You have a lunch bucket?"

I tried to picture the elegant professor coiling his legs under a squirt-sized table, munching carrot sticks and bologna sandwich tri-angles without crusts. Chewing raisins and sipping apple juice from squeeze pouches. The image nudged a tender spot in my heart.

"We have matching boxes. Dora the Explorer." He shoved flounder chunks past the sigh. "Then I stay for about twenty minutes, watching Tommy play. When they go down for a nap, I leave."

"That's good, Sam. Real good." I wanted to say something richer, but chewing beef was a better alternative than blubbering raw senti-ment.

Sam went on: "At first Tommy seemed so lonely. When I'd arrive, I'd see him standing in a corner, hands behind his back. Like he'd been bruised and battered by the whole world."

"Which is true, in a way," I said. When he nodded, I reached for the coffee carafe and refilled my mug.

No need for evasion or soft-pedaling. So much of the boy's routine had changed without explanation. New school, new playmates, new home, no mother. How did losing a parent compare to losing a child? Was Tommy's pain muted because he'd known his mother for less than three years? Could he already sense the torque in his future? The spin away from a path he should have taken? I couldn't devise an equa-tion that would reveal those dynamics. A wave of raw need surged over me. I wanted to hold Monica again. It would be enough to touch her face one more time. I clamped my teeth to stifle the groan.

Sam coughed. I veered to another lane. "What do the teachers say?"

"They say he's coming out of his shell. Every day is better than the one before." Sam pushed peas on his plate into a mound, then smashed it with his fork.

"It's good you can be here for him. You're the continuity he needs now."

"Yeah, I hope that's true." He puffed his cheeks, then wiped his mouth with a paper napkin.

He raised his eyes, bright with tears. A smile skipped into view. "Tommy has made friends at Blue Bird in the past week."

"That's good," I said, too quickly. Another gulp of coffee blocked the sniffle.

"Two little girls, Isabel and Jennifer. They speak with him in Spanish, which seems to help. They taught him to call me abuelo or abuelito."

Now my eyes watered. "Yes, the Baca twins. They attended day care in Q-Town with Tommy. Then their mother moved them to Robbinsville."

Sam's brows bent in confusion. "How do you know them?"

I swirled a tomato wedge in vinaigrette. I couldn't bring it to my mouth, so I gathered a long breath. "Their father is Carlos Baca. He is—was—a friend of Hector Ramírez."

"Christ." Sam spit the words like acid. "Circles of fucking hell in this town."

"Yeah," I said. "Nobody escapes."

Sam sawed at a sprig of parsley half hidden under the flounder. I attempted the tomato again, dropping it on my tongue in hopes I'd be able to chew it this year.

Now that we were knee-deep in misery, I decided to plunge us up to our necks. "I saw Leo this afternoon."

"Where?"

"At the apartment complex where he and Tommy live."

"You went to their place?"

"No, I ran into them on the way out of someone else's apartment."

Sam squinted. He knew I was aiming at something and having

trouble hitting the mark. "Spit it out, Vandy. Who's this 'someone else'?"

I whooshed, then spilled. "Pepper Sheridan."

"Familiar name. Who is she?"

"Pepper was a friend of Ivy's."

"And now?"

"And now she's a friend of Leo's."

He took a long gulp of coffee. "That's not what you mean, is it?"

"No. Pepper is his lover."

"Since when?"

"For at least a year." I tried to minimize the grim story. But shaving the time didn't cut the insult.

"Did-did Ivy know?"

"Yes, I think so. Pepper believed she did."

"That explains a lot." The corners of his mouth folded into crevasses. Above the grizzle, his cheeks paled to ash. Another portion of sadness to bear. But no surprise or anger this round.

"How so?" I asked.

"I remember what Ivy told me on the ride to the airport . . . that week . . . before she died." He stalled under the weight of memory.

"What did she say?" Leaning on the table, I shoved aside my plate.

He coughed to loosen the story. "She said she planned to get a divorce."

I nodded. "And what else?"

"Ivy said she had important information she intended to use to extract a good divorce settlement from Leo."

"Did she say what that information was? Was it details of the affair with Pepper?"

"I don't know what the information was. Maybe the affair. Maybe something else. But she sounded confident. Chipper. Like a kid who bought the test answers before the exam. Like she had the world by the tail." He paused; the smile tipping his lips didn't reach his eyes. "Like she had Leo by the balls."

"Nothing specific? Are you sure it was about Leo?"

"She didn't say anything definite. But it had to be about Leo, didn't it?" He looked at me for the first time in many minutes. "It had to be something big, some blockbuster thing to compel him to give her what she wanted."

"And what she wanted was lots of money."

"Yes, Ivy told me not to worry. She said she'd put the squeeze on Leo. The alimony she'd win from him would provide a solid financial foundation for herself and Tommy. Thanks to what she knew, their future was secure."

Sam sniffed. I could see tendons flex in his neck. He worked his jaw, popping muscles in front of his ears.

"That was the last time I saw her. My beautiful, perfect girl."

When I touched the knuckles on his right hand, they bulged under my fingers. I squeezed, watching the waxy knobs bunch and relax.

He muttered, "You've got Leo's motive now, don't you? He wanted to be free from Ivy."

"Yes, Pepper was the pull." I bit a ragged cuticle on my index finger.

"But not enough?"

"Pull, yes. But I want to know about the push. It's a long fall from dissatisfied to murderous. I want to know what shoved Leo."

"You've got more digging to do."

"Yes. To go to the cops, to upend their narrative, I need more."

For a while, the coffee captured our misery. I studied the stains on the rim of my mug. Sam ran a fingernail on the cracks threading over the handle of his. He waved at Roxanne for the check.

Our troubled mood infected the air in our booth. I watched Roxanne's face slide from frisky to morose when she arrived with the dessert list. Sighing, she ditched the peach cobbler tease.

As Sam paid the bill at the counter, I walked toward the entrance. The cell buzzed in my pocket.

I fat-fingered the phone until I slid it open. The screen read: *Glendale Memory Care Center.* I didn't recognize the number. Not Keyshawn Sayre's line. Or the phone in my father's apartment. My heart galloped. Ceiling lights battered my eyes. I listened to the voice on the other end of the line.

Sam held the restaurant door open. Cold whipped my face. Sweat coated my palm and the phone slipped to the cement step. He stooped and handed it to me.

"What's the matter?" he said. "You look sick." He pressed fingers to my shoulder.

I gulped twice. The oxygen cleared my head; the breeze opened my throat. "My father has disappeared."

"What do you mean?"

"Evander walked away from Glendale. Escaped. No one knows where he's gone."

CHAPTER **THIRTY-EIGHT**

I wanted to race to Glendale Memory Care Center. Find my father before the dark swallowed him whole.

In the car, trembling fingers botched my efforts to buckle the seat belt. I made it on the third attempt. I offered to drive Sam Decker to his motel, but he insisted on coming with me.

"More eyes and hands for the search," he said. "Let's go."

We tore from the parking lot, scraping curbs and potholes as we rolled. Automatic pilot switched on. For fifteen minutes, the Jeep found the corners and side streets without my direction.

My mind found Evander. He couldn't be far, only a few blocks beyond the iron pickets enclosing the campus. He was out there. Waiting for me. Perched on a park bench, drumming his fingers on his knees. Or leaning against a lamppost, basking in the cold yellow veil of light. Maybe he'd followed a deer into a wooded patch and was sitting on a fallen log, waiting for me to find him. Maybe my father would recognize me when I came to fetch him. *Evander, meet Evander. Shake hands, kiss, hug.* A breakthrough just like I wanted. It could happen.

We galloped into the Glendale lobby. Men and women stood in clusters with their heads lowered over phones. Murmurs echoed from the vaulted ceiling, interrupted by bleats or yelps. I scanned the tight circles. I wanted to find a black face or a brown one. Somebody who knew my father and cared about his disappearance beyond the calculations of litigation and liability. A stench of sweat and fear rolled across the heated space. A white man aimed his eyes at me, pointing a chin, then a finger; another man confirmed with hunched shoulders. They knew I was the daughter. The responsible one. The aggrieved one. Maybe, if luck fled like this demented old Black man, the bereaved one.

I saw Keyshawn Sayre's head jerk above the group. He strode to us and grabbed me by the arm. "Vandy, thank God, they reached you."

"What the hell happened, Key?"

He pointed at a clutch of attendants in wool coats and puffer jackets. "We're organizing a search party." His phrases beat like a storm against my forehead. "We've mapped a two-mile diameter area around the center. Divided it into six zones. We'll cover each zone in groups of five. You can join me."

His eyes were unfocused behind a mist of tears, his breath humid on my cheeks.

I stiffened; my stomach twisted under my heart. Squeezing my lids to stop the tumbling, I shouted, "Whoa, hold on." I pounded on Key's chest. "Tell me what happened."

He blinked twice. His eyes cleared. He tugged me toward reading chairs in a quiet corner. Sam followed, perching on the arm of my chair. Keyshawn and I sat facing each other, his knees braced against mine.

"I noticed Evander wasn't in the dining room at six-thirty." Keyshawn said. "He usually walks down to dinner by six. If I'm here, I help him select his meal, sit with him for a while. But if I'm not around, another staffer steps in. Evander's not much on conversation, but he does enjoy the company."

Keyshawn looked up at Sam, noticing him for the first time. He reared in the chair, mouth clamping shut, nostrils flaring.

No time for elaborate introductions, I said, "This is Sam. He's a friend. He's here to help."

Key nodded and continued: "I went to Evander's apartment to check. I thought maybe he'd fallen asleep or gotten distracted by some TV show. He wasn't in the apartment. I walked every hall on the fifth floor, checked the library, the craft room, the movie theater. Nothing."

When he sputtered to a stop, I squeezed his knee. Did he think I blamed him for this horror? Maybe the fear in my eyes registered as accusation. Resting bitch face translated anxiety as anger.

I tried a smile, but it flattened. "When did you all realize he was missing?"

"After we searched the grounds. Inside the fenced perimeter. Twenty minutes ago, we notified the police. Bobby'll be here soon."

I craned to catch Sam's eye. "Bobby Sayre is Keyshawn's brother. And chief of police in Q-Town."

Sam nodded, mouth compressing to a line. I remembered his dinnertime curse: *Circles of fucking hell in this town.* And my answer: *Nobody escapes.*

Keyshawn continued, "But we're not waiting for QPD. We move into the two-mile perimeter now. The cops can expand the search area with their officers."

I wanted to ask how Evander had dodged all the protocols and slipped away from Glendale. Had he been seen outdoors? Had he worn a coat when he left? Why hadn't a single staff member at the front desk noticed him passing? How many exits were there in this building? What did security cameras at those doors reveal? How the fuck had this disaster happened?

But I kept my question simple: "How long do you figure Evander's been missing?"

"One hour, maybe two," Key said. He winced and looked at his knuckles.

"Jesus Christ," Sam blurted, "it's fucking cold out there."

Keyshawn's blazing eyes swept the lobby. He spotted his colleagues moving toward the revolving doors. One woman gestured with a gloved hand. He stood and zipped his parka. He was ready to charge. My questions could come later. If I wanted to join the search, I had to hold my fire.

Keyshawn handed flashlights to me and Sam. We set off on foot from the locked gate separating Glendale from the saner precincts of town.

In hour three of the search, I switched sectors. I'd seen enough of woodland. Nothing of Evander.

Flanked by Sam and Keyshawn, I tramped through open fields of soybean stubble. Our boots churned the snow into mud as we moved. Rodents rushed from their burrows, darting between the light beams we waved across the landscape. We stumbled around last fall's corn maze, tripping over pumpkin carcasses and lost mittens. Stands of pin oak, maple, and pines yielded nothing except startled deer, their eyes flashing like hazard lights on a car dashboard. We skirted two frozen ponds, tranquil as coins dropped in mud. Their banks were camouflaged by stalks of cattails and deadheaded Queen Anne's lace. I saw a fox lead her three kits to an invisible den. After her babies disappeared beneath a tangle of vines, the vixen paused to study us. As we walked on, she flicked her tail and vanished.

On the edge of another clearing, I kicked at a rotten tree trunk. Wood chunks pelted the ground. This was the fallen log I'd imagined my father would choose as his park bench. Why wasn't he waiting here for me? Wind whipped particles of branch and bark across my face. I tugged the shirtsleeve from inside my coat and dabbed my nose and brow. No one was looking, so I wiped my eyes, too. We were explorers, and the night was virgin territory. Finding Evander was our El Dorado. Tears had no part in this expedition. I puffed a jet of air toward my right eye to whisk away the last tear.

Keyshawn sat on the log. "We need a break. This is as good a spot as any." He gazed across the field at a line of black trees guarding another forest.

I accepted the permission to pause I couldn't grant myself. I sat, leaning close to him so there was room for Sam. But he strode four yards away, raking his torchlight over the dented grass.

I pressed my mouth against Key's shoulder. "I thought we'd find him by now."

"We will," he whispered. "Just a little while longer."

Behind us, I heard Sam crunch dried leaves. His voice boomed from the darkness. "How'd a self-respecting town like this let so much wilderness nestle right inside the city limits?"

He pointed his torch over our heads at the verge of trees in the distance. Still in lecture-hall mode, inflected with wondering warmth: "Look over there. Primordial nature cheek by jowl with housing developments and highways. You'd think the real estate industry would gain the upper hand. From here, it looks like civilization's lost this round."

He won a laugh from me: "Says Florida Man. You've got alligators rambling onto your backyard patio looking to make lunch out of Cousin Billy Bob."

Sam sat beside me. "You need to travel more. We're not all rednecks down there."

When I dipped my head to his shoulder, he hitched. He turned his face to murmur against my knit cap. "If your dad's out here, we'll find him."

Between them, Keyshawn and Sam had bolstered my spirits. They were right. We needed to move. Evander wasn't searching for us; we had to find him.

CHAPTER **THIRTY-NINE**

I wanted to fire up our search for Evander. Five minutes' rest meant my father wandered alone for five minutes longer in this freezing weather. Muddling and moongazing wouldn't win the day. We needed to move. I fastened my hands on both knees to rise from the log. My phone blared in my coat pocket. Maybe news, maybe a break. Unzipping cost three more buzzes. I slapped the cell to my ear.

"What?" I shouted.

"Where you at, Ms. Vandy?" Ingrid Ramírez's chirp sliced through my head. "I been trying to reach you. You busy?"

Standing from the fallen tree, I began, "Ingrid, you caught me at a . . . a bad time." When my voice hitched, my search companions, Sam and Keyshawn, closed ranks around me.

Ingrid's Boss Girl flex continued. She wanted a late-night update from her employee. How could she think I'd be eager to debrief on the Hannah investigation at this hour? Easy. Kids were citizens of vampire country; night was their natural element, and they never carried watches.

Wind gusting around my ears muffled her response. "What's up? You sound like shit."

I explained my father's disappearance in four sentences. There was nothing she could do. No need to delay the resumption of our search with detailed reportage. I should have expected Ingrid's reaction. I didn't.

"I'll look on this side." Flat, hard, no room for reversal. Ingrid wasn't asking, she was telling. "My friend can drive."

"In Abbott's Landing?" I didn't want to debate geography and the stamina of eighty-six-year-old men. "Too far from Glendale."

Ignoring my lame-ass protests, she skipped to issuing assignments. "You need to check out the cemetery. You looked there yet?"

I stiffened my objection. "Too far. At the rate he walks, it'd take my father half a day to get there from Glendale."

"Maybe. But don't underrate him." I heard Ingrid inhale, the breath softening her next words. "How long's he been gone?"

Too fucking long. "At least five hours, maybe six or seven." My knees wobbled as I said the numbers out loud.

Both men stepped closer. Keyshawn gripped my elbow as I sagged.

I hated showing weakness. I was the pro, the law enforcement veteran, the PI with the iron stomach and head. I'd seen gore, dealt with loss and death. Softness was not on my résumé. But now I wobbled like a newborn lamb. With good reason, sure. I could cut myself some slack. But a feeble move all the same. Still, I appreciated their support. An "I got you, girl" without the pity or macho power play.

"You with a search party? Or by yourself?" Ingrid asked, old-head energy flowing. How had a sixteen-year-old become the mother in this exchange?

"Sam and my friend Keyshawn are with me."

"Good." Muffled phrases followed; she was speaking to someone in the room. She hacked to clear her throat. "Yeah, you go to the cemetery. I'll check you in one hour."

I grunted and hung up without a word. I was too tired to argue. The kid was right. Evander might have aimed his trek beyond Queenstown's historic center. Our old house was in the Flats, the Black quarter of town. I'd grown up in a modest bungalow there. He'd grown senile there watching his wife die. We'd buried my mother and my daughter in the cemetery opposite Bethel AME Church. A ramble to the Flats might make sense in Evander's jumbled mind.

After slurps of transparent coffee in the Glendale lobby, Keyshawn and Sam crowded into my Jeep for the trip to the Flats. We were a team now, my ride-or-die crew. Hollows below Keyshawn's eyes had darkened to maroon batwings. Sam looked beat, too, his lips gray as oysters. I managed a bathroom break without glancing in the mirror. So I judged my appearance by the grimaces on their faces: I was a twelve-car smashup. Hideous.

I parked across the street from the entrance to the church. At the iron gate, I removed my gloves. We weren't vandals, but irrational respect said the disruption was reduced if I pushed with bare hands. The gate swung smoothly, oil on my fingers testifying to the care lavished on this graveyard. I said a silent thanks to the Bethel congregation and entered.

A cement ribbon curved toward the far corner of the cemetery, moonlight glinting off threads of ice between the pavers. We resumed the formation we'd established during our earlier march: I walked in the middle, on the path, which had been shoveled clean. Sam and Keyshawn trudged through unmarked snow, fifty yards on either side. They dodged around the close-laid gravestones, sometimes tripping on tree roots bent like knees at irregular intervals. I wondered if either man was superstitious. Would they resent me for staying on the cleared walk while they dislodged ghosts and haints?

I led toward the northeast section, where my mother and daughter were buried. As we moved further from the streetlamps, scents replaced sight. The air smelled of moss mingled with crushed berries. I hoped Evander had tramped to this deserted corner. Maybe he celebrated these eternal ties, the way Mexican families picnicked on the graves of their loved ones on the Day of the Dead. Did he feel more connected to Alma and Monica than to me, his last living relative?

After ten minutes' tramp, we reached a stone bench. I sat, propping one heel against the carved lion's paw supporting the seat. This was my limit. Pain flicked from shins to hips as I settled on the cold block.

I pointed toward a shadow under a muscular oak tree. "That's the gravestone for my family."

The men stepped toward the granite marker, approaching the way they'd tiptoe to the cradle of a sleeping baby.

I didn't need to view the tablet; I'd put it there. Ash-gray stone flecked with white, shiny and broad. Chiseled letters softened by serif script across the top of the slab. I knew the inscription: MYRICK. Bold and proud. Below, lines curved like rivulets through the stone: ALMA MARIE, LOVING WIFE, DEVOTED MOTHER. Then the freshest strokes: MONICA ALMA, BELOVED DAUGHTER.

Monica's name had been cut into the space originally planned for my father. Despite the haste, the stonemason did fine work on the squeeze job. I remembered watching him carve those delicate strokes, dust rising in silver mist as the letters emerged. Grief sliced me now as it had then: Monica should never have been there; the engraving was a memorial to waste. But when he finished, the carving made her name look elegant. I took comfort from that beauty. And from the symmetry of the doubled ALMA, the shared name bracketing their connection like graceful bookends. I didn't need to see the grave now. I knew space remained on the lower half of the granite slab for my father's name and mine, when time claimed us.

I saw first Keyshawn, then Sam, touch the arched crown of the gravestone. Evander was not here. I lowered my head to my hands and wept.

For thirty minutes, we stalked through the other sections of the cemetery. We had little hope, but we completed the job. Why would Evander skip the Myrick grave to visit a stranger's resting place? Even for a demented man, that wouldn't make sense. As expected, he wasn't anywhere.

Swirling rain and snow pricked our faces as we returned to the cemetery gate on Quincy Street.

Sam took the back seat this time. In the rearview mirror, I watched him pull his knit cap over his eyes, then stretch his upper body along the bench in search of rest. Cold stinging my fingers made it hard to turn the ignition key. I pumped the pedal and cranked the heater to blast. Just as the first burst of warmth flared from the vent, my cell buzzed. I looked a plea at Keyshawn next to me.

His eyelids fluttered with exhaustion as he pulled the phone from my pocket. "Yeah, this is Vandy's phone. Who is this?" He put the caller on Speaker.

Ingrid's voice bubbled from the phone: "We found him. We got him. He's okay. We found him."

"Where are you?"

"The water tower. The shed next to the reservoir. Come get us."

I yelled, "Oh my God, yes."

Keyshawn hollered, "Thank God. Bless you, girl."

Sam pounded the headrest behind Keyshawn. "Move," he shouted. "Move."

CHAPTER **FORTY**

I counted two beats. They seemed like centuries. Sam's breath stroked hot on my neck. "How far?" he asked.

"Ten minutes, if I follow the law." I reeled the car into a U-turn. "I'll make it five."

Wheels skittered on icy patches at the intersection. We flew by the marble Union soldier guarding the entrance to the Flats. I busted through two red lights and three stop signs before slowing to cross Route 130. Traffic had evaporated. At three A.M., Queenstown was tucked tight in bed.

I felt the weight of the water tower before I saw its bulk out-lined against the clouds. I sped down the straightaway toward the reservoir's yard. Four blocks of slick asphalt stretched like an airport runway. I didn't slow as we flew through the double-wide opening in the fence. Inside the yard, I veered toward the wood-shingled shed hunched in the shadow of the tower. I pumped the brakes; the Jeep shuddered to a halt.

"There they are," Keyshawn screeched. He pointed toward the shed.

I saw my father walk from the shack's open door. Ingrid leaned against his left side, her shoulder under his arm like a crutch. Evander canted sideways but strode with his chin high. His face was smooth, open. Was that a simper playing on his lips? As if he'd designed this scenario just so, the dramatic ending a scripted climax of his inven-tion. Director's cut. Roll the credits. Cue the exit music.

I jumped from the car, yelling. I heard boots crunch the gravel behind me: Keyshawn and Sam in support. I ran through the headlight
beams toward my father.

Evander's head was bare, revealing the glower of his eyes. With
Ingrid's cheek against his chest, I could see his flannel shirt was buttoned to the throat. A light-colored coat was draped over his right
shoulder.

I buried my face in his chest, clamping my arms around his waist. I
squeezed until I heard him gasp for breath. Until I felt his heart pumping our blood, his and mine, through his veins. Ingrid bent her head
to my shoulder; her purple ball cap tipped, then fell to the ground. I
opened my right arm to enfold her.

I raised my head to murmur into his shirt. "Why did you go,
Daddy?"

The whine sounded like a child's protest. As it should. I was the
wounded person here, not Evander. I'd been scared; I wasn't ready to
bear the grief he'd thrust upon me. I wanted him to know I'd been
afraid. I wanted him to understand me. To admit he had caused my
fear. During those hours he'd been away, I felt orphaned. I wanted
him to know me, to know how much I hurt.

Keyshawn raised a hand to stroke my father's head, then his cheek
and neck. He leaned to whisper, "Evander, where'd you go, man? We
been all over, looking for you. Why'd you take off like that?"

Sam stepped to our circle but stayed a pace away. Ingrid broke
away and ran to him. They staggered backward in a tight embrace, his
face buried in her hair. I thought I heard him say, "Good girl."

Evander said nothing. As I hugged him, he gazed over my head,
taking in the rumbling car and the spherical outline of the old water
tank above us.

After a minute, I looked to Ingrid. "Thank you," I said. "Thank you
for saving my father."

She nodded, then stooped to retrieve her hat.

I saw Evander's eyes fire with excitement. He stretched his right
hand toward the girl, his fist grabbing air. The camel-hair coat on his
shoulder slipped to the gravel. He clutched and released his fingers.
He wanted the ball cap. Maybe he was cold after so many hours

outdoors. Maybe he believed his balding head entitled him to all hats; they belonged to him, by right of age and pedigree.

Ingrid extended her cap to him. Evander took it, settling it on his scalp at a jaunty angle. He patted her hair.

"Ivy," he said. A grin broke across his face. "Thank you, Ivy."

I saw Sam jolt, his elbows jerked as if by wires. "What did he say?"

I blew a long sigh, shutting my eyes. "It's play with Ingrid." Preparing to explain made my head swim.

"What do you mean?" Sam's voice quivered.

"Ivy visited Glendale as a church volunteer," I said. "She met Evander and they used to exchange ball caps. When he saw Ingrid's hat, it reminded him of his play with Ivy. So now he makes Ingrid trade caps the way Ivy did."

Sam pressed a hand to his throat. "Oh. I see." The fog in his eyes said he didn't.

I crouched to pick up the coat Evander dropped. I held it to Keyshawn. "This isn't one of his. Where did this come from?"

"Never seen it," Key said, shaking his head. He moved to Evander and gripped his elbow. "You got me freezin' out here, man."

They walked toward the Jeep. I watched my father slide onto the rear bench. Key closed the door, then trotted to the other side. He sat next to Evander. After buckling their seat belts, he waved at me through the side window.

I wanted to go. But I wanted the mystery solved. "So where was this coat when you found him?"

Ingrid said, "He was lying under it when we found him in the shed." She turned to point at a car parked beside the shack. "My friend Ethan drove me here."

I hadn't noticed the beat-up blue Toyota Corolla idling nearby. I could make out the profile of a teenager behind the wheel. I decided in that instant this Ethan person deserved all the things in the world.

"What made you come here?" I asked.

"Lots of kids hang out here. You know, for privacy. The shed's a safe place. Our getaway room." She looked toward Ethan, a smile flickering for the first time. "I figured maybe your dad decided to come here, too. After scouting Abbott's Landing, we drove here."

"And you found him." Obvious, but waves of gratitude swamped deeper thoughts.

"Yeah, he was lying on a mattress, under a blanket. Curled up. Not asleep. Just humming and twiddling his fingers. He didn't seem worried or even cold. Like he was waiting on a park bench for somebody to walk by and find him."

I turned the coat, looking for the label. Ralph Lauren. Size six. Genuine tortoiseshell buttons on the left side. I recognized this coat. Whiffs of lavender and citrus lifted from the lapels. I knew that fragrance. I'd smelled it on two different women. One must have given the perfume to the other.

I dangled the coat by the metal chain below the collar. "And this? Where'd you find it?"

"Evander was lying with one arm stuck in the coat sleeve. It's too small for him. So he kept it on one arm."

"Okay, got it," I said.

True. I got the message contained in this coat. A communication meant for me alone. From an adversary I hadn't realized I was fighting. I wouldn't share the message with the others. Not yet.

I hugged the girl. "Ingrid, I appreciate you. You're a superhero. My hero."

She sniffed. Two tears rolled down her cheeks. "I'm glad . . ." She shivered. "I'm glad I could save somebody." She raised her face, her brother's eyes drowning below heavy lids.

Sam said, "Let's get out of here. It's cold as fuck." He didn't smile, but he'd recovered some fragment of his spirit.

Sam and I watched Ingrid and her knight Ethan dart away. I rolled the coat into a bundle and stowed it in the rear of the Jeep. On the road to Glendale, Keyshawn phoned his brother to alert the police that Evander had been found. I dropped Sam at his motel, with a hug for his support and a promise to phone in the afternoon. No morning duties for us.

At the memory center, Evander was greeted as a conquering champion. Blankets were thrown over his back; he was pushed into a wheelchair and hurried to his apartment. Kitchen staff delivered two trays heaped with cafeteria food to remind the wayward resident why he should never, ever roam. I suppressed flashes of anger as we moved through the adoring crowds. They'd let him escape. Or be taken. This debacle was on them.

Keyshawn offered to spend the night with Evander. I said I'd stay; this was my father, my family. The sofa was good enough for me.

After helping his charge into pajamas and under two coverlets, Key brought a pillow and blanket to the living room for me.

"You sure you're all right, Vandy?" Fatigue slurred his words.

"I'll be fine." *You're a good man,* I wanted to say. *The best.* "No worries. Go home and sleep for a thousand years. We done good tonight." I hugged him hard to show I was still strong.

After Key left, I reheated the meatloaf and stabbed it into a pile. Picking at the brown rubble, I sat at the kitchen counter and thought about what I'd learned.

I recognized the camel-hair coat. It belonged to Josephine Hannah. I'd seen her wear it many times, including at the memorial service for Ivy Hannah. The scent on the collar belonged to her, too. I remembered the lavender/citrus fragrance from when we met at the murder house, reviewing the facts of the case.

I also recalled noting this scent on Pepper Sheridan. It struck me at the time as being too matronly. But if Pepper had received a bottle as a gift from her lover's aunt, she might have worn the perfume out of loyalty.

I knew there was only one way Evander could have acquired that coat. Mayor Hannah had given it to him when she took him from Glendale.

I would check the security camera footage tomorrow. I was certain I'd find nothing of value. I was sure the mayor had shuffled her captive through an unguarded back door, beyond the view of the cameras. Had Leo Hannah alerted his aunt after our argument this afternoon? I didn't know. But I was sure she'd abducted my father to send me a message; she gave him her coat to make sure the message was delivered. She wanted me to stop my investigation of Ivy Hannah's murder. The threat was clear: she could harm the people dearest to me if I continued to push.

I shoveled the remains of the meatloaf into the garbage pail. I dumped the plastic plate in the sink for tomorrow's attention. After a gulp of water and a splash on my face, I settled under the blanket. I scrunched the pillow into a bolster and craned my neck into the indentation.

After a minute, I rose and pushed open the bedroom door. My father was sleeping, snores ruffling through a smile on his lips. I folded the hem of the coverlet across his shoulders and stroked his arm. Then I kissed his forehead. He smiled and rolled on his side. My father was safe, but seeing him at rest revived all the anxiety of our search. My fear he had been injured or killed. The haunting belief that I might never see him again. The dread that my father would never hold me in his arms again, never steal grapes from me or watch me play chess again. The horror that I might have lost him without ever hearing him say my name again. I returned to the living room and lay under the blanket; this time its warmth enveloped me. I stretched my legs. My toes finally stopped tingling from cold.

I thought about the coat bundled in my car. Message received. Message rejected. I knew who had abducted my father. Who had tormented him with cold and neglect. As I twisted under the blanket, I felt the warmth of my flesh convert to rage in my heart. This injury to my father—to me—could not be allowed to stand. Not only would I continue to drive my investigation, I intended to crash it right into city hall.

I wanted sleep and a clear mind for my audience with Mayor Josephine Hannah.

CHAPTER **FORTY-ONE**

When I stalked into the mayor's office at three-thirty Monday afternoon, I'd erased most of the damage of the preceding day and night.

Four hours' sleep in my father's apartment. Slow Sunday pampering Evander with food and idle talk. Shower at home, a restless night in my own bed, wading through oceans of dreams in which Monica, swathed in gold rags, pointed the way to Evander's grave. Another shower to erase the clammy sweat. Jump into my everyday armor of denim and black wool. But I kept the boots uncleaned and unpolished. The stains meant I hadn't forgotten. The anger wasn't washed away. I wanted to confront the woman responsible for abducting my father. Maybe Evander's forced ramble hadn't frightened him, but it scared the hell out of me. I wanted her to answer. I wanted her to pay.

I chirped at the mayor's assistant as he stood behind an ocean-liner desk. "No, I don't have an appointment." The fear I'd felt when my father disappeared had congealed into cold rage.

My smile was broad and phony. The assistant's smirk was feline and as tight as his pin-striped suit. He swept a hand under the straw thatch brushing his brow. He looked at my mud-caked boots and winced.

Yes, I was dirty, tired, too. Anger drummed behind both ears. My fingers twitched with suppressed energy. If this jerk tried to block me, I'd crush bones. I saw his eyes fly toward a closed door on the left. The mayor was in. Before he could invent a lie, I swung around the desk and elbowed the door. It fell open. Snarls trailed me as I crossed the threshold and slammed the door behind me. I spun the lock to be sure the cat-assistant wouldn't disturb us.

Josephine Hannah was seated at a desk smaller than the boat in the outer suite. Her workstation resembled an overturned refrigerator, black surfaces opaque and highly polished. A twenty-inch HP laptop lay flat on the left side. A pad of white legal paper was anchored by two Montblanc pens on the right. Behind her was a credenza support-ing a pitcher of water surrounded by four crystal tumblers. The official seal of Queenstown hung above the credenza.

The mayor didn't stand when I barreled in. She didn't act surprised to see me. No raised eyebrows or gaping mouth. No flush exploding on her cheeks or fingers scrabbling against palms. She didn't seem happy, either. A tilt to the left dislodged one hank of hair; sweat dotted the black roots. The magenta of her knit dress drained her face to sliced-pear pale. Above brown eyes, the thick fringe of lashes batted furiously.

"Sit, Ms. Myrick." She waved at two chairs made of molded plastic and metal, designed to discomfort guests. "I've been expecting you."

I leaped to essentials. "I would have returned your coat, but I fig-ured I'd keep it as evidence."

"Evidence of what, may I ask?" Cornered and overly polite.

I wondered if she'd launch into a full-blown confession, like a Bond villain bragging of plans for global conquest and annihilation of the hero. Her sneer showed that she was cooler than Goldfinger. Concessions, if any, would be scant and cagey.

I said, "You kidnapped my father Saturday. We found him wearing your overcoat."

"What makes you think the coat was mine?" A non-denial denial. Cute.

"I recognized it. Camel-hair. Designer label. The collar was cov-ered in your perfume." I sniffed to mime my technique.

Pursed lips and narrowed lids. "My perfume?" Sliding eyes meant she was genuinely puzzled. Hannah stumped: point for Myrick.

I thrust the shiv. "Yeah. Lavender with a twist of lemon. It's yours."

She stiffened, as if I'd accused her of using the wrong silverware at dinner. "Of course. That's L'Air d'Avignon. My nephew gave me a bottle for Christmas several years ago."

"And then you gave the same fragrance to his girlfriend. So sweet."

Croaks escaped her mouth. "I did no such thing. What a disgusting thought."

"And yet I smelled the identical scent in her apartment Saturday. Maybe Leo gifted her the same perfume he gave you." I smirked to twist the knife. "Family ties in a fluted bottle. How lovely."

She spun the chair, reaching for the water pitcher behind her. I heard two gulps, then a murmured "Stupid boy." Another swig to gain time.

When she swung around, sallow replaced green in her cheeks. She set the half-empty water glass next to the laptop. "This proves nothing."

"Wrong." I jabbed a finger into the desk. "Your coat on my father proves you took him. And you left him to die of exposure."

"But he didn't die." Another non-denial. She leaned forward, banging elbows to the desk. "You found him, with help from your little minions."

I wondered who had briefed the mayor on Evander's rescue. Had she spoken with QPD Chief Sayre? Or with someone on the staff at Glendale?

I skirted that detour. "Why did you take him?"

"Evander and I are old friends." A dodge, but the history intrigued me, so I didn't object. "We've been in each other's orbits since his early days on the force. You might say we're almost family."

"That why you visit him regularly?"

"Yes. Even though he doesn't recognize me now. It's my duty as a close friend to visit when I can. During the years after Alma's death, I took it upon myself to see he was properly cared for." She sharpened her gaze. "You were away from Queenstown for so long and he needed old friends. I stepped in."

As she'd intended, guilt panged through me. I squeezed my hands to control the flinch. "But why now?" I huffed twice to suppress the squeak. "Why kidnap him now?"

"*Kidnap* is a harsh word. I prefer *jaunt*." The upper lip twitch might have been a smile on a decent person. "Evander and I went for a ride. An excursion. I hoped a visit to the water tower—seeing our little shed again—might jog his memory. When I let him out of the car in front of the Glendale gate, I assumed he'd go inside. Instead, he chose to wander." She sighed, long and billowy, like a disappointed mother.

Our shed? Jaunt? What crap was she slinging?

"Bullshit," I snapped. "You took him, drove him miles away, and dumped him on the side of the road. That's how you treated your 'old friend.'" The last words curdled on my tongue.

"Supposing that is the case, why would I do it?"

"You wanted to get my attention." I was panting, angry. I didn't care if she noticed. "That's what the coat stunt was all about."

She raised her eyebrows. "And do I have your attention now?"

"Yes." I shifted forward on the hard chair.

"Then listen." Now the smile was full-toothed. I could count her molars. "I don't repeat myself. It's inefficient and weak."

"I'm listening. What do you want?"

"I want you to drop your investigation of the death of my nephew's wife."

"Don't you want to get to the bottom of Ivy's murder?"

"Of course I do. She was family. *My* family. That means everything to me." She bunched a fist on the legal pad. "The police and prosecutor closed the case weeks ago. That hideous little Latin person stalked her. Then he killed her."

"That's not true." Feeble, so I added, "I'm building a case to prove Hector Ramírez didn't murder Ivy."

The mayor cackled, a wild peal that battered my ears. She relaxed into her chair. "Your imagination is fertile. Or should I say, *fertilizer*. Evander was a great man. Real police. He'd be embarrassed by you. With your cheap stunts and tasteless conjecture. He always wanted to give his name to a boy. Too bad he didn't. Your case is full of shit. The sooner you recognize that, the better for everyone."

"Everyone?" I balanced on the edge of my seat. This was the heart of our meeting.

"Yes, everyone you know."

"Are you threatening me?" I wanted her focused on me, not my friends.

"No, I'm telling you facts." She pulled on a hidden drawer. She slid a manila folder onto the desk surface next to the closed computer. "Here's what you need to know."

She opened the folder. I leaned forward. It was empty. Chuckling, she said, "You don't think I keep a written file on your associates, do you?" She tapped her temple. "It's all up here."

"Why would you collect information on my friends?"

"Unpleasant incidents can happen, even in the most peaceful of places. Queenstown is no different." She slotted her eyes left.

She walked to the picture window overlooking the town center. She stroked her hands along the window ledge, leaning until her nose almost touched the glass.

I stood from my chair to follow her gaze. Snow-covered shops and a church steeple crowded the banks of Lake Trask. The scene looked innocent, like a Currier and Ives engraving.

The mayor said, "For years, gossip suggested I disposed of political enemies by having them dumped in the lake." A chuckle fogged the windowpane. "Ludicrous. Nonsense generated by childish minds. But the fear factor helped my career. Helped me serve Queenstown. I never denied the rumors." She tugged the cuffs of her dress, then smoothed creases over her wide hips.

Seated again, she swung on me. "But unpleasant things do happen to people who cross me."

"Unpleasant?" I tensed in my chair.

"Let me make a list for you." She pushed the legal pad toward me. "You may want to write it down, if your memory isn't as good as mine." She nudged a pen until it rolled to the edge of the desk. "Keep the paper, return the Montblanc. It was a gift from the governor."

"Stop the kidding, Jo." I liked the way her head snapped at the familiarity. "Say what you want to say."

She held up her index finger. "Your friend Mavis Jenkins has a nice business at Kings Cross Tavern. If she were to lose her liquor license, the bar would fold." She bobbed the forefinger at me. "I also understand Mavis dreams of expanding the restaurant to enclose the patio for all-season use. Maybe the city council needs to tighten those zoning restrictions, hmm?"

I sucked in breath but said nothing.

The list continued, with a second finger in the air. "Then there's your partner, Elissa Adesanya. Child of African immigrants makes good. What a heartwarming story." Her eyes drilled a spot over my shoulder. "Elissa derives a third of her business from work for the town and county. If that were to dry up, she'd have to close shop." A smile as frosting for the poisonous cake. "An attorney relies on the recommendations of satisfied clients. What would happen to poor Elissa if her clients became . . . dissatisfied?"

"You're threatening to put my friends out of business? Is that it?" My stomach galloped, spewing bile to my mouth.

"You're paying attention. Good." Her brows lowered until the glint of pupils was curtained by lashes. "Now let me continue."

I gulped and nodded.

"Keyshawn Sayre has a checkered criminal record. He hangs on to his job at Glendale because of my kindness. I'm on the board of directors, you know. Maybe his job goes poof, hmm?"

"That's ridiculous." But it didn't sound impossible. Fear seeped into the tight places in my heart. I closed my eyes for an instant so she couldn't see the dread. And I couldn't see her face.

The move didn't stop her. "Is it? Or perhaps the Q-High principal cracks down on drugs. His investigation discovers prescription opioids in the locker of Ingrid Ramírez. How do you think a drug conviction would affect her chances to transfer to the Rome School?"

I knew Ingrid wanted to apply to the prestigious private academy for her last two years of high school. How had Hannah learned about the girl's hopes?

I stood and pushed the chair with my calf. It tipped over. I jammed both fists on the desk. "You're threatening the future of a child? A girl whose only offense is seeking justice for her dead brother?"

Hannah's grin broadened. "I'm sure my colleagues on the Rome School board of trustees would hear that sob story with considerable interest."

Anxiety rustled the hairs on the back of my neck. I hissed, "This is sick." To break the tightening trap, I circled the fallen chair, fists pounding into my thighs. "You're sick."

"Calm down. Listen. Think."

I stomped to the side of her desk. "Go on."

She raised a thumb for the last point on her list. "Sam Decker is a pompous overeducated jerk. But he's a loving grandfather. I understand him. He's like me. I know family means everything to him. Blood kin or not, family is all. Same for me. Family is the world to me." She swallowed, her eyes reddening with emotion.

She swiped perspiration from her brow, lowering the veil she'd lifted. "Decker wants custody of Tommy. I can prevent that." She pointed at me, aiming her vitriol at my gut. "Understand this. I have connections in county and state child protective services agencies. One word from me and they learn Decker is a twisted pervert."

My stomach jolted. I struggled to rein the quiver in my voice. "Because I'm investigating the death of his daughter?"

"You keep digging, I'll stop him from seeing Tommy ever again." She reached a cell phone from inside the desk. "I can have QPD issue a restraining order against Decker tonight." She brandished the phone like a torch. "He'll be blocked from visiting Tommy at day care tomorrow."

"You wouldn't," I whimpered.

She clapped the phone on the desk. "Try me." Her lips stretched until I could see pink gums framing upper and lower teeth. The incisors were brighter than the dinge circling her pupils. "You mess with my family, you pay the price."

Ashes coated my tongue. What had I done to my friends? Was this investigation worth their damage?

Yes. Voices reverberated in my mind. Sam's tenor, Ingrid's soprano, blending to a single note. *Yes.* This case was worth the pain. *Yes.* I'd never heard Ivy Hannah speak. But the small firm voice tolling now was surely hers. *Yes.* Their voices propelled me. Their cause converted my dread to anger.

I lunged at Hannah, sweeping my arm through the air. "Goddamn you to hell."

She screeched and shrank into her chair, her eyes raking the ceiling, then the window.

I heard the door lock rattle. The assistant pounded the wood, yelling.

Heat rolled in my ears. I grabbed the water glass and threw it at the wall behind Hannah. The crystal crashed against the town seal, then the pitcher. Water splashed on the mayor's neck, glass shards tumbling to the carpet. Her shriek blistered the air.

The wooden door exploded; splinters flew from the frame. Two white men in suits burst into the room. I heard babbling behind them. The assistant and four women poured into the office, surging toward me. One of the suits clamped my biceps in an iron grip. Knuckles under my armpits, he lifted me until only my toes touched the carpet. I recognized the muscle man: Tidy Sutton, my groping attacker. His high school pal and fellow goon, Jake Hughes, scowled beside him. Hughes dug his fingers into my forearm.

Jo Hannah stepped toward me. I saw tendons bulge at the hinge of her jaw. She thrust her face to mine. She whispered, "Evander deserved better than you."

Weighted by her curse, I felt my stomach twist, then drop below my belt. I kicked, my boots striking air.

Like enraged hornets, the mayor's team circled. The hum swelled to a roar.

"You all right, Mayor?" The assistant's voice piped above the buzzing.

No, I wanted to shout. *Can't you see she's batshit crazy?* I lurched against my captors' fists. I slammed my boot heel into a shin.

Hughes screeched. Hopping on one foot, his grip on my arm loosened.

Sutton growled in my ear, "We warned you, Myrick." He dug his thumb into the nerve above my right elbow.

Pain shot to my wrist. I stilled, settling my boots on the rug.

Sutton relaxed the pressure. He muttered, "Good girl." He drilled for nerve again. Fire flicked my arm. "You learning?" he asked. He released, but pain still snaked under my skin.

I gritted my teeth to block the groan.

Hannah's lids skinned back over bulging eyeballs. Red wires marbled the yellow around her pupils. She leaned toward me, gargling low in her throat. "Get her out of here," she snapped.

Spittle flecked my chin. Her fury smelled like raw meat in a butcher shop.

Sutton shook me. "To the police?" He sounded eager, a war dog straining at the leash.

"No," The mayor's head swung left to right. She hacked wet from her chest. "Toss her out. The curb's good enough for this trash."

Hughes and Sutton hustled me from the fourth floor, their breaths clammy against my ears. In front of the municipal building, they found a yellow-stained snow pile between two QPD squad cars. I landed face-first.

CHAPTER **FORTY-TWO**

After the shower and shea butter, the oatmeal supper and white satin pajamas, I dropped into bed, bone tired. I rubbed both wrists until the cream's nutty aroma erased the stink of Hughes and Sutton from my mind. But not the memory of what they'd done to me. When they beat me. When they pushed my face into piss-filled snow. When they told me I was rubbish, powerless, unworthy. I'd deal with them. Their moment would come. Tomorrow, next week, next summer. I'd be ready.

I lay spread-eagle under the quilt, wanting its weight to smooth the edges of the day, the way strokes from my mother's hand pressed comfort into my back as I drifted to sleep. I breathed, my mouth damp against the quilt, hoping to catch her chamomile trace in the cloth's frayed squares.

As I often did on cold nights, I rolled Monica's sweatshirt into a chubby parcel and cuddled it in the curve of my waist. The terry cloth smelled like peaches, from the pink lotion she used on her hair. She'd been gone only an hour. Or maybe a year? So much had changed since then.

I glimpsed a flutter of wings on the rooftop beyond my window. Shadows wavered, then darted. Perhaps the owl from my backyard oak had begun her evening prowl. Like me, she hunted for clues, following veiled signs in pursuit of prey. I thought about how much had changed since I'd taken Ivy Hannah's case.

Before, my hunt was devoted to finding entertainment for a night.

Sex was a retreat; a flight to numbing pleasure. I was skilled at the game, and I enjoyed the escape. If I even learned the names of those men, I forgot them the morning after. Now I was different. I wanted real connections. I liked working with Sam Decker. I recognized my pain in his, but the anguish didn't overwhelm me. His agile humor, his take-no-bullshit attitude pushed me in a good way. Also over the past weeks, I had revived a shaky connection with my high school boy-friend, Bobby Sayre. Did that mean anything beyond annoyance and nostalgia? And there was Key. I'd uncovered a side to Keyshawn Sayre I'd never noticed before. I'd always discounted him as the troubled straggler, seen in him a portrait of underachievement. Now I found Key wasn't a bundle of unrealized potential. He displayed empathy and revealed self-examination, badges of a man in full. Maybe he'd changed. Or perhaps it was me: I'd grown up. I'd lost so much. Was I ready to risk losing again? I clenched my fingers, driving nails into the Heart line of my right palm. Not yet. Not now.

I sat, gathering knees to chest. On either side of my feet, I smoothed the furrows in the quilt. A cloud cloaked the moon, then flew on. Light seeped through the lace curtains like drops of mercury from a shattered thermometer.

I thought about my father. The ugly twists of the Hannah case made me wish for a breakthrough with him. Before, I'd abandoned the idea of ever connecting with him. We'd never be as close as I'd hoped. I was never going to be the boy he'd wanted. I'd figured Evander was lost forever to the shadows of creeping disease. Now, after the abduc-tion, I wanted to keep trying with him. We couldn't be perfect, never the Evander duo of my dreams. But we still might be something of value to each other. Maybe even make a family again. I wanted what-ever shreds of comfort I could grab from my father now.

I unrolled the worn sweatshirt and held it by the shoulders, tilting it from side to side. In the moonlight, I saw the sleeves flounce, the hem bob and ripple. Like a girl, dancing.

This case had brought me to Ingrid Ramírez. Her energy refreshed me. Her determination in the face of devastating loss inspired me. In-grid made me believe my life could be different. Not better, but new.

I'd learned more. I reached for my phone on the side table to search for the Robert Frost poem Sam had shared. As I read, the blunt syllables and simple images tumbled through my mind in Sam's voice:

> Nature's first green is gold,
> Her hardest hue to hold.
> Her early leaf's a flower;
> But only so an hour.
> Then leaf subsides to leaf.
> So Eden sank to grief,
> So dawn goes down to day.
> Nothing gold can stay.

I stretched flat under the quilt, feeling the cool pajamas slide over my legs. Sleep floated like satin across my mind, and I drifted away.

Next morning, the ten-minute drive to my office unspooled in a blur. I was fixed on phoning Sam, Key, and Ingrid to update them on my work and plan new steps. With my father safe, I squared my sights on the mayor. I wanted her punished for endangering Evander.

As I reached the intersection of Abbott and Center Streets, I slammed the brakes. A crowd jostled in front of Kings Cross Tavern. I parked at the photography studio and darted catty-corner across the street to the packed sidewalk.

The tavern's windowpane lay in bright fragments on the sidewalk. I tramped glass as I angled toward the door for a closer look. Serrated triangles jutted from the top of the frame under the awning. I pushed aside two men to gape into the dark interior.

"Mavis, you here?" I shouted into the bar. Was she inside? Had she been hurt in the assault? "Mavis?"

No one answered. I jerked the door. It was locked. Panic rising, I returned to the open window. I could see glass scattered on a table below the window. Four bricks lay in nests of shards on the floor. I saw three clear plastic baggies filled with dark mounds. Clay? Potting soil? Two baggies had torn; their soft contents spilled onto the pine boards. A gust lifted the blended odors of roasted peanuts and manure to my nose. Dung for sure. Depending on how sick these night raiders were, they'd flung either animal or human shit.

Around me, the crowd pushed closer. When a woman elbowed my ribs, I cursed until she retreated.

I glimpsed a familiar face near the bar. Leaning on the open windowsill, I yelled at the cook, "Pepe, is Mavis there?"

He wagged his head like a beaten dog. His mouth sagged. Then a stream of frost carried his words. "No, she's gone with the police to file a report."

When I stepped back, I trampled toes. I balled my fists, ready to attack. Someone needed to pay for this damage. A large hand squeezed my shoulder. The man towered over me, black eyes flashing.

"We've come to help," Satish Rajaram said. The pharmacist pointed at his wife beside him. "Nina bought boards at Home Depot."

She flashed a smile. Under her teal glove, a sheet of plywood flexed on the ground. Boards were stacked against the wall on the other side of the door. Two men positioned a ladder, ready to nail boards over the violated window.

I felt the fight impulse evaporate. "Did you see what happened?" I figured Dr. Rajaram might have spotted the culprits from his store across the street.

He raked fingers through his black hair and sucked his teeth. "No, when we arrived at eight, the damage was done."

"Did you speak with Mavis? Was she all right?"

"Yes, we talked with her for a few minutes. She was uninjured." He looked to his wife for confirmation.

Nina nodded as she rummaged in a satchel slung over her shoulder. Her hair sprang in dark waves from the hem of her pink beret. She said, "Mavis looked shocked, absolutely devastated. I asked if she needed anything. She told me, I just want to find those . . . um, those bad people." Her milky cheeks glowing, Nina chuckled. "That's not the word she used, of course."

I smirked, sister-pride warming me. No doubt Mavis wanted to catch the motherfuckers as much as I did. I thanked Satish and Nina Rajaram for their support. She hugged me, then moved toward a clutch of men. I saw her distribute hammers and boxes of nails from her canvas bag.

Watching his wife organize the work crew, Rajaram shrugged. "It's what neighbors do. Mavis would do the same for us."

I said, "You have any idea who did this?" I wanted to leap to conclusions, but collecting evidence was better.

"None. There's no trouble at the tavern." He sighed. "Mavis was elected chair of the Center Street Merchants' Association last month. First time one of us has led the group." Solidarity was sweet, even if small-scale. Rajaram made *tsk-tsk* sounds as he spread his fingers. "I know a few whites grumbled. But the tavern is a Q-Town institution. Why would anyone want to damage it?"

I remembered Mayor Hannah's threat against my friends. I figured this was the first step in her campaign of destruction. She'd struck fast, maybe to preempt my action.

"Can't answer that yet," I said. "But I'm going to find out."

"Good." Rajaram slapped his gloves together. He looked at the pewter sky. "Snow's predicted for this afternoon. We need to board up before the storm." Pulling a plywood sheet from the stack, he wrestled it toward the broken window.

I sidled toward the ladder. Maybe I'd lend a hand. Or at least offer a word of appreciation. Spare a moment to be neighborly. Act cool. Hannah was within reach. Reacting before thinking wouldn't help Mavis and might exact worse punishment for the others. I'd find the mayor soon enough. The crew sounded like woodpeckers tapping at a furious pace. Angling to avoid the ladder, I spotted a notable pair of boots on the fifth rung. That mud-daubed green alligator skin, those two-inch underslung heels. The hell.

I pounded the left boot, then craned my neck to hail its owner. "Get down here, Darryl. On the double."

Baffled at first, my one-night cowboy stepped off the ladder. Then dusty pink surged over his cheekbones as recognition struck.

I growled, "Yeah, it's me, Darryl." I grabbed the lapels of his barn jacket with both hands. Conjecture fiddled in my mind. He might know something I could use. When Darryl sputtered, I jammed my knuckles into the soft underside of his chin. "Let's talk," I said. My guess rooted into theory. Then a plan bloomed. This might work.

CHAPTER **FORTY-THREE**

I pushed Darryl backward around the corner of the tavern into the parking lot of the First Federal Bank of Queenstown. He gargled, my fist against his Adam's apple blocking speech. I shoved him into the walk-up ATM counter. He squawked when the metal ledge bumped the small of his back.

As he bent, rubbing his throat, I stepped a pace away. His eyes were closed; I fidgeted in my coat pocket, pushing record on my cell phone. Yesterday, anger made me blow my shot at recording my tête-à-tête with the mayor. I'd capture this next talk.

I couldn't see the workers nailing boards to the frame of the tavern's broken window, but I could hear their muffled orders and even a laugh as I advanced on Darryl.

"Tell me what you know about this." No questions, no explanation of my reasoning. "You tell me. Or you tell the cops. Your choice."

Darryl straightened, pushing the flop of blond hair from his eyes. "What makes you think I know something?"

"You're not here by accident," I barked. "You didn't stumble across the scene of the crime by chance and decide, out of the goodness of your little old heart, to stop and nail boards to a broken window."

He coughed and sniffed.

I continued, "You know how that window got broken and why. And you know who did it." I tapped the scruff on his chin. "You feel some kind of way about what went down. That's why you joined the hammer-and-nail crew." Impatience made me pinch his dimple. A little pain to speed our talk. He was a tough guy, he could handle the hurt. "So spill."

"It wasn't supposed to go down like it did." His voice was hoarse, with a dollop of tears.

"What was supposed to happen last night?"

"The plan was to paint the tavern door."

"Paint it?"

"Paint words . . . Um, bad words . . ."

Petering out left the blanks for me to fill in. "Like *nigger*? Those kinds of words?"

He bobbed his head. "I brought the paint. See?"

He pointed at the needle-nose of his boot. It was dotted with black splotches. I'd mistaken the paint for mud.

"We pulled in front of the tavern about four-thirty this morning. I pried open the can in the bed of the truck. Spilled some on me." He glanced at his boots, digging a toe into a rut below the ATM machine.

"What happened then?"

"They tell me, 'Forget the paint. We got better ways to tune up this uppity bitch's joint.'"

"Bricks, right?"

His blue eyes widened in wonder. "How'd you know?"

"I saw two bricks in a heap of glass inside the bar." I wanted to add, *Duh*. I felt sorry for him. He wasn't even KKK, only a wannabe follower. Almost sorry.

"Oh, yeah." Darryl squinted as he appreciated my logic. "I didn't throw 'em." His voice dwindled. "Only watched."

"And the bags of shit? That your contribution?"

His jaw fell until I could see the tongue flap against his molars. "That wasn't me." His eyes flounced east and west as he pulled more words. "Honest. I didn't do it."

"Your pals exercising their free speech rights?"

Frowns billowed across his forehead. "I don't . . . I mean . . ."

I switched gears. "What's your name? Your last name?"

Confusion—not about the name, the why—made his eyebrows sail. "Newcombe. I'm Darryl Newcombe."

"Okay, Darryl Newcombe. Here's the bonus round question. For the grand prize money: who was with you on this raid?"

"I . . . I can't say."

"Can't say? Or *won't* say?"

"I'll pay hell if I squeal. You gotta know that."

I snorted. "I know you're gonna pay for this when I run you in." I leaned, breathing into his face. "Now you have a choice, Darryl. You go it alone. Like a video game first-person shooter. All down to you. No backup."

He grimaced, then chewed his lower lip. He scraped two fingers over the stubble on his neck.

I had him. I pointed at a spot between his eyes. "Maybe your pals bring you flowers and chocolate while you cool your ass in county jail. Six months, one year. More?" I doubted he'd get that kind of time, but exaggeration was my cudgel. "Or you tell me who led this attack. If you steer me right, I'll put in a good word for you with the cops. You pay a fine, a few dollars, that's it." I whisked my hands together, easy-peasy.

His cheeks ballooned. Then he exhaled. "You can't let on I ratted. Promise me."

"I'll keep your name out of it," I lied, guilt-free.

He exhaled. "It was Ted Sutton and Jake Hughes who called me last night. They set up the gig."

No shock there. As in their high school days, the Knights of the New Round Table rode in gangs.

I said, "Sutton and Hughes. My beat-down buddies, right?"

Darryl blushed and rubbed fingers over his mouth. "I didn't know they were going to hurt you like that. I swear."

"I believe you, Darryl." *Softheaded or softhearted. Flip a coin.* I patted him on the cheek. "You got penance to pay."

His face crumpled. "Yeah, I do," he whispered.

"Here's how you start. Give me the addresses for Sutton and Hughes."

As Darryl recited, I typed the details into my cell. I asked a few more questions. He gave me good answers. Then I said, "Step two: hand me your phone."

"What for?" His jaw dropped like I'd asked him to sacrifice his first-born son.

"I trust you. You're not going to warn your good buddies, are you?"

"No, of course not. For sure." Saucer eyes. His innocence game was strong.

I turned my palm up. "Even so, eliminate the temptation. Hand over your phone."

He tugged at his jeans pocket, then dropped the Samsung Galaxy onto my glove. "I want it back."

"Absolutely." I grinned. If he'd known me better, he'd have registered the cheesy smile as faux. Too bad we weren't that close.

"You got a password, Darryl?"

His mouth pursed sweetly around "four-three-two-one." I could have guessed, but confirmation was nice.

"Good. Now get to nailing those boards." I jerked a thumb over my shoulder.

He scooted around the corner and rejoined the work brigade.

I crossed the street to my car. I was pissed. At dim Darryl and his bigot boys. At myself, too. I should have seen this coming. I should have protected Mavis. Were my other friends already on the hit list for today? Time to move on these shit-slingers. While heat spewed from the dash, I checked my phone. The recording was good. Next I tapped Darryl's cell to message his vandal partners. Hughes and Sutton got separate texts: Cops are on to us. Meet me at your house. Two pm. We need plan.

Quick thumbs-up from both thugs. Sutton added a horse-toothed smiley face.

I stowed Darryl's cell in the glove compartment. Then I used my own phone to call QPD chief Bobby Sayre.

Payback time was now.

CHAPTER **FORTY-FOUR**

I hoped the fifteen-minute ride from police headquarters to Jake Hughes's house would give Bobby Sayre time to cool down.

After all, I'd offered him a choice: go with me or I'd confront my attackers alone. Either way was fine with me. I told him what I'd learned from Darryl Newcombe. Hughes and Sutton were behind the vandalism of Kings Cross Tavern. And the same dynamic duo had assaulted me. When Bobby griped about evidence, I played him the recording of my interview with Darryl. Law or no law, I intended to deal with Jake Hughes and Tidy Sutton. Payback was overdue.

I'd hoped Bobby would see things my way. I'd even let him drive the unmarked sedan. But he was still pissed when we pulled in front of Hughes's gray-shingled house. Sweat gleamed on his bald head.

"I don't like this, Vandy." He bent to look past me to the splintered wood steps and junked fridge on the porch. "I ought to go in with you. Make it official."

I didn't want Bobby to come with me. I wanted to protect him, give him a screen of deniability. He was police. I wasn't. I could go places QPD could not. I could do shit Bobby could not. And shit needed to get done.

I said, "You'll make it official soon enough. Let me get my shot first."

"*Shot?* You packing?" He scanned my chest and lap as if he had X-ray eyes.

"I don't carry a gun. You know that." I glanced at the house to the left. Quiet and dark. Same on the right. Good. The sidewalk was empty, too. "I want him alone. Ten minutes. After that, if I don't come out, you charge in like gangbusters. Deal?"

"Deal." Mumbled into his uniform collar. He looked at his watch. "You got nine minutes."

I walked on the ice-mottled driveway beside the house. Fat snowflakes dropped on the dirt strip dividing the cement. I stepped around a mud-splattered red Dodge Ram. Humiliating memories jiggled inside me. Any of my DNA still stuck to the grooves of the truck bed? At the end of the drive was a one-car garage, covered in gray shingles to match the main house. This was the place Darryl told me to search.

I scrubbed a circle in the grimy glass of the door and looked inside. I could see a rubber garbage bin and a covered barrel. Lifting the latch, I stepped into the narrow shed. A bare bulb dangled overhead. I snatched the chain. The fixture swung, casting bars of light into the gloom. Good. I wanted Hughes to know I was here. I wanted his dread to start now.

The place looked like the set of a low-budget slasher movie: gloom, grime, and lots of blades. I saw a gas lawn mower under a tarp, two snow shovels, a handsaw, and a pickaxe. I pulled aside a rake and a push broom. Plenty of ready weapons here. Overturned flowerpots nestled against sacks of potting soil and mulch along one wall. A tricycle missing one wheel and a plastic dollhouse complete with a white family of four were stuffed into a crate. Christmas decorations filled three cardboard boxes. Moving deeper into the garage, I saw an empty wheelbarrow stationed over a pile of bricks. Hughes's contribution to the raid on the tavern. Had he donated the shit, too? A long-handled scythe leaned against the cart. Behind a bag of grass seed, I found what I was looking for.

The iron cannonball was black, its surface pockmarked with age and corrosion. I brushed aside cobwebs, then touched a finger to the relic. Flakes drifted to the floor. This was one of the cannonballs stolen from the Civil War monument guarding my old neighborhood. I knelt beside the iron sphere. Images of the marble soldier darted through my mind. I remembered how his keen eyes seemed to flicker as he defended us. I remembered how the violation of the monument stung our community. The punishment I intended to inflict now was for my injuries. And for the damage done to the tavern. But all those years ago, these fuckers had desecrated our neighborhood. This retribution was for the Flats, too. For every Black girl and Black boy who'd walked by that defiled monument year after year, wondering why they felt ashamed and powerless. Like I had.

The garage door rattled. I stood, shoving aside the wheelbarrow. I grabbed the scythe. When the hinges creaked, I stripped off the safety sheath. The crescent blade shone in the dim light.

Jake Hughes crept into the shed. He blinked, dazed. Dust swirled between us. He rubbed his eyes.

I pushed the wheelbarrow. It clattered toward his legs.

He sidestepped into my path. Into my plan.

I thrust the blade to the soft gap under his jaw. "You move, I cut out your tongue."

He burbled, eyes wheeling to find my face.

I nudged the scythe's tip to his Adam's apple. "Test me." I poked. "Go on."

He pushed palms against the air, as if to repel me. "No, no. I . . ."

"Don't talk. Listen." I prodded his flesh. "Understand?"

"Yes, yes." He flapped his hands beside his ears.

"You stole that cannonball." No need to tip my head, he knew what I meant. "Defaced town property. No statute of limitations."

He inhaled to object. Dumb move, player.

I nicked the skin under his ear. Two drops of blood danced over my blade. "Breathing is talking. Stop."

He gasped, then hummed agreement.

I inched forward, pressing harder. "You broke windows in my friend's property today. You tossed shit in the tavern. You deny it, I cut your lobe." I slid the blade to the cartilage guarding his ear. "Snip. Snip."

His eyes bulged. He wriggled his head to concede. Getting smarter by the second.

My voice rose. "A week ago, you and your pal beat me. A warning, you said. You didn't wait for my answer. Here it is."

I drew the blade along his jaw. A scarlet thread jumped on his skin. Beautiful, like fine stitchery on satin. I wanted to see blood ooze, so I pressed metal until the red line glittered.

He yelped; drool leaked into the grizzle on his chin.

My time was done. Bobby would bust up our party any minute. I lowered the scythe to Hughes's chest and shoved. "Move."

He started to turn. I barked, "Face me. Walk backwards. Let me see your eyes."

We stepped down the driveway. Backwards perp walk. Hughes stumbled twice; I tapped the blade under his chin to encourage him. After the second fall, he walked with arms outstretched for balance. A taste of shame for the vandal.

I saw Bobby jump from the sedan. When we reached the sidewalk, he jerked Hughes's wrists behind his back and slapped on handcuffs.

"You okay?" Bobby asked.

Hughes said, "No, she—"

"Shut up," Bobby said. "Jacob Hughes, you are under arrest for vandalism and assault."

When I bounced my eyebrows, he added, "You get your rights read to you at the station."

Pushing Hughes into the rear seat, Bobby said, "Sit back and enjoy the ride. This train's got one more stop."

I'd broken Jake Hughes with no fuss. Would his pal Tidy Sutton be as easy to crack?

CHAPTER **FORTY-FIVE**

Ted Sutton's house was tidy. Maybe his high school nickname had prescriptive powers. White-painted bricks covered the one-story structure, which had no raised porch, no metal awning. The dark blue door met the walk over a simple stone threshold, shiny with ice. On either side of the flagstone path, green crocus shoots poked through the snow. Boxwood hedges flanked the door, clipped to waist height.

As before, Bobby Sayre remained in the car, engine running. I had ten minutes to get the job done.

I walked to the rear of the house. I carried the handle of the scythe in two fists, balanced like a fighting staff across my body. I hoped Sutton followed the practice of most homeowners: Queenstown wasn't the Wild West or New York City overrun with dark throngs; here doors stayed unlocked until bedtime.

I stepped into the kitchen. The light was on; a teakettle strained toward the boil. Where was Sutton? I stepped over a cat's saucer, licked clean, on a rubber mat beside the refrigerator. Litter-box pong coiled with the pine-fresh scent drifting from the counters. An orange mug rested near the stove, a Lipton tea tag draped over its rim. Tidy must have left moments before I entered. The kitchen was small, a possible trap. I wanted the living room, so I chose the door to the left.

In front of the brick fireplace, I bent to inspect the two iron cannonballs Darryl said I'd find there. As with the one in Jake Hughes's garage, the black surface of these stolen mementos was flaking with corrosion. Green dust drifted to the hearth and smeared my fingertip. Three decades of anger and shame curdled in my mouth.

I heard the slap of bare feet on wood planks. I stood, my back to the fireplace.

Sutton tramped into the room, then halted. He stared at me, his amber eyes bulging. Without his sidekick and the armor of a business suit, he looked shrunken. I remembered him as a high school titan: the brawn cloaked by swagger. He'd intimidated me then. Now his bulk had melted to flab. He seemed ordinary—confused, even scared. A drop of pity for him cooled my anger. I sniffed to erase the moment. He'd stomped my gut, threatened to rape me. Pity was high school; I'd graduated from that bullshit.

Sutton wagged his head, gaze crawling over the picture window and sofa. While he searched the wallpaper stripes for answers, I paced to the center of the room.

I raised the scythe, tapping the point to his flannel shirt. He contracted his belly; I poked until I struck rib.

"What the fuck," he yelled. He slapped at the blade, then retreated toward the kitchen door. "Get the hell out of my house."

I pressed my weapon into his gut, driving until his back hit the wall. "First we talk."

"I got nothing to say to you, bitch."

"Good. You listen instead." I dragged the tool down, ripping the shirt. I could see a red stripe of blood pop below his sternum.

He howled. His fingers fumbled at the torn fabric. "You cut me, you goddamn nigger. I'm bleeding."

Heat surged up my spine. Blue flecks jumped behind my eyelids. The bastard wanted to double down on the insult. I was ready. I flipped the scythe. The wood handle pointed toward Sutton. Muscles bunched and flowed as I swung. My club laid two swats to his head. One blow smashed his left temple, that was for assaulting me. The other strike pounded his chin. That was for the shit he'd poured in the tavern.

The shocks thwacked his head into the doorframe. Eyes spinning, he slid down the wall until his ass hit the floor. Blood poured from a gash on his forehead. The chin wasn't cut, but instant swelling there said the bruise would be impressive. Good start, but I itched to do more damage.

The teapot shrieked. Sutton's knees jerked and his lower lip fell. Saliva dribbled onto the purpling lump.

"Don't budge," I said. I hustled to the kitchen, removed the squealing kettle, and swiveled the stove knob to off. I returned to study my captive. As ordered, he hadn't moved. I squelched a cackle of triumph. No time to celebrate. Not yet.

Tidy blinked when I leaned to push my knuckles against his nose. He didn't roll his head to evade my touch. His pupils widened as he focused on my mouth. Nice. He was ready to cooperate.

I crouched, my face level with his. "You said you didn't want to talk. Then you called me *nigger.*"

When I squeezed the knob on his chin, he moaned. An apology? No way. Retracting three hundred years of insults wasn't his MO. Maybe he'd plead for mercy. Waste of breath.

"I'm not asking about the cannonballs you stole." I jerked my head toward the fireplace. "That's old business. The police will sort you on that."

To give him a good look, I raised the scythe to his nose. He squirmed, belly wriggling; his hands waved like flippers. But he held his head still. Good boy.

"I want you to tell me who ordered you to trash the tavern this morning."

"I-I can't . . ." He sighed. Sweat pooled in the dent of his collarbone.

I shifted my grip on the handle. "You can. Unless you want another thrashing." My right fist slid up the pole to choke the metal collar below the blade. I pressed iron to the tip of his nose. "Do you?"

He rotated his head slowly, testing for pain. Blood poured beside his left eye. He didn't lift his hand to stanch the flow. Drops fell on his clavicle and rolled beneath his shirt.

"Your boy Hughes is a good gardener. Keeps his tools clean." Grinning, I touched my left index finger to the blade. "This edge is sharp. Bet it'll give you quite a shave." I laid the metal against his cheek. "Want me to try?"

"No. Please." A chorus of wails. His answers improved by the minute. Gave me hope for the future of our conversation.

"Start again," I said. "Who gave you orders for the hit?"

"I can't tell. My sister'll lose her job at Glendale if I tell." Whines looped around his words like snakes.

I remembered Sutton's sister, Laurette Brandt. The yoga instructor helped me build my case by tipping me to the regular visits Ivy Hannah paid to my father. Not her fault she was kin to this scum. Gratitude flickered, then died. I also recalled the connection to his boss.

"Mayor Hannah is on the board at Glendale," I said. "She'll fire Laurette if you squeal. That it?"

"Yeah," he sniffled. "Laurette can't afford to lose another job." He wiped knuckles across his left eye, painting blood into his sideburn. Red turned the yellow fur orange.

"I understand. You're in a bind. But here's how I see it. You tell me Hannah ordered the brick toss. Or you don't. Either way, I'm going after her."

I clenched my jaw. I couldn't do anything to protect his sister. She was collateral damage in this fight. I felt sorry for Laurette. But not sad enough to stop. Maybe her brother would tell her about the beatdown he'd given me, about the way he'd trashed the tavern. Perhaps Laurette would forgive him for getting her into this mess. Maybe not. My vengeance wasn't derailed by pity.

Tidy whimpered and hunched his shoulders.

My voice surged. "The mayor will blame you no matter what. Maybe she'll punish your sister. Maybe not. I don't know. I *do* know this: if you cooperate, I'll see the law goes easy on you." Simple to sound honest; I had no power to enforce the promise.

I glanced at my watch. "You got two minutes before a big Black cop busts in here thinking you hurt me. Trust and believe, you do *not* want to be on the receiving end of his fury." I winked, but no smile. "So what's it going to be, Tidy?"

He lifted his eyes toward the window. From his angle on the floor, I knew he couldn't see the sedan parked outside. Only gray branches against a snow-laden sky. But when tears brimmed on his lids, I figured he was imagining the beatdown Bobby Sayre would give him. In one minute. I was picturing it, too. Nice visuals.

"Okay, yeah," Tidy whispered. Racial reckoning was not on his wish list today. "What do you want to know?"

"Who ordered you to trash the tavern this morning?"

"Mayor Hannah."

"Did she say why?"

"No, just told me to get some of the boys and bust up the place. That's all."

"What else did she tell you to do?"

He shifted to pull a plastic baggie from the back pocket of his trousers. "She told me to wait two, three days. Then on her mark, I was to put this junk into the locker of some girl at the high school." White pills rattled when he shook the bag.

"Whose locker?"

"I don't know. Some Mexican bitch named Angela, Inger, something. It's written here." He extended his arm.

Through the plastic, I could make out the tight scratches on a slip of paper inside the baggie. Ingrid Ramírez. I'd assumed the worst, but seeing her name scrawled there snatched my breath. Reality, that nasty bitch, was poised to choke my friend.

Tidy continued, "The mayor said talk with the vice principal. Said he'd get me to the right locker. All I had to do was drop the pills in this chick's locker."

Ingrid Ramírez was the target. Prescription opioids were the weapon. Escalation in the terror campaign Mayor Hannah had threatened yesterday. She was waiting for my move. If I struck, she'd hit hard. Mavis today, Ingrid next week. On and on until I stopped.

"Anything else on your to-do list?" I gripped the scythe to contain the tremor in my fingers. My BS detector was dialed to high. If Tidy fudged the truth, I'd split his cheek.

His eyebrows pinched as he thought over the assignment. "No, the mayor didn't give me any more jobs for now. She said she'd be in touch later with more orders depending on how things turned out."

"You mean, depending on if I quit digging, right?"

Tidy's eyes bulged, but he said nothing.

I pinched his bruised chin. "You tell the mayor I'm not quitting. Not now. Not ever."

A groan ruffled his lips. He bent his brows, eyes shifting as if memorizing my message for his boss. It wasn't that complicated, but nice to see him make the effort. He plucked at the rip in his shirt, lifting it from his blood-dabbed skin.

Tidy's gaze swept the floor. With his downturned mouth, he looked sad his role as a stool pigeon had come to such an abrupt end. Like he wanted to give me more, but he couldn't push his imagination to invent jobs out of thin air. Serving as my messenger boy would have to fill the gap.

"Okay, Tidy. We're done here." My tone was soft, like a burned-out coach at the end of a losing season. "Let's go."

I helped him to his feet. Gripping an elbow, I steered him to the front door. When I opened it, a wall of cold hit our faces. He squealed, "But I need shoes. My coat."

"No, you don't." I pushed him past the storm door. Like a ballerina, he tiptoed on the icy stone threshold. As he walked the path, he made neat prints in the snow. Once he pirouetted to catch his balance. I wanted to snap a picture, a dispatch for the internet. Humiliating and viral was a thing, right? Maybe Ingrid could teach me to post on Tik-Tok. But my escort was waiting.

At the curb, Bobby leaned on the front headlight of the car. He dangled handcuffs from a beefy fist. The way Bobby's hand engulfed Sutton's skull as he shoved him into the car sent shivers along my spine. Revenge was bitter, according to my mother's life lessons. But today it tasted thrilling.

The ride to the municipal building fell quiet after I used three short phrases to outline Sutton's tavern vandalism confession. I didn't mention the plot against Ingrid, nor did I tell Bobby I'd sent a message to Mayor Hannah. If I had, he'd have told me to stand down. I was done taking orders. From him. From anybody. I'd punished Sutton and Hughes as I wanted. The surge of emotion that propelled me drained away, replaced by exhaustion. Now I was bone-tired. But the job wasn't done.

Rain mixed with snow, slapping the windshield. The boys in the back seat shrank into opposite corners like boxers at the end of round 14. Hughes was behind me, out of view. But I could see Sutton's red-faced pout when I glanced in the rearview mirror. I pressed my temple against the windowpane. The handle of the scythe rested on my knee, bumping as we rolled. My trusty blade deserved a name, something noble like Excalibur. Or Punk-Destroyer. I'd think on it tonight.

Nearing my house, Bobby asked if I wanted to be dropped off.

I wanted my bed, my quilt, and a mug of chamomile tea. Instead: "No, I need to check something at QPD evidence lockup. I'll go with you."

"You can't get in without my permission."

"Then give it to me." So what if I sounded like an eight-year-old? This was important.

"Don't push me, Vandy." His eyes raked the oncoming traffic as if he wanted to incinerate every vehicle. "We'll see when we get there."

At QPD headquarters, I went to Bobby's office while he delivered the two men for processing. I'd give my written statement before the end of the decade. Now I wanted to sort my thoughts on next steps. I knew one thing for sure: to advance my plans, I needed even more cooperation from the chief of police.

CHAPTER **FORTY-SIX**

When Bobby Sayre walked into his office an hour later, he looked ten years older. A dull cast shrouded his skin, throwing the gray flecks of his beard into high relief. He dropped in the swivel chair behind his desk and rotated to face the wall.

I crossed from the window to stand between two guest chairs before the desk. "What's going on, Bobby?"

"Jesus, Vandy. You really did a number on Sutton's head." When he swung around, his eyes were tight and hard. "I had to give the bastard two phone calls instead of the usual one to shut his squalling. Then I dealt a fistful of favors to get the intake officer to modify a description of the damage. The mug shots are bad as fuck."

I lowered my gaze to study a crystal baseball glove anchoring a stack of papers. I wasn't going to apologize. Sorry was for when we'd wrapped the case. But for my plan to work, I needed Bobby on my side. I gave him a version of the truth: "Sutton threatened me. I hit him. I didn't mean to put you in a bind."

"Well, you did." He leaned both elbows on the blotter, propping his head in his hands. "You fucked me up good."

I winced as my stomach dropped. I retreated, plowing around the conference table at the far end of the room. Returning to my spot before the desk, I sighed. My only way out was forward: "I need—we need—to get the cell phone belonging to Hector Ramírez."

"What are you talking about?"

"He had a phone in his pocket when he died. I saw it on his body in the murder room. We need that phone, Bobby."

"Why?"

"What brought Hector to the Hannah home that morning? No one has provided a solid answer to that. The prosecutor never asked. The cops never investigated." I hitched a breath. I didn't want to sound like I was accusing QPD of dereliction of duty. But I was.

Bobby squinted. He caught the implications of my reproach. "What's your theory?"

"I think Hector was invited to the Hannahs'. His friend thinks so, too." I'd detail Carlos Baca's claim later, if needed. For now, I stuck to the simplest account. "Why else would Hector drive there?"

"Maybe he was stalking Mrs. Hannah, like her husband said."

"If he's a stalker, why did Ivy let him in the house?" My words fired like buckshot. "She was no fool. If she was afraid of him, she'd have bolted the lock when he rang the doorbell."

I pulled my phone from my pocket and thumbed through the photo gallery. "Here are the two mugs I saw on the dining room table that morning. Hector was drinking coffee with Ivy. Not attacking her."

Bobby scrolled through the pictures with pursed lips. "You think Ivy called Hector? Invited him?"

I tilted my head to the right. "Or maybe Leo used Ivy's phone to send him a text." I recalled how easily I'd fooled Hughes and Sutton by using Darryl Newcombe's cell to post bogus messages.

"Hector knew Ivy. He liked her," I said. "He worked with her as a church volunteer. If he thought she was inviting him to her house, he'd have come."

Bobby set my phone on the blotter. "He was invited to his own death?"

"He'd have walked right in, big smile on his face."

"And you're saying Ivy let him in?"

"Maybe she was surprised to see him. She hadn't invited him, so an unannounced visit would have puzzled her at first. But Hector was a friend, a valued worker in her organization. She'd have brought him to the dining room, offered him a cup of coffee. Sat at the table chatting with him."

Bobby stared at me, eyes bloodshot. "In your scenario, who did Leo strike first?"

I paced in front of the desk, twisting my fingers as I roved.

"He would have separated them. Together, they might have overcome his attack. Leo needed them apart. So he called Ivy to the kitchen on some pretext."

When Bobby's brows shot up, I shrugged and rolled my eyes. "Maybe he couldn't find postage stamps. Or he needed the pediatrician's phone number. Mislaid their checkbook. Anything domestic but urgent to draw her away from Hector."

"Then he walked to the dining room, made Hector kneel, and shot him in the head?"

"Right." I swallowed bile rising in my throat.

"When Ivy heard the uproar, she ran in, and Leo clubbed her."

"That's how I figure it." I spread my fingers, palms up. "This sequence explains why Hector's body fell so far from Ivy. If Hector was hitting her, as Leo claimed, he wouldn't have fallen eight feet away."

"Then Leo phoned 911 and launched his act?"

"No, first he phoned me. I was part of the plan." Stupid launch of your private eye career, Myrick.

"To be a witness to the scene?"

"Yes. To back his story. Then he called 911. It's the only way to make sense of the evidence."

I figured the Hannahs had roped me into their plot because I was new in town, with few resources and no clout. My connections were outdated. I had scant insight into current local issues or personal dynamics. Jo Hannah pushed Leo to hire me because she thought I could be manipulated into providing cover for the murders. She believed my ignorance made me the perfect dupe. Hannah was right, as far as she went. But she'd stopped calculating before the final bell. My comeback was now.

"And you're saying QPD blew the investigation?" Bobby hissed. "That shit's hard to push at this stage."

"Hard, maybe. Impossible, no." I leaned on the desk. "You know I'm right. This makes sense. We examine Hector's phone, we find the truth."

"But you got no motive. God damn it." He banged the wood surface. The loud report made me jump. "Give me more than farts and piss, Vandy." Palm flat, empty. "What would drive Leo Hannah to kill his wife and an innocent man?"

I worried knots of hair at my nape, tugging one until it snapped. "I-I don't have the whole picture."

"Fuck. Even if I wanted to believe you, I can't." Bobby pressed fists to both temples, then drew his palms over the crown of his head. "Not without something solid."

I stared at the long fingers gripping his scalp. "Do that again, Bobby."

"What?"

"Drag your hands over your head." I made the gesture and he followed suit.

I said, "Key told me you shaved your head to hide your bald spot."

"Yeah, what of it?" He frowned and stroked his scalp like I'd insulted the bare skin. "Our dad went bald early. I didn't like the look, so I started shaving." He jutted his beard. "What you driving at?"

I slapped the desk. "I know what Ivy saw."

CHAPTER **FORTY-SEVEN**

I stepped toward Bobby Sayre, arms outstretched, fists tight. Silence wrapped his office as the weight of my words plunged between us. I knew I was right. I wanted him to feel the same certainty. Gusts batted a branch against the windowpane. We both gasped at the brusque noise.

He recovered first. "What the fuck you mean, you know what Ivy Hannah saw? When? Where?"

I scrubbed a finger across my right eye. "She saw the bald spot on her husband's head."

He sniffed. "My wife knows I have a bald spot. So what?"

"I saw it, too, the first day I met him. Leo's bald patch is unusual. Kidney shaped, like an old-fashioned swimming pool. He wears his hair scraped across the top to hide the spot. But it's distinctive."

"You think Ivy teased him about going bald?" Bobby snorted. "That's rotten, but no motive for murder."

"Ivy met another man with the same unusual balding pattern."

"Who?"

"Evander Myrick." Heat pounded my forehead. I swallowed, acid stinging my tongue.

"Shut up," he spat. "What are you thinking?"

"Ivy Hannah played a game with my father every time she visited him at Glendale. She switched baseball caps with him. She'd fix his hat on her head." I touched my cropped hair. "Then she'd set hers on his head. She studied Evander's bald patch. She recognized it was identical to Leo's."

The vertical crease between Bobby's eyes deepened. "And?"

"She made an educated guess. About male pattern baldness. Just like you inherited your bald spot from your dad, Ivy figured Leo inherited his." I dropped onto a chair, fingers gripping the armrests. This next part hurt. Hard. "She guessed Evander is Leo's biological father."

"Fuck me," Bobby muttered.

"There's more." My heart tattooed unruly thumps. Fury? Disgust? Shame? I shifted my jaw to quell the tide of nausea. "Ivy could have searched Glendale records to discover my father's full name. It's Evander Lionel Myrick." I inhaled, then swallowed. Why was this so tough to say? "Leo's name is Leonard Joseph Hannah." I smiled for the first time that afternoon. A sneer at the ugly joke. "Leonard is a variation of Lionel. Someone named Leo after his father."

Bobby muttered, "And you're going to tell me who that someone is, right?"

I remembered the family resemblances: black hair, pear-shaped figures, large eyes with thick lashes, command-and-control personalities. It fit.

"Only one candidate," I said. "Josephine Hannah."

"Not his aunt. His goddamn mother." Bobby groaned, slumping behind his desk.

I nodded. "Exactly."

I shifted in the chair. I took no triumph from the revelation. Plenty of regret. I rubbed my thumb into my hairline to tamp a headache blooming over the right temple. I remembered an explanation Leo threw at me during our row in the Robbinsville apartment building: *Aunt Jo said I ought to get to know you better. Hang with you. Like we'd become pals.* At the time I dismissed the sneer as nonsense. A stupid comment from a cornered man. Now I recognized this as his expression of bitter truth. He was my family, my brother. I wondered how long Leo had known he and I were half siblings. Did his wife tell him? Or his mother?

Bobby grabbed a ballpoint pen from a drawer. He etched a circle in the blotter, digging deeper with each cycle until he'd torn the thick paper. He poked at the rip, lifting it.

He sighed. "What do you figure Ivy did with this . . . information?" His lips curled over the last word like he hated it as much as I did.

"I think she blackmailed Leo and his mother."

"Blackmailed them for what? What did she want?"

Now I was on firmer ground. Talking about someone else's relationships instead of my newfound family ties. I'd been a single child all my life. Then, with my mother in her grave and my father draped in permanent night, I'd become a quasi-orphan. Now, without warning, these new connections were thrust upon me. The Hannahs, celebrated and feared, were yoked to me by blood. My almost family. I figured the Hannahs didn't want me. I knew I didn't want them.

I leaned forward, eager to share my conclusions about Ivy with Bobby. "Ivy knew Leo was cheating on her with one of her girlfriends. She wanted three things: a divorce; a big alimony settlement; and full custody of their son."

"Why not give Ivy what she wanted? Why resort to murder?"

"The Hannahs are all about control." I went nasty to drive my point. "You know that better than I do."

Bobby had shared with me his interactions with Mayor Hannah. He'd let me see the shame he carried because of his failure to curb her corruption. Now I wielded those revelations like a club. I felt bad, but I needed him to follow my logic.

Bobby's shoulders stiffened to halt the cringe. He wagged his head. "No lie there."

I plowed on. "Leo refused to give up his son. He wanted freedom from Ivy. But only on conditions he set. He wouldn't permit a despised wife to dictate terms to him."

"And Mayor Hannah, what did she want?"

"She has one big goal: protect her family. To do that, she wanted three things. Hide her adulterous affair with Evander. Keep her illegitimate child secret. And assist her son with his double life."

Bobby sighed, then scrubbed his eyebrows. "Of course. Leo's passing," He glared at me as if this minstrel show were my fault. "And the mayor wants to help him do it."

No need for a Black cop and a Black PI to rehearse the lifetime of advantages Leo had gained by passing as white. I hiked my shoulders and raised both palms to the ceiling. *Light, bright, sure looked right.* The boy profited from white privilege; what're you going to do? We couldn't end racism in America this round. Maybe next week.

I said, "Exactly. Jo knew as long as Ivy breathed, the blackmail cloud would never disappear." Perspiration slipped down my spine. I rubbed my lower lip to quell the nausea. "Even if Ivy got everything she wanted in the divorce settlement, she still posed an existential threat to the Hannahs."

"Ivy could fuck their lives anytime she chose."

"Right," I said. "The only way to end the danger was to kill her."

"But why murder Hector Ramírez? He knew nothing, posed no threat of any kind. Why did he have to die?" Bobby clenched both fists like barrels. A drop of sweat trickled beside his ear.

I stiff-armed from the desk. My chair tottered on two legs. I set it on the carpet with a thunk.

"Leo and the mayor wanted to get away with murder," I said. "They needed a fall guy. Hector was perfect. He was an immigrant, an outsider with brown skin and a dodgy employment history. That's three strikes against him in Q-Town. Horrific violence like that, everybody would buy the Latino guy did it."

Bobby groaned. "And killing Hector guaranteed he couldn't defend himself."

"The Hannahs didn't reckon with his sister, Ingrid," I said. "Or Ivy's father."

"Or you." Sweat popped on Bobby's nose. After a moment, I saw his eyes ignite as lines around his mouth eased. He barked, "Let's go."

"Where?"

"You want Hector's cell phone. It's in the evidence lockup downstairs. Let's get it."

He slammed the chair against the wall, crossed the room in three strides, and grabbed his uniform jacket from the hook behind the door.

Hand gripping the doorframe, Bobby looked at me. "I'm gonna do my job. Like I should've done years ago." Breath harsh, eyes glittering. "I'm gonna nail these sonsabitches."

Before I could jump from my seat, he disappeared into the hall.

I slung my coat over my shoulders and raced after Bobby. He trotted to the elevator, elbows wide. The corridor was crowded. Junior officers flattened against the wall as he bowled past. When I chugged to his side, he was punching the down button like it was Leo Hannah's face.

CHAPTER **FORTY-EIGHT**

The QPD evidence lockup packed half the basement of the four-story municipal building.

A floor-to-ceiling wire screen caged the area from the hall. A hinged door on the right controlled access through the screen. Inside the cage, the clerk's desk sat at the head of a row of metal shelves. Eight such rows extended the length of the room. Next to the door was a chest-high opening in the screen. Through this wood-framed window, the evidence clerk received deposits and fielded requests.

When we hit the basement, Bobby Sayre burst from the elevator, shouting. "Richards, get me the box on the Hannah case." He pushed his chest against the wood ledge and raised the decibel level. "Everything you got."

The uniformed officer sprang from his desk, overturning the metal chair. Instead of righting the seat, Richards, cherry-cheeked and grinning, disappeared down the fifth row of shelves.

I pressed close to Bobby's right shoulder, breathing hard. I flapped the open lapels of my coat to cool down. If we found Hector's phone, we'd be closer to wrapping this case. If it was gone, we'd stumble. Not the end of the investigation. But its direction hinged on what we'd find in this dusty cavern.

The clerk hustled into view a minute later, lugging a large carton. "Here you go, Chief." He plunked the container on the ledge and stepped back as if it contained dynamite. Maybe it did. I leaned forward, rubbing my nose to stifle a sneeze.

After checking the label, Bobby fiddled through the cardboard box. Eyes narrow, fingernails scrabbling over plastic and paper, Bobby looked like an adventurer prying open a treasure chest. Genie's lamp or JLo-size gem? Ancient scroll or Nazi-frying device? All I wanted was the freaking cell phone. I glimpsed transparent sacks filled with clothing and shoes. I saw the two coffee mugs, one still stained with Ivy Hannah's pink lipstick. Pens, greeting cards, spoons, toy trucks, napkins. Even the hammer, splotched with dried blood and hair. These horrific souvenirs forced images of the Hannah house death room through my mind.

Bobby bellowed, "Where's the damn phone, Sergeant?"

I cringed, swallowing disappointment. Was I wrong? Had we been close? Or was this rollercoaster ride doomed to take another swerve?

"I think it's not there?" Richards lifted his voice. He rubbed the spikes of his brown crew cut. His eyes searched the elevator door beyond our heads. Maybe he hoped replying with a question would get him off the hook. Wrong.

"Who's been in this box?" Bobby poked the air in front of the clerk's nose. "Show me the intake chart."

I knew each transaction was recorded. Every time someone added, removed, or examined items in an evidence file, the action was logged, either on paper or on the computer. I hoped for Richards's sake his catalogue was accurate and up-to-date.

"Sure thing, Chief." The officer brought a laptop to the counter and pried it open. After a few finger flicks, he rotated the computer to let Bobby inspect the database for the Hannah evidence box.

"This record shows no one touched this box since January 31." Bobby's voice sounded warm, like he was soothing a colicky infant. "Is that right, Sergeant?"

From memories of our high school fling, I recognized Bobby's tone. Slow and gravelly meant danger. A plunge to ice signaled Code Red.

"Pretty much . . . yeah, it's accurate." Richards brought his thumbnail to his teeth for a good gnaw.

"I'm going to ask again," Bobby said. Low, clear, and cold like the moon setting over Lake Trask. "And if you lie again, Richards, you're off the force. Understand?"

Anxiety gripped my gut, and I wasn't even under fire. Bobby wanted the cell phone as much as I did. Gratitude rushed over me. I was lucky to have this man on my side, believing in me at last.

Bobby glared at his subordinate. "Did anyone get into this box since January?"

Dark crescents wet the armpits of his uniform blouse as Richards reevaluated his career options. "Yeah, okay. Someone did come by asking for that file."

"Who?"

"Mayor Hannah." The sergeant swiped the back of his hand across his mouth as if to smother the name.

"When?"

A whimper: "This afternoon."

"Did the mayor remove anything from the box?"

Richards grimaced, upper lip stretched over dry gums. "She told me not to say."

"And I'm ordering you to answer me," Bobby snapped. "What did she take?"

"An evidence bag with a cell phone."

"That all?"

"Yes, sir. That's all she took." Richards grinned, cheeks flaming. I saw his chest sink over a sigh, as if he'd completed a tough math problem. He thought he'd salvaged his career. From the grimace twisting Bobby's mouth, I wasn't so sure.

I asked, "When was she here?" I figured Tidy Sutton had used one of his phone calls to warn the boss. And convey my message. Now she knew I wasn't quitting. I'd pushed her over the edge.

The sergeant blinked in my direction. I wasn't sure he'd registered my presence until that moment. Black woman dealing questions like a boss? No way. Double Black authority figures was a bridge too far. Richards's lower lip flopped in a pout. He shook his head, rejecting my request, my uppity existence. Would we be stymied by this micro-bigot?

"Answer her," Bobby said. The dismissal threat loomed.

Richards looked at his Timex, whimpering, "They left here twenty-five minutes ago."

"Who's *they?*" I knew, but I wanted confirmation.

"The mayor was with Mr. Hannah."

"God damn it to hell." Bobby banged the counter. The laptop jumped, then fell to the floor. Our hopes crashed with it. Every minute Richards yakked gave the Hannahs another minute to escape.

Bobby ran to the elevator. I tore after him.

Punching the up button, Bobby looked over his shoulder at the clerk. "If this goes south, Richards, I'm coming for your shield."

Bobby only wanted to fire the fool. I wanted to kill him.

When we barged into the mayor's fourth-floor office suite, the assistants snapped their mouths shut as if they'd choreographed the stunt. One woman flipped a sheet of paper, but the rest froze as Bobby advanced into the room.

He stopped at the desk of the top assistant, who delivered his feline smirk, languid gaze sweeping from me to Bobby. "Chief Sayre, so nice to see you today. How can I help you?"

"Is Mayor Hannah here?" Bobby said.

"Why, no. I'm afraid she's gone for the day." Gooey, sweet tones.

"Where'd she go?" Bobby's voice was deep-freeze stiff.

"I'm afraid I couldn't say." Cat eyes crept toward the window, narrowing as they traveled. *Afraid* was the operative word. Something was outside, something he hoped we'd miss.

From my position, I could see aluminum sky. I wanted to know what the assistant feared I'd find. I stepped to the window and looked down. The parking lot encircling the building was half empty. At five forty-five, most civil servants had left for home.

In a reserved space near the main entrance, I spotted a familiar vehicle, Josephine Hannah's navy blue Lexus. I saw the mayor slip behind the wheel. The car backed from the row. As it pulled into the Y-turn, I caught Leo Hannah's profile in the passenger side window.

"She's running, Bobby," I shouted. "Let's go."

We had a shot, slim but real, to catch the Hannahs. At the building entrance, we split in hopes of boosting our chances. Bobby ran to the mayor's parking space. I retrieved the Jeep from the visitors' lot. When

I arrived to collect him, Bobby sighed, his eyes raking the pavement in despair.

"Any idea which direction she went?" I asked. Giving up was not on my card. Not yet.

He shook his head. "No. When I got here, they were gone." He flopped beside me and slammed the side door. "We should try her house." He rattled the address from memory.

"She'll want to destroy the cell phone," I said. "She knows it's valuable. That's why she took it."

Bobby shivered. He wore his uniform jacket, no overcoat. "She might throw it in the municipal dump. Or the lake."

"Maybe the creek beside the high school," I said. I reached for a blanket crumpled on the floor behind my seat. This was the blanket my father wrapped over his shoulders when we rescued him three nights ago. "Take this."

I thought Bobby might pull a macho stunt and refuse the cover. Instead he draped the blanket over his chest and buckled the seat belt on top.

"Those motherfuckers are going to get away with this, aren't they?" he mumbled.

I squeezed his forearm. "No, we'll figure it out." I sounded more confident than I felt. I couldn't bear to have Bobby fade on me. Not now that we were moving as a united force. I shifted gears.

My phone rang. I braked. "This better be important," I snapped at the cell's slick face.

"Vandy, it's me," Keyshawn screeched.

My head swimming, I poked the speaker button so his brother could hear. I said, "What's up, Key?"

"They took your father. I would have stopped it. I didn't know. I didn't see it. I would have stopped them." His babble tottered on the edge of incoherence. "It's my fault. I'm sorry."

Bobby yelled, "Key, stop." When the phone went dead, he resumed, "Start. Making. Sense."

I heard Keyshawn inhale. Gathering his emotions, struggling for control. Just as I was. His next words came slow, as ordered. "Fifteen minutes ago. I went to Evander's room. He wasn't there. I asked at the front desk. They said he'd gone for a ride. I asked who took him. They said Mayor Hannah."

"Jesus Christ," Bobby moaned.

I was incensed. This was violation, pure and simple. I asked, "Did anyone hear where they were going? See which direction they headed?"

"No," Keyshawn whimpered. "Nobody saw nothing. Heard nothing." He paused. "Except."

"Except what?" I wanted to rip the words from his mouth. But I kept my voice steady. "What did you hear?"

"Laurette the yoga lady said something funny."

Bobby's eyes bugged in exasperation. He tightened his fists on the seat belt.

I held my breath until fake calm cooled my question: "What was funny?" Was Tidy Sutton's little sister Laurette going to provide another valuable assist? I didn't have time now. Maybe next year I'd laugh at the irony.

Keyshawn replied, "She said she saw the mayor with Evander. They were walking through the lobby, arm in arm. She heard the mayor say to Evander, 'We're going to a family reunion.'"

Bobby exploded. "What the fuck does that mean?"

"I don't know, man. All's I got is what she said." Tears dripped through Keyshawn's words.

I tested my voice around a gulp. "That's good, Key. Real good. Thank you."

"You gonna find him, Vandy?" I heard agony in my friend's voice.

"I hope so." I shook my head at Bobby, who closed his eyes. "I'm going to try."

I stabbed the phone shut and dropped it into the cup holder.

"What's that fucked-up shit about some family reunion?" Bobby's nose reddened. When he sniffed, his eyes watered. I didn't want him crying, not now. Not when my gut was grinding with a new round of grief. To save us both, I grabbed for the nearest notion.

"I have an idea," I said. "I know where they're headed." Just an inkling, not big enough to be called a clue. But I was desperate. I shot anyway: "To Robbinsville."

He huffed. "What's in Robbinsville?"

I jerked the gearshift into drive. "The Blue Bird Day Care Center. They're going to get Tommy Hannah."

I had to be right. Right?

CHAPTER **FORTY-NINE**

We crossed Queenstown dodging through light traffic on side streets. If my hunch was right, the Hannahs were only fifteen minutes ahead on the road to Robbinsville.

But at Fells Creek Trail, the turn into Route 130 jammed us. The southbound side was a frozen river of red taillights.

Bobby voiced our only hope. "They're caught in this mess, too." He squinted against the low-angled sun.

"If I'm wrong . . ."

"You're not," Bobby said.

"If they're headed somewhere else, we'll never catch them."

He pressed his phone to his ear. "I'll issue an APB for the mayor's car." He dialed headquarters and gave the order. When he hung up, he said, "We'll have eight squad cars on the streets in three minutes."

I sighed and raised my hand to block the sunset glare. This little fleet of Queenstown police vehicles wasn't enough to corral a determined runner. On the other side of the highway, northbound traffic flowed smoothly. If they were headed that way, the Hannahs could be thirty miles up the road in New Brunswick before we reached Robbinsville to discover our error.

But would Leo Hannah consent to flee without his son? I gambled he'd push his mother to collect Tommy for the flight from Queenstown. The boy was her family. I figured whatever Jo Hannah was planning, she'd want to include her grandson.

If I was wrong, we all lost. If the Hannahs disappeared, there'd be no resolution for Ingrid Ramírez; her brother would forever be labeled a killer. Or for Sam Decker, whose daughter's death would never be explained. If the child vanished, Sam would never be able to claim custody of his grandson. I wanted to capture Jo and Leo Hannah for my clients, Sam and Ingrid. For Ivy, I wanted the cell phone which could prove how she died.

Our parade of cars inched past an auto body shop, a Liberty gas station, and the abandoned Molly Pitcher Diner. I knew the lineup by heart: after the puppy mill and two long-haul trucker motels, we'd hit the Sweetheart Chocolate factory. When the creamy fumes of milk and cocoa wafted through our air filter, we'd be halfway to Robbinsville.

Pain rumbled between my eyes. I squeezed the bridge of my nose.

I said, "Call the Blue Bird Day Care Center. Tell them to hold Tommy Hannah. Even if his father insists, they must not let Tommy leave."

Bobby thumbed through websites until he found the phone number for Blue Bird's Robbinsville facility. He put the call on speaker.

"This is Chief Robert Sayre of the Queenstown Police Department. Who am I speaking to?"

"Ann Varney, sir."

"Ann, I need to speak to your director. It's urgent."

"She's in a meeting with a parent. Can I take a message?"

"No. Interrupt the meeting. Right now. This is police business."

"Hold on, please. I'll see if she's available."

Bobby exhaled, staring at the cell. Red forked the whites of his eyes. He'd have jumped through the phone to choke Ann if he could. Lucky for her we were stuck six miles and twenty minutes away.

A new female voice broke over the line. "Chief Sayre, this is Felicity Brent. How may I help you?"

"You have a boy, Tommy Hannah, enrolled there, right?"

"Yes, he's one of our students."

"Good. Keep him."

"What do you mean? *Keep* him?"

"Don't let him leave the premises. Under no circumstances, understand?"

"Tommy's already gone home for the day. He left about . . ." I heard her mumble to an associate.

Bobby's forehead shone with sweat. He brushed the beads across his scalp. I thought he'd explode before the director returned to the phone.

Felicity Brent said, "I'm told Tommy left with his father ten minutes ago."

"What do you mean?"

"I mean what I said: Mr. Hannah picked up his son ten minutes ago. I'm looking at his signature on the sign-out form. He was late. Thirty-five minutes past our mandatory pickup time. So Mr. Hannah had to sign the checkout register and the late-penalty agreement. He'll have to pay a fine. We charge twenty-five dollars for every half hour beyond the designated pickup time. That penalty may seem excessive, but it's the only way we . . ."

Her bureaucratic blather cranked into overdrive as Bobby punched off the phone.

"God damn it to hell." Bobby dropped his cell next to mine in the cup holder. "Where to now?"

"I'm guessing south," I said. A fast drive beyond the Jersey border would test cooperation between jurisdictions. Hannah could play any bureaucratic tangles to her advantage.

"You think they're headed to Philly?"

"Or further. Maybe Wilmington. Even D.C."

Bobby's phone buzzed. The report from his deputy delivered the obvious: the blue Lexus hadn't been sighted in Queenstown. Bobby thanked the woman and signed off.

We chugged toward Dinah's Diner, a blue-and-yellow landmark on the border of Robbinsville. The road eased to the right, straight into the sun.

I slowed as white flashes shot from the bumper in front. I tipped my head to escape the glare. A blur oozed by on the left. Was that car blue? I pumped the brake and turned to look. Navy Lexus speeding north. Jo Hannah bent over the wheel. I saw my father's face in the rear window.

"There," I shouted. "Other side. Look!" I jerked a thumb at my window.

Bobby twisted under the blanket. "Yeah! That's her." He pointed ahead. "Take the U-turn at the jug handle. Next block on the right, past the diner."

I glanced at the northbound lane. Hannah had disappeared. Delay was not my game. I wanted the shortcut.

I edged the Jeep forward. I wrenched the steering wheel until its nose angled into the lane on my left. A Nissan honked but braked. I saluted thanks, then darted in front. I rolled one car length. The cement curb of the median strip was cracked, a chunk missing. I drove for the gap. If this was snow, I'd vault the curb. If ice, I'd skid into the Nissan.

I stomped the pedal and charged. The snow mound caved. We bowled onto the embankment. Relief pounded my chest. Maybe we'd caught some luck at last.

I drove north on the median strip. For two blocks, cars on both sides honked and flashed headlights. Without the setting sun in my eyes, my headache pain lifted. I saw muscles on Bobby's jaw flex as we bumped over bare spots and ice chunks. He craned to spot an opening in the traffic stream. When we drew parallel to a Conoco gas station, he raised a hand, then chopped it forward. Yes, my time, my luck. I shot the Jeep into the gap.

Northbound traffic to Queenstown flowed like ribbon slipping from a gift box. But the Hannahs' car had vanished.

"Call her," I said. "You've got her private number. Get her talking."

"You think she'll turn herself in?"

"Surrender? No. She's wild now. Desperate. Determined to destroy everything. Her whole family." My family, too. The remnants of my world. The last ones who'd known me or owned me, loved me or hated me, were in that car. They were mine. I wanted to catch them.

I stuttered the next words. "But she might slow. G-give your team a chance to catch her." We were ten miles above the speed limit. I added five more. Teeth clenched, I barked, "Do it. Call her."

Eyes bulging at my fervor, he said, "Yeah, it's worth a try."

Bobby alerted his deputy to Jo Hannah's approach to the outskirts of Q-Town. Then he pulled a new phone from the breast pocket of his shirt. "My private cell. She'll pick up if I call from this number."

Hannah answered on the first ring. Breezy, she chirped, "Hey, Bobby, can't talk now. Catch you later."

"Jo, I need to see you now. Where are you?" He punched the speaker button, turning the phone away from the window to reduce traffic noise.

"It can wait until tomorrow." Cheery, like she was on a picnic.

"No. It can't," Bobby gritted.

I glanced at Bobby. His lower lids quivered. Then the eyes went cold. "Jo, I need you to pull over now. Let Evander, Leo, and the boy out of the car."

I heard her gasp. "How do you . . . Where are you . . . ?"

No safe answer to that. Bobby was talking to a speeding time bomb. He switched subjects. "I know you don't want to hurt anybody, Jo. Let them walk away. Then you and I can talk."

I heard murmurs behind her; Leo was speaking. His garble cranked higher, pleading.

Then a new voice boomed, "Hannah." My father. Maybe he knew who she was and what was happening. Did he want to stop her?

I heard Tommy's squeak burst into giggles. Two voices—father and grandmother—rose to shush the child. I swallowed, then glanced at Bobby. His mouth gaped in horror as he stared at the cell.

Jo Hannah spoke through the phone. "Bobby, you don't understand. You don't know the story."

"Explain it to me."

"Is she with you?"

"Who?"

"Evander's girl." I could hear the sneer through the distance.

Bobby raised his eyebrows at me.

I nodded. If she wanted to hurt me, let her take the shot. Anything to slow her escape.

He hissed, "Yes, she's here."

"I want her to know, too," Jo purred.

"I hear you." I squeezed the wheel, bracing for whatever story she wanted to deal. What could be worse than the sordid tale I'd already uncovered?

"Good."

Leo gibbered, a groan, more wails.

Jo yelled at her son: "Shut up. This gets said. You listen. Maybe you'll learn something, even if it's too late now."

Bobby soothed her rant. "We're all listening, Jo. Tell us."

She pitched her voice high, as if reciting a bedtime fairy tale to a restless child: "At the start, I was good at auditing. Mid-level, but I made the financials sing. Big firms offered me jobs. Boston, Hartford. But I loved Queenstown. I wanted to stay. I wanted to do good here."

She hacked. I heard the hum as her window lowered. She cursed at a passing car. As the pane rose, I heard wind whistle. I strained to catch a clue to her location, but the chance evaporated.

Jo continued. "When I met Evander, he was married with a three-year-old daughter." She chuckled. "I was happy to find someone who couldn't marry me. I was ambitious. I didn't want the chains." She snickered. "But I liked the sex. Oh, we had some good old times, Evander and me."

She screeched, "You hear that, Vandy?"

"Yeah, I heard you." I bit my lip. Pain stopped tears from falling. Bobby glanced at me. I stared through the windshield. The Jeep hit a pothole. I wrenched the wheel to control the shudder.

Jo said, "When we first got together, I lived in an apartment. A rabbit hutch with gossiping neighbors on every side. So we would meet at the shed near the old water tower. Not swanky, but clean and private. Then I bought my own house and we had the safety we wanted."

Her voice shriveled to a whisper. "When I took him to our shed this week, I thought he might remember. Me. Us. Something. But he didn't. Nothing . . ."

Bobby groaned. He lifted the phone until his mouth brushed its surface. "Jo, you don't have to do this."

She yelled: "You mean, shut up? Is that what you want, Bobby? Trying to protect Evander's little girl, are you?"

"I just want you safe, Jo," he said.

"Liar," she snapped. Then her voice cooled around a new taunt. "I knew all about you from the start, Vandy. You and your mother were the limits on our fun."

I coughed, spittle dotting the steering wheel. "Yeah, I get that." I cut my answer to disguise the sickness welling in me. Her legend left me heartsore, history-shorn.

Jo continued, "Pregnancy wasn't part of the plan. But it happened. You lucked out, Leo. I could have had an abortion." Short barks. Was she laughing?

I looked at Bobby. He touched his temple to the side pane and closed his eyes. His breath fogged the glass.

"But my hippie sister offered, and I accepted. I had the baby in Maine and left him with her. When he was older, I got him into the Rome School and paid for the whole preppy ride. Sweet deal, right, Leo?"

I broke into the silence. "Did Evander know?"

I wanted to learn the truth, the reality my father had buried for decades.

"About Leo?" She cackled down the line. "You decide. You're the private eye, chew on this: while you were at college, Evander attended all Leo's lacrosse and wrestling matches. And every track meet. Do some detecting with that, Detective."

The wheel spun under my fingers. I wiped the left palm on my jeans.

I remembered my mother's warning decades ago: *Trust is like sponge cake, sweet but squishy. You craving that sugar, but the foundation goes soft when you step.* Alma knew, I felt it now. All those years. She knew about the adultery. The second family. She figured out the identity of her husband's only son. All those years, she didn't trust me with the truth. Waiting, watching, perhaps hating. Until the facts gnawed her from the inside out. My heart revved as sweat pooled at the base of my spine. Evander wasn't the father I'd imagined. The man I'd longed for all these years. I knew that now. But he was still my one. The father I wanted.

Foul breath caught in my throat. I hacked, then pumped the brake. The Jeep swerved across the lane, control slithering through my fingers.

Bobby grabbed the dashboard, eyes on my face. I'd scared him. When I righted the car, he returned to present troubles. "Let them out, Jo. They haven't hurt you. Let them go."

"Stay out of this, Bobby. My call, not yours." Her voice dropped to a rumble. "I got hurt, all right. Ivy tried to *destroy* me. Stuck-up blond bitch. I couldn't let that happen. Not to me."

We neared the Walmart exit on the edge of Queenstown. Bile burned my tongue. I veered toward the broad parking lot. As we pulled to a lamppost near the garden department, my stomach plunged. I opened the car door. With one foot on the brake, I vomited onto the pavement.

Bobby gripped the steering wheel. I heard him jerk the stick from drive to park.

I righted myself and wiped a sleeve over my mouth. Eyes damp, I nodded at him, I eased the door shut.

Bobby rumbled into the phone, "Come to my house, Jo. Let's talk there." Soft, an easy swing to the phrases. Like he was enticing a friend, not distracting a lunatic. "We'll fix tea. Sip a little bourbon."

"Don't try to handle me, Bobby."

"I want to see you, Jo. Let's talk."

"Nice try, Chief. No deal." She hooted. "I've got to wash away this mess." Another laugh. The same wild cackle I'd heard in her office. "Catch you on the other side."

The mayor hung up. Nausea surged a bitter wave in my throat. Could I find her before she destroyed her family and mine?

CHAPTER **FIFTY**

My head swam. On the Walmart parking lot asphalt, yellow lines shimmied under a gauze of snow. I closed my eyes to stop the whirl-igig. "Bobby, take the wheel."

Unsteady, unsafe. I stumbled from the Jeep. We switched positions for the race toward Queenstown center. Night dropped as we steered past an abandoned hardware store and Bethel Cemetery's city of tombs.

"She can't be far," he said. "Where do you figure she's going?"

Slumped against the side window, I squeezed my eyes to block the dazzle of oncoming traffic. "She wants to destroy Hector's cell phone. She said she'd 'wash away this mess.' Maybe she's headed to Lake Trask."

"Good call."

Bobby's approval, tiny as it was, calmed my stomach. The churning stopped. My head cleared and I could watch the cars again. We had a chance. That's what I heard in his voice; that's what I wanted to believe.

After five minutes of speeding, we pulled to the intersection of Abbott and Center Streets, facing Kings Cross Tavern. Traffic was sparse. We were too early for dinner congestion and too late for the rush-hour bottleneck. Not good. A traffic jam might have slowed Jo Hannah's flight. How far had she sped before we reached this intersection? Was the lake still her target? Maybe I was wrong about her direction. She could be halfway to New Fucking Brunswick by now.

I pointed at an inlet beyond the tavern. We were here, we might as well try. "Circle to the library. We can see the whole north shore of the lake from there."

Bobby turned left, guiding the Jeep over a stone bridge to the parking lot fronting the squat building. Lights from the main reading room painted our faces orange as we jumped from the car. We ran to a bench overlooking the lake. The water was black, but snow on the banks glittered like a festival in the moonlight.

"Do you see her?" Bobby asked. His words pelted between breaths as he swung his head.

Stomach jumping, I shook my head. He couldn't see my movement, so I said, "Nothing. I was wrong."

We trudged to the car, defeated. Sick crawled up my throat. I paused at the cement drinking fountain that anchored a small plaza in front of the library. Could I get a drop of water to clean my sour mouth? An icicle hung from the spigot. I poked the frozen spear until it dropped into the basin. No water. Disgusted, I spat into the bowl. I touched the icicle again. Slick, jagged, wet. Could this be the answer? Yes, I needed this break.

"The water tower," I shouted. "That's where she's gone!"

I raced for the Jeep and slid behind the wheel. As I careened into a U-turn, Bobby slammed the door shut. He called for backup as we rolled.

When we gained the avenue leading to the water tank, I saw red light streaming from a dark sedan ahead. The fleeing car sped over squares of light from houses bordering the street. Was it Hannah's Lexus? I jammed the accelerator. Forty, forty-five. The sedan leaped, increasing the distance between us.

Bobby pounded a fist to the dashboard. "It's her!"

Gleaming asphalt stretched four blocks to the water tower's chain link fence. The car gobbled pavement as it surged forward. Was she accelerating to beat my pace? I hit an ice patch; the Jeep sideswiped a parked station wagon. Bobby tilted. I wrestled to correct the swerve. As we righted, the Lexus dashed through the opening in the fence.

I heard her engine clench, then churn. Wheels spit gravel as the car accelerated. With no words for the unfolding horror, I screamed, my throat raw.

Hannah drove straight at the west leg of the water tower. No slip, no brake, no waver. The madwoman's trajectory was true. I saw the pillar vibrate with the impact. The car's bumper hugged the metal pole. Above the hood, the leg folded like a paper straw. Twelve feet in the air, a dark crease dented the pole's blue paint.

I pumped the brakes four times, steering the Jeep into the fence a hundred yards from the tower. Bobby and I ran to the crumpled Lexus. I wanted to save as many as we could. Even if Hannah intended to kill them all. We circled left to the rear door behind the driver's seat.

My father was inside, banging on the window. Bobby picked up a concrete chunk and jabbed the glass with its pointed edge. On the second blow, the window fractured. I elbowed the glass until it collapsed. Reaching inside, I jerked the handle, opened the door. Oven-hot air poured onto my face. The gust smelled of fear and shit and blood. Evander struggled to swing his feet, carrying the child under his right arm like a football. I pulled him upright. My voice was weak. "You're safe, Daddy. Run." Could he hear me? The blank planes of his face told me nothing. I reached to touch his shoulder, to shake him, but he turned away.

Without a word, my father strode from the car, Tommy's head bouncing against his stomach. Bobby ran to Evander's side. Halfway to the fence, I saw him take the boy from my father. My family was safe. What about the others?

When I turned back to the Lexus, the driver's door was ajar. I saw Jo Hannah limp under the water tower. I called to her. She moved with jerks and hitches, arms flailing, head lolling. "No," I screamed. She couldn't get away. Not after all this. "No." Metal groans drowned my shouts.

Reaching the north leg, Hannah grabbed the guardrail of a ladder, her face raised toward the flat belly of the tank. As she climbed, I saw her jaw work. She was yelling at each rung. She stopped to press her face between steps, mouth gaping as she shouted. A hundred feet in the air, she crawled through a hole in the scaffolding that girdled the reservoir. I watched her pace along the platform. She trailed one hand on the giant barrel. As if awakened, the tank shook. Near my face, steam spewed from rents in the car hood. Oily smoke smeared my nose. I heard a rumble as the stricken pole tilted, ripping its base from the soil. It balanced like an uprooted tree. I ran toward the passenger side door. Had Leo Hannah joined the others at the fence? Was he trapped inside?

As I bolted around the trunk, the car screeched, then bucked. The door hung on one hinge. I pried it open.

I saw Leo flat on the seat, faceup, his legs hidden.

He gasped, gore filling his mouth. "Help me."

Debris from the busted air bag stuck to his face. On his neck, silver fragments glittered like reptile scales. This man, my brother, trapped by twisted metal. I lowered my face to meet his eyes.

He lifted his hand to grip mine. His fingers were cold. Where we touched, blood slimed our skin.

Leo killed, he maimed, he wrecked. But I still wanted to save him. My father's son, my family. I tugged. The car moved; he didn't. Through the cracked windshield, I saw a gap in the hood. The engine block had disappeared. Impact rammed the engine into the cab of the car. Leo's pelvis and legs were pinned under the twisted metal.

"Help me." His breaths sputtered, soft and shallow.

Smoothing hair from his eyes, I shook my head. I wanted to say I was sorry. Sorry I couldn't save him. Sorry I never knew him. Sorry we never had the chance to find each other as children of Evander Myrick.

He arched his back. I thought he was heaving his crushed legs. But when he rolled his eyes toward the rear seat, I knew his mind was elsewhere.

"Tommy," he groaned.

"He's all right, Leo. He's safe." I could say that much, offer that drop of comfort.

I stroked his head. He whispered. I couldn't make out the words. I pressed my cheek to his damp face. He repeated the mumble, then patted his heart. I thought he was thanking me. Even though I couldn't save him, he was grateful. My eyes blurred at the unexpected gesture.

But then he pulled a plastic bag from the inner pocket of his coat. He pressed Hector Ramírez's cell phone into my hand. Gasping, I leaned to kiss Leo's cheek. I swiped my eyes, mixing his blood with my tears. I hoped he won a bit of grace with this ending.

From far away, Bobby's voice stabbed my ears. "Run, Vandy. Now!"

I crawled from the wreckage on knees and one hand, the phone clutched in my left fist. Overhead, struts groaned as they stretched, then split. Loose bolts plunked like hail onto the car hood.

Closer, another voice boomed: "Run, Vandy."

I scuffled through the gravel, flying toward my father's bass rumble: "Vandy, run!"

At the Jeep, I stopped, wheezing. The reservoir howled behind me, a keening animal cry. Did I hear a human scream twisted into the strange sounds? As I turned, the water tank crashed, swallowing the Lexus into its steel gut. Against the black sky, I saw plumes of snow trace the tower's collapse.

Roaring water flooded the yard. The surge hit my thighs. I couldn't break my fall without dropping the phone; the wave pounded me flat. I thrust the phone above the tide.

Fresh water brewed with snow and pebbles in my mouth. I swiped at the grit; blood salted my tongue. Mine? Leo's? The flood subsided, swirling toward the shed at the end of the yard.

On my knees, I watched water stream past the fence onto the sidewalks and lawns across the avenue. I climbed to my feet, using the links for support. Wobbling, I grabbed at my throat. I couldn't lose it now. Not like this. I felt thin wires roll under my fingertips. Monica's necklace was still there. I exhaled.

Beyond the gate, I saw my father standing next to Bobby. Frost spewed from their open mouths. Eyes goggling, Tommy squirmed in Evander's arms, pointing at the twisted wreckage. Mud splashed the pants of both men to the knees.

When I reached them, my father murmured, "Vandy."

His eyes burned into mine. He recognized me, saw me, wanted me. He touched my face, painting streaks of warmth from my eyelid to my lips. I'd worked my whole life to win this moment. Evander knew me.

I gasped; the caress was so unexpected, so new. His arm wrapped across my shoulders. He squeezed hard. I buried my nose into my father's chest. He smelled like soil and sweat and all my oldest memories. Without leaving my father's embrace, I slipped my arm around Bobby's waist. He had stiffened my resolve, backed me with his own brand of courage. He was new family now. I pulled him tight to my side.

CASE CLOSED

CHAPTER **FIFTY-ONE**

TEN WEEKS LATER

One golden Saturday in mid-May, I met Keyshawn Sayre at the drinking fountain on the little plaza in front of the Queenstown library. I'd invited Ingrid Ramírez to join us for lunch at Kings Cross Tavern. It was fifteen days since we three last got together.

The walk around the end of the lake to the restaurant took ten minutes; Key and I were early, so we waited on the park bench facing the water. Triangles of light jumped from the rippling surface; silence between us let my mind drift back.

Plenty happened in Queenstown after the water tower fell.

Two weeks after, sudden temperatures in the eighties baked the neighboring lawns dry. Silt formed dusty wave patterns across the avenue.

One noon, I walked those four blocks, hoping to confirm what I'd experienced that night. Facing the fence of the utility yard, I dropped to one knee. Clawing the silt with my fingernails, I deposited the grains in the pocket of my denim jacket. I saved that souvenir grit in an amber bottle that I stored on the ledge behind my kitchen faucet.

After three days of frenzied coverage of the Q-Town calamity, the TV news teams scuttled toward a new catastrophe.

According to the official account, Mayor Hannah and her nephew, Leo Hannah, died in a horrific accident after skidding into the dilapidated water tower. Their mangled bodies were recovered from the debris. Journalists dug up reports from the city engineer documenting the decrepit state of the old tank. No mention of Evander Myrick or Tommy Hannah's close escape from the disaster. QPD Chief Robert Sayre fixed it so my name was left out of the reports.

An overflow crowd attended the joint memorial service for the Hannahs. In her will, Josephine Hannah left a million dollars to the Rome School, half a million to the Queenstown public library, and the remainder of her estate to her nephew. As Leo's heir, Tommy Hannah received $3.8 million. No one asked how dedicated public servant Jo Hannah acquired her fortune. And as she wanted, no one learned the truth about her nephew's parentage. Her family remained protected.

After what was called the tower tragedy, Queenstown became a magnet for disaster-porn fans. Tourists traveled from across the state to gawk at the twisted rubble. Savvy local kids set up card tables at the site, hanging their homemade signs from the chain link fence. Iced lemonade, seventy-five cents a cup. For fifty cents extra, visitors got eyewitness accounts of the calamity. As if these were the ruins of Pompeii, one eighth-grader sold pencil sketches of the wreckage. Clever renderings, buck-fifty a pop. I bought one and stuck it in my box of family souvenirs.

By the time the county health department lifted the boil-water advisory, orange, red, and pink azaleas rioted across Queenstown. I filled vases in my living room and bedroom with heavy-headed rhododendron blossoms from the bushes beside my front porch.

A month after the tower deluge, the first lawsuits were filed against the municipal water authority by homeowners hoping to win reparations for flood damage to their basements.

Nobody offered compensation to the four of us. We'd witnessed the fury unfiltered. From the few who learned the truth, we got shoulder thumps and head pats. Lots of "atta boy" and "oh, chile." No one wanted to hear about death. I didn't blame them. We were the infected, spreading contagion if we talked. Irony sketched a circle around us: Evander and Tommy had no words for what they'd seen. Bobby and I found safety in silence.

After the shock, I needed comfort. Bobby was there: distraction in a familiar package. Bad move, but on brand. We claimed three weeks of solace. We never talked much; sex was our conversation. I didn't want more; he didn't ask for less.

The fourth time he visited my house, Bobby brought a cardboard shoebox filled with scraps of paper. I lit the gas fireplace in the living room. We burned all the receipts, notes, and lists documenting Jo Hannah's kickback operation. That evening, sweet smells of ink and carbon wafted upstairs to my bedroom. I hope Bobby felt cleansed by the burning.

On the lawn edging the library plaza, a fat Canadian goose honked at its mate, disrupting my memories.

Keyshawn shifted on the bench beside me. He stretched his legs toward the sloping banks of the lake.

"You look good," he said. He gazed at my peach camp shirt and light-wash jeans. Eyes pinned on his fingers meant he was fishing for a compliment.

I delivered: "You, too." His sky-blue knit shirt made the praise easy. "How you been keeping yourself?"

"Chillin'. Laying low."

Our nightly electronic chess match continued. But when I visited my father at Glendale, Keyshawn was not around. New schedule? Avoiding me? No point asking Evander to explain the change. My father remained jolly but mute. He smiled each time I entered the apartment. When I bent for a kiss, he patted my cheek. I wanted to believe he recognized me. But after the water tower fell, he never said my name again. Everything and everyone had receded behind the curtain. Now Evander lived in the sunlit present tense, always cheerful, forever vague.

Fidgeting on the park bench, I asked Keyshawn: "Anything new with you?"

Did Key know about me and his brother? Did I care what he thought? Goose bumps prickled my neck. Yes, his opinion mattered.

"Nah, nothing much." Keyshawn's gaze narrowed as he studied his phone. "Time to start for the tavern?"

"Sure," I said. Guessing why he was reticent, I welcomed movement as a diversion. I didn't want to talk about Bobby and me, either.

At the intersection of Abbott and Center Streets, we spotted Ingrid leaving the Queenstown Pharmacy. She carried several newspapers folded under her elbow. She was wearing a spring variation on her usual gear: aqua-and-gray camo leggings under a green barn jacket. The black combat boots were replaced by high-top sneakers, also black, splattered with yellow daisies.

She hitched the backpack on her shoulder, waving as we crossed the street.

"You see this?" She unfurled a paper and thrust it toward us.

I'd seen the Q-Town *Herald* when it came out Friday afternoon, but Keyshawn shook his head and seized the tabloid.

Ingrid pointed at the lower right-hand corner of the front page. The picture of her brother was the same head shot the newspaper published four months ago, only smaller this time.

But the headline was what Ingrid tapped: HECTOR RAMÍREZ EXONERATED.

The article was brief and as accurate as we could wish. Forensic examination of Hector's cell phone revealed a flurry of messages the day before his death. He received five texts from Ivy Hannah's phone inviting him to visit her house for coffee the next morning. The time fixed for the appointment was precise: eight-thirty A.M. More messages early that morning confirmed the appointment. Police investigators concluded Hector wasn't a stalker. He hadn't broken into the Hannah house. He never attacked Ivy. He'd been invited to be the fall guy. A dupe deceived by his killer, Leo Hannah. I remembered Leo phoned me—his other stooge—at nine thirty-five that morning. I figured by the time Leo called me, Hector had been dead half an hour.

"I bought extra copies for my mother," Ingrid said. "She cried and cried last night. Tears of relief."

I opened my arms; Ingrid rushed into them.

She mumbled into my chest: "Thank you."

"You're welcome." I nuzzled her frizzy hair, then wriggled my face, so when we pulled apart, my cheeks were dry again.

Smiling, Keyshawn said, "Ladies, you got me starvin' out here." He threw puppy eyes toward the tavern.

Ingrid stashed the newspapers in her backpack. She linked arms with me and we turned to cross the street to the restaurant.

A small, clear voice darted in our direction. "Ingy, Ingy, wait!" Tommy Hannah ran at Ingrid. He fastened his body to her leg like a leech in a blue-striped T-shirt and red corduroy overalls.

"Tommy, hold up." Sam Decker trotted behind his grandson, laughing. "You know how to greet a friend. And that's *not* what I taught you." He winked at me.

The boy detached himself from Ingrid. He stuck out his fingers for a proper shake.

She pumped his hand. "Hola, Tommy. Qué pasa? Cómo estás?"

"Muy bien, gracias, Ingy. Y tú?"

Inspired by Tommy's manners, we shook hands all around and exchanged greetings in Spanish. Sam had clipped his beard into a proper goatee; its salt-and-ginger highlighted the sparkle in his eyes. No complaints from me about the trim cut of his red sweater and faded denims. He looked the part of Cool Grandpa to perfection.

It was more than an act. In an emotional hearing the previous month, Sam had won temporary custody of Tommy. The family court judge ruled the boy must remain in Mason County until final adjudication of the case. I knew Sam rented a bungalow in Abbott's Landing, a few blocks from the apartment where Ingrid and her mother lived. And about ten minutes' drive from my home. I wondered if he planned to stay in Queenstown past the summer. Did he want to take Tommy to Florida for a fresh start? Change the boy's last name from Hannah to Decker? But these were questions for a private conversation, not for now.

I glanced at Sam through lowered lashes. One item I scratched from our agenda: were sparks between us real or imaginary? I remembered what I'd said to Elissa about Sam months ago: *He's grieving and lost. Angry and frustrated. And not looking for a hookup.* Sharp insight then, even better thought now. Letting the sizzle sputter to extinction protected us both: him from disappointment, me from risk. I toed a crack in the sidewalk as my ears heated with embarrassment.

"Ingrid, your lessons are paying off," Sam said, cheeks radiant as he looked down at her. "Tommy's Spanish improves every day."

Off my raised eyebrows, she explained: "We worked out a barter deal. I babysit Tommy four afternoons a week. Sam tutors me for SAT prep."

Frowning, the boy objected: "I *not* a baby."

Ingrid crouched to eye level. "You're right, Tommy. You're my friend." She stroked his hair.

"Good trade," Keyshawn said.

Ingrid stood and smiled at her private prof. "Sam helped tons with an essay I wrote."

"What essay?" I asked. We could have delayed our catch-up session until lunch. But a PI never sleeps on a mystery, no matter how small.

"I applied for transfer to the Rome School." She rolled her eyes to downplay the ambition. But the flush on her cheeks meant this was serious.

"Good on you," I cheered. "You deserve this." I was glad she'd stuck with the plans she'd told me about weeks ago.

Sam said, "Her essay was superb, no help needed from me."

Ingrid sighed and pulled on her fingers until the knuckles cracked. I thought she was being modest to dodge a compliment. I was wrong.

She said, "Writing about Hector was hard. The toughest thing I ever tried." She dashed a hand over her brow. "But important."

Sam squeezed her shoulder. The furrows at her hairline smoothed.

Searching for my own comfort, I traced circles on the underside of my wrist. Should I take that chance? Write about Monica? Maybe writing would ease the loss. Stitch the girl-shaped hole in my heart. *Better than the bad moves I'm making now.* I rubbed the back of my neck until the pain fled.

Tommy pulled on Sam's cuff. "Let's go, Grandpa." He pointed up the block.

As he leaned in the boy's intended direction, Sam invited us to a housewarming party at his place the next Sunday. Keyshawn fiddled, but accepted after I did.

Sam stroked his beard, twisting his mouth to one side. "Do you think Chief Sayre would accept an invitation? I'd like to have him. He's been a tremendous help through all this."

Before I could wonder if this was a trick, Keyshawn blurted, "I bet Bobby'd come, for sure." He glared at me. "If Vandy did the inviting."

Sam and Ingrid hiked their eyebrows and rotated in unison toward me. Nope, not telling. Private eye's private business.

Deflecting like a pro, I asked Sam to join us for lunch.

"No occasion," I said in answer to Sam's question. "Just celebrating springtime in Q-Town." Bubbly, like a tourism brochure.

"Can we get a rain check?" Sam's glance followed Tommy as he scampered away. "Story time at the Curious Cat every Saturday." He pointed with his chin at the entrance to the children's bookstore. "If we miss the reading, Tommy'll throw a tantrum they'll hear all the way to Princeton."

Beaming, Sam trotted to catch his grandson. They waved from the shop entrance and disappeared inside.

Ingrid, Keyshawn, and I crossed the street to the tavern door. While they entered, I lingered under the new canvas awning. Classy green-and-white stripes. My girl Mavis boosting her style game. I stepped toward a workman applying gold trim to the green letters on the new pane in the picture window.

Darryl Newcombe had swapped his fancy alligator-skin cowboy boots for white sneakers. I watched a drop of metallic paint splash on the clean toe.

"Don't mess up, Darryl," I said. I meant the new kicks. And the fresh start I'd given when I recommended him to Mavis. *Softheaded or softhearted. Flip a coin.*

He snapped a salute, then mouthed a silent *Thank you.*

The restaurant was jammed. Tourists mingled with townspeople in such a stew, I couldn't complete my usual racial census of the room. The tavern never took reservations. But I'd convinced Mavis to hold a table. We skated past the waiting line to a spot in the rear.

We ordered cheeseburgers—blue for Keyshawn, cheddar for me—and salmon Caesar salad for Ingrid. Catch-up talk was easy, even loopy, despite the absence of booze. I taught Ingrid the recipe for Clean Tom Collins. She hated the club soda, but admired my resolve, toasting me with iced green tea. Key guzzled a bucket of Dr Pepper.

I saw a stranger chatting with Mavis at the bar. His side-eyes and her flying fingers were directed at me. So I wasn't surprised when the man approached our table. Thin and white as a pipe cleaner, he was overdressed in a black-on-black suit. A Tom Hanks–ish openness to his face convinced me to ask him to sit.

"I'm Charles Dumont," he said. "We haven't met, but you come highly recommended." He glanced at Mavis, who saluted from behind the cash register. Maybe I'd start giving her commissions.

I sipped my Collins. "Flattery works, Mr. Dumont. What can I do for you?"

"I'm the director of the Rome School. And I need your help."

Ingrid and Key flinched. I knew why Ingrid reacted; her stake in the school was clear. But what threw Keyshawn? Testing, I introduced them to Dumont.

Hearing the names, he bounced in his seat. The silverware on the table rattled as a grin broke over Dumont's hangdog face.

"Ms. Ramírez, I am delighted to meet you at last." He pumped her hand like they were line judges at Wimbledon.

To me, he said, "Several weeks ago, Ms. Ramírez submitted a stellar application package. Two days ago, our admissions committee enthusiastically recommended acceptance."

Ingrid gasped. She looked from me to Keyshawn. Russet flowed over her cheeks as her jaw dropped.

Dumont beamed. His voice dipped even further into formality: "We look forward to welcoming you to the Rome School this fall, Ms. Ramírez." He inclined his head in a short bow.

Behind her hands, Ingrid squeaked, sipping air as she shook her head. "Thank you *so* much."

Like the Easter Bunny, Dumont delivered more surprises. He turned to Keyshawn.

"And, Mr. Sayre, it's good to finally put a face to the name. You're already something of a star in our buildings and grounds department." He tipped his head toward me. "We've been short-staffed this year, forced to delay vital maintenance projects while we scraped by. With the addition of Mr. Sayre, we're on the move again."

My mouth opened twice before words spurted: "Come through, Key. Big ups." I closed my eyes to prevent them popping from my head. If this wasn't his dream job, it was damn near perfect.

Ingrid clapped her hands, then crowed, *"That's* what I'm talkin' about." She slapped her palm to Key's. "Way to go!"

He rumbled into his shirt front. "Thanks, Mr. Dumont."

"My pleasure, welcome aboard."

Now we were all chummy like old home week. I wanted my gift from the Easter Bunny, a new job. "What can I do for you, Mr. Dumont?"

"I have a little problem I hope you can solve."

"Give me the outline. We'll go from there."

"Last Tuesday, someone broke into a locked display case in the school's main hall. The cabinet holds sports trophies dating back a hundred years."

I hummed approval of Rome's respect for ancient athletic prowess. "And now?"

"Two of the oldest trophies are missing." Dumont blinked. "I want you to find out who stole them."

"And recover the trophies?" I asked.

"Yes, of course." Dumont fiddled his fingers like a knitter.

Four brown eyes blazing, Ingrid and Keyshawn torched my forehead. With these new ties to the Rome School, I didn't have an option.

"Mr. Dumont, I'm happy to look into your little puzzle. Come to my office Monday morning. I'm above the pharmacy." I pointed out the front window. "We can discuss details then."

Ingrid fished one of my business cards from her backpack and gave it to Dumont.

When the head man left, she jumped from the table. "I've got to call Mamá . . . and Ethan." She skipped toward the alcove leading to the restrooms.

Unease settled like a shroud over the table. Keyshawn dragged his gaze toward the bar, then the picture window.

I leaned forward, arm extended, palm up. I wanted him to take my hand. We were still friends, right?

"Evander's going to miss you, Key." I tried a smile. It froze, then drooped. "When were you going to tell me about your new job at the Rome School?"

He stared at my hand. "The same time you spilled about this . . . this *thing* between Bobby and you." Through his teeth, the word *thing* sounded ugly. Shame throbbed in heated waves from my gut to my cheeks.

Three weeks of solace, come and gone. An affair? No, not even a fling. Nothing to report. Nothing I'd share. Key wanted to hurt? I'd oblige. I withdrew my hand, lowering it to my lap.

"Not your business," I said. Maybe I did owe Keyshawn, but this wasn't how I'd pay. I tapped a finger to stop the angry twitching of my eyelid.

"My business, if I make it mine."

"No," I said. "You can't." Key was a good guy, but not my guy. I wouldn't chance it. Couldn't bear the risk.

I stood, turning a tight circle, so he could see I was free. I moved quickly to hide the wobble in my knees.

I clamped my arms to my sides as I finished the revolution. "Bad moves, no strings," I said. "My brand. My way." I released the breath I'd been holding and caressed the gold letter M at my throat. I'd already lost the world; I refused to risk losing more.

Key slumped in his chair, piercing beef scraps with a fork.

My heart clattering in my chest, I walked to the bar to settle the bill. Old-school cash. Four twenties, keep the change. Along the slant of my eyes, I watched Keyshawn stride to the door. His jaw was set in fury, no backward glance for me.

I hitched a hip on the barstool and waited for Ingrid. When she returned, joy flashing from her eyes, we walked onto the sunlit road to retrieve her bicycle.

ACKNOWLEDGMENTS

My deepest gratitude to my agent, Josh Getzler, whose confidence and energy made this book happen. Thanks also to Jonathan Cobb and the rest of the stellar team at HG Literary, who had my back in so many ways. The invaluable guidance of editor Madeline Houpt at Minotaur Books prompted Vandy's spirit to shine with vigor and clarity. Maddie's touch was delicate, her insights unerring. Many thanks to the skilled Minotaur/St. Martin's Press team, whose copyediting, design, and promotional expertise launched this work into the world with a shining face.

This book benefited from thoughtful comments by writers John Burgess and Carolyn Marie Wilkins, who brought their outstanding craft skills to early readings. Developmental editor Sarah Monsma had worked with me on four previous fiction projects before turning her meticulous eye to sharpening *Trouble in Queenstown*. This time around, her suggestions, always gracious and accurate, were invaluable.

I owe a big debt of gratitude to the bookish communities of Sisters in Crime and Crime Writers of Color. The generosity of friends and colleagues in these organizations proves the oft-stated maxim that it takes a village of pen-wielding, advice-doling, cheerleading writers to raise a book. My oldest circle of friends, Oberlin College classmates Marcie, Beatrice, and Karen, have been unflagging sources of enthusiasm and fun. Look how far we've come!

What can I say about my family except that without the support of my brother Steven and my children Adam, Nick, Rachel, and Matt,

I wouldn't have had the inspiration to push on to finish this book. And a shout-out to my cousin, Esther Myricks, who founded a little private security agency in the Bronzeville neighborhood on our beloved South Side of Chicago in the 1970s. Esther didn't tackle murder mysteries, but I borrowed her grit, drive, and warm heart to create the fictional Jersey private eye who bears her name.

Above all, my heart rejoices that I've been able to share this amazing journey with my husband, John Vincent.

ABOUT THE AUTHOR

STEVEN C. PITTS

DELIA PITTS worked as a journalist before earning a Ph.D. in history from the University of Chicago. After careers as a US diplomat and university administrator, she left academia to write fiction. *Trouble in Queenstown* is the first book in a new mystery series featuring Black private investigator Vandy Myrick. Delia is also the author of the Ross Agency Mysteries, about a Harlem detective firm, and several short stories. She's a member of Sisters in Crime, Mystery Writers of America, and Crime Writers of Color. Learn more about Delia at DeliaPitts.com.